True Privilege

THE UNHOLY REALM

DR. KARYN DARNELL

ISBN 978-1-956001-87-7 (paperback)
ISBN 978-1-956001-88-4 (hardcover)
ISBN 978-1-956001-89-1 (eBook)

Printed in the United States of America

A special thank you to Jessica Coleman and Michelle Schofield Romero for helping with the editing process.

"True Privilege" Endorsements

"Another epic franchise on the scale of 'Lord of the Rings' and 'Narnia' has been born."

- Authors Digest Daily

"Dr. Darnell writes like a true Protégé of Lewis and Tolkien."

- Franchise Book Weekly

"Finally, a woman writes a book that TRULY empowers Women."

- Women Writers Association

"Who would have thought one woman could fight slavery with the weapon of her imagination."

- Platinum Books Critics

"This work is truly inspired."

- Big Book Magazine

Contents

Freedom to Captivity

Chapter 1

ARRIVAL TO AMERICA: AUTUMN 1899

ELLIS ISLAND TEAMED with immigrants, tired in body but exhilarated with hope. Majestic sea birds flew above, casting momentary shadows over the crowds. New arrivals disembarked the ship from Europe with sea-weary legs and sleepless eyes.

Naomi clutched the ship's cold metal rails with a firm hand that steadied her gait.

"Come along," she urged as her husband Thomas lagged behind, taking in the crowd.

Thomas held their daughter Purity's hand. A child of eight years old, she was lovely with piercing green eyes and flowing brown hair.

A misty fog of ocean spray settled on their clothing. Dampness and a chill set in that only a warm fire could ease. The ship's smokestacks released a final deafening blow, reminding the newcomers that one journey was over and a new one was commencing.

Naomi and Thomas drew close, huddling their daughter Purity between them for warmth and safety. It was a new world with challenges, uncertainty, and adventure ahead.

"Thomas, stay close. I can't afford to lose you in this ocean of people," Naomi begged her husband.

"We're finally here," Purity said, looking up to Papa Thomas as they made their way down the ramp.

Rachel, a stunning teen from Russia, followed the little family. She was on her own and befriended them on the journey across the sea. Naomi was fit; no one took advantage of her curves on the voyage. Plenty of the men gave Rachel that lusty eye as the ship rocked back and forth, reminding them of other things.

"Get away! I'll gut you if you get too close," Naomi had warned the men about Rachel more than a few times along the way. She even batted away a few as they made their way off the ship.

"Rachel, you're like fresh meat, drawing flies. You don't have an ounce of sense traveling alone," Naomi scolded like a doting mother.

"But Roberto's coming. To be his wife, who would think twice? It's a new life," she said in broken English. Rachel gave Naomi a loving squeeze.

"You're better than my own Mama. I'll never forget you," Rachel said with tears welling.

"Don't go soft on me, girl. You've been my constant worry. You'd better come with us if you know what's good for you," Naomi coaxed as they moved on.

In a sea of people, they waited patiently in long lines. The immigrants answered questions through interpreters. Then with sighs of relief, officials stamped their paperwork at each station.

An official looked over their long Croatian last name.

"Who could pronounce this? I'll shorten it to Thomascovich," the official complained. He slashed the last ten syllables from the unpronounceable name.

Thomas nodded in submission, accepting the shortened version.

"America. A new name. A new life. Same wife," he said, pulling Naomi in close. He landed a light kiss on her neck.

"Not the time, man," his wife complained but returned his advances with a gentle hug.

"Move forward," the official said, trying to make progress.

A Jewish family they had befriended on board trailed behind. Natasha Weinstein, their seven-year-old daughter, adored Purity and followed her everywhere. Her father wore a Kippah that covered a balding head. At times he wore a prayer shawl and rocked back and forth in prayer.

"As God leads, this is our home." Mr. Weinstein was full of hope as he stared into his wife's eyes.

Purity took Natasha's hand in hers.

"Thanks for being my friend."

"When can we play dolls again?" Natasha asked.

"Soon, I promise," Purity replied.

An official waved his hand for the group to stand in the observation line. Doctors wearing white medical coats scanned each one for disease and infection.

"Over here," a doctor motioned for Naomi, Thomas, and Purity to come.

"One at a time. Open your mouths, stick out your tongues," the doctor ordered.

They opened wide without hesitation as children obeying a staunch parent.

"Looks good." The doctor then examined their skin, scalps, and ears for diseases. He pressed a cold metal stethoscope to their lungs, and they breathed deep.

"Lungs' clear, move ahead," he announced and moved down the line.

"Welcome to America! Next," the official bellowed, blindly stamping their documents while others stood by waiting their turn.

Mesmerized, the two families huddled together a distance away from the Statue of Liberty. As one, they stared at her majesty, and the fiery torch held high. The gravity of the venture hit each heart differently, from staggering anxiety to the overwhelming feeling of an uncertain future. The sum worth of their possessions weighed heavy in small suitcases.

"We made it Thomas, but we left everything and everyone behind." Naomi squeezed his arm even tighter as though somehow it eased the stress.

Thomas kissed her cheek.

"There's nothing to go back to, my love. And you can write the folks back home."

Natasha's father recited a Jewish prayer, "Blessed are you, Ha Shem, our God, King of the Universe, the Good and Doer of good."

Rachel made the sign of the Cross over her chest and looked up to the sky. Natasha and Purity remained silent spectators, like little lambs among a giant crowd.

"Thank you for the prayer, good man," Thomas said with appreciation.

He sang an upbeat song, "America" from his heart to anyone who would listen.

> Why look back when our future is waiting
> No second-guessing, we made it, let's embrace it
> The future is waiting, let's make it something grand
> We'll arise from despair to declare
> We made it in America, we made it in America
>
> There's no turning back
> Hope for today, building our tomorrows
> It's time to let go of every sorrow
>
> Step-by-step, moving forward
> We'll arise from despair to declare
> We made it in America, we made it in America

Papa Thomas ended on a high note, greeted with applause from those who stopped to listen. Other travelers shared their own hopes. Unaware, black crows landed on lamp posts and fence tops nearby, appearing to glare at the newcomers. The sky darkened as clouds dimmed the light of the sun. Evil lurked, despite so much good happening around them.

Mave Murdock, a beauty in her day, looked about with sinister shifting eyes. She made her way through the throngs of poor European immigrants, searching for a specific target. Shrouded in an elegant hooded blue velvet cape, she pushed her way through the crowd. The hood covered lackluster dark hair whose glory faded long ago. Her darting eyes, light in color but dark in spirit, searched for what seemed a treasure. They landed on Natasha—the intended prey finally found.

Adrenalin pumped through Mave. With focused intention, she pulled a handful of wrapped candies from a deep pocket—tiny presents of temptation. It was alluring bait for any child used to having nothing. Like a fisherman casting a net, she tossed the bait to the intended target, hoping for a bite. The shiny wrapping caught the girl's attention. Natasha slipped from her father's grasp.

"What luck. It's all mine," Natasha thought. She picked up one deliciously wrapped treat after the other. Her homemade doll lost all appeal and dropped from distracted hands in pursuit of a more tangible pleasure.

Natasha unwrapped the first piece, pushing it in her mouth. The chocolate, caramel, and peanut crunch saturated her taste buds. She hungrily scoured the ground in search of more delicious treats. Led along the path of Mave's making, she wove through the crowd of new immigrants as if nothing were more important. Mave continued the seduction, waiting for Natasha to turn a blind corner.

Natasha's parents were distracted with hugs, tearful farewells, and good wishes.

"We'll catch up soon, this isn't goodbye. We'll be opening the deli soon. Come in for a sandwich," Mr. Weinstein said, shaking Thomas' hand.

"Sounds delicious. Yes, we'll be in touch," Thomas replied.

"I think we're missing some papers." Naomi shuffled their papers with anxiety. A few pages escaped her shaking hands and scattered on the wind. Thomas rushed after the floating pages.

"Woman let me handle this," Thomas said aggravated.

"What time is the train to Bristol coming?" Natasha's father called after Thomas.

"Within the hour," Thomas answered, gathering the crumpled documents.

Unlike her distracted parents, Purity saw Natasha leave and followed behind. Natasha rounded a corner that led down a corridor of small buildings. Purity ran after her 'forever friend' and stopped cold when she saw Natasha kicking and screaming before being overpowered. Mave's bony fingers covered the child's mouth, preventing blood-curdling screams as she was dragged off.

"Let her go. Help! Help!" Purity screamed in a fit of anxiety.

The noise from the large crowd muffled any protests. Purity looked about, realizing the futility, and pulled a slingshot from her belt. She placed a shiny stone from her jacket pocket in the launcher. Squinting one eye, she aimed and fired the stone with precision. It sliced the side of Mave's head, leaving a bloody gash. Purity ran with intention and lunged for Natasha's staggering oppressor.

"You, monster! Let my friend go," Purity shouted, pounding Mave's staggering body with her fists.

The dark-haired beast, Mave, fought back with angry slaps, refusing to release the child. Like a pit-bull, Purity bit the soft flesh of the woman's hand.

"Ouch. You little dog. You're mine too," Mave threatened. But her hand throbbed, and blood dripped down her face, blinding her view. She released Natasha and pulled a handkerchief from her cape to wipe the blood.

"Bloody mess," Mave complained.

Purity yanked at Natasha's clothing to pull her friend from danger. They raced down several corridors in search of a place to hide. The girls glanced over their shoulders at the sound of a chase. Mave's face contorted like a witch, and she resembled an old, winded horse, grunting and panting. Purity dumped over a nearby mop and bucket.

"You spilled the water. We're in trouble," Natasha protested.

Purity grabbed her friend's collar and pulled her onward.

Mave raced after them. As she hit the water, her feet hydroplaned and slipped from beneath her. She crashed with a tremendous thud against the wall.

Around the corner, Natasha stumbled.

"I can't go any further," she complained.

Purity eyed a possible hiding place—an open door to a janitor's closet. She helped her friend hobble to the hideout.

"Don't make a sound. I'm going for help," Purity warned and closed the door.

Unseen evil lurked as Mave watched from the shadows. Like a rabid dog licking infected wounds, she wiped the blood from her head with her sleeve.

Once Purity was out of sight, Mave made her move.

Natasha cowered in fear as the closet door slowly opened. Mave's long bony fingers reached in to take her captive.

"Get away from me," Natasha yelled, throwing kicks and punches that caused no harm.

Purity raced through a long corridor, looking for help. A bright fiery ball of light appeared in front of her. It morphed into an illuminated child angel with fluffy wings and a golden gown.

"What are you? Who are you?" Purity asked in fear.

The angel pulsated with golden rainbow colors.

"My name is Ora. Go back. Natasha needs you." Purity's eyes widened, and she turned around.

Moments later, something hit the back of Mave's head with the force of a hammer. Waves of nausea and pain radiated down her spine to the depths of her toes. Her body crashed to the floor like a tree falling with a violent thud. She was rendered unconscious.

"What took you so long?" Natasha asked Purity, who stood beside Mave.

"Sorry, my friend. I shouldn't have left. I was told to come back."

Purity slid the slingshot into her jacket pocket.

"Who would know such a thing?" Natasha wondered.

"A light that speaks."

Purity pulled Natasha over Mave's motionless body.

"Was it scary? I've never heard of such a thing," Natasha said, limping along.

The two girls made their way through the mob of immigrants frantically looking for their parents. Natasha saw her doll crumpled on the ground. It was crushed, dirtied, and trampled. With one swoop, she rescued the mangled toy with as much vigor as her own rescuer.

Natasha starred at the doll's cracked face.

"Purity, my friend. Don't ever leave me."

"You're safe now. Hurry along." Purity feared they were lost.

To the girls' relief, they found their parents chit-chatting with ease, surrounded by thick crowds.

"Child, you're shaking," Naomi rattled when she saw Purity.

"I'm fine, Mama," Purity said, easing her mother's worries.

"Natasha, we've told you about wandering off. We were getting worried," Mr. Weinstein sounded with concern.

"A witch hurt me, but Purity rescued me." Natasha pulled a wrapped candy from her pocket.

"Never take candy from strangers, foolish child," Mrs. Weinstein warned and hit the candy from Natasha's hand.

Natasha's father looked to Purity.

"You saved us from disaster. Bless you."

"I'm glad she's safe," Purity said with humility.

"Trouble, trouble, and we just got off the boat," Naomi said, clutching her husband's arm.

Natasha pulled a small music box from her carpet bag and presented it to her friend. Purity opened it, and a small statue of a couple ballroom dancing popped up. Purity admired the couple spinning around and around as music played.

"Thank you, Natasha. But you don't have to."

"I'll never forget how you saved me." Natasha beamed at her friend.

Rachel, who still stood with the two families, frantically looked for her fiancé, Roberto, amidst the crowds.

"Come with us, girl. You hardly know the man. Marriage is hard enough for adults, let alone a child. What's the rush?" Naomi insisted.

"I'll never forget you, but I'm in love. I'm getting married." Rachel hugged her new friend's goodbye.

"Are you sure Roberto's coming?" Naomi asked with concern.

"Roberto's a man of his word," Rachel boasted.

"Rachel. Rachel, my beauty," yelled a handsome young man with dark hair and eyes. He wore a fine suit and carried a bouquet of flowers.

Rachel ran into his arms, relieved to see him. They embraced—two love-starved hearts, finally united.

"He actually exists," Thomas said to the others.

"I fear for her. Senseless girl," Naomi said, focused on the young man some distance away.

"Looks like love to me," Thomas said.

"Oh, Papa. She's a mail-order bride. They're nothing but strangers," Naomi said in their Croatian language.

'Papa' was Thomas's name of affection, and he responded to it with pride.

"Not for long, by the looks of it. Let's go. The train's waiting. Shadow Brook Estate, here we come." Papa Thomas glanced at his gold pocket watch.

Rachel, the rare beauty, gave one last wave and never looked back.

Branded

Chapter 2

ROBERTO AND RACHEL made their way through the crowds near the New York seaport. He carried her luggage like a perfect gentleman. Rachel clung to his arm like a princess in love with her prince.

"I've missed you. I can't wait for our wedding. My beautiful bride," Roberto exclaimed.

"It will be the best day of our lives," Rachel responded.

About a half a mile away, they made it to Roberto's horse and buggy parked on a busy street.

Rachel stroked the horse's mane and admired the buggy.

"You must be rich to afford such a luxury."

"You're easily impressed. My bride deserves the best, and you'll have it," he said, flattering her.

"You're too generous," Rachel said shyly.

Roberto placed her belongings in the back of the buggy and climbed up. He offered a helping hand, like a doting husband. Rachel reached for him, and with a quick yank, she slid onto the leather seat of the horse-drawn buggy.

Roberto raised her hand to his lips and kissed it gently.

"You're captivating, my love."

He slapped the reins, and they were off through the crowded streets. After a few miles, they stopped in front of a fancy New York hotel. Rachel looked up in awe.

"There's nothing like this back home."

"Forget about home. There's nothing but surprises ahead," Roberto said, avoiding eye contact.

As he helped her down from the buggy, he pressed her close, kissing her in heated passion.

Rachel pushed away.

"Stop, we're not married yet."

"Forgive me. It's hard to wait," Roberto responded, sounding mischievous.

A few black crows landed on the horse-drawn buggy and began squawking. Clouds appeared out of nowhere, dark and misty. Rachel looked up and cringed at what looked to be a large, skeletal-faced entity etched in the clouds.

"Do you see it, Roberto? It's the face of torture," Rachel said with terror.

Looking up, he too noted the strange sight.

"It's nothing. No torture in these parts. Only pleasure, my dear, only pleasure." He took her arm and escorted her inside the luxurious hotel.

"You forgot my bags. You're hurting my arm," she complained as he pulled her along. A wave of fear swept over her.

"Sorry, dear. Don't worry. The bellman will get your bags." He reluctantly released the hold on her arm.

Ornate marble covered the hotel floors. Crystal chandeliers sparkled from the ceilings. In the lobby were lavish furnishings, large oil paintings, and plush area rugs.

Rachel paused to admire them.

"Magnificent. I've never seen such wealth."

Roberto stopped as if tolerating the delay.

"Only the best for you. But first things first. I have a few friends I want you to meet."

He stole another short kiss.

"Anything for you," Rachel said with affection.

They climbed an elegant staircase to the second floor. With each step, Roberto's countenance became more devilish. A translucent, dark figure overshadowed his being. He knocked at suite number six, and the door opened.

Roberto violently pushed Rachel inside.

A group of men waited for her with hungry eyes. They were obviously wealthy, wearing expensive business suits and puffing on cigars. Some reclined on fine tapestry couches while others sat in well-upholstered leather chairs. Two stained glass oil lamps, ornamented with dangling crystals, lit up the smoke-filled air.

Loathing translucent spirits of greed resided on each man, appearing as smoky black shadows, coiling around their heads and necks.

Roberto shoved Rachel on a couch with a hard push and started the sales pitch.

"Name your price. I've sampled the merchandise, and you'll have no disappointments with this one. Just what you ordered."

"Shut up. Who asked for your opinion? We do our own inspections," Mr. Wells' flabby, middle-aged abdomen jiggled as he moved. His receding hairline, deep facial lines, and dull eyes made for haunting expressions. He held a stack of money in his hand.

A wave of terror shook Rachel as his voice vibrated through her body.

"You're a Judas! Let God strike you," Rachel yelled at Roberto.

"Sorry, change of plans. There won't be a wedding, but definitely a honeymoon," Roberto boasted with a tone of savage lust as he fettered her hands and feet in chains with angry yanks and pulls.

"Liar. You devil! Don't touch me," she cried.

Roberto retaliated and tore some of her clothing, exposing a firm, trim figure.

"How's that for a soft touch," he mocked.

"Get your hands off me. I'm no whore," she howled with embarrassment.

"You got your wish. I'll be the first man you're going to make happy," Roberto joked.

"Not so fast. That privilege goes to the highest bidder," Mr. Wells interrupted, belting Roberto in the mouth.

"Pigs, all of you!" she cried, holding her torn clothing to cover tender breasts.

"She'll bring in a fortune," one observer said, eyeing her silky skin and curves.

"Bidding starts at a hundred dollars firm," Mr. Wells grunted.

"One hundred fifty," said a man from the shadows.

Another bidder raised a hand.

"Two hundred."

"Two hundred twenty-five," a rough-looking gangster chimed in.

An elderly gentleman wearing a pin-striped gray suit raised a deformed hand full of cash. The hand was foul in texture and form, having only a thumb, pointer, and middle finger. It looked like a claw, unsuitable for humans. An expensive hat was pulled low, hiding his full identity.

"Two hundred fifty dollars, plus first rights. Let's call it a honeymoon," he said as he waved the cash in the air.

The others refused to match that, and the bidding was suddenly over.

"A quick sell to the highest bidder," Mr. Wells said, pulling the money from the twisted hand.

"I want her branded to prove my ownership," Rachel's owner demanded.

In a few moments, a man came forward with a small bucket of burning coals. In it sat a hot poker embossed with the letter 'M.'

"Dirty dogs!" Rachel shrieked, trying to wrestle loose from the chains.

The hot iron burned red as the man lifted it from the coals.

The new slave screamed and wrestled against her captors.

"Shut her up," Mr. Wells insisted sternly.

"She's a fighter. Not good in this business," an onlooker said.

"There's no getting out of hell," sneered the man holding the poker as he pressed the hot branding iron firmly into Rachel's right shoulder. Her flesh sizzled like raw meat frying, leaving a bright red impression of the letter 'M' burned deep into exposed tissue. Rachel screamed in agony, now rightfully marked as a commodity to be sold.

Strands of Rachel's luscious wavy dark hair matted as tears saturated her flawless skin. She clutched her shredded clothing even tighter as though trying to cling to her last moments of sanity. The life she had known had been swept away in a moment. Finally, shock set in, and a catatonic gaze clouded her once clear blue eyes.

The chains hanging from her wrists clanged with the slightest movement. The smell of burning flesh lingered in the room.

There was another knock on the door.

Once again, a young woman was pushed in and landed on the floor in front of the well-entertained audience.

"Start the bidding," Mr. Wells insisted.

"Get her ready for me," Rachel's owner demanded, pointing his deformed hand to the adjacent bedroom.

Another man pulled on Rachel's chains, dragging her past co-conspirators who refused to intervene.

They left her alone, closing the door.

Her heart broke with no escape in sight. She sang, "Freedom Cries" like a lonely dove.

> Ahh, ahh, chh, woo, woo
> Freedom, freedom, who's keeping me from you
> My captors don't care, I'm sold for abuse and despair
> Will I survive this dark night of the soul
>
> Oh, freedom cries, freedom cries for me
> Is it possible to die but still be alive
> My eyes can see, my lungs can breathe
> But my soul, my soul has died
>
> Oh, freedom cries, freedom cries
> I can only imagine what I'm forced to do
> Day and night to earn my bread
> She looks and wonders why
>
> Oh, freedom cries, freedom cries for me
> There's no one to find me as I die
> God in heaven send an angel
> To rescue me from these chains
>
> Ahh, ahh, woo, woo, ahh, ahh, woo, woo
> Freedom cries, oh freedom cries

Suddenly, the door was kicked open. Rachel's owner stepped in, still disguised by his large hat. The door closed behind him with an eerie squeak.

He moved to the bed. Softly, his deformed hand stroked her cheeks then moved down her neck.

"Freedom, find me as I die!" Rachel yelled, only to be silenced by a vicious slap.

A loud banging sounded on the hotel door in the other room. Mr. Wells checked the gun in his suit jacket, and with a heavy hand, turned the knob. He sucked in a breath at the gory sight. Mave stood before him—a bloody mess panting in pain.

"What the hell happened to you? And where's Natasha? Her father owes me for fronting the deli expenses, and she's the final payment," Mr. Wells' questioned.

"She had a little bodyguard. Next time I'll get 'em both."

"You may have blown our cover. Did anyone see you?"

"I can't say. The port was crowded. Let's sit on this till the girl gets some curves," Mave said, afraid of punishment.

"Good idea. Just remember you're working for me, and I expect results," he threatened with a hand lifted, ready to strike.

Shadow Brook Estate

Chapter 3

TEN YEARS LATER: SHADOW BROOK ESTATE, BRISTOL, RHODE ISLAND, 1909

NARRAGANSETT BAY SPARKLED like diamonds dancing in the sun. Sailboats skirted across the gentle waves with precision. Seagulls hovered above, eclipsing deep blue skies, as a refreshing wind blew over the rocky beaches of Bristol, Rhode Island.

Shadow Brook Estate held captivating views of the bay, surrounded by landscapes of manicured gardens and picturesque fountains. Trees, neatly trimmed shrubs, and scattered bursts of floral delights lined the long drive leading from Ferry Avenue to the mansion.

The Wisedor family owned the property and relished in the opulence of their success. They were entrepreneurs who owned businesses in town—one manufactured fine china dinnerware, and the other was a shipbuilding company. The enterprises were established over a hundred and fifty years ago.

A shiny luxury car pulled off Ferry Avenue and made its way to the house.

"The Wisedor's have arrived! Start lining up," yelled a gardener trimming a bush.

The call reached the ears of a young maid who was sweeping the grand porch. In turn, she scampered inside, reporting, "The Wisedor's have arrived. Prepare to meet them."

Alexis, a young maid with an African complexion, stopped scrubbing the marble floor in the grand garden sanctuary.

"Oh, dear," she said. Hopping up, she wiped wet hands on her apron.

Other maids, hearing the news, abandoned their tasks in the kitchen, dining room, and grand parlor. They joined the others who scurried to the entrance and formed a greeting line in front of the mansion. Each stood at attention with backs straight and hands clasped in their proper place.

Naomi Thomascovich was fit to be tied. After ten years of hard-earned service, she finally worked her way up to the position of head maid. She poked her head out the kitchen door of the mansion. Her countenance appeared disturbed and impatient. There was still a hint of her accent from the old country of Croatia.

"Purity, where are you?" her mother called.

There was no response.

Purity, now eighteen years old, with flowing, brown, sun-glistened hair and blazing eyes, sported a shapely trim figure. In the mansion, she slid down the ornate banister from upstairs and rushed into the ballroom.

Natasha, seventeen years old, was dust mopping the wooden floor with a few other maids.

Purity pulled a towel from a cleaning basket and tied it in knots like a ball for sport. Then grabbing a mop, she made a wide swing and hit the rag ball over to Natasha, interrupting her work.

The two batted the rag in wild competition, smacking it back and forth with great fun. The other maids joined in for the game. Then the mood shifted into a dance.

Purity turned her mop upside down on its handle and bowing before it, pretended it was a handsome gentleman. The music of a fine orchestra played in her mind.

"I'd be honored to dance with you, fine sir. You're my dream come true," Purity flirted, batting her long thick eyelashes.

One of the maids began whistling a little ditty they all began to dance about and sing, "A Call to the Ball."

It's a call to the ball, it's time for romance
My prince is asking for a dance
With a touch of his hand, I'll melt in his arms
It's a call to the ball, let's dance and romance
Hear the music and song, come along to the ball
It's a great time for all, a dream come true
He's the best, and yes, I won't settle for less
For my prince is asking me to dance

We'll dance and twirl and give a shout
When my prince is here, there is no doubt
We'll dance on air, to the clouds and stars
Hitting every beat with ready feet
It's a call to the ball, let's dance and romance

He's handsome and strong, doing no wrong
When I look into his eyes, my life comes alive
It's love at first sight, where there is no fright
Take my hand, twirl, and give a shout
Let's dance, my prince, till we're sore and tired
Living out our days, till we're old and gray
It's a call to the ball, one and all

It's our turn to live and laugh some, too
Working our fingers to the bone
Breaking our backs and nails, too
With my prince, we'll escape
Riding on the stars to forever and back
Oh, the tales we'll tell, where there is no lack
I'll dance with my prince and give a shout
It's our turn to live and laugh some, too
It's a call to the ball, let's dance and romance

The maids danced around and around the grand ballroom. With mop heads up and love-struck eyes, each envisioned their prince. They dreamed of attending a fine gala and wearing elegant gowns.

Purity danced on with a mop in hand, swaying back and forth in awkward rhythms, a real klutz. She tried her best to glide with style around the other maids but stumbled more than once over clumsy feet.

Suddenly, she snapped from the fantasy and returned to the rolled-up towel. And smacking it back and forth again, she gave it a final whack to the other maids. The dusty ball sailed through the air, and thinking fast, Natasha ducked, avoiding a swift hit.

Naomi entered the ballroom in frustration, looking for the rest of the staff. In regretful horror, the dusty ball smacked the head maid's nose like a punch. A cloud of dust sprayed in more than a few directions before she dropped to her feet.

All the maids stopped dancing.

"Enough of this. Take your positions. The Wisedor's have arrived," Naomi said as she wiped the dust from her face.

The fantasy was over, and the maids fluttered past Naomi.

"I'll be right there, mother. Let me pick up this mess," Purity said reassuringly and started picking up mops and dust towels.

"I'll believe it when I see it. Time's wasting. No more excuses," Naomi muttered and left the ballroom.

Purity stayed behind, humming and dancing as she cleaned. Her steps were awkward and uncoordinated, but that didn't stop her from trying. She sang, "The Wisedor's Have Arrived."

> The Wisedor's have arrived
> Oh, what a surprise
> Who cares, big deal
>
> The Wisedor's have arrived
> Backs straight, look alive
> Your wish is my command
> A little here, a little there
> Do as you're told, or it won't go well

The Wisedor's have arrived
Big deal, who cares
Follow their orders, do your chores
Working my fingers to the bone
From dawn to dusk, there is no rest
The Wisedor's have arrived, big deal
The Wisedor's have arrived, who cares

Purity was the last to join the line of fortunate 'help' working at Shadow Brook Estate.

The Wisedor family took many excursions as their wealth afforded the luxury of frequent vacations. They were returning from a short get away in Newport.

The front passenger door of the luxury car swung open with haste. Generally, Mrs. Wisedor waited for the butler to open it, but not today. She was preoccupied with a mental list of things to do before the dinner party that evening.

The butler opened the driver's door. Mr. Wisedor crawled from behind the wheel, wincing and stretching the kinks from his back. He was tall, middle-aged, and still handsome, with dark hair.

He liked driving and refused a chauffeur for the family outings. He circled the luxury car inspecting it for any imperfections. With a white handkerchief, he wiped away any road dust like a doting fanatic.

Mr. Wisedor was preoccupied but not with thoughts of the dinner party. It was his business enterprises that demanded constant attention. He dreaded his return to work the next morning and relished in the knowledge that he would be retiring soon. The stacks of paperwork and never-ending problems no longer held any appeal or challenge. Favor, his responsible son, would continue in his footsteps when the time was right.

A fresh wind gently brushed Purity's sun-bleached strands over her angelic features. Her breathing finally relaxed from the mad dash to welcome Shadow Brook's royalty. She reached for her mother's hand and held it gently. Then her attention shifted ever so slightly to Papa's frail body and ashen color a few feet away.

He coughed in wild fits, trying to suppress a racket of phlegm gurgling in his chest. His lungs wheezed in protest, and his body swayed in weakness.

"Don't worry, I'm fine," Papa said, noticing his daughter's concern.

Papa toiled long hours each day, rotating through the vegetable garden and fruit orchards. He was a man of the earth with the ability to grow lush gardens and produce. Other estates far and wide came and bought the work of Papa's hands—the excess produce. Papa possessed the secrets to grow the best. He even spoke to the plants, encouraging them to grow and rebuking surrounding weeds with an angry yank.

He cared for the horses and livestock too. The animals came running when they caught a glimpse of Papa coming. Treats of barley and oats flowed from his deep pockets. He fed them little bits while inspecting for sores and ticks. He talked with them too, as though knowing their language.

Purity released her mother's hand as her heart swelled with anticipation in seeing her friends from childhood—none other than Favor and Victoria Wisedor, the son and daughter of Mr. and Mrs. Wisedor. Purity had grown up with Favor and Victoria. They always seemed to find each other on the grounds and instantly fell into cat and mouse adventures as Purity avoided more chores and Favor and Victoria dodged tutoring lessons.

The butler opened the rear passenger door.

The Wisedor's daughter Victoria, twenty-one years old, bounced off the black leather seat with eagerness as she climbed out. She was an attractive young woman, with dark blonde hair and blue eyes.

Natasha reached for Victoria's belongings and was ready to grant any command.

Then he stepped out—Favor Wisedor, the most handsome, eligible bachelor in Bristol. At twenty-three years old, he was the epitome of fine breeding. His build was athletic, accentuated with dark curly hair, olive skin, and large brown eyes. Favor was primed for the future responsibility of carrying on the family fortune.

Purity thought of flying kites with Favor a few months before. Their kites flew high and tangled in the air, quickly spiraling out of control. Rushing over, he covered her soft hand with his, and together they pulled the kites from a rocky disaster.

"Let me help you, Purity. Our kites are entwined. Don't worry, it'll be fine," Favor said with sincerity.

"Thank you, Favor," she said with admiration.

Favor's eyes scanned the line of estate help and finally rested on Purity.

"It's good to be back. Thank you for your service," Favor said to the staff with appreciation. He straightened his jacket, and a butler helped gather some of his personal items.

Purity escaped the line-up and hid behind large pillars. She watched his every move and sang in low tones, "Most Eligible Bachelor."

> The most eligible bachelor in town
> There he is without a care in the world
> Dressed to the hilt without any guilt
> Handsome and dashing about
> He's bored with such fashion
> And lacks reaction to anyone looking his way
> Cause he's the most eligible bachelor in town
>
> If his mother had a say, he'd marry today
> To a rich socialite with matching estates
> Oh, the plotting and planning, to find the right one
> For the most eligible bachelor in town
> He's handsome and dashing
> Oh, isn't he smashing
> Cause he's the most eligible bachelor in town

Mrs. Wisedor's main goal was to marry her two children to the most deserving estates within the next few years. She was plotting engagements and grand weddings. The family was known for hosting the most extravagant galas in the area. An invitation to a Shadow Brook Estate event was a coveted honor.

Mr. Wisedor looked up and down the line of help. With a salt-and-pepper mustache eclipsing tight lips, he addressed the servants with respect.

"Good day," he paused with a grunt.

"The estate appears well kept. Thank you for your diligence."

Then he waited for his family to gather their things with the help of the maids. His duty done, he couldn't be bothered with anything else but a good cigar and a cup of black coffee.

Alexis graciously held Mrs. Wisedor's elegant silk coat with a mink fur collar and gathered a few small bags.

"Alexis, get my hat and dress boxes," Mrs. Wisedor demanded, galloping past like an old racehorse. Her large bellowing hat caught the wind, and in midair, Alexis caught it. Mrs. Wisedor's light-brown hair was arranged in a flowing style of elegance. With piercing brown eyes, she belted out orders for the dinner party.

"I want the appetizers served at five o'clock, dinner served promptly at six, and dessert offered by seven. Do you understand?" Mrs. Wisedor commanded Naomi, who followed behind with subservient attention.

"Not to worry," Naomi reassured her Mistress.

Once inside the stately mansion, Mrs. Wisedor continued bellowing anxieties as she rushed to the kitchen.

"Coffee, coffee," she ordered, sitting at a small table. A maid placed a fresh cup before her within seconds.

"Let's go over every detail." Mrs. Wisedor's lips puckered, addressing the head maid. She pulled a lengthy list from her pocket.

"My eyes are getting worse. One moment," Mrs. Wisedor said, squinting while removing a fine leather spectacle case from her purse, then gently settled the wire-rimmed eyeglasses on her nose.

"The finest families of Bristol are coming," she said with pride.

"Rest assured, all the preparations are on task," Naomi tried to sound convincing through her aggravation.

"The guests are arriving soon. Everything must be perfect," Mrs. Wisedor bellowed the song, "Impressions."

Impressions, impressions, nothing but the best
The party's about to start, let's get it right
Making sure it's fit for the rich and famous too

Impressions, impressions, nothing but the best
We're expected to impress, or think of the stress
We're the privileged, just like royalty
Perfection is expected from taste to touch

It's a show to impress, our splendid wealthy guests
Think of the gossip, if anything goes wrong
Our reputation's at stake, make no mistakes

Impressions, impressions, it's nothing but the best
The invites are like gold, so we've been told
Rubbing elbows with the best, with our heads held high
It's all about impressions, impressions, impressions
Perfection is expected from start to finish
Impressions, impressions, impressions

Unaffected by the rush, Mr. Wisedor retired to the elegant grand parlor. He puffed on a fine cigar, sipped on fresh-brewed coffee and braced for a long boring evening. He never worried about the details or preparations of the endless events at Shadow Brook Estate. He left everything to his wife.

Nothing excited him anymore, for he accomplished the task of increasing the family enterprises by four-fold in just one generation. He was satisfied yet discontent and not sure why.

Elusive Escape

Chapter 4

FAVOR TIPTOED DOWN the long back hallway passing over-worked maids. His mother's irritated voice echoed through the mansion.

"Such incompetence. You're going to dry the roasts. Turn the heat down. Are the cakes ready? What about the dinner rolls? Must I oversee every detail? Good God!"

He slipped out the large ornate front doors of the mansion and headed for the stables. Rozzie, his horse, snorted in recognition as Favor approached.

"Hey, boy. Easy now," he said, gently stroking the horse's neck.

Favor was a trained equestrian who skillfully slipped a bridle over the horse's nose and slid a saddle on his back. In moments, they were off, gliding across the acreage of Shadow Brook Estate. He wanted desperately to get away, even if it was only for a few moments.

* * *

At the house, Purity tiptoed around the other maids in the kitchen and exited the back door. She headed to the family cottage a stone's throw away. After collecting her small Bible, she peeked her head out of the cottage door. When the coast was clear, she took off in haste, desperate to avoid detection.

Running through the acreage, she envisioned someday leaving Shadow Brook Estate to see the world. She slowed her pace and began to sing, "Change."

Change, dear change, I can feel you on the wind
Pick me up, flying like a kite
Time's on my side, but seasons keep passing me by
Oh, change, dear change, let's get going
Don't wait till I'm old and gray
Let's do this thing called life today
Change, change, I can feel you on the wind
Stop passing me by, I'm ready to fly

Change, oh change, I can feel you on the wind
My heart's ready to see this whole world
Let's change it for the poor and needy too
The pampered and spoiled don't deserve my toil
I'm leaving this place for good

Change, oh change, I'm ready for you
I hear you whispering, someday
You're coming, be patient, I'll win
I'm watching, I'm waiting, doing all I can
Pick me up, let's fly around the world
Change, oh change, I can feel you coming for me

Purity decided it was time to make some decisions about life and her future. Looking up, she questioned her Maker.

"But where do I go? What if I had opportunities and choices? Why do I have to work without anything to show for it?" she thought.

"I trust you for a change—to do the impossible. Until then, it's another night of backbreaking work."

She repeated out loud the often-spoken lines, "I'll take your coat. More wine? Another serving? Can I take your plate?"

"If I could save enough money to open the school, then things might be different," she thought.

Wandering further than anticipated, Purity ended up by the only lake on the property, fed by a flowing stream. The galloping of an approaching horse shattered her thoughts.

She darted behind a large pine tree, hoping to escape notice. The horse snorted. Nearby, brittle twigs snapped under hooves. Holding her breath, she slouched down, hoping for invisibility.

It was Favor, with whom she had spent so much time playing games as children. In the remote woods of the estate, they were equals, sparring, jostling and competing. They romped through streams—racing away from imaginary foes—and fished the lake, roasting their catch on makeshift campfires. It was childhood adventure at its best.

Now, as young adults, they knew better than most to avoid being seen together. How Purity yearned for the old days—there was no going back, but the affection that started in a child's heart still lingered. The blush of love rose whenever he was near.

Favor glided off the horse with the agility of a fine athlete. He tied the reins to a nearby branch and headed for the lake. From her hiding place, Purity sang in low tones.

> There he is without a care
> The most eligible bachelor in town
> Dressed to the hilt, without any guilt
> Handsome and dashing about
> He's bored with such fashion
> And lacks reaction
> To anyone looking his way
> Because he's the most
> Eligible bachelor in town

The low singing stopped as she watched him start to strip. Embarrassed, she covered both eyes—only to spread her fingers a moment later, unable to resist the spectacle. Taking off his jacket, shirt, shoes, and socks, Favor plunged into the cool lake wearing just his pants. She watched him swimming about without a care in the world, resentful.

"I'm trapped. He'll see me if I run. Must life always be so tormenting," she thought. Remaining as a frozen statue, she watched him splash about.

Then surfacing from another cool plunge, he spotted her.

"Who goes there?" he sounded with alarm.

"It's me, Purity."

"Excuse me. I didn't see you," he said, emerging from the refreshing water. He struggled to put on his shirt.

With deflected eyes, she pretended not to notice his bulging muscles and well-defined physique. She could take it no longer and fled the scene in thunderous haste.

"I insist you stay," he loudly petitioned.

"I'm serving tonight," she responded almost in melody. He chased after her, slipping one shoe on at a time.

"But it hasn't started yet," he insisted.

"Slow down. Ease your pace," he demanded, grabbing her arm.

Reluctantly, she obeyed.

"Shouldn't you be getting ready for the dinner party?" she asked, looking into the eyes of the man she had grown to love.

"Yes. But first, some peace. As usual, Mother has worked herself into a tizzy."

"And you expect pity from me? What I wouldn't give for half your opportunity." Purity's voice resonated with disappointment.

"I'm ungrateful. Is that the implication?" He narrowed his eyes in a joking fashion.

"You said it yourself," Purity said, playfully sarcastic.

"The estate's demands are getting heavier by the day. I'll be taking over soon, which means more pressure. I don't know how much time we'll have together," Favor said with sadness.

"You're right. Everything's changing, and I don't think there's anything we can do about it. My heart aches already. Meanwhile, you seem to be having all the fun lately."

He noticed the Bible she was holding.

"My life consists of more than fun. I see you brought your favorite book," he said, touching her hand softly. She nodded with affirmation clutching her Bible close.

"Yes, and thank you for teaching me to read it," Purity said with admiration and set it down.

"I trust your studies are advancing with our tutoring sessions. You've always been a fast learner. And I want to thank you for helping Victoria with her studies. She insists you're the only one who understands her learning deficiencies," Favor said with admiration.

"Yes, dear Victoria. I've learned so much from her too. Promise you'll teach me everything you know before you go off to a stuffy job," Purity tugged at his shirt.

"Only if you win. To the tree and back," Favor said and bolted toward the white pine tree a few hundred yards ahead. It was a familiar challenge, acting as children once again.

"No fair. You cheated. I'll never catch you," Purity said, chasing after the man who held her very heart.

Favor didn't let up. Stretching with long strides, she followed behind, huffing and puffing. She realized he was no longer the boy she could compete against.

He tagged the tree.

"I won. You're slipping," he said.

As he turned to her, she barreled right into his arms, breathing heavily. Her momentum spun them around a few times.

Favor held her tight until she could steady herself. He didn't want to let go. Their lips drew near, hearts beating as one.

"Tell me your dreams, Purity," Favor said, looking into her eyes.

"Someday, I'll start a school for the poor. Then I'll see the nations—wherever the breath of God blows. Will you come with me?" she asked in a whisper.

"I have obligations here," he sighed, a bit convicted, and released the embrace.

"But I must say, I admire your dreams." He was impressed with her strength and intellect, despite her lack of formal training.

"You've always been my biggest supporter," Purity said with admiration.

"I see your passion. I'm sure your parents are proud of your kind heart."

"My parents dream through me. I'm all they have. I don't want to disappoint them," she said, peering deep into his eyes.

"You won't. How could you? I know God can move anyone to do great ventures beyond themselves." Not many of the young women in his circles cared about making a difference in anyone's life but their own.

"Now about teaching you everything I know—let's continue to keep our tutoring sessions a secret. Deal?" He extended a firm but gentle hand.

"Not a word to anyone," Purity said, shaking his hand.

"Agreed then." He raised her hand and kissed it gently.

Then pulling a buck knife from his pocket, he carved his initials in the tree—an F, then a W.

"What are you doing?"

"I, Favor Wisedor, pledge to help Purity Thomascovich in all her adventures," he said with intention as he carved a capitol P, then T, under his.

"Do you really mean it?"

"Don't ever doubt me," he said with a grin.

"Have I ever," she said fondly.

Favor looked back toward the lake—it was still, unlike his heart that beat wildly.

"My grandfather called the lake 'Destiny.' He proposed to my grandmother just there," he pointed with pride.

Purity soaked up the serenity of the lake. It was one of her favorite spots.

Favor observed her as the sun sent dapples of light through the tree above. They played over her sweet face like dancing fairies.

She turned to him, and he faltered.

Clearing his throat, hoping to clear his head, he said, "Meet me here, tomorrow, after lunch. For our next lesson, I want to focus on reading analysis. Ask yourself a few questions. The first is, "How do I apply this to my life?" You never want to read for reading's sake alone, but you must train your mind to analyze. The second question is, "What is the author trying to say to the world? How is he moving your soul?"

Purity nodded as though following his logic, but she didn't hear a word spoken. With a steady gaze deep into his eyes, she wondered about the depth of his soul. As they grew up together, her parents struggled while his maintained a splendid lifestyle.

"Do I really know his heart, now that he's a man?" she thought.

He broke her gaze.

"It's late. Mother will be vexed. I must leave," he said, remembering his dreaded obligation.

"See you at the gala," Purity called after him as he ran off toward the lake.

She rushed back to her Bible and picked it up. She ran through the lush green grasses back toward the mansion, and the song, "True Privilege" flowed from her heart.

> Privilege, true privilege
> What I'd give for a smidget of it
> True privilege, at my fingertips, but never mine
> You belong to those who don't care, cut the ties
> Let's see the world, don't hold me back
> Blue skies, mountain tops, there has to be
> a better day coming my way
>
> Privilege, true privilege wants to know
> Who ya gonna help, who ya gonna heal
> Take some time for the forgotten souls
> Lonely hearts, wasted years
> Broken dreams tearing them apart
>
> Privilege, true privilege, it's not all about me
> But to give to those in need
> If I had true privilege
> What would I do, where would I go
> True privilege, it's never too late
> To start caring from the heart
>
> Privilege, true privilege
> Stars sparkling in the sky
> Where's my breakthrough
> It doesn't come easy and won't be abused
> Just give me a chance
> I promise to go to the dark places too
>
> True privilege, here I am
> Teach me your ways without delay
> You've wasted your time
> On the selfish and blind
> I'm not hiding from you

Privilege, true privilege,
What I'd give for a smidget of it

Favor gathered his things by the lake, jamming them into Rozzie's saddlebag. He mounted the horse and kicked his side.

"Let's go, Rozzie." He obeyed and took off into a gallop.

It wasn't long before he caught up with Purity as she ran through the open fields.

"How about a lift? It's getting late." He extended a strong hand, keeping a steady pace with her.

"No, I mustn't. Have you forgotten I'm only a maid?"

"You're too stubborn," he said without malice.

She slowed, and in an instant, his hand caught hers. With one motion, he pulled her up in front of him on the horse. She looked back, giving a meek smile. The wind blew her soft brown strands over his face, and he inhaled her fragrance.

"Let's go." He snapped the reigns, and they were off.

Favor held Purity tight to steady her.

"Slow down," Favor warned as the horse seemed to be showing off for Purity, raising his legs and prancing along.

"Cut it out, Rozzie," he said sternly, and the horse responded.

Favor looked about for unseen eyes as Purity was rarely alone on the acreage. She took in homeless boys—hid them in the woods on the property and helped them survive. He pretended not to know about the enterprise.

They spied on every tutoring lesson. Surely, they were lurking about somewhere, masters of camouflage and small warriors always equipped for a battle with bows and arrows strapped to their backs and knives at their sides. Just as he thought. He saw them watching, trying to remain hidden. They peered through heavy shrubs, tall grasses, and hung on high tree branches.

Purity was their 'Princess' by every definition—the overseer and helper in all their struggles.

"We have company," Favor whispered in Purity's ear.

The wind of his breath blew shivers of new sensation down her spine.

"It must be your imagination."

31

His grip around her waist tightened, and for the first time, he held her close with the perfect, legitimate excuse.

"I don't want you falling," he said with concern.

She smiled up at him. She was all that was good. Yet her kind deeds didn't stop with the boys. Purity and her mother Naomi helped the poor in Bristol. Those whose bodies reeled under the demands of heavy labor and poverty. They practiced herbal medicine taught by the Narragansett tribe.

Favor recalled the distant memory of when their relationship with the tribe began. Shortly after the Thomascovich family became servants—ten long years before—Naomi took the children for a stroll on the acreage. She was holding Purity with one hand and Victoria with the other. Favor lagged behind, catching insects and bottling them in a jar for his next fishing outing. Suddenly, they heard a child weeping.

"Shush," Naomi motioned with a hand.

They followed the soft wailing and discovered a beautiful Indian girl. She was distraught and quite miserable. Cautiously they approached.

"Are you alone?" asked Naomi.

The girl was wearing a leather dress decorated with beadwork and feathers. Matching moccasins adorned her feet. She cried even harder, not understanding the white woman's words.

The risk of kidnapping by roaming scoundrels who hated the retreating, dwindling tribe was real. Naomi gently took the Indian girl's hand like a loving mother.

Eventually, they found her father, who was searching frantically with a small army of warriors. Chief Wolf dropped to his knees and raised hands of praise at the sight of Fair Dawn.

"Fair Dawn," he cried in relief as she rushed into his arms.

Knowing some English, he communicated his sincere gratitude, "Your kindness will never be forgotten."

This was the beginning of a long and trusting relationship between Naomi and the tribe. Even after the tribe left the area to escape life on the reservations, Naomi still used their medicines to heal those in need.

Many nights, Favor was awakened by the noise of a wagon being loaded with needed supplies for nearby farms and cottages of the other estates. The hired help couldn't afford trained medical doctors, those who attended the paying kind.

Sometimes he would jump from his bed and don a black hooded cloak. It mantled his head and shoulders, shrouding his identity. It wasn't his goal to be discovered but to understand a world devoid of the opulence and opportunity to which he was accustomed.

In the darkness, Favor trailed behind the wagon and the old, worn-out horse that bore the load.

"What a contrast of character between his own mother and the young women of society. They claimed social standing and merit by financial advantage alone," Favor often thought.

Undetected, he secretly gazed through the smudged, fogged windows of the unfortunate. Many a night, he strained to get a glimpse of Purity holding a newly delivered infant. Favor was an unseen witness to the sick who were treated with herbal remedies concocted by Naomi or Purity. They often prayed, reciting healing Scriptures.

"By His stripes, you are healed. You'll live and not die to proclaim the praises of the Lord," Naomi declared over the sick.

Most revived that same night, others after a few days. He'd been told the help was born to work, struggle, and live in the shadows of acceptability. They were overlooked by the world and its standards of what it was to be, "Women of Society."

Purity shifted in Favor's arms, and the memory fled. He saw that they approached the small cottage where Purity's family lived. It was just a stone's throw from the estate's back kitchen door. The mansion's eclipsing enormity and the fading sun cast shadows over the cottage.

"Hold up," he said, pulling the horse's reigns. Rozzie's pace slowed to a stop by Purity's small family cottage.

He didn't want to let her go. Who was this dazzling young woman he was holding? She didn't need jewelry or stately garments to express her qualities and beauty. Her adornment, it seemed, came from a quiet and humble spirit, yet she had the strength of a lion. What was it about Purity that pulled on his heart? Was it the harsh reality of her life—the grueling work schedule? Or was it her purity, learned by parents with firm convictions? Holding her saturated his being with a peace he'd never felt before. Something in his heart was changing—about life and its meaning.

He released his hold on Purity's waist. His hands helped guide her body to a safe landing on the ground.

"Don't forget your books tomorrow," he said and kicked the horse's side to advance.

"Tomorrow." She couldn't stop herself from smiling.

* * *

From the grand parlor bay window, Mrs. Wisedor noticed the exchange between Favor and Purity. Moments before, she was enjoying tea. Now, any fiber of tranquility had fled. Her eyes hissed at the sight of her son barring an open shirt and holding one of the maids.

"It's reprehensible. The rumors will spread like fire, ruining his reputation," she howled and burst into an aggravated song, "Reprehensible."

It's reprehensible, reprehensible
What's he thinking, it's like fire on dry wood
Crickle, crickle, crack, crack
Like a puff of smoke gone forever
His reputation ruined, never to come back
A little crickle here, a little crackle there,
There's a fire burning, oh, what a slap

It's a nasty burn, to set him back
It's crickle, crickle, crack, crack
Crickle, crack, oh, what an attack
Our son with a maid, the scandal's front page
Can't you hear the talk of the town
Life would never be the same
It's too hot to handle, what a burn
Crickle, crack, crickle, crack, crickle, crack crack

What is she plotting, to gain romance
I can hear it now, crickle, crack
Nothing but a laughingstock to the crowd
Looking down their noses with great big frowns
It's a sure attack, we would never survive
I can hear it now, talk of the town

Hot off the presses, oh, what next
Crickle, crickle, crack, crack
It's reprehensible, what is he doing
The rumors and shock would never ever stop
Mocking our name to smithereens
Crickle, crack, crickle, crack, crickle, crack crack
That's what you get with a silver spoon
Mixing with the classes is taboo
What's he thinking, it must be stopped
Crickle, crickle, crack, crack
I hope it's all an act
The rumors and the shock would haunt our days
Do you hear me husband

"In God's name, Wife. What's the problem now?" Mr. Wisedor asked without eye contact. He was reading the newspaper, trying his best to ignore his wife's constant complaints and gripes.

Moments later, Favor strode past the parlor entrance with a hop in his step.

"Favor, come here at once!" his mother's voice cracked in frustration.

"There she blows again," he thought out loud. He hesitated momentarily, then marched into the room, ready to battle.

"Where have you been? The guests will be arriving, and you're ill-prepared to greet them. Get changed." She eyed his bare chest and wet pants.

"Yes, Mother," Favor huffed.

"It's not acceptable to associate with the hired help."

"Purity was in the woods. It was getting late, and I was concerned for her safety."

"Her safety. Who do you think you are? Her guardian angel? You've been born to privilege. Don't jeopardize your reputation for foolish crushes. We're not paying Purity to roam the countryside with you. She has no business on a gentleman's horse," Mrs. Wisedor said with spite.

"All you care about is what others think. Well, if I'm such an embarrassment, I'll stay to my room tonight," Favor snapped back. He knew she'd never stand for his absence.

She inhaled deeply, and every line on her face deepened.

"Your presence is mandatory. You're born to privilege—with its expectations and prohibitions. To pollute generations of distinguished society with subordinate relations is an atrocity. Some have been disowned for less."

"I'd rather be disowned than fall into your web of plotted proposals," Favor replied as he stormed out of the room.

Mrs. Wisedor turned her frustrations toward her husband.

"And you didn't say a peep."

"I'm not bothered by it, woman," Mr. Wisedor said, irritated. He took another puff of his fine cigar.

"Will you ignore his improprieties? Your son needs to start thinking about a proper engagement," Mrs. Wisedor ranted.

"Don't involve me with your plotting. Stop treating our son like a boy. He's a capable young man, ready to make his own decisions."

"Yes, but he must have guidance."

"I don't care what he does as long as he makes this estate plenty of money," Mr. Wisedor said sternly.

* * *

Favor retreated upstairs to his elaborate bedroom. It was decorated with finely carved furnishings, silk bedding, and expensive rugs. He was sulking and flustered as he washed up.

His Valet noticed his sour mood.

"Your Mother's at it again, I see."

"Did you marry for love?"

"There was no other option. Money wasn't an issue. Not so in your case. If your mother has her way, love will have nothing to do with your marriage—it's merely an economic investment. But times are changing. Don't settle for an empty marriage. Your parent's marriage was arranged and look how happy they are," the Valet said, cracking a smile.

"Thanks for reminding me," Favor whined. He sang, "My Head Has a Price" as the Valet watched.

My head has a price, and it won't be nice
If they ever get their way

Let the auction start, sell me for a price
To the highest bidder, I'm sold

My future's on the block, to be hocked
Whatever happened to love and passion
They say it will come in time
God help me if I'm settled
With a girl I can't stand
Who's only looking for something grand

My head has a price, and it won't be nice
If they ever get their way
But answer this, where's love in all of this
Do I live for approval and ignore my heart
Estates must match, or it's all a scratch

My head has a price, and it won't be nice
If they ever get their way
I don't care if mother's as wild as an ox
And father's sly as a fox, I'll resist their plans
Will I ever be free to choose my way
It's time to stand and be a man

Let the auction start, sell me for a price
To the highest bidder, I'm sold
My head has a price, and it won't be nice
If they ever get their way

Favor dressed, still humming the song. His strong hands buttoned a fine starched dress shirt, and the Valet handed him a silk tie. The image in the mirror reflected a dignified young man.

"I dread these events. I'm treated like a commodity. Who's going to stand the closest to me or talk the longest? Is there any glimmer of interest in my eyes? Then the complaints start. Why haven't you come to court? Shame on you. And my parents encourage the masquerade," Favor rattled in protest.

"Protocol, I'm afraid. Don't expect things to change without a fight," the Valet insisted.

* * *

After leaving Favor, Purity entered her family's meager cottage. The door slammed behind her, and she leaned on it for support.

"Does he want me like I want him?" she asked out loud and closed her eyes, dreaming.

Papa was resting in his chair in the other room.

"What was that Purity?" he asked in curiosity.

"Papa, I was just talking to myself. I was dreaming again," Purity said, slightly embarrassed.

"Don't let anyone steal your dreams. Someday, you'll move on. Life will be better for you. I know it," Papa said in admiration.

"You've always been there for me. I love you, Papa." Purity leaned down and hugged him.

"You're my very heart," Papa said and coughed a bit.

"I better get going or I'll never hear the end of it from Mother." She released him and went to her room to wash and put on a clean uniform.

In a few moments, she was out the door and on her way to the mansion. The kitchen door opened to a flurry of maids preparing a scrumptious meal for the grand party. Some baked bread, others cut vegetables and fruit, and Naomi checked the roasts in the ovens.

"Where have you been?" Naomi asked Purity.

Purity avoided eye contact.

"I needed some fresh air."

She grabbed a clean apron and tied it tight around her waist. She felt again the sensation of Favor's embrace. Only minutes before, his arms had curled around the very spot the apron now occupied.

It was best not to dwell too long on it. She and Favor could never be together.

Purity moved to the dining room. As she prepared the flower vases on each table, she thought about seeing the world. In her mind's eye, she boarded a ship with her hair blowing in the wind, destined for a great adventure.

"As God's Word stands, nothing will stop me," she mumbled under her breath. She danced around the elegant tables, singing, "Spirit Move Me."

> Spirit move me to where I belong
> My life's a big waste in this place
> I'm moving forward before it's too late
>
> Catch me if you can, I'm ready to fly
> I'm dreaming big, going where I belong
> Dancing on the clouds and to the moon
> Spirit move me to where I belong
>
> Eagles soar above the storms, so why can't I
> This is my lot, I'm told, so why complain
> But I've got gifts to give outside these walls
> Catch me if you can, I'm dreaming again
> Flying high to the sky, dancing on the moon
>
> Spirit move me where I belong
> I was made for more than this
> Spirit move me to where I belong
> I'm dreaming, flying high to the sky
> Dancing on the clouds and to the moon
> Spirit move me to where I belong

Favor interrupted Purity's work as he passed through the dining room. The other maids quit their chatter and quickened their work in his presence.

Favor's gaze rested on Purity's frame. Their eyes met. Her hands trembled as she tried to arrange roses in a vase. There it was again, an attraction neither of them knew what to do with nor fully wanted to admit.

"Roses are my favorite," Favor said, plucking a red rose from the arrangement. Snipping the stem, he tucked it in his lapel. Then he pulled another rose and slowly handed it to Purity.

"Mine too," Purity whispered, struggling to find her voice.

* * *

In the grand parlor, Mr. and Mrs. Wisedor were dressed in formal attire, ready to meet their guests. Mrs. Wisedor detected footsteps and glimpsed Favor exiting the dining room.

"I hope you've come to your senses," she raised her voice, reaching him in the hallway.

Favor entered the parlor.

"Come in," Mr. Wisedor said in an inviting manner, hoping to ease his wife's bitter mood.

"Let me speak first. I'm grateful for such privilege. Rest assured, my heart's here managing the estate. I would never jeopardize that," Favor said, making eye contact with his father.

"You've never shamed our family name. I'm honored to pass it on to you," his father said with approval.

"However, we're responsible for upholding the finest standards and beg you to heed our advice. Dear Favor, try not to look so bored with the young ladies tonight," Mrs. Wisedor said with a serious tone.

"After watching your blissful relationship, getting married isn't my top priority, Mother. Forgive me for sounding disrespectful, but I won't be forced into an economic arrangement that suits your appetites."

"Listen to reason, dear Son."

"Mother, stop trying to control everything and everyone," Favor rebuked his mother's pride.

"Will you ignore his defiance?" Mrs. Wisedor said, scorning her husband's complacency in the matter.

"Let's stop the arguing and have a wonderful evening. Is that possible?" Mr. Wisedor said, grinning.

"Yes, dear. But we must be united on this issue," Mrs. Wisedor said with urgency.

"You'll find a worthy match or else. We won't be robbed by blood-sucking fortune hunters," Mr. Wisedor caved to his wife.

Full Possession

Chapter 5

A FEW MILES AWAY in the same town of Bristol, dark clouds gathered over the Coevet Estate. Despite its grand architecture, well-manicured lawns, and gardens, an evil shadow covered the acreage.

Ahaba, "Prince of the Air," and his demon army, hovered in the clouds above, sensing fresh prey. They desired to rob, steal, and destroy.

"I smell a foul soul waiting to be devoured," Ahaba growled as his hordes drooled and sniffed the scent of weak, struggling flesh.

Deep within the majestic walls of the mansion, the echoes of a conversation hummed in a luxurious bedroom. A young woman stood in contemplation. Her name was Jezzabella Coevet, but friends called her Jezzie. Her soft hands glided over an hourglass figure while peering into a full-length mirror.

"Who could resist such temptation? It's a shame. I'm in love with a man I can never have, and I don't know what to do about it," Jezzie remarked under her breath, appearing distraught.

The chambermaid overheard and wanted to help.

"You can never be confident in finding love. Ask for vexing powers to get your way from ancient powers," the chambermaid said.

"I'll do anything to win him," Jezzie sounded with desperation.

"I'll show you. Repeat after me," said the chambermaid while lighting some candles on the table. She pulled a black silk scarf from a deep pocket and placed the candles on it. Her eyes rolled back in a demonic trance as she sputtered and mumbled wild chants. She called on the power of ancient, wicked spirits.

At first, dispelling the idea, Jezzie resisted in fear, but then in desperation, she repeated the chant.

"Ancient spirits of deception send your power. Give me all I want for all of me. All I want for all of me. All I want for all of me." She lit the last candle, committing her allegiance to any dark power that could help secure forbidden love.

The chanting echoed out the window and billowed on the wind. It tickled Ahaba's ears as he looked for another soul to devour. In a gruff voice, he bellowed an ominous sound, and his evil army joined in. The demons sang, "Full Possession."

Full possession, full possession, is our specialty
Grant her wish, she deserves our best
I bet she'll like our curses too
You sold your soul for selfish gain
And what a price you'll have to pay

With full possession, full possession
We'll teach you a lesson you'll never forget
Full Possession, full possession
With all its pain and torture too
How we love to torment too
What a delight to ignite
Full-blown nightmares in your soul
So, don't take fright but sit tight
Cause you ain't seen nothing yet

Full Possession, full possession, not a pretty sight
When it's all over, they won't know it's you
Cause it's full possession, full possession
We'll help you get love at a price
You'll regret this day for the rest of your life
A few spells here, our crafty ways there
We'll torture your soul for the rest of your days
You'll pay big for asking us in

It's full possession, full possession

How we love taking a life straight to hell
We'll snuff out your light without thinking twice
You're ours to possess, you gave us full rights
You've given your soul to whet our appetites
We'll make you crazy till you sing the blues
You've lost your mind and body too
You think it's a joke until judgment day
When you'll repay everything we've done for you
Full possession, full possession, just our specialty
Grant her wish, she deserves our best
I bet she'll like our curses too

The evil hordes laughed, responding eagerly to the self-inflicted curse. In an instant, their shadowed, misty dark forms filtered into the bedroom through the open windows.

"Grant her desires," Ahaba said, with menace in his dark eyes.

Translucent to the naked eye, the wicked spirits pounced on Jezzie like piranha's eating fresh meat. She felt strangely assaulted as the heavy, cruel, and deceptive spirits ravaged her soul.

Jezzie's body contorted and twisted as they took full possession. She screamed and writhed in pain. A feeling of nausea erupted, drenching her clothing in a pool of perspiration. The chambermaid blew out the candles and stared with contempt.

"Full possession—just what you asked for." The maid's eyes glowed red. She locked the door behind her as she left and scampered down the hall as if nothing had happened.

Moments later, loud banging jolted the bedroom door, rattling Jezzie's nerves.

"Jezzabella. Open this door at once," her mother's voice rang with impatience.

Jezzie clutched her aching stomach, staggered to the door, and struggled to unlock it.

Mrs. Coevet entered with purpose. A translucent, unclean spirit wrapped around her neck like a snake. Another hopped on her back. She was immediately breathless and grabbed her back in pain. It slowed her momentum slightly.

"Sit down," Mrs. Coevet commanded in frustration, trying to ignore the back-breaking pain.

Jezzie, like a fearful child, obeyed and plopped in a nearby chair.

"Listen to me very carefully. Tonight, we have the honor of attending a dinner party at Shadow Brook Estate. It's a serious moment in the history of our family. As you know, our efforts to align with the Wisedor's wealth have eluded our grasp in the past. However, as fate would have it, we have another chance to prove our worthiness. Your father and I insist you secure an engagement to Favor Wisedor, if possible, tonight. Most men only want an ornament for a wife, so you'll suffice," Mrs. Coevet said, balancing Jezzie's chin with an index finger. Then she kissed her daughter's forehead with a gesture of motherly love.

"You want me to marry Favor Wisedor?" Jezzie asked, still dizzy.

"I insist your beauty isn't wasted on an inferior marriage. Favor's the most eligible bachelor in Bristol, and I refuse to have his affections set on anyone else. So, do your best," Mrs. Coevet's voice softened.

"But, I'm not in love with Favor. My heart belongs to someone else."

"Listen to reason. Look around, because we're running out of time. Our ship is sinking, and our options are few. We're going broke. It all depends on you." Mrs. Coevet opened a closet, pulled out a seductive lace gown, and threw it on the bed.

"Mother, listen to me. The man I love is penniless, but I think he loves me."

"Ask yourself something, can you make it working for a living? This isn't about love. It's about survival," Mrs. Coevet said convincingly.

"You've made your point," Jezzie nodded in surrender.

"We're leaving in an hour."

Hidden Seductions

Chapter 6

A few hours later, distinguished guests arrived promptly at Shadow Brook Estate. The mansion swelled with the rich and affluent from Bristol and the neighboring cities. They entered in splendid fashions and with great enthusiasm.

Mr. and Mrs. Wisedor stood in the reception parlor, warmly welcoming each guest.

"The Coevet's of Bristol. Mr. and Mrs. Coevet, their daughter Jezzabella and son Franklin," the butler announced with a commanding voice.

"We're honored to be invited to the great Shadow Brook Estate," Mr. Coevet said, nodding ever so slightly.

"It's an honor to host the owners of Coevet Estate," Mrs. Wisedor replied before he moved on to the next guest.

The young and pampered tossed their silk and velvet capes into Purity's arms. She wasn't recognized as a person, only as one obligated to serve their every whim.

"If I find a wrinkle on it, you'll be reported," Jezzie threatened, handing over her cape.

"Yes, of course," Purity answered as Jezzie sauntered away. Then in spite, Purity rolled up the elegant cape and threw it in the corner.

"You'll get us fired," Natasha rebuked Purity for such frivolous behavior.

"I'm looking after your Papa tonight—your mother's orders. I hear he's getting worse," Natasha said with sincere concern.

"I didn't want to leave his side, but Mama insisted I needed to serve tonight." Purity's eyes welled with tears.

* * *

Mrs. Coevet hovered close to Mrs. Wisedor as the evening began.

"Surely you've noticed Jezzabella?" Mrs. Coevet asked and glanced toward her daughter a few yards away.

"She's stunning. You must be so proud," Mrs. Wisedor said, pressing her hand-held eyeglasses firmly to weak eyes.

"Indeed. You're looking at years of preparation and refinement—the very essence of culture. She's refused several marriage proposals and is waiting for the right one. So, how is Favor?"

"Quite well. Very soon he'll be taking over the family business ventures. Increasing our profits is the main priority. His aim is to maintain the reputation of the Wisedor family fortune."

Mrs. Coevet found it hard to catch her breath, imagining the sheer glory of aligning with such wealth.

"I'm sure he'll exceed your expectations. Our estates match quite elegantly, and our profits are thriving," Mrs. Coevet boasted. Then in high anxiety, she raised her ornate fan and, with great thrusts, fanned tiny beads of perspiration accumulating on her forehead and upper lip.

"We must have tea this week. It appears we have common goals that can't be ignored," Mrs. Wisedor insisted and gave a subtle wink.

Jezzie worked her way through the crowded ballroom. She approached Victoria, Favor's sister, with the elegance and style of a cultured woman.

"Victoria, it's been too long. Thank you for inviting me to spend time with your family."

"I wasn't aware you were invited. It's news to me," Victoria responded, startled.

Jezzie's eyes locked on Favor across the room. Her mind raced with plots.

"I'll marry you, and what a prize you'll be," she thought, fully absorbing the stately mansion with its elegant, expensive furnishings, exquisite architecture, chandeliers, and magnificent staircase.

"Someday, it will be all mine," Jezzie said, plotting under her breath.

"What was that?" Victoria said in alarm.

"The pleasure's all mine, to be in your esteemed presence. I must say hello to your brother. It has been an age."

* * *

Favor stood in the midst of elegant young elites, staring past them as though in another world. He tried his best to look interested, especially when his mother was nearby.

Purity approached with a tray of wine glasses, and he picked up a glass.

"Hello, Purity. You're looking ravishing tonight," Favor said with an expression that was hard to read.

"Thank you, sir."

"And your studies? How are they coming along?" he asked, breaking all etiquette.

The young elites around him snarled at giving a mere maid attention.

"A maid studying? Who's heard of such nonsense?" one of the spoiled and pampered mocked.

Favor was merely baiting the young socialites, challenging their deeply held prejudice for his amusement.

"Quite well, sir," Purity answered Favor and then moved on serving others.

Favor felt heavy eyes staring and looking around, the mystery was solved. He caught a glimpse of Jezzie coming his way.

"What is it about her? Looking at her caused most men to melt with desire," he pondered.

Favor braced for her usual gestures of seduction and promised enticements, though he'd not been the unlucky recipient of her regard in some weeks. He wasn't sure which Jezzie he would get tonight.

Jezzie raised her hand to his lips, hoping he would kiss it.

"Ah yes, Jezzabella Coevet," Favor said. Bypassing a kiss, he politely shook her hand.

"Friends call me Jezzie, as you well know. Where have you been all these months? I haven't heard from you in quite some time. You haven't called or come courting. Shame on you. But no worries, there's time to redeem yourself. I was hoping to explore Shadow Brook Estate with you." She straightened his tie and moved her hands slowly down his suit's lapel.

Favor looked intently into Jezzie's eyes and felt a strange, alluring vexation. It was as if she was reading his mind, drawing him into an unavoidable vortex of desire. The woods were his place of solace, where heaven touched down with divine revelations. It was his favorite place to think, dream, and explore. It was where turmoil became peace and striving ceased to exist. He knew every inch of it, especially by Lake Destiny, which was far enough away from most intrusions. It was a world he wasn't sure Jezzie could understand. A strange desire to take her there grew in his soul the longer she stared into his eyes. Her eyes seemed almost red as if red-hot flames danced within.

"Your eyes," Favor stuttered, feeling lightheaded and confused. His stomach rolled, feeling pulled by unholy desires. An unseen, evil spirit rested on Jezzie's shoulder. Slowly, like a vapor of seduction, it wrapped around Favor's neck, drawing them together.

"Yes, I'll give you a chance," he thought, without knowing why.

Jezzie snapped her fingers in front of his eyes as though wakening him to a new reality.

"Hello? Anyone home? It's as if you haven't heard a word I've said. Oh, enough. Let's dance," she said laughing, as she dragged Favor onto the ballroom dance floor. In perfect step, they blended in with the other couples.

* * *

Purity observed Favor and Jezzie while stacking a serving tray with dirty wine glasses.

"Good heavens, maid. Watch your step," an annoyed older woman said with a throbbing foot just stepped on by Purity.

"So sorry," Purity apologized.

Favor and Jezzie glided by her, floating in style and elegance, both well trained in ballroom dance. Jezzie was the picture of fine breeding, and Favor was just as handsome.

"The Coevet's are hoping for an engagement," a nearby guest boasted secretly.

"I've heard the rumors. Jezzie's after Favor, and she always gets what she wants," another guest chimed in.

Purity overheard the shocking revelations. Tears threatened as waves of new emotions crashed over Purity's breaking heart. Her maid's clothing squeezed tight like a constricting python, slowly asphyxiating any hope for the future. It represented a prison locking her into an existence of mediocrity and repetition with no hope of advancement.

Purity gazed at her image in a nearby mirror. Staring back was a humble maid holding a serving tray surrounded by socialites dressed in the highest fashion. Once again, she imagined what it would be like to attend such an event. To wear a beautiful gown, adorn her hair, and dance with Favor. He was the man who poured so much into her as a teacher and mentor.

The serving tray slipped from her shaking hands, crashing to the floor with a heavy thud. The half-filled glasses splattered crimson wine on the fine gowns of those nearby.

"What a clumsy maid," one of the guests spouted.

"Forgive me," Purity said and pushed through the ballroom guests wanting desperately to get away from her lot in life. She tripped in the crowd and landed hard on the floor.

"Inexcusable behavior. Wretched maid," a young socialite loudly proclaimed.

"Such incompetent help," a gentleman said with disgust.

Purity rose slowly from her knees and saw that Favor gawked in unbelief.

"She must go. Fire her immediately. What an embarrassment to you," Jezzie proclaimed as she twisted her arm through his.

"Back to dancing. Back to dancing. Don't let this spoil the night," Mrs. Wisedor said with embarrassment.

As the dancers move back onto the floor, she lowered her voice to Purity.

"Get to the kitchen where you belong."

Purity pushed past faces of ridicule and headed to the busy kitchen. In her haste, she crashed into Alexis, who was busy reloading trays with fruit, crackers, and cheese.

"Slow yourself. None of us want to be here." protested Alexis.

Purity ignored her friend and headed straight for Naomi.

"Mother, I'm leaving," Purity said, realizing the wrath to follow.

"I'm bushed, and you're leaving. What's gotten into you?" Naomi glared with annoyance.

"It's my job to take care of Papa." Purity said, thinking quickly. Without waiting for approval, she rushed out of the kitchen.

The cool night air hit like a slap of sobriety, making it difficult to catch her breath. Purity's soul screamed in protest against the invisible barriers preventing life as she dreamed. She paused, peering through the stately ballroom windows at an unattainable existence. The music was faint but still audible, giving a melody to a world filled with pomp, glamour, and pride. It was a place reserved for those with position, power, and opportunity. None of which she possessed. Purity sang, "Invisible Girl."

I'm the invisible girl, the laugh of the party
In a world of glitz and glamour
Don't remind me of my fantasy
It's an unattainable world beyond my fingertips
For the elites and the snobs in their fancy charade

I'm made to serve their every whim, but who cares
Give me your coat and wine glass
I'll take your plate and salad dish too
I'm the invisible girl, does anyone see me
It's an unattainable world, beyond my fingertips
For the elites and the snobs in their fancy charade

It's a life beyond my reach
Reminding me of constant defeat
I could never earn my way in or land the right guy
I'm the invisible girl, just walk on by
It's their snooty fruity club of deceit and guile

They're too good for the help, so don't even try
Keeping the wealth for themselves is their style

Turning a blind eye, leaving others behind
It's an unattainable world, beyond my reach
For the elites and snobs in their fancy charade

I'm the invisible girl, is it my skin or the class I'm in
I'm an untouchable girl, I could never win
I'm the invisible girl, carrying the world
Where do I fit, where do I belong
How could I ever win his heart, it's keeping us apart

It's an unattainable world, beyond my fingertips
I'm the invisible girl, do I even matter

Purity finished the song, watching through the window as Favor danced in perfect step with Jezzie.

"I know the plans I have for you. Plans not to harm you but to give you a hope and a future," a voice sang softly on the wind. She'd heard the voice before but didn't know its origin.

"Please, tell me who you are," she whispered, looking to the night sky. A quiet calm settled like a refreshing mist.

* * *

At that moment, high above, a chariot, whose wheels spun with fire, was advancing with lightning speed. It was pulled by four white horses, galloping through space over galactic storms. It carried Captain of the Lord's Army whose very presence illuminated the dark universe. He was driving the chariot hard over solar winds with the reigns firmly placed in his scarred hands. He was coming from the New Earth, far above the created galaxies, from the third heaven where all things created were spoken into existence with declarations of "Let there be." He headed toward the old earth that was passing away, on a mission.

"I know the plans I have for you. Plans not to harm you but to give you a hope and a future," the Captain sang out. It sounded like thunder vibrating the earth below. His appearance was magnificent, like a King. He was dressed as a warrior, wearing a helmet and body armor engraved with the names "King of Kings, Lord of Lords."

He was accompanied by five child angels—Rocco, Josiah, Sergio, Kaleb, and Toby—who appeared between the ages of ten and twelve years old. Each angel was of a different ethnicity. Rocco was African with dark skin and a dimple on each cheek. Josiah was Caucasian, with a ruddy complexion, blue eyes, and dark brown hair. Sergio was of Asian Indian descent with tan skin, black hair, and big black eyes. His chiseled jawline framed handsome features. Kaleb was Asian with jet black straight hair and black eyes that slanted handsomely. Toby was American Indian with brown skin, brown eyes, and a smile that exposed a jolly heart. They were dressed in a similar fashion with helmets and body armor. Each one illuminated the light from their great Captain. They were on a mission.

"On your first assignment, may your wings grow to the size of your hearts. Five means grace, so I'll call you a Ring of Grace," the Captain said to the five angels.

Following behind were the great archangels Michael, Raphael, Gabriel, Ariel, and Azrael. They appeared with large, feathered wings, each clad with body armor embedded with precious jewels of diamonds, rubies, sapphires, and turquoise, set in gold. Galactic weapons attached with magnetic titanium adhered to their backs, waists, and thighs, giving ready access to annihilate Ahaba's evil forces. The weapons were made of rare metals from the New Earth and were loaded with heat dissolving lasers. As they flew through the universe, the weapons recharged with galactic radiation.

The archangels flew close to the chariot of fire as bodyguards. The wars in the universe were worsening as evil principalities fought for control.

* * *

Purity opened the cottage door and shifted roles from maid to a loving daughter.

"Papa, I'm here," she practically shouted as she ripped off her apron and threw it on a kitchen chair.

"Natasha, it's your turn to work the kitchen."

The young maid sitting by Papa's side looked relieved.

"Take care. I'll check on you tomorrow," Natasha said to Papa and rushed from the cottage.

Before her was Purity's dreaded nightmare coming to pass. For several months she'd watched Papa Thomas fade away. His strong, agile body bent low under a spirit of infirmity. They tried everything—even an expensive doctor's visit—but there was no diagnosing the mysterious illness that attacked his lungs. It chipped away at his vitality each day, until there was hardly anything left of him. She wiped his feverish brow with a cool, damp cloth and lifted a cup of water to his cracked, dry lips.

"I'm headed where all things become new," he said, coughing wildly.

Tears welled in his daughter's eyes.

"Papa, don't say it."

"Take care of Mother. Promise me. Finish your studies with Favor. Let him help you." Papa winked slowly as though any movement was difficult.

"I promise I will."

"You're already a great teacher. You've taught those orphan boys well," Papa's voice withered in volume.

"I love them like my own sons, Papa," Purity said, tearing up.

"I'm so proud of you. I believe in you," he said in pain.

"Get my pocket watch."

Purity reached in a drawer and pulled out an engraved gold pocket watch. She placed it in his shaking hand.

"It's yours," he whispered.

"No, Papa. I can't take it. I'm calling the doctor. God, please help," she cried, panicked.

With his last bit of strength, he forced the watch in her hand.

"Open the curtains. I'm going to the New Earth," he gasped.

Purity pulled the curtains, exposing the starry night sky.

"The New Earth. Papa, rest. You're not making any sense."

With spiritual eyes, he was able to see the chariot of fire entering the earth's atmosphere.

"They're coming for me. The New Earth is more real than you'll ever know," Papa Thomas gasped. He gazed at the evening sky with a faint smile and nodded as though in sweet surrender.

"Tell me about it, Papa," Purity said, wiping his brow.

"I'm not afraid. I'm waiting for you, Captain," Papa said with a weak smile, gazing out the window.

"Who's coming, Papa?" Purity looked out the window, trying to understand.

"The Captain and his mighty angels. I'll be watching over you. Don't worry." Papa raised his hand, gently stroking Purity's cheek. He fixed his final gaze on his only child. Then his spirit disengaged from his diseased-ravaged body, ready to leave with the angels.

The Captain appeared, translucent in form, as a mighty warrior whose armor was worn from many battles. His five archangels landed beside their King. The Captain took Papa's hand and, for a moment, they hovered close to Purity in translucent radiating light. Then the Ring of Grace manifested as small warriors. When Papa saw the angels and the majestic Captain, he nodded in understanding.

"I'm ready." Papa placed an invisible hand on Purity's head momentarily.

In a blink, Papa, Captain, and the angels were at the chariot whose wheels appeared as flames of fire. The child angels helped strap Papa into one of the chariot's red velvet seats.

"Just a safety precaution. The galactic winds are fierce," the Captain said and winked.

The child angels peered over their shoulders and saw their wings grew a little bigger.

"That was easy," Rocca said, surprised.

"Not too bad for our first assignment," Toby said, hopping into the chariot.

"Up and away! To the New Earth," the Captain shouted as the chariot took flight. A small cloud of gold dust showered Purity as they departed.

Unaware of the scene that just took place in the spirit realm, she choked out the song, "Oh Papa."

> Oh, Papa, Papa, don't go, I need you here
> Without your love, I'm like an orphan child
> How will Mama and I survive
> The labor's too hard, the hours too long
>
> Oh, Papa, Papa, I love you too much
> To ever say goodbye, but if you must
> Fly, fly, fly away, to a better day
> The New Earth's calling, spread your wings

Oh, Papa, Papa
If you have to go, I understand
Fly like a bird to your resting place
You'll blaze like a star in the universe

Oh, Papa, Papa
Promise one thing, to shine over me
Till I see you again in heaven's bright light
So, fly, Papa, fly, fly to the New Earth

A few days later, Purity and Naomi buried Papa. His wooden casket was loaded onto a horse-drawn wagon decorated with flowers that hid the old dry wood. Naomi wept from a shattered heart. Purity tried to console her mother.

Slowly, with agonizing steps, the funeral procession wove through the city of Bristol and inched up the road to the pauper's cemetery. The hired help from surrounding estates wore dark colors of brown, black, and dark gray. Everyone realized survival would be tougher now that Papa was gone.

The preacher took his place by the grave. It was deep, with a mound of earth piled beside it.

The Wisedor family attended Papa's funeral and helped supply food for the dinner afterward. Favor joined the commoners, gripping the casket by one of its ridges, lowering Papa to his final place of rest.

Mourners threw flowers into the darkness. They landed on the casket with a gentle thud.

"There's a time to live and a time to die. From dust, we were created. To dust, we will return. He has gone to his eternal dwelling with the Savior," the preacher prayed.

Purity found it difficult to comprehend anything. Her eyes shifted to Favor, and their eyes locked as though understanding the other's pain. Purity watched as Jezzie clutched Favor's arm even tighter. Victoria's comforting hand on Purity's shoulder, though welcome, did little to ease the pain.

Purity took notice of Mrs. Wisedor, who looked as if on patrol, ready to combat any unwanted approach. Mr. Wisedor stood next to her, stoic and unflinching at the death of a trusted servant.

When the pastor finished, friends and coworkers offered condolences.

Favor embraced Naomi, who was more like a mother to him.

"Papa Thomas will be greatly missed."

Then looking to Purity, he reached with one smooth movement for her hand. He had never approached her publicly in this manner. As their hands melted together, an intense emotion surged through their souls, far deeper than expected.

"My deepest regrets, Purity," Favor said, embracing her trembling body. She molded to his body, collapsing in his arms, weeping. His masculine hug pushed past any grief, confirming all she tried to deny. He gently kissed her forehead, which surprised them both. He quickly let her go, not wanting to bring notice to his actions

Awakening

Chapter 7

PURITY STOOD NEAR the shoreline of Narragansett Bay. The stately mansion of Shadow Brook Estate loomed behind in shifting shadows. With a blank stare, she watched ships in the distance plow through frothy white waves. They were headed to the Bristol harbor loaded with cargo from around the globe.

It seemed like only a breath of time since her family arrived as poor immigrants. The memory of stepping onto Ellis Island returned, saturating her mind with all the new sights and sounds of hope. She remained transfixed for quite some time, appearing like a statue, except for her hair and clothes billowing in the fresh wind.

"How fortunate to have settled on this estate with the Wisedor family," she thought.

Other immigrants were not as blessed and ended up living in the squalor of tenant housing in New York City. As a child, she was unaware of those desperately clinging to the hope of opportunity on distant shores.

If it was up to Purity, she would have turned the ship around and headed back to the old country of Croatia. She longed for her grandparents, who were probably working the garden or preparing fresh-baked bread for dinner. Or maybe it was evening, and they were rounding up the livestock for another night's protection. Her heart ached with longing to return to life as it had been—to security and their loving embrace—but that was not an option.

Her thoughts were disrupted by the haunting vision of sailors carrying another covered body on a stretcher. Family members wailed behind, drying endless tears. A loving spouse placed a small wooden cross on the deceased's chest before making its last journey into the sea below.

"Open wide, jaws of the sea. Another dreamer dead and gone." Purity's words were swallowed by the howling wind.

The harsh reality of the voyage was inescapable. Most were stricken with influenza shortly after departure. The passengers tried to avoid the flu by moving away from others, but there was no place to go. It was the ceaseless rattle of coughing, vomit, and odors of the sick. The groans of despair drove a person mad from lack of sleep and hopelessness. Someone was always going stir crazy and screaming out just when a good sleep was setting in.

Naomi held Purity tight, saying, "Don't mind it, dear. Drift off, drift off, child." It must have been the warm embrace and rhythm of a mother rocking a tormented child that brought any solace. Her whispered prayers echoed with the wind, "Lord, spare us. Don't leave us, Jesus, Jesus, Jesus."

Years later, the terrors of such a journey were only fading memories. Purity walked the rocky crags of Narragansett Bay as visions faded in and out like the tossing waves.

Her mind shifted to recent horrors. Something that had happened mere days after burying Papa.

"Take Favor his lunch," Naomi had demanded a few days prior.

A lunch basket in her hands, Purity had scurried along Bay View Avenue, relishing in the new adventure. She'd found the three-story factory where Favor worked. It was whitewashed in color, with large windows covering the front of the building. A sign that read "Wisedor Dish Factory" hung over the double door entry. Purity had stepped inside for the first time since her family began working for the Wisedors.

It had been horrifying to see scores of teens and young children appearing overworked and gaunt. She's approached one of the emaciated teens.

"Where's your family?" she'd asked with curiosity.

"They're dead, miss," the teen had replied with sorrow.

"How did you get here?" she'd persisted with a hushed whisper.

"On Mr. Wisedor's ship."

"It was their ship? Are you sure?" Purity had asked, surprised.

"They own ships and work us like slaves. They promised a new life, but work is all we know."

"What's your pay?"

"Pennies a day. Some food and a blanket for sleep. Same with the rest," he'd answered and deflected his eyes.

"Where are you from?" she had pried.

"Over the ocean, Poland."

"Get back to work," Dagon, the floor manager, had yelled in a threatening tone. He'd raised a hand to strike, but another young worker nearby had distracted him with a coughing fit.

"Stop your bloody coughing," Dagon had raged without sympathy.

A teen carrying a heavy box near her had almost fainted.

"Are you ill?" Purity had asked while helping steady his balance.

"Hungry, miss," he slowly answered.

Just then, two-floor managers had passed with a stretcher, carrying the body of a child covered by bloodied white linen. A trail of blood had spotted the floor.

"What happened?" Purity had asked, peering into the eyes of another boy.

"Another accident. Don't worry. He'll be replaced. The work never ends."

Horrors of death, cheating workers, and children used and abused. And the Wisedor's tolerate such injustice? She'd been inflamed with righteous anger.

"What the hell are ya doin' here?" Dagon had barked when he noticed her gawking. He'd roughly grabbed her arm.

"I'm a maid from Shadow Brook Estate. I've brought Favor's lunch," she had said, raising the basket as if proof of the mission.

He'd grabbed for the basket.

"I'll take it to 'em."

"I insist on delivering it, as ordered to do," she'd announced, clutching the basket to her frame. Just then, Favor had erupted from the office and intervened.

"Dagon, enough. Purity come this way."

The office was tastefully decorated. It was furnished with brown leather chairs, a large mahogany desk littered with papers, and rows of wooden file cabinets lining the walls. Expensive oil paintings hung about, and busts of great noblemen added to the room's elaborate decor.

"Pull up a chair. There's enough for both of us," Favor had coaxed.

"I've lost my appetite. Don't you realize what's going on here? Right under your nose?"

"I don't work here much. I'm mainly at the shipyard. Father restricts me to the office. The managers work the factory floors. What's the problem?"

"Forgive me, but it's hard to ignore the abuse of children and your workers."

"Abuse? I don't know anything about it, but I promise to look into it."

"Thank you, because I can't believe you're a willing participant. Please, don't turn away from so much suffering. You're either too scared to confront the bloody terror, or you're fine pretending hell is burning everywhere but here."

"Purity, sit. Take a breath."

"Please excuse me. My mother needs my help at the estate," Purity had responded and left the office.

The awful memories from that day continued haunting, chasing like basset hounds on a wild hunt. The emotional storm they caused eclipsed the beauty of the long afternoon walk. Purity continued down the rocky shoreline, stumbling about as though in a heartbroken trance.

Suddenly, the sound of laughter breaking over the dunes shattered the awful memories. She'd almost crashed a party. With quick reflexes, she collapsed on the sand, hoping to escape notice. The voices were loud and recognizable.

"Favor, try mother's favorite dish. You won't be disappointed," Jezzie coaxed in a flirtatious way.

"It's quite delicious," she heard Favor say.

"Seriously. How inconvenient," Purity said in a testy manner.

She peaked her head over a dune and spotted Favor having a picnic with friends by the scenic bay. A few sailboats were moored on shore, resting from an afternoon of sailing.

Jezzie was there, doing everything in her power to attract attention.

"Will you be traveling abroad this summer, Favor? Hopefully, you'll be home for the holidays. Tell us you're staying. It's simply not the same without you."

Before he had the opportunity to answer, she spoke.

"What's blowing over the dune?" she asked, gazing at a strange sight.

Unbeknownst to Purity, her long hair was blowing wildly in the wind, but her body was hidden.

"That's strange," Favor said and ran to the sight. In moments, Favor was standing over Purity with his masculine arms folded over his chest. He saw his beautiful maid and was amused.

"I was taking a walk. I'm so sorry, sir," Purity said.

"What a pleasant surprise. Care to join us?" he asked with a sincere tone.

"No, thank you."

He gently grabbed her arm.

"Can we talk about the other day? You were upset."

"There's nothing to say." She pulled her arm away and ran in the opposite direction.

"Who is it, dear?" Jezzie inquired.

"No worries. Don't be alarmed," he responded, watching his maid flee.

Son's Camp

Chapter 8

PURE RELIGION IS looking after the orphans in their distress.

"Son's Camp" had been formed, one by one, as the homeless boys had stumbled on the remote acreage of Shadow Brook Estate, nestled in the woods far away from the mansion. To their good fortune, Purity had found them and helped to survive in obscurity. Most of the boys had come from hopeless situations—parents who were dead or didn't care. At Son's Camp, they had become "Brothers," able to escape unrelenting work and abusive homes.

"Hurry, a storm's coming, take the rope, and tie the knot like this," Andrew, one of the sons, said to his brother Danny.

"Like this?" Danny responded, tying the rope securing a small tent between two trees.

"That's close enough," Andrew said, helping the boy tighten the rope.

Other sons worked feverishly, covering tapestry bags filled with clothing and food supplies. It appeared a downpour was coming as the sky darkened above. The camp was surrounded by large boulders and a thick forest of Shagbark Hickory trees concealing its location.

Beyond the trees, a few boys were practicing archery with bows and arrows. Others were unloading fresh rotisserie chickens from the fire pit in the center of the small camp.

The wind increased around Son's Camp. Suddenly, the Captain's Ring of Grace touched down, manifesting in translucent form near the fire pit.

"Lunch, anyone?" Sergio asked the other angels, elbowing his counterparts.

The boys were unaware of the angels and continued loading the chickens in large cooking pots.

"Not now. Let's take a look around," Rocco responded.

The angels elevated with ease, their wings flapping like hummingbirds. They hovered above, watching the boys drop their pursuits to protect the camp from a downpour.

A strange boy wandered close to Son's Camp, looking for shelter from the approaching storm. He was about ten years old, scruffy faced, and hardened from life's cruelties. His father had been killed in a coal mine a few months earlier. A desperate mother, unable to provide, farmed most of her children out to friends and relatives. An old spinster had taken him in, but before long, despised the sight of him. So, he ran and never stopped.

Purity's first son, David, had been adopted five years before. He was a master hunter and raised his bow and arrow, listening for prey. It gave him great pride in bringing fresh meat into camp for the younger sons. He was only a few years younger than Purity, but she watched out for him like a mother and bossed him like one too. His father was an alcoholic who had kicked him out, and his mother had died years before.

The Ring of Grace flew overhead, witnessing a disaster about to happen. They held their shields around the strange boy, trying to prevent an accidental kill by David.

The bushes shook, alerting any seasoned hunter that fresh prey was close. The harder the boy pushed to break through the angels' invisible force, the noisier the rustling leaves.

David swiftly drew his bow back even further and squinted one eye, instinctively readied for the emergence of prey.

"One more move, and it's dinner time," David whispered.

Instead of fresh meat, the boy appeared weak and bone thin. He spotted David and ducked for cover, diving into the dirt.

"I beg you, hold your fire. I'm looking for work, not trouble," the boy called out.

"That was too close. What's your name?" David demanded, blowing out a sigh of relief and lowering his bow.

"My Mama named me Burden. My daddy died in a black hole. I don't mean any harm."

"Come on, boy." David clutched the boy's ragged jacket and yanked him back to camp like a criminal.

Purity tended one of the sheep in camp, surrounded by her boys. Small raindrops began to wet her clothing. A chill of cold was beginning to set in.

"What a nasty wound," she said, noticing maggots crawling in the sore on its hind leg.

David broke her concentration.

"Hey, Purity. I've found a trespasser. He calls himself a Burden.

"Watch your attitude. We're all trespassers in some way. Don't forget it," she warned.

"He's a tramp and has no right on this fine estate," David sounded with arrogance.

"Like the rest of us with no rights here. Where's your mercy, David? We're all on the edge of homelessness. How are we any better than this poor boy?" she rebuked him.

The boy's eyes were almost swollen shut from lack of sleep. He was a mess from head to toe, with filthy tattered clothes and festered sores that cracked his lips and oozed yellow pus. It appeared he hadn't bathed or eaten a solid meal in weeks.

"He carries a stench," David said, scrunching his nose in protest.

"What's your crime, boy?"

The boy found it difficult to make eye contact and looked to the ground.

"Born poor. Mama couldn't afford me. Daddy died in a black hole."

"From this day forward, I name you Jonathan, which means a gift from God. You're no longer a burden, son," Purity said and embraced the boy.

"I don't know how to thank you," Jonathan said, tearing up.

"You can thank me by being a good son," Purity said, kissing the boy's forehead.

"David, take charge of him. Clean him up and feed him. He's going to need ointment for those sores. Let him heal before you start training him."

"At your service," David said, quickly changing his tune.

"David, I appreciate everything you do, but remember, I have the final say around here," Purity said with authority.

"Your wish is my command," David said with respect.

"I promise I won't disappoint you. I'll work hard and mind my manners," the boy pledged.

The angels placed transparent hands on the boy, and he was immediately strengthened. Then a job well done, they disappeared.

"Tell Alexis and Natasha we've got one more and to prepare a bed for him. That storm is not waiting for anyone," Purity said, looking up at the darkening sky.

* * *

As the days passed, David taught Jonathan how to be a warrior—everything from shepherding, archery, hunting, and reading. He excelled rapidly.

There were twelve sons in all—Matthew, Mark, Luke, Jonathan, Paul, Danny, Andrew, Timothy, Barnabas, Peter, Joseph, and of course, David, the eldest who looked after them all.

In time, the hard walls of rejection collapsed for Purity's sons. They rested in her commitment to them. They found the peace of God's Spirit in Son's Camp, sheltered from the family storms of Shadow Brook Estate, or so they thought.

One day, the sons went fishing at Lake Destiny on Shadow Brook Estate. It was far enough out of the way that no one feared being found. A few of the sons watched from high trees with ram's horns in hand, ready at a moment's notice to warn others if someone was approaching.

Dagon, the scoundrel from the Wisedor Dish Factory, went unnoticed as he peered through the thick trees, watching the boys. Their dog, Ozzie, a boxer, sounded the alarm with a furious bark.

Dagon approached on horseback, swinging a rope and casting threats.

"Lazy boys," he said with dark eyes.

Invisible shadowed creatures hovered on the man's back and coiled around his neck. They appeared as translucent, withered beings, and they prompted evil deeds.

David blew the ram's horn, sounding the alarm. As one body, the sons scattered and ran for cover, grabbing rocks, homemade slings, and their bows and arrows. They knew exactly what to do as warriors and had been trained for emergencies against predators—man or beast.

"Get off this property. You're trespassing. I'm putting you to work," Dagon yelled.

Jonathan, unable to avoid his quick grasp, was easy prey.

"You'll get a good price, boy." Dagon swept him off his feet, yanking him up on the horse.

"Let me go!" Jonathan screamed, fighting his captor.

The evil man was pelted with arrows and stones. He released Jonathan, who fell from the horse unharmed.

It wasn't long before the whole incident was reported to Purity, Natasha, and Alexis.

"Did you recognize the man?" Purity asked David.

He turned away, reluctant to answer.

"What are you trying to hide?"

"It was Dagon. He works at the Wisedor Dish Factory. No doubt, he was looking for free labor to work their factories," David said with spite.

"Greed has no limits. How could Favor allow this?"

"What makes you think he cares? Your schoolgirl crush on him has blinded you."

"My affections are none of your business." Purity turned to the other sons.

"You've been trained to set the captives free. God has a plan and purpose for your lives. By saving your brother, Jonathan, you've done heaven's work today."

"Revenge on Dagon," David yelled.

"Revenge on Dagon. Revenge on Dagon," the sons chanted in unison.

"Hold your peace. Hold your peace. I'll deal with this, but you have every right to defend yourselves," she instructed.

Moonlighting

Chapter 9

LATE ONE AFTERNOON in Bristol, Purity left the pawnshop with a heavy heart. She tucked the crisp bills into her purse. She hated selling Papa's prized gold pocket watch, but it was a matter of economics. Her sons needed a constant supply of goods. They needed coats, boots, and warm blankets if they were going to survive another harsh winter. Handing Papa's prized pocket watch over was painful, but she realized he would approve of the sacrifice.

Purity walked through Bristol, surrounded by bustling crowds. The newest cars scurried past horse-drawn buggies and wagons. Shops of all kinds, from bakeries to the general store, lined the busy streets.

An unshakable loneliness crept through her soul. She longed for Papa. Life without his income was unbearable and the money wouldn't go very far with so many mouths to feed. It was time to get a second job but doing so would mean putting off her dreams a little longer. Even so, it had to be done. She knew just where to go—Mave's of Bristol—more than a few blocks away. She'd noticed a "Help Wanted" sign posted the week before.

That evening, Purity returned to Shadow Brook Estate and entered the small cottage. Her mother was dozing in Papa's old chair. Naomi's head bobbed back and forth, snoring in rhythms of snorts and grunts. Purity tiptoed past her.

"Where you been, girl?" Naomi asked, breaking the silence.

"I had business in town. I want you to know I applied for a second job at Mave's of Bristol. There's an opening in the evenings for kitchen help."

"I've heard rumors about that place. It's not safe."

"And who cares about our bills? Papa's gone, and I have mouths to feed. I'm going for the interview tomorrow." Purity tried to sound convincing as she knelt at her mother's feet.

"I love you, Purity. How much can a heart take? I can't lose you too," Naomi said wrapping her arms tightly around her only daughter.

"I love you too, Mama. I'll be fine. You'll see." Purity kissed Naomi's cheek.

Later the next day, after working at Shadow Brook Estate, Purity headed to town. She sat in the office at Mave's of Bristol hotel, waiting for the interview.

Chin Lu, an Asian beauty, served tea.

"She's coming," Chin Lu said with a heavy Asian accent.

Just then, Mave Murdock burst through the door and picked up her application from the desk. Neither remembered the other from years before on Ellis Island. Due to a decrepit heart, Mave had aged fast. Her thin hair was dried and gray, her skin wrinkled, and her waistline thick.

"So, you're an experienced maid. I see you work the day shift at Shadow Brook Estate."

"That's right, but I need the money. I'd appreciate the kitchen position," Purity said, trying not to sound too desperate.

"Of course you would," Mave said, staring at Purity's full bust line and angelic features.

"There's room for advancement here. If things work out in the kitchen, so be it. If not, there are other ways to make a fortune."

"How's that accomplished?" Purity asked naively.

"Another time, another day, for that discussion. You're hired." With that, Mave left the office.

"You make lots of money here. No problem. See you tomorrow," Chin Lu said in broken English as she collected the tea service.

Purity walked through the bar area on her way out. Seductive whistles echoed from a few interested customers.

"You don't belong here. This is no place for the church going kind," said a young ballroom dancer. Purity snubbed the warning and headed for the front doors.

To her right, Mave stepped inside an ornate black wrought iron elevator and entered a code with a long bony finger. Slowly, it began to rise to the second level of the hotel. Purity caught her staring down at her with a look of seduction. It wasn't the place for the church-going kind, but at this point, economics forced the decision.

* * *

Purity worked at least three nights a week at the hotel. One of her favorite times in the evening was watching the escorts dance with the patrons. Men from all backgrounds filtered through Mave's of Bristol. It was ballroom dancing at its best, with a live band. They danced to the Waltz, Fox Trot, Grizzly Bear, and Turkey Trot.

Tonight, the band filled the place with a ragtime beat and sang, "Bee-Bop, Sassy-Frass."

> It's time to kick up your heels, shake it loose
> Beata-boop, boop, bee-bop, sassy-frass
> Find that rhythm, grab a hand, shake it loose
> Forget your worries, dance your heart away
> Life's too short, the troubles never end
>
> Bee-bop, sassy-frass, beata-boop, boop, boop
> Kick up your heels, shake it loose
> Drop what you're doing, dance, dance, dance
> Tap your feet, clap ya hands, find that rhythm
> Dance, dance, it's beata-boop, boop, Bee-bop
> Sassy-frass, beata-boop, boop, boop
> Crazy, feel the beat
>
> Life is grand, dancing to that sassy, frassy
> Gotta go rhythm, beata, boop
> Crazy, don't stop till you get it right
> Play it boys, all over again

Mandy was a real looker, with shiny blonde hair and piercing blue eyes. Mave had hired her as the lead dance instructor to teach the escorts the newest dances to keep the customers happy. She glided across the floor with a tall, classy, toned figure, like she really knew her stuff. Purity wondered how such a talent ended up at a joint on the seedy side of town.

As Mandy floated across the floor, teaching a new dancer, her knee gave out. In a world of pain, a few girls carried her off the floor.

This had happened before, but Mave kept her around because rumors circulated, she used to be a professional dancer.

"Quick. Get a chair and a cold towel," Purity said, giving orders to a few dancers.

"Don't make a fuss. It's an old injury and flares up when I least expect it," Mandy grunted in pain with a New York accent.

"You've got some slang. Where are you from?" Purity asked.

"I'm a New Yorker from way back, but don't mind my accent," Mandy said, grunting in pain.

* * *

A week later, Mandy had recuperated and was back training the girls. Purity swayed to the music, watching the dancers move with perfect choreography on the dance floor.

Mandy blew a loud whistle interrupting the dance practice.

"Hey, kid. Do ya wanna dance or not? I can teach ya," Mandy asked out of nowhere with her thick accent.

Purity eyed the pretty blonde with apprehension as she wiped a table and collected dirty glasses on a serving tray.

"Are you talking to me?" Purity asked, playing dumb.

"No. I'm talking to the wall. Sheesh," Mandy joked.

"I wouldn't mind learning."

"Some of the girls are busy tonight. I'll teach you a few dances. Then, you're on your own. Don't worry. The customers know there's no messing around unless you're willing," Mandy said, hoping for a positive response.

"Messing around. I'm not here for that," Purity said, gripped with fear.

"Don't worry. I'll keep an eye on you. Besides, you'll make more money in tips than working in that hellhole kitchen. You have orphans to feed, don't you?"

"How do you know?" Purity asked with surprise.

"There's eyes and ears everywhere. They'd be dead on the streets without you. Do it for them," Mandy encouraged and dragged Purity on the dance floor.

"Who can trust rumors?" Purity said.

"Hit it, fellas," Mandy yelled at the band.

"Follow me. Watch your posture. Move your feet. One, two, three. One, two, three. Head tilted, back straight. Remember, no free pressing. If they hold you close, that's extra money."

"No man's pressing me," Purity protested with apprehension.

"That's your decision. Just focus on your dancing," Mandy said with a laugh.

They circled around the dance floor. The other dancers snickered at Purity's inexperience and clumsy feet.

"I can't get the steps," Purity sighed in frustration.

"It's like you have two left feet and no rhythm," Mandy said, trying to make light of it.

"I'm a lost cause. I better stay in the kitchen."

"You're some kind of a klutz. Sorry, kid, I call it like I see it. We'll keep working on it. Your looks will make up for no talent."

"Thanks for the encouragement, but who's going to work the kitchen?" Purity asked, dreading the wrath of Mave.

"I'll take care of Mave. Just dance for the tips. You won't be sorry," Mandy said, giving a wink.

Later that night, customers crowded the bar and dance floor. Purity was in the kitchen scrubbing pots, second-guessing the whole thing.

"Hey, kid. It's time for on-the-job training. Come with me," Mandy said, poking her head in the kitchen.

Purity dried her hands and followed Mandy down a long hallway. They entered a nicely decorated room filled with ballroom dance gowns and matching dance shoes. Purity was astounded by the expensive apparel.

Mandy grabbed a fancy dress from a rack.

"Here. Get dressed. What size shoe are you?"

"I'm not sure. I've never worn fancy heels."

Mandy sized up her feet and pulled a pair of sparkling silver patent leather shoes from a shelf.

"Here, put these on."

"These are the real deal. I bought them in France when… well never mind. Consider them a gift."

Mandy picked up a make-up brush. She dabbed it in soft beige powder and brushed Purity's face with quick strokes.

"Make-up. I've never worn it. Mama would just die," Purity shook in guilt.

"Well, Mama's not here, is she?" Mandy sounded a little flustered.

"A little powder to start, blush on your cheeks, and a spot of lip color. The customers will like it. When they ask you to dance, put your hand out for a tip. Then again, if they want another go-round."

As Mandy applied the make-up, Purity grew curious.

"What were you doing in France? These shoes must have cost a fortune."

"That's where my world ended. No use remembering what could have been. A dream that came to nothing. The rest ain't worth talking about," Mandy said, with a noticeable drop in mood.

"I understand. I don't know what's worse, a dream that never happens or one that's cut short."

"Both are pretty sad, but what do you know about disappointments? You get to work at that fancy Shadow Brook Estate," Mandy said, giving Purity a wink.

"Fancy for them. I'm just the help, and they remind me of it every day." "There," Mandy said, placing the make-up back on the table.

"I'll let you dress." In a moment, Mandy was gone.

Purity held her stomach in an attempt to calm her nerves.

"Make-up and dancing with men. Mama's going to kill me if she finds out. Shh, it's our little secret," Purity said out loud, pressing a finger to her lips while looking into an ornate mirror.

Rising slowly, she slipped into the ballroom dress made of blue silk with lace trim embellishing the neck and hemline. Then in awe, she picked up the sparkling silver ballroom dance shoes. She slid on one shoe at a time. They were a perfect fit. Purity walked around, overwhelmed with her transformation. As she gazed into a full-length mirror, her countenance saddened, and she sang, "Girl in the Mirror."

Who is that girl in the mirror
Is that really me, staring back
I can't believe I'm here
Dancing for tips and a laugh
Who is that girl in the mirror
Is that really me, staring back
All my fine dreams are slipping away
I've become someone I don't even know

Is that really me in the mirror
Am I living a fantasy and a lie
When I was a child
I dreamed of my Prince come true
But, like sand falling through my fingertips
I'm losing a grip on my soul way too soon

Is that really me in the mirror
I'm someone else in a moment's time
I wonder how a girl like me ended up like this
God, where's your plan if my life's in your hands

Who is that girl in the mirror, is it really me or a lie
Why can't I find my place in this crazy ole' world
It's nothing but a fight trying to survive
Somehow, I'm trying to keep my mind

Who is that girl in the mirror
Is that really me, staring back
I don't know myself these days
My bones so tired, I'm too young to retire
God help me find my way, as it all fades away
Who is that girl in the mirror
I don't know myself these days

Purity tore her gaze from the mirror and headed to the dance floor.

She stood looking like a princess by the crowded dance floor as the music played. A handsome man took her hand and began moving with the upbeat sound. Then remembering, she held out her hand and looked intently into his eyes. He slipped her a dollar bill.

"You must be new?" he asked, looking her up and down.

"It's my first go-round. I only know one dance, and that's pretty shaky," Purity said, surprised by the easy cash.

"Maybe I can teach you a few things," he said, and off they went.

He was an experienced dancer and gave Purity some impromptu instructions. Before the shift was over, her tip bag was full. She was excited about the possibilities of providing for her family.

That night, Mandy dropped Purity off at the entrance of Shadow Brook Estate in her brand new 1909 car.

"Great car. You must be doing something right," Purity said, looking it over.

"Keep dancing, and it just might happen for you. See you tomorrow," Mandy said, bidding goodnight.

Purity stumbled in the darkness, making her way up the long cobblestone driveway. It was quiet enough to finally listen to reason. She contemplated her decisions.

"God, I don't know what I'm doing," she thought.

Gently, her hand steadied the bobbing tip bag hanging from her waist.

The cottage door creaked as Purity entered the small, dark kitchen. She washed, slipped into a nightgown, and rubbed her aching feet before falling into bed.

She glanced at the music box on her dresser, and golden swirls of sparkling light wisped around it.

"I'm seeing things," Purity whispered and hobbled over with sore, blistered feet. She lifted its lid, and music played. The tiny ballroom dancers popped up and spun round and round.

"What I'd give to dance like that," she said, closing the lid and returning to bed. She pulled the blankets high around her neck and descended into a deep sleep.

The Captain Sings

Chapter 10

In the deep dark of night, Purity was lifted from her bed by rainbow Light Beings who resembled angels. Beautiful colors radiated from them, spilling into the dark room. With a wave of their hands, she floated in a weightless state.

"Bring Purity up here," a voice thundered from above.

"Yes, Captain, Purity's coming," one of the Light Beings answered.

The Captain, mounted on his white horse, hovered above, surrounded by his vast army and sparkling stars. He sang a lively tune, "Captain's Love Song," as Purity ascended.

> My love, come away, come away with me
> I'm Captain of the Lord's Army
> Come away, come away to far-off galaxies
> Where the sun and planets shine by my design
> Welcome to the New Earth
> Where each one comes, turning death to life
> For I'm Captain of the New Earth
> Where my people never grow old or tired
>
> Up through the universe where wars arise
> My arms are open wide, I'll fight by your side
> Come to my world, open the radiant gates
> I'll meet you there by the white sandy shores

Look my way and be mesmerized
With just one glance of my fiery eyes
Get ready to run, I've got plans for you
For I'm Captain of Lord's Army
Ruler of the New Earth

My love, come away, come away with me
I'm Captain of the Lord's Army
Come and fly to far off galaxies
Let's dance on the stars, till Kingdom come
Just you and me, like shooting stars, we'll go far
I've heard your cry, so don't be surprised
When all your dreams in an instant come alive

Come away, come away, my love
Set your sails, catch the wind
Ride the river in my world
Catching the sights with delight
I'm Captain of the Lord's Army
Mighty in battle, able to save
Where the mountain of my witnesses
Are watching from above
United with song till the victory's won
I commission you to save the slaves
For justice and doing right

For I'm Captain of the Lord's Army
King of the New Earth
Once you arrive, you'll thrive in my light
Trust me for it all, victory's been won
My love, come away, come away with me
For I'm Captain of the Lord's Army

The Captain and his army vanished in the night sky. The Light Beings lifted Purity to the towering rooftops of Shadow Brook Estate. She woke in their presence, but oddly, wasn't afraid.

"Am I dreaming?"

"Hush. The enemy has sharp ears," one of the Light Beings said, putting a radiant rainbow-colored finger to her lips.

Two huge eagles waited on the roof, surveying the territory with their keen ultra-sonic radar vision and hearing. Laser rays of deep blue light beamed from their eyes, reaching miles in every direction.

"Any sign of Ahaba and his evil army?" a Light Being asked the eagles, Keenan and Valor.

"I'm not detecting their chaos," Valor answered as sonic blue light beams jetted from his eyes. Keenan kept on task and continued moving his thick neck to and fro, sending out more rays for enemy detection.

Favor, fast asleep, was awakened by what sounded like heavy footsteps on the rooftop above. He sat up with a quick start, jumped from bed, and lit a candle in haste. He bolted from his room and made his way to the small door leading to a narrow staircase to the roof. The low flame from the candle swayed in the gentle breeze as he stepped into the dark open air.

Favor spotted the enormous eagles and rainbow Light Beings. He rubbed his eyes in disbelief.

"I've lost my mind," he thought and ducked out of sight.

The Light Beings slowly lowered Purity on Keenan's slippery, soft feathers. The eagles were kind, and their wingspans massive.

"Who are you? Where did you come from?" Purity asked, still half asleep. Keenan turned his large, feathered head, and with one eye, focused on his passenger.

"I'm Keenan, and my brother's name is Valor. Nice to meet you, Purity,"

"The angels are Bright and Star," Valor said, introducing the Light Beings.

"You talk, too. Nice to meet everyone. Where are we going?" Purity asked with enthusiasm.

"We're going to where all things become new," Valor said with a smirk.

And with that, the eagles took a running start over the mansion's rooftop, flapping their wings for a lift into the night sky. The roof rumbled under their stampeding feet, shaking the mansion below.

Mrs. Wisedor woke in horror and shook her husband violently. He was snoring heavily and spoke a few unintelligible words.

"Wake up. The roof's falling in," Mrs. Wisedor said, fearing they would be crushed.

"What's going on?" Mr. Wisedor mumbled, still shaking heavy slumber.

Then all was silent, and the shaking stopped.

"It felt like the end of the world," his wife bellowed in fear.

"Back to sleep, my dear. The sky's not falling yet," Mr. Wisedor blundered and rolled over.

The eagles ascended the heights, flying through the atmosphere. Bright and Star morphed into brilliant colors, encapsulating the two eagles and Purity with a protective magnetic shield.

"I love your colors," Purity said to Bright and Star.

"And we see your light," Bright Star answered merging into one being—a large bright star.

"It's time to fly high, above all your troubles and strife," Keenan started to sing.

"I'm ready for my dreams to come true," Purity said with sleepy eyes.

The higher they flew, the tighter she held on, clutching the soft feathers on the eagle's back. Purity was electrified by the sights of a living universe filled with billions of stars and spinning galaxies. Behind her, the old earth that is passing away appeared smaller and smaller.

The eagles and Bright Star sang, "Fly, Fly Away" and swayed in a fun dance as they glided on the wind.

> It's time to fly, fly, fly away
> Leaving your troubles and strife
> It's time to fly, fly, fly away
> Shake, shake, shake it off
> Your blues and heavy heart
> We'll show you the way
> To live out your days
>
> Wind under our wings
> Headed for a brighter day
> No more looking back
> On what you can't change
> It's time to fly, fly, fly away

Set your sights on what's to come
It will blow your mind
Till Kingdom come, it's time to ride
On the rays of the sun
Through the blue gates, till heaven's come
The great beyond is calling your name
Oh, the stories you'll tell from above and beyond
Shake, shake, shake it off

It's time to fly away, fly, fly, fly away
The trials are just a test of faith
You've got nothing but the best
Heading your way
Shake, shake, shake it off
Stand up, be brave, you're almost there
It's time to fly, fly, fly away

The enemy tried to block your way
Shut the doors and lock you out
When all seems lost, you'll know the way
And journey find your rightful place
Shake, shake, shake it off
It's time to fly, fly, fly away
It's time to fly, fly, fly away
Above all your troubles and strife this day
Shake, shake, shake it off

They traveled light-years of distance in moments, singing and bumping along on the atmospheric waves of the universe. Vast galaxies began to blur as they passed out of time.

When they broke through into interstellar space, a different weightless atmosphere enabled the eagles to fly without flapping their wings. They soared on invisible energy that carried them effortlessly along. Purity's eyes grew heavy, but she fought exhaustion, not wanting to miss gigantic galaxies and massive stars.

Valor and Keenan slowed in what appeared to be gloriously colored gas clouds of vibrant pinks, orange, blues, and yellow light.

"What is this place?" Purity asked in awe.

"This is where the stars are born," Valor answered.

Just then, a bright light flashed, and a tiny star was birthed.

"A baby star is born?" Purity asked in delight.

Keenan and Valor nodded in affirmation. Purity reached out and held it momentarily in her hand.

"That's enough. Let it go," Valor said.

Purity blew it from her hands, like blowing a kiss. Then Keenan whisked her away.

"We must go," Keenan said as though pressed with an important matter.

Time lapsed, and there was no fighting a summoning sleep, melting deep into her soul. Its peace was so overwhelming that all the cares and concerns of life faded away. She finally burrowed into Keenan's feathers and fell fast asleep. Keenan looked back momentarily as though a mother hen watching over a chickling. Purity talked in her sleep, mumbling words in faraway dreams.

Purity did not know how long or how far they had journeyed through the vast universe. She woke with a start as eerie sounds from interstellar space pierced her ears with a thunderous, rapturous noise. She poked her head from the soft feathers, and gusty winds pelted her face. Looking about, she tried to focus on the endless stars and planets ahead. Far in the distance, a brilliant planet appeared, in colors of iridescent blue woven into a golden shining atmosphere. It was surrounded by erupting splashes of glistening fire.

As they drew closer, majestic, radiant blue arches towered above, suspended on the dark energy of the universe. It was the gateway into a different universe. A force field of entrancing power allowed only those with permission to enter.

Moments before they entered the mystical arches, the massive eagles were hit by an overwhelming host of evil. Keenan increased his speed and made abrupt flying maneuvers to avoid an onslaught of fiery arrows. Valor tried his best to fight off the assailants with his massive wings. Bright and Star pulled weapons appearing like bows and arrows from their backs and fired multiple rounds of laser-sharp arrows at the enemy.

A blinding light shone from Purity that hurt the eyes of the enemy.

Ahaba, Prince of the Air, ordered his troops to attack.

"Stop Purity! Attack! Attack! Snuff out her blinding light." His features were skeletal and twisted in a scowl. Fiery darts spewed from his mouth and hands. The darts hit Purity's gracious escorts with an onslaught of force. Ahaba grunted out the evil tune, "Purity's Light."

> Purity's light is no delight
> Make her brightness go away
> She shines like heaven
> Blinding our eyes in burning pain
> She must be stopped, so fire the darts
> She's a threat to our deadly ways
> Shoot the darts, through the heart
>
> Purity's light is no delight
> Make her brightness go away
> Fire the darts, and snuff her out
> She'll be given powers to devour
> Our darkest hopes and plans
> She has no idea what's ahead
> She'll be used to stop monstrous plans
> Purity's light is no delight
> Make her brightness go away

Ahaba's forces hit even harder with wave after wave of fiery darts. Star and Bright encapsulated them with a magnetic field that covered them like a webbed blanket—it's shield repelling each strike.

Warriors of Light poured forth from the majestic arches in countless numbers. They rode on creatures resembling horses with faces appearing as lions that roared in battle. They wore body armor, helmets of gold, chest plates of silver, and held swords of fire. They were soldiers in The Captain's army and inhabited the glistening planet below called the New Earth.

Their shields extinguished the viscous darts of the enemy.

Ahaba battled and regrouped with hordes seven times more powerful. In a violent skirmish against the light and dark, Purity proved again and again to be a target.

"Stop Purity forever! Snuff out her light!" Ahaba shouted with nasty snarls. His forces drew weapons with mounted bows to strike the defenseless beauty.

The mighty Warriors of Light fought gallantly, trying to protect Purity with their fiery shields. Fiery arrows hit both eagles, and some of their feathers ignited with flaming fire. Purity held on tight as Keenan tried his best to remain in flight. The ride was rough, like a bucking horse out of control. She was almost thrown from the eagle's back and struggled to hold onto his sleek feathers.

Purity tried to put out his burning feathers.

"Ouch, that's hot," she groaned as the flames burned her hands.

Keenan shrieked with loud squawks, in agonizing pain. Valor battled and tried his best to protect Keenan as the protective shield from Bright Star was torn to shreds.

The Warriors of Light continued to repel the onslaught of unrelenting attacks from Ahaba's dark forces. But despite all their defenses, a fiery dart hit Purity in the right shoulder with bone-crunching pain. The force of it toppled her from Keenan's back. Her body was catapulted with such force into the dark energy of the universe that she was rendered unconscious. Her blood flowed, drop by drop, into a weightless atmosphere.

The Warriors of Light raced against Ahaba's dark forces to reach Purity first—wanting to preserve her precious life.

Captain of the Lord's Army appeared, riding on his majestic white stallion. The archangels surrounded him, appearing as warriors of fire. Michael, Gabriel, Raphael, Ariel, and Azrael drew galactic weapons that resembled high powered sonic bows with arrows of burning fire.

"We're here for the clean-up," Gabriel said, relishing the fight.

"Just say the word, Captain," Michael said, engaging his bow.

The other archangels followed suit, rallying for a battle.

"I release the archangels to battle," the Captain shouted.

"For our King and the New Earth," shouted Raphael.

The archangel's rushed into battle with the Captain's army. Ahaba's army put up a miserable defense.

"Retreat! Retreat!" Ahaba shouted, realizing in the Captain's presence that Purity was out of reach.

The dark forces obeyed and retreated into the dark energy of the universe howling in the loss.

The Captain was kingly, handsome, and a "Warrior above all Warriors." Instantly, he was translated by Purity's side with just a thought. Sliding from his horse, he stood on dark matter, determined to save this special vessel. He retrieved her with a forceful hand and noticed she wasn't breathing. Pulling her motionless body close, he inhaled a deep breath and blew life back into her lungs. His breath appeared as a misty golden vapor. Purity's chest once again rose and fell with life.

Her blood continued to flow on the weightless atmosphere as he held her tightly with one arm. His hands, scarred from previous battles, morphed in appearance, like glowing fire that emitted healing power. With a gentle touch, he first cauterized the wound to stop her bleeding. Then, he healed the blistered burns with strokes of seamless energy.

Bright Star and the eagles appeared again. The great Captain gently handed Purity over to their care. Bright Star encompassed her in rainbow light, like a baby wrapped in a blanket, and placed Purity on Valor's soft feathers. Keenan was too badly injured to carry the extra weight.

The archangels flew close by, keeping guard as the eagles and Bright Star approached the high radiant blue arches. Purity rested as though in blissful sleep.

The force field of gold and silver guarding the entrance allowed them to pass. As Keenan passed through the majestic arches, his wounds began to vibrate. He was revived and restored instantly. The awful burned, bloodied wounds were covered over with pink flesh, and his feathers grew. Valor flew close by his brother through the peaceful atmosphere. They descended into the fresh, misty skies of another world with breathtaking landscapes, snow-peaked mountains, majestic waterfalls, and scenic countryside.

Purity was gently placed in a large sailboat. Multiple sails billowed in the wind as it moved down a winding river at a steady pace. The waters glistened with colors of silver, gold, blue, pink, and purple. An entrancing breeze continued to flow, penetrating every cell of her body.

Moments later, the sound of singing flowed through her sleep world. It reverberated over the land and every mountain and filled every valley. It was a sound that awakened every fiber of her soul. Voices were singing, "New Earth."

> Welcome to the New Earth
> Where the generations come

All toil's done, the battle's won
The books are opened
His thoughts revealed

Welcome to the New Earth
Rewards to the faithful
From death to life
All is gain, no struggle remains
Welcome to the New Earth

Purity woke, humming the tune. She sprang forth as though rising from the dead. For the first time, her eyes caught sight of the New Earth—a world of indescribable beauty. Her bloodied clothing instantly changed to a shimmery rainbow-colored dress that sparkled with gold and silver. She peered over the side of the boat. Her reflection in the water was more beautiful than ever before.

She was awed by the sheer majesty of deep blue skies, with streaks of pink, purple, and orange. Above, glowing planets orbited so close it seemed possible to reach out and pull one down.

Keenan and Valor circled overhead and waved goodbye with a flap of their wings. Bright Star ascended gradually and joined the light of the sky above, fading into its brilliance. The archangels returned to the universe, ready for new battles.

Purity grabbed her shoulder, remembering the piercing pain, but there was no injury there.

"Am I dead or alive?" she questioned, feeling her face, arms, and hands.

The sailboat ran aground with a thud on the edge of the riverbank, knocking her body to the boat's floor. Gathering her faculties, she hopped out and began exploring the wide-open spaces filled with lush forests and exotic animals. She peered through some brush.

The ground began quaking under her feet, sending vibrations through her body.

"What's going on?" she thought. In sheer terror, she hid in the brush.

A vast army passed through the territory right before her eyes. They were soldiers, male and female, dressed in armor-clad uniforms, riding in rank on white horses. They appeared battle-weary as though returning from a long journey. Despite exhaustion, they sang, "Captain of the Lord's Army" with all their might.

> He's Captain of the Lord's Army
> He gives the victory
> Captain of the Lord's Army
> He gives the victory
>
> We stand, we fight
> We give it all our might
> Until the battle's won
> Until the battle's won
>
> He's Captain of the victory
> He sees the battle through
> Gifting those who fight
> With power and insight
> Not caving into fright
> His army stands tall and bright
>
> He's Captain of the Lord's Army
> He gives the victory
> Captain of the Lord's Army
> He gives the victory

As they passed, some warriors spoke of a recent battle.

"We could have given the victory, but they failed to trust and believe," said a warrior.

"Believing for the impossible guarantees the victory."

"They defeated themselves, victims of fear. Refusing the Captain's power to win was their doom," a gallant warrior sighed in grief.

Purity backed up slowly and ran, leaving the army far behind. She raced through the forest and headed back to the river's shore.

The billowing white sails flapped in the soft wind as the boat remained moored on the beach. Purity's feet crunched on the soft white sand. Stopping abruptly, she noticed a mighty warrior next to the boat. It was Captain of the Lord's Army, but Purity didn't know it.

He stepped into the river and dipped a golden challis into the water. He appeared war-torn, with perspiration and a muddied complexion. He wore a chest protector labeled "Righteousness" and a helmet with the word "Salvation" engraved upon it. A large sword hung from a belt engraved with the word "Truth." His boots were knee-high with gripping short spikes for traction on each sole. He was fit with muscles that flexed at the smallest movement.

One step at a time, Purity backed up slowly, trying to escape his attention.

"How was the journey?" he asked, gulping down the cold refreshing water. He filled the cup again and splashed his head and body.

"Are you talking to me?"

"Is there anyone else around?" he questioned.

"Where am I?" Purity asked, keeping a safe distance.

"It's called the New Earth, where all things become new."

"Am I dead? Is this heaven?"

"This is the New Earth. All are not here yet. You're here for a while. Many are on the way, and others won't come for generations."

"Thanks for clearing everything up," Purity said sarcastically.

He approached, holding the cup in his right hand. His blazing eyes penetrated deep into her soul. Under the enormous weight of his gaze, she dropped to her knees. His war-scarred hand lifted her chin gently.

"You're looking for direction. You've got a lot of questions. We all have battles and victories ahead. Choose your battles carefully. And look to the Captain, who always knows what to do."

"The Captain came for my Papa. Please, take me to him. I need his help."

The Captain returned to the river and filled the golden challis with cool water again. His armor shifted, exposing his back and deep scars. The mere sight of it took her breath away. The warrior read her facial expressions as he turned to offer another drink.

"Don't be afraid. I'm a warrior. The battles can leave scares."

"Your battles have been many. The sight of them is frightening."

"I'm a frontline warrior. I get hit first but watch out for the revenge." He extended the cup.

"Have some living water. It will bring life to all you're going to accomplish. Drink deep. Drink it all."

Purity took the cup and peered into the liquid.

"What are you worried about? A little seaweed?" the Warrior joked.

"Very funny." Hesitantly, she drank it down. It was smooth, like silk, and tasted like an irresistible grape juice. By the time the cup was emptied, her mind cleared, and any weariness left with her next breath.

"If it's living water, then my body too." She clutched the cup with both hands and stepped into the river.

He submerged her body under the passing current. After a few seconds, he pulled her up, revitalized. Her lungs burst with exhilaration. Their eyes locked.

"Remember, you're never alone." He breathed on her, releasing what appeared as golden particles landing on her skin.

Her eyes shifted in distraction as a large flock of doves flew close overhead.

"What's your name?" She looked back to the warrior, but he had vanished.

"Come back. Don't leave me here alone," she shouted. Purity's heart swelled with a love she had never experienced in her short existence. It was different than the romantic love she had for Favor—far superior and unexplainably more profound. How could this new love be so complete? But there it was, in an instant, a love so high and deep, once you were in it, you never wanted to leave its all-consuming power. It felt inescapable, as wide as it was long, able to span the eons of time, even beyond her last breath. In full surrender to it, she sang, "Forever Changed."

> I'm forever changed, with one look in your eyes
> You stole my heart right from the start
> How could it be, a love so deep
> I've struggled to find all my life
> My bitter soul wasted away
> Until I met you, until I met you
>
> The sound of your voice, the beat of your heart
> The touch of your hand has given me life
> I'm forever changed, with one look in your eyes

You stole my heart, right from the start
With one look in your eyes, I'm forever changed
I'm renewed, like a bird set free from a cage
To live again, to love again, my hope's renewed
All my dreams come true
With one look in your eyes, I'm forever changed
You stole my heart, I'm strong and set free
Return my love with open arms
And we'll set the world on fire
With one look in your eyes, I'm forever changed

* * *

Purity woke in her dark bedroom in the cottage, gasping in shock. Her hair and nightgown were soaking wet.

"Was I really there?" she asked, trying to comprehend the journey. She set her head back on the pillow and fell fast asleep.

* * *

On the New Earth, in his great palace, Captain of the Lord's Army peered into a basin of pure living water. He placed his scarred hands over it. The water stirred and illuminated the image of Purity sleeping in her room.

"Rest my love," the Captain said with affection.

His focus was distracted by an ominous presence behind him. The Captain turned with a precise, sharp motion.

Standing before him was Ahaba, "Prince of the Air," from the old earth that is passing away. His grotesque skeletal features exuded a rancid smell of death and dripped green and yellow secretions. In a flash of anger, Ahaba drew a sword that projected flames of sulfur. He thrust it near the Captain's chest with violent force.

"You're slipping. I invaded the New Earth without resistance," Ahaba boasted.

The Captain gazed with laser focus into the beast's dark eyes. The evil Prince dropped to his knees under the intensity of such a gaze.

"You're here because I allowed it. Welcome to the New Earth, a place you'll never enjoy," the Captain taunted.

Ahaba broke from the agonizing gaze and with a quick maneuver, jumped to his feet. He slashed his sword at the Captain, who evaded the strikes with swift moves. Captain lifted his right hand, and a fiery sword instantly appeared. They fought a brutal battle for several minutes, crashing into furnishings and slicing everything in their path.

"I've had enough fun. It's time for you to go," the Captain huffed.

"I'll kill Purity. She'll never fulfill her destiny," the evil Prince threatened.

"She's one of my chosen ones, to set the captives free. I know the plans I have for her. No weapon formed against her will prosper. My light on her will never cease to burn your eyes."

Ahaba screamed in pain and dropped to his knees. With a final blow, the Captain catapulted Ahaba through a massive sky window.

Hearts Revealed

Chapter 11

THE TEENAGERS WERE promised work and the opportunity to learn English. Each stumbled over the other, clutching their sparse belongings as they disembarked the large ship in Bristol's harbor.

"Come on, come on," a sailor barked.

"Get going before you're spotted. Boys in the wagon. Girls with the lady."

The male teens were loaded in a waiting cattle wagon.

"Where are they going?" the driver asked Mave.

"Wisedor Dish Factory. Ask for Dagon," Mave said with a glare.

The female teens lined up in front of Mave, who appeared more sinister each day. Her wiry hair, aging skin, and piercing eyes evoked distrust and fear in the captives. Mave's nails dug into and pinched the human cargo while maneuvering them in the desired direction.

"Follow me," she hissed as a cruel scowl descended over her countenance. The teens followed down a long back alley, littered with garbage, scampering rats, and the smell of foul sewage. They climbed a narrow staircase and disappeared behind a heavy door.

Inside, two men approached. One held each captive in a vice grip while the other tore the clothing from their right shoulder and pressed a hot iron into their skin. Screams erupted, and the air reeked of burning flesh. They were branded with the letter 'M.'

* * *

On his way home, the sailor noticed a boy shaking from the cold and begging for bread.

"What's your name? Where ya headed?" the sailor asked.

"Orion's my name. I have nowhere to go," the boy looked down with hopeless misery.

"I bet you're hungry," the sailor taunted and then pulled some red grapes from his pack. He dangled them like a carrot in front of a horse.

The boy gulped them down with ravenous hunger.

"You can sleep on the street or come to my place. How does that suit you, boy? I can put you to work in the morning. You have to eat, so you have to work."

In desperation, the boy nodded in agreement.

"Where's your father and mother?" the sailor hissed.

"I don't know."

The boy's face and hands were dirty, and sores filled with green pus festered on his scalp.

"Disgusting," the sailor moaned.

Slowly, the child followed his only hope of survival down the street and into a small, musty apartment.

"Come in, and keep quiet," the sailor barked. He heated some water on the stove and poured it into a basin, then grabbed a clean towel from the shelf.

"Scrub your filth. Here's soap, a towel, and a nightshirt. Let me see those sores. I have some sulfur ointment that might help. Isn't this better than being on the street?"

The boy washed and put on the over-sized nightshirt. Then the sailor used some gauze and applied the ointment to the oozing sores.

"All done, there's your bed. Get some rest. You're working tomorrow," he commanded, pointing to a small pallet on the floor.

"Where, sir?" inquired the boy.

"You'll find out soon enough," he growled and threw the boy a blanket and pillow.

The next morning the streets of Bristol were jammed with cars and horse-drawn wagons. The sidewalks were crowded with folks headed here and there.

The sailor's voice sounded with no conscience.

"Get up, get dressed, and let's go." The man tossed a uniform at the boy. It was dingy gray and a little oversized, but it would do.

It was a short walk to the Wisedor Dish Factory. The old sailor dragged Orion in by the collar. Dagon, the manager, exchanged a handful of cash with the sailor.

Ahaba hovered over the factory with his evil army. They clanged their war weapons, celebrating the birth of another slave. Ahaba reached down through the factory's roof with fingers appearing as misty black snakes. The wicked spirit gripped the necks of Dagon and the sailor. Both men gasped momentarily as the hold tightened. Ahaba's horde sat on the roof, watching with penetrating vision. Then once the exchange commenced, they flapped their bat-like wings and flew away, one by one, laughing hysterically.

Dagon threatened the sailor, "Not a word to anyone. I have friends you don't want to meet."

"Not a word. I like my beer money," the sailor said, shoving the money into his pocket. The sailor left, escaping into the crowds on the busy Bristol streets.

Dagon grabbed Orion by the collar and dragged him up to the third floor.

"Get to work, boy."

Immediately, other boys began to show Orion how to wrap the fine dishes. Tears flowed from the boy's eyes.

Revelation

Chapter 12

A MISTY FOG COVERED the Bristol harbor leading to Narragansett Bay. Mr. Wisedor sat in his luxury office at the shipbuilding yard. It was the end of another long day.

Favor tapped on the office door.

"Come in," his father answered, happy to see his son.

"We have business to discuss. Sit down."

"Do we?" Favor asked as he sat.

"I'm officially releasing our business enterprises into your competent hands. I'll check on the affairs from time to time, but as of today, I'm retired. You'll handle the day-to-day now. Of course, the managers will still report to me regarding the labor force."

"Retired. I didn't expect this so soon. I'll take over under one condition. I need access to all the records."

"That's not possible, and I don't want to argue," Mr. Wisedor insisted, as though he had something to hide.

"Then find yourself another replacement. I'm not going into this blindfolded."

"You have a way of getting what you want. You're too much like your mother. Take my advice. Leave things alone, and you'll be handsomely rewarded."

"Enough of the family secrets. What are you trying to hide?"

"Your mother will have a fit, but I don't care. You're of age, and it's time we discussed all the family business ventures. Pull the ledger from my top drawer," Mr. Wisedor said begrudgingly and handed the key over.

Favor unlocked the desk drawer and pulled out a thick ledger.

"When's the next cargo shipment from Cuba coming in?" Mr. Wisedor asked.

"Cargo shipment from Cuba?" Favor thumbed through the pages.

"We're the proud owners of a sugar cane plantation there. The fresh cane makes the best molasses for rum production. And I'm happy to announce that we own the only distillery in Bristol.

"I wasn't aware we owned a plantation in Cuba or a rum distillery. Where's the factory?"

"It's called Bristol Distillery on Chestnut Road. I've been meaning to take you there when the time was right. I'd say under the circumstances, that's now. We'll head over this week."

"Very well. Give me the records, and I'll give you a full report of our earnings, gains, and losses by next week. I'm hoping to inject fresh ideas into the order of things," Favor said, grabbing a stack of records from the desk.

"I didn't ask you for fresh ideas. Everything is set up to run the way I like it. I just need your oversight, not micromanagement. Do you get that, Son? The managers will continue to report to me. We have our own understanding."

"Calm down. We don't have to change everything at once," Favor said, annoyed.

"So, when's our ship coming in from Cuba?" Mr. Wisedor questioned again.

Favor thumbed through the pages of the ledger.

"Looks like tomorrow. According to this, it's loaded with sugar for the rum and men for cheap labor."

"Perfect timing. We received an order for a large ship to be built by next fall. We're going to need a full labor force. You're the new boss, and I'm officially retired. Somewhat, that is. It's time to start enjoying life." Mr. Wisedor pulled a heavy key ring from his jacket and plopped it in Favor's hand.

"Here are the keys to our buildings." With that, Mr. Wisedor left the office.

Favor put the keys to work, and like a detective, he opened the locked file cabinets. He searched vigorously through all the records. Eventually, he left the office with a briefcase full of business ledgers and headed to Shadow Brook Estate.

It was late when Favor entered the dimly lit mansion. He went straight to the library and piled the business ledgers on the desk. Some of the records were from previous decades.

He sat down and began looking over the numbers. What he found was incriminating. He was sickened by reports of free or cheap labor, recorded deaths, and injuries at the shipyard, fine china, and rum factories. Then he found a record dating back to slave voyages.

In the wee hours of the morning, Favor had fallen asleep, his face buried in the ledgers. The Captain hovered above him and reached into his dreams.

Favor was on a ship headed to West Africa in the year 1808. The ocean breeze blew through his hair as he stood on deck, marveling at the beauty of the coastline.

The ship docked at a large port. Lines of chained black slaves stood on the dock waiting to board. It was as if Favor could read their thoughts.

"My mother and father will miss me forever," one teen thought with his head bowed.

"My wife's pregnant. I'll never see her again, or my child," a young man thought, looking straight into Favor's eyes.

"I was raped and beaten by my captors," a female teen with a battered face thought as she gazed into his eyes.

Favor woke from the nightmare with a jolt. He fell from the chair to his knees, repenting.

"God, what have we done? Forgive my forefathers. They were criminals at best."

Invisible to Favor, Captain placed his fiery scarred hand on Favor's heart, causing him to feel a deep conviction. Favor sobbed for some time and then went to bed.

* * *

Early the next morning, Purity oversaw dusting the main floor of the estate. She carried a basket containing clean dust towels, furniture oil, and a feather duster. She started in the dining room, moved to the grand parlor, and then entered the library.

She wiped the fine busts of Abraham Lincoln, George Washington, and Thomas Jefferson with a damp white cloth. Carefully, she feather-dusted the ornate wooden frames encasing exquisite oil paintings of ocean scenes, family portraits, and the French countryside.

Next to be dusted was the large cherry wood desk. She gently dusted around the stacks of business ledgers. One of the open books caught her attention. It was titled "Triangular Trade, 1790 to 1820."

"What's this?" Purity thought and read through the document quickly. She saw the other ledgers and found a hiding place in a window nook where she could look them over.

Her hiding spot was not as safe as she'd thought, for Mrs. Wisedor happened upon her and stared down at her with suspicion.

"What are you doing? Our records have no business in your clutches."

"I'm doing my job, dusting and rearranging the clutter, that's all," Purity answered, trying to defend her actions. She stood and sat the three ledgers down on the desk. Picking up the feather duster, she dusted around the paper clutter.

Mrs. Wisedor squinted, calculating her next move. Before she could say another word, the interaction was interrupted.

"Come at once, my dear. I need you," her husband yelled from the grand parlor. She knew from experience not to keep him waiting.

"If you want your job, leave our family business alone," Mrs. Wisedor threatened and retreated in a whirlwind.

Purity gasped a sigh of relief. Quickly, she picked up the ledgers and stashed them into the cleaning basket. She covered them with a clean white dust towel and headed for the small cottage.

Once inside, she set the basket on the table. Purity opened the ledgers, one by one, inhaling the information. A newspaper clipping dated April 4, 1900, from the Bristol Times Newspaper, rustled free from the ledger as a gust of wind blew over it from the open cottage window.

She grabbed hold of it.

"What's this?"

The article was titled "Wisedor Slave Trade." It read: "Between 1790 and 1807, there were 934 recorded slave voyages sponsored by

Rhode Island merchants. The ships carried over 106,000 slaves from their homeland in Africa. Eighty percent of this slave trade was carried out from the ports of Bristol, Newport, and Providence. The Wisedor family was responsible for most of the slave voyages originating out of Bristol, Rhode Island, between the years 1790 to 1807."

Purity was shocked but continued reading.

"During this time, the family used slave labor in all their enterprises. The triangular trade brought in a fortune at every port. It started with harvested sugar from the Cuban plantation that was brought back to Bristol and distilled into rum. The rum was then exported to West Africa and sold along with guns and furs to purchase slaves. Then the slaves were transported back to Cuba to replenish the plantation with labor and to pick up a fresh harvest of sugar cane. The cargo was brought back to Bristol, including some slaves, to start the process all over again. Each triangular trip brought in hundreds of thousands of dollars."

* * *

The next morning was cold and foggy at the Bristol deep-water harbor overlooking Narragansett Bay. A foghorn blew, and the lighthouse beamed penetrating shafts of light to a ship emerging through the misty waters.

Purity watched, with her coat buttoned, collar pulled high, and a hat tucked over her eyes. A black leather satchel hung over her right shoulder, weighted with the three ledgers.

The ship approached slowly, navigating into the harbor. Torturous groans grew louder as the ship docked. Translucent, billowing dark figures from Ahaba's army hovered above as though strengthened by the stench and misery below.

The face of Ahaba appeared as a translucent skull in the dark clouds above. He transmitted a spirit of hopelessness over those huddled inside the ship.

The ports men yelled directions to the ship's sailors.

"A little to the right. Bring her in straight away."

Large ropes were cast, and several ports men tied the ship to the dock. The human cargo, from European countries, shuffled off, frightened and exhausted from the long, nauseating voyage.

"We need twenty-five men at the rum factory, twenty-five men at the dish factory, and two hundred and fifty to stay here and work the shipyard. We have an order for another deep-water ship to be built," a dock supervisor yelled.

"Yes, sir," a ports man replied and began organizing the new arrivals.

Purity watched as the men were loaded into wagons, waiting to be taken to the factories. The remaining two hundred and fifty men waited in the cold fog.

The evil hordes from above raised their hands toward the familiar beauty and hissed. Others flew over to Ahaba and pointed to Purity's presence. Every time he looked her way, he was blinded by her light.

"The Captain's light shines on her. Off with her head," he shouted at his evil soldiers.

He extended a wicked hand to strike, but the young angel Josiah shot a fiery arrow his way.

"How dare you interfere," Ahaba roared.

"We're a Ring of Grace, sent by Captain of the Lord's Army to protect Purity," Josiah said, aiming another arrow.

Instantly, Ahaba was surrounded by four other translucent child warrior angels shining with full-body armor with raised weapons. They sang as one, "Ring of Grace."

> We're a Ring of Grace, a Ring of Grace
> Commissioned, tried, and true
> We're making sure Purity's protected
> From the likes of you
> Don't mess with us, we're tough guys too
> We may be small, but don't be fooled
>
> We're a Ring of Grace, a Ring of Grace
> Standing tall against you goons
> Fighting strong, we'll whip you too
> We're a Ring of Grace, a Ring of Grace
> Commissioned, tried, and true

"Toby, Rocco, Kaleb, and Sergio, show your stuff," Josiah yelled.

The five angels battled against Ahaba's forces, clashing in power over the harbor. During the battle, many dark spirits entered the supervisors, ports men, and sailors. Their facial expressions changed to that of vicious intent as the spirits took hold of their souls.

A supervisor shouted to the new slave labor.

"Hear me, men. Your work begins now. If you run, we have your documents. No one will hire you, and the police will jail you. I guarantee you'll have food and a place to lay your head, but your debt for passage needs to be repaid."

"We paid for passage. We were promised jobs. Are we slaves just off the boat?" an immigrant yelled.

A sailor nearby hit the newcomer who'd shouted the objections, knocking him to the ground. The other immigrants joined the fight, wild fists flying in protest against the port's men and sailors.

Purity approached with caution, treading lightly over the unequal wood planks leading to the shipyard. It was her plan to remain hidden behind stacked crates and barrels filled with cargo, but one of the supervisors spotted her as she took notes.

"What the hell are ya doing here, miss?" He rudely grabbed the notebook and shredded the pages.

"There'll be no record of these affairs. Get going before I throw you to the lions. Better yet, I'll call the police," he growled.

"Go ahead. Call the police. I'll wait. I'm sure they'd like to know about your labor practices," Purity said without fear.

"Any complaints, take it up with Mr. Favor Wisedor. He's in charge of this fine establishment," he glared with distaste.

Purity didn't press her luck with the supervisor. Stunned to hear of Favor's new position, she left and hailed a taxi.

"Bristol Distillery, Chestnut Road," she ordered the driver.

On the way, Purity opened her satchel and pulled out one of the ledgers. It outlined the business practices of the distillery. She read through with interest. She was astonished by the distressing details of her employer's family history.

Visions of black slaves working the sugarcane fields in Cuba invaded her mind. They swung machetes with powerful strokes to harvest the cane.

"They're still enslaving today. They thrive on cheap labor and debt bondage the workers can't afford to pay off. Modern slavery. That's what it is," Purity thought, feeling nauseous.

"We're here, miss. Bristol Distillery," the driver barked.

Purity stepped out of the cab and stood in front of a large factory. Several spouts of white steam flowed into the atmosphere from the chimneys. The building was constructed of red brick with massive wooden garage doors for easy entry. The premises were surrounded by black cast iron fencing. Purity found the main gate and boldly entered the premises.

Inside the main building, she saw at least three hundred men making rum. Their clothes were filthy and marked with large stains of perspiration—the air saturated with the smell of heavy body odor. Many pushed heavy carts loaded with molasses. Others carried heavy sacks of sugar cane from wagons parked in the yard.

A manager approaching with suspicion.

"Didn't you read the sign? No trespassing, miss."

"I was interested in buying a supply of rum," Purity said, looking the place over.

"Oh, is that a fact? What does a pretty thing like you want with rum?"

"Are you turning a customer away?"

"Never. We mainly export globally, but we supply some venues throughout the country," the manager said as he eyed the beauty.

"Where do you find your workers?" she asked, trying not to sound too intrusive.

"All over the world. Once they come, our retention is high."

"I imagine with no choice," she said, walking out.

"Hey, what about your order?" he called after her.

Nearby, one of the workers tapped his co-worker's shoulder.

"Look, enough juice to blow the house down." He exposed two sticks of dynamite tucked in his belt.

"Revenge for running us like slaves."

With a deep raspy voice, he sang, "Blow the House Down."

Blow the house down, blow the house down
Here's nasty revenge, for the pain we're in

100

Working us like dirty dogs, we'll get 'em in the end
Light the fuse, raise the roof, here we go
Up to the sky, in a cloud of smoke

Blow the house down, blow the house down
They deserve disaster, for the pain we're in
We're treated like slaves, smelling like pigs
Working from dawn to dusk
What sweet revenge, what sweet revenge
Blow the house down, blow the house down

"Warn me before she blows," responded the co-worker with a sinister laugh.

Church Service

Chapter 13

PURITY WALKED WITH her mother to church, tired and worn. Time was passing and she prayed for a new season to commence in her life. She loved the changing of the seasons but somehow felt left behind.

A feeling of heaviness flooded Purity's spirit. Deep remorse weighed on her heart as she fully understood the abuse that was occurring all around. Mave's of Bristol hosted some of the worst sufferings. Purity replayed some of the unsavory escapades in her mind.

A few days prior, she had taken a break from dance practice and had gone to the kitchen, her only thought to quench her thirst. A few Korean teens were being pulled through the kitchen door by Mave. They were chained together and blindfolded. Chin Lu opened the door leading to the basement. The teens were forced down the stairs like captured animals. They cried out for help in Korean.

"There's no hope for you. If you work, then you can eat," Chin Lu scolded in their native tongue.

Five strapping men appeared, each handing Mave a stack of money.

"What's going on?" Purity had demanded. Mave slammed her against the wall, slapping her on each cheek.

"Just a little business transaction. It's none of your business. If you work here, you're deaf and dumb. Say anything, and you'll go missing without a trace," Mave had growled while holding Purity in a vice grip.

"Take your paws off of me." Purity shook herself loose from the ironclad grip. But instantly, another firm grip pulled on her clothing. It was one of the men holding a handful of cash.

"I want this one," he'd begged Mave.

"Be my guest. Break the girl's spirit after you've had your fill."

The man started pulling Purity down the basement stairs.

"Let go of me," Purity screamed, putting up a fight.

Mandy suddenly appeared and intervened.

"You're not taking her, or I'll kill you myself." Mandy sounded like a mama bear on attack. She pulled Mave into a headlock and grabbed a knife from the counter so fast it made everyone's head spin.

"Do what she says," Mave commanded.

The man released his grip on Purity.

"Let's get out of here," Mandy said, grabbing Purity by the arm.

Unfortunately, the teens were taken away. That evening, Purity and Mandy reported the illegal activity to the police department.

"Yes, we'll investigate," an officer promised them, but no one ever came.

Naomi and Purity stopped momentarily and gazed at the large cross on the church's steeple. A deep conviction tormented Purity's spirit as she thought about dancing with the men at Mave's hotel. They often made unwelcome advances with tight hugs and lustful propositions. Each week, Purity purchased the needed supplies and clothing for the boys, but it was all taking its toll.

"I need a way out, but the boys have needs," Purity prayed under her breath.

"What was that?" asked Naomi.

"Nothing, Mama. Let's go. The service is about to start."

"Purity. Purity, good morning," Victoria called, standing near her family. The Coevet's stood by the Wisedor family. Jezzie glared at Purity with loathing and tightened her grip on Favor's arm.

"I'm surprised you're up so early. Aren't you tired from all that bar dancing at Mave's of Bristol?" Jezzie's voice rang out for all to hear.

The Parishioners turned and gasped at the revelation.

"Bar dancing? Is it true?" Favor asked, searching Purity's eyes. The revelation shattered his wholesome thoughts about his friend.

"I won't be condemned by those abusing the poor. I'm dancing to support a charitable cause."

"You whore. Who's abusing the poor? You dare strike the hand that feeds you? And what charity is worth ruining your reputation?" Mrs. Wisedor said in retaliation.

The crowd looked on in horror.

"My daughter's no whore. Let's hope she can find a better night job," Naomi said, trying to defuse the situation. Quickly, grabbing Purity's arm, her mother pulled her away.

Once settled on a pew in the church, Naomi leaned over in a hushed voice and started to rant.

"Trouble. Trouble. We could be evicted and unemployed in one moment. You know Mrs. Wisedor's moods."

"I can't quit Mave's of Bristol. We need the money."

"You'll get us fired, and then what? We'll both be dancing whores. How about trusting God for those orphans? Maybe he can do a better job providing for them," Naomi chastised her daughter.

Purity stared at the large cross above the altar. She said a silent prayer.

"Captain, I can't go on. I hate what I'm doing, but I have mouths to feed."

* * *

The Wisedor's settled in a pew nearby. The Coevet's followed, sitting next to them. Favor couldn't take his eyes off Purity, who was sitting a few pews away. She appeared distraught. Jezzie squeezed Favor's arm, holding on to him like a scared child whose life depended on his approval.

"Your reputation's at stake. You need to fire Purity and her mother," Jezzie whispered in Favor's ear.

A fog of witchcraft hit his mind.

"Did I ask for your advice?" Favor questioned in whispered annoyance, feeling a wave of nausea.

A scowl wrinkled her face that was difficult to hide. Mr. and Mrs. Coevet heard the remark and looked worried.

The service started, and soft music blanketed the people. Pastor Ezra felt the tug from the Holy Spirit.

"Come to the altar and surrender your lives to God," he called out. Pastor Ezra and his beautiful wife Rebecca stood together, holding hands near the alter.

Parishioners slowly move to the front. They swayed together as one, surrounded by a heavenly presence. Some were crying, while others appeared somber.

Favor's eyes followed as Purity stepped out from the pew, her eyes and hands lifted toward heaven. One step at a time, she walked to the altar in surrender. Favor's eyes remained fastened on his childhood friend. A look of admiration covered his face.

Noticing the object of Favor's gaze, Jezzie abruptly stood and stepped out, hoping for the same admiration. Her mother winced in disbelief and wanted to stop her daughter from surrendering to anything but her wishes.

"Sit down before you embarrass us all," Mrs. Coevet whispered loudly and grabbed her arm.

Jezzie shook free from the restraint and walked down the aisle.

A translucent spirit from Ahaba's dark realm wrapped around her throat and racked her body with fear.

"You belong to us," the spirit whispered in her ear.

A cold hatred iced over her empty heart. She stopped, unable to take another step.

Favor stared with a look of distaste, his stomach turning in her presence.

* * *

A soft melody played on the piano. Purity fell on her knees in sweet surrender at the altar.

"I give up. My plan's not working," she prayed, with eyes closed and lips trembling.

A heavenly presence swept over her, and Purity was taken up to the New Earth—her spirit instantly translated to the above and beyond on the New Earth but her body remained at the alter.

"Captain, I'm here. I must meet with you at once. Please come for me," she yelled.

The wind whispered through the trees.

"Come to me, my love," the Captain's voice echoed on the wind.

Purity started walking toward the voice. For hours, she made her way through the exotic landscapes. Finally, she came to the gates of an enormous city of splendor. Large regiments of the Captain's army were there celebrating another victory.

"Maybe I'll see the warrior who gave me living water to drink," Purity thought.

A great warrior stood at the entrance of the gates.

"Your filth detains you," he warned, staring at her muddied clothing.

She lifted her soiled dress with dirty hands. A look of shame covered her face.

He summoned one of the maidens saying, "Change the filthy rags."

The maiden took Purity to a palatial building—into a beautiful room furnished with carved wood furnishings and royal blue satin couches with matching draperies.

The maiden opened a closet full of splendid apparel and pulled out a gorgeous gown.

"Hmm, this one suits you. This gown should please him."

"Please, who?" Purity questioned.

"Captain of the Lord's Army. You must be radiant in his presence. He's returned from a long battle, and it's time to celebrate."

"Will I meet him today?"

"If he desires to meet you. But it doesn't hurt to ask."

"How can I ask someone I've never met?"

"He hears your thoughts and every whisper. Keep asking, seeking, and knocking. He's the giver of every gift and makes dreams come true. Clean up first, and then put on the royal clothing. Your search has come to an end," the maiden said while helping Purity prepare.

"It doesn't make sense, but I'll take your advice. Captain of the Lord's Army, I want to know you. Please meet me today," Purity said as though whispering a prayer.

"Hurry, girl. Get ready. You don't want to miss him. The warriors are celebrating new victories and preparing for battles ahead. But don't worry, all the battles are won, for he is a mighty captain," the maiden declared.

"If the Captain makes dreams come true, then I can't live without him. And a few gifts couldn't hurt either. I've also been looking for a warrior. He was badly scarred, and he gave me living water. Can you help me find him?" Purity asked as the maiden fixed her hair.

"Don't worry about finding him. When the timing's right, he'll find you."

"But I don't even know his name."

"It's all about timing, so don't fret," the maiden said, taking Purity's hand. She led her back to the triumphant celebration and disappeared.

"Come back. I don't want to enter alone."

Hesitantly, Purity entered a palatial hall. It was elaborate, with enormous marble pillars, ornate granite flooring, and flowing blue, white, and purple draperies. Fine furnishings and elegant tapestries filled the place.

It was crowded, with strong and vital warriors, male and female, from the heavenly army. None of them seemed to notice her presence, nor seemed to care. She watched them sing, play joyous music, and dance with celebration. They talked of their battles, and most of all, the victories.

Purity walked close to a group of warriors who suddenly erupted with laughter. She hesitated and backed up, bumping into what felt like a wall. She turned around and recognized the warrior standing a few feet away.

"You gave me living water."

"It is as you say," the warrior said with a twinkling look in his eyes.

"And your name? Before you disappear again."

"I'm Lord of the Dance. Shall we?" He extended hands that bore deep scars.

Purity took his strong, scarred hands. They felt amazingly soft.

"Maybe we should just talk. I've got two left feet and no rhythm."

"Ask for a worthy gift, and it will be granted here on the New Earth."

"Well, to start, how about dancing?" Purity asked.

The music started, and her feet followed along in perfect sync.

"My feet know what to do," Purity said, surprised.

"What else do you want?" asked Lord of the Dance, enjoying her delight as they danced.

"I need to meet Captain of the Lord's Army. He makes everything possible, so I'm told. I've got mouths to feed and could use some help. And I have dreams to start a school and see the world."

"So, you're asking for dreams to come true? But are you willing to fight for them? The Captain battles through the brave. You have to believe He gives the victory."

"I do believe, but help me with my unbelief," Purity said anxiously.

"The Captain knows the plans and purposes for your life. Do you believe that? As you step into the plans, you join him in the battle."

"Well, if he's got a plan for me, that's hard to believe. The only plan I see is people dying as slaves, and no one lifts a finger to help."

"It's always darkest before the dawn. The battle rages, but the victory's already won. Remember, the more you stand to defeat darkness, the more you'll be attacked. But don't fear. When you fight for injustice, the Captain of the Lord's Army will battle by your side. You're never alone."

"But how will I know he's with me?"

"Listen for the sound of his mighty army, like the sound of the rushing wind. He'll fill you with courage and strength. That's how you'll know," he said, looking intently into her eyes.

"Can you ask the Captain to help me?" Purity begged.

"Ask him yourself," Lord of the Dance encouraged.

"I beg you, take me to him," Purity asked with urgency.

"If you believe He exists, he's already near. I know this—he's gifting you with a new weapon for the fight."

"I didn't choose this fight. And I'm tired already. The more I help, the worse it gets for me. Enough about new weapons."

"Sometimes, the battle chooses you. Remember, any talent can be used in the fight," Lord of the Dance said, sounding very wise. The dance ended, and he disappeared into the crowd.

* * *

The Bristol church service was long over, and the congregation was gone. The afternoon sun streamed through the stained-glass windows, emitting rainbow reflections that danced on the walls.

"It looks like rainbow stars, flashing in record speed," Favor said, playing softly on the piano. Bright Star was there, bouncing from wall to wall, and giggled at the observation.

"Did you hear that? It sounds like laughing," Favor said to Pastor Ezra and his wife, Rebecca.

"It's just the sun reflecting from the windows. And there must be children playing outside," Rebecca said.

Purity still laid on the floor before the altar. Suddenly, she rolled about, her legs and arms moving as if dancing the waltz. Pastor Ezra wasn't quite sure what to make of it. Favor left the piano and stood over her, perplexed.

"Do you think she'll ever come back?"

"Looks like she's dancing," Pastor Rebecca said with uncertainty.

Purity woke with a start and sat straight up—eyes wide.

"Where did you go, girl?" Pastor Ezra pressed with urgency.

"The New Earth. Guess what? Captain of the Lord's Army has a purpose for my life," Purity said with confidence.

Favor didn't quite know what to make of her.

"The Captain and the New Earth, where all things become new, are mentioned in the Bible. I want to hear all about it," Rebecca said.

"I'm feeling a bit weak. I'll have to share another time," Purity answered, holding her head.

"Of course. Just tell us when. The above and beyond can take your breath away. Shall we go, my dear Rebecca?" Pastor Ezra asked, taking his wife's hand.

"Yes, dear. Purity, if you're looking for a purpose, come with us to China. We're starting an orphanage. We're leaving soon," Rebecca shared.

Purity looked heavenward.

"Captain, show me the way."

"You have a purpose on the estate. Sometimes the greatest mission field is in your own backyard. Who's this Captain, anyway?" Favor asked, extending a hand and helping Purity from the floor. He pulled her in close, gazing into her eyes. Their lips drew closer.

"The Captain fights our battles and makes dreams come true. What are you doing here, Favor? I thought you were with Jezzie," she said groggily.

"I thought I'd stick around. Let's get back to the estate. I don't think you're feeling well."

Favor drove Purity back to the estate. The conversation was sparse, as though both were upset and deep in thought. Minutes later, they pulled into the drive of Shadow Brook Estate. Favor pulled over before reaching the horseshoe driveway, trying to avoid detection.

"You've skipped our tutoring sessions. Why?"

"I can't stand to see you with Jezzie. It seems her powers have darkened your soul," Purity said with keen insight.

"I don't know myself either. My parents are trying to force my hand. Pray for me."

"You're always in my prayers. Until you sort things out, I feel it's best if we're not alone. Please understand." Purity opened the car door and stepped out.

"You're being unreasonable." Favor called after her.

* * *

The next evening, Purity stepped onto the dance floor at Mave's of Bristol Hotel. Mandy was teaching a new dance, and the steps were complicated.

"Hit it, boys," Mandy shouted at the band.

After a few minutes, one of the dancers complained.

"I can't get the steps, Mandy. Show me again," the beautiful escort asked.

"Here we go again," Mandy said. She reviewed the steps, slow at first and then faster to get a feel for the rhythm.

Purity was usually in the back, struggling with the steps, but for some reason, today was different. Her feet moved in perfect rhythm with the beat. Purity moved through the other dancers.

Mandy watched in awe.

"You've got this." Mandy took Purity's hand, and off they went on the dance floor, doing a variety of freestyle.

"My feet have a mind of their own. I can't take credit for it," Purity explained.

"Looks like you'll get triple the tips tonight," Mandy joked.

Discovery

Chapter 14

SHADOW BROOK ESTATE was breathtaking in all its splendor. Jezzie and her mother rode thoroughbred horses through the acreage. They journeyed through meadows, hills, and forest areas. The majesty of the estate was almost palpable.

They stopped on a high hill overlooking the grandiose views of the mansion. Clothed in the finest riding attire, they held their heads high as if entitled to it all.

"Shadow Brook Estate.

"It's fit for a queen," Mrs. Coevet exclaimed.

"Call me Queen Jezzabella then," her daughter boasted with a sly chuckle.

"How close are we to getting a proposal from Favor? I'm working on Mrs. Wisedor. She's quite fond of you," Mrs. Coevet said with confidence.

"Favor is so annoying. I've done my best to weasel into his heart with no luck I'm afraid. I'm prepared to make the sacrifice, to marry a man I don't love. And he's aware it's his duty to choose a bride with money," Jezzie said with spite.

"Let's hope the wedding happens before we go completely bankrupt. Without a bailout, we're doomed to poverty, and neither of us has the strength to work for a living. The love will come later, and if not, at least you'll have plenty of money," Mrs. Coevet said in a gloating fashion.

"It's full-blown deception, but living as beggars is far worse," Jezzie said with a mischievous smile.

They rode on basking in the beauty of such plush acreage. Mrs. Coevet noticed smoke billowing from a grove of trees nearby.

"There's a fire, let's investigate. We can't afford to let Shadow Brook burn," Mrs. Coevet said with a worried groan.

"You read my mind mother," Jezzie answered and trotted ahead.

They followed the cloud of smoke through a thick forest. The sound of ram's horns echoed through the trees. A light misty rain had fallen earlier, and the area was damp with low hanging misty fog.

"It sounds like a call to battle," Mrs. Coevet said with some reservations. They passed under a makeshift wooden sign, suspended from trees with old ropes. It read, 'Son's Camp.'

"Son's Camp. What's going on here?" Jezzie asked in a disgusted tone. A rage surged through her selfish bones.

Son's camp was saturated in misty fog and dampness. Wet clothing hung on sagging ropes tied from tree to tree. Makeshift tents bellowed in the wind, filled with blankets, pillows, and carpet bags stuffed with supplies.

Tables made of driftwood, covered with damp ornate table clothes, sat abandoned. Lanterns hung from ropes strewn from tree branches. A fire in mid camp burned with five plump chickens roasting over it.

"Disgusting squatters," Jezzie yelled while dismounting the horse. A foreboding shadow was cast over her countenance, contorting her features.

"Come out at once," Mrs. Coevet yelled, looking about.

"Mother let me handle this," Jezzie said cautious of her mother's safety.

Ahaba's army appeared in the atmosphere as dark translucent wispy spirits. They hovered above the trees and suddenly morphed into black crows. A transparent spirit, resembling a snake, coiled around Jezzie's head. She lifted a hand to her forehead, as though faint from a pounding headache.

"Trespassers show yourselves," Jezzie raged with indignation. The dark spirit slithered around her neck and squeezed in a suffocating fashion. She walked about the camp breathless and leaning against a tree tried to catch her breath. The unseen oppressor found pleasure causing such discomfort. Her search for the vagabonds continued, despite her chest starting to tighten. Mrs. Coevet remained on her horse, disgusted by the mess.

"I'll have this camp cleared by nightfall. I command you—show yourselves," Jezzie yelled. A minute passed, and Purity stepped out from behind a tall oak tree. She was dressed in a long tan buckskin dress, with a fur sash crossing her chest. On her back rested a quiver of arrows with a bow attached. Strapped to her waist was a knife in a leather holder and a homemade slingshot. She appeared radiant with compassion.

Fearlessly, Purity approached the hostile intruders and prayed silently, "Captain, I need your help."

"Step forward, sons," she commanded. One by one, the boys stepped forward from behind trees, boulders, and tall grasses. David swung from a rope suspended from the oak tree, barely missing the elite intruder.

"Beg for mercy, or we attack." He drew a sword.

"You dare enter our camp with insults?"

Above, Captain of the Lord's Army appeared on his white stallion. He stared Ahaba down, and raising a hand, light beams projected, blasting the enemy back into submission.

The Captain drew his golden sword and raised it in the air.

"You want some of this? Come get it."

Ahaba whistled for more evil hordes, and the dark forces multiplied in an instant.

The Ring of Grace manifested in a large tree, each angel clinging to his own branch. They appeared as child warriors, wearing body armor, chest protectors, shin guards, and quivers of arrows slung over their shoulders with their glistening bows.

They jumped down, ready for battle. Undetected by the human eye and ear, they taunted Ahaba's army.

"Retreat. You have no power over Purity," Toby yelled to the wicked spirits.

"Touch her sons, and it's off with your heads," Rocco threatened. The wicked spirits flapped their wings in protest, ready to battle.

"Back to hell where you belong," Kaleb shouted.

The dark foes hissed as the Ring of Grace fired razor-sharp arrows with lightning speed.

"Attack," Ahaba yelled, and a fight ensued above the treetops.

A raging wind blew through the camp. Five lightning strikes hit, thrashing and bumping into each other overhead. The sons were amazed by the ruckus it caused.

"What is it?" Andrew asked, looking at his brothers.

"A storm's coming," Danny said as the trees swayed.

Purity tried to ward off a bloody conflict before the storm hit.

"Let me handle this," she warned David, who was momentarily distracted by the lightning and heavy winds.

"Well, well. It's the bar dancing whore, living in filth," Jezzie mocked, surveying the unkempt boys and muddy mess.

"Let me explain," Purity tried to defend the enterprise.

"This is shocking—to set up a squatter's camp on Shadow Brook Estate. How dare you? I'll have this squalor cleared by nightfall." She pulled down a rope with hanging clothes as though she owned the place.

"Does Favor know about this?"

"That's none of your business."

"No, of course not. This is your secret mission, taking in the unfortunate. What a caring soul." Jezzie moved aggressively toward Purity.

In response, the sons drew their bows and arrows. Jezzie and her mother withered in response.

"Hold your fire," Purity shouted. Reluctantly, the sons withdrew their weapons.

"You'd rather see my sons begging or dead on the streets? Alive, they're some help to this estate," Purity pleaded with Jezzie.

"You call them sons. These delinquents wouldn't hesitate to kill, as we just witnessed. Don't you realize? In a short time, all this will be mine."

Jezzie pulled a knife from her belt and dove at Purity.

Purity tackled Jezzie to stop the attack. The two wrestled rigorously, preventing the sons, who had drawn their bows again, from taking an accurate shot.

Purity forced the knife from her attacker's hand, causing it to drop to the muddy ground. David dove for it, batting it out of Jezzie's reach.

Evil spirits, appearing as wispy shadows, attacked the sons, whispering in their ears, "Attack. Revenge. Death to your enemies."

Many of the sons waited for just the right time to strike the invaders. Hate and revenge embittered their souls, stirring up old emotional wounds of abandonment.

"Death to you, Jezzie," Andrew yelled and lunged at her. The other boys joined in.

The Ring of Grace sliced away at the harassing spirits with their fiery swords. Miraculously, the sons' eyes were opened to the spirit realm just before an irreversible strike against Jezzie occurred. The angels stood before them, appearing as child warriors holding swords of fire. Purity's sons dropped their weapons and fell backward.

Josiah stepped forward and warned them, "Death will only take you captive. Fight this battle with prayer."

The sons rose from the ground and raised their hands toward Jezzie, releasing united prayer. Immediately, they were filled with a heavenly language. Blue flames hovered over each of them, and every son had his own strange dialect—at times sounding like earthly languages such as Mandarin, Arabic, and Hebrew. As they spoke forth this strange new sound, only interpreted by heaven, the sons grew stronger, and the enemy forces weakened. The Ring of Grace, emboldened by the son's solidarity in spiritual power, went through the camp and extinguished every wicked spirit.

"Wallow in the filth. It's where you belong," Jezzie gasped with labored breathing. She was unaware of the spiritual war around her. She turned to Purity.

"I'm aware of your plans. I know all about your tutoring sessions with Favor. He may be teaching you science or math, but what are you teaching him? You little whore." Jezzie lunged at Purity again, but some of the sons held her back.

"I've heard enough," Purity scolded and lunged at her accuser. David pulled her back to prevent further violence.

"I bet you'd give anything to trap Favor—to free you from slaving away as a despicable maid. Come to your senses. You don't belong in Favor's world. There's no hope for you, your so-called sons, and your destitute mother. You're a maid by day and bar dancer by night."

"You're the one who doesn't belong here. Get out of Son's Camp," Purity shouted.

"Clear this camp and resign from your position at once. Your mother too. Otherwise, I'll be forced to tell Favor about your little life of squalor," Jezzie threatened as she mounted her horse.

"The Captain rebuke you. You have no power over my fate," Purity shouted in retaliation.

"We'll see, you pathetic tramp. The last woman standing wins," Jezzie said with a smirk. She and her mother galloped away.

"Hold your weapons," Purity yelled as her sons engaged their bows, ready to strike.

With a heavy heart, Purity ran into the woods. Reaching a clearing, Purity withheld no emotion. She descended into a frenzy of song, belting out, "Dear Captain

> Captain, dear Captain, I need to hear a word
> I can only wonder where you are
> Cause the fighting's getting dirty
> And we've gotta take a stand
>
> Forgive me for my disrespect but
> It's looking like we're gonna lose
> If I'm standing for injustice
> Then I need your mighty power
>
> Where's the wind I'm supposed to hear
> And weapons to avenge my enemies
> Cause the devil's dancing dirty
> And I'm in his target range
>
> Captain, dear Captain, I don't know what to do
> I thought you heard my every whisper, even to the clouds
> Captain, dear Captain, I need your mighty power
> Where's your presence, if you're standing by my side
> I thought you heard my thoughts and whispers
> You can't forsake me now

Purity searched the sky in wretched hopelessness. Tears of broken agony trickled down her cheeks.

"Maybe you're too busy fighting other battles?" she said, feeling forsaken.

Black crows squawked on tree branches in a mocking rhythm as the sky grew dark. The heavens were silent but for the distance rumblings of thunder.

One by one, her sons knelt by her side, each calling out prayers, intermixed with their new language from heaven.

"Captain, we've heard of your great army. Come fight for us," David prayed.

"We're not alone. Cast away your doubts. We saw them. There were five angels with swords of fire," Andrew said with amazement.

The other sons all agreed, and one by one, gave witness to heaven touching down.

Danny, one of the youngest sons, tried to explain.

"Mother, they were boys like us, but warriors. They killed the enemy like this." Danny thrashed his arms and legs about in warrior fashion. The other boys joined in, mimicking the Ring of Grace.

"You saw five angels fighting for us?" Purity asked.

"I've never seen anything like it. Powerful in battle and mighty in strength," Andrew said, confirming the vision.

"And the new language? What is it? Where does it come from?" Purity asked.

"It must be from your great Captain because the angels responded. Somehow, they understood us, and it helped them fight the dark ones," Andrew said with amazement.

"Captain, you answered our prayers. Forgive me for doubting you," Purity repented.

Deception Revealed

Chapter 15

JEZZIE RODE HER horse recklessly through the acreage toward the mansion.

"Hurry, Mother," Jezzie called out.

"Slow down," Mrs. Coevet begged, fearing the horses would stumble.

"Wait till Favor hears. What a pleasure to see his reaction. Even better, I'll volunteer to help with the eviction."

They reached the estate's vast gardens.

"I'll handle this, Mother. Go on," Jezzie insisted with a wave of the hand.

They parted ways on a narrow path leading to the mansion. Then Jezzie rode on. She looked for Favor on the porches and covered verandas of the house.

"Where's Favor?" she barked at one of the gardeners.

"In the garden, overlooking the bay," he responded and then returned to his work, cleaning out a flowerbed.

* * *

Favor was in deep thought, standing by a large statue of an angel, his right hand perched on one of its wings.

"Favor, Favor, it's urgent. Your grand estate is in jeopardy," Jezzie said as she dismounted her horse.

"What's happened," he asked in alarm.

"I was viciously attacked by criminals on your property." She feigned panic and fell into his arms.

"They'll be hunted and tossed into jail. This won't be tolerated," Favor said, noticing her tattered, dirty clothing. He saw a foreboding darkness over her countenance, and her eyes seemed to glow red.

"That's just to start. You have squatters and juvenile delinquents on this grand estate. My mother and I were almost their victims. You're being used by an unscrupulous, self-centered, deceptive whore who has no regard for your property. And your gracious parents know nothing of this, I'm sure. It's a scandal," her voice raced to hysterical heights.

"To whom are you referring?"

"Who else? Your maid, Purity. She's running a camp on this fine estate and lives in wretched filth with complete ease."

"And what do you suggest?" he asked with a hint of mockery in his voice.

"I suggest you evict them immediately."

"Evict them immediately," he repeated her suggestion.

"I was hoping you might feel some compassion toward them," he said, staring into her vacant eyes.

"You knew about them?"

"I suggest you take a few orphans in yourself. Wouldn't that be grand? Imagine Jezzie thinking of someone other than herself."

"I'm full of compassion. That's why I'm here."

"Show me an ounce of it. But we know that's out of the question, isn't it? You wouldn't want to exert energy that won't profit your plans."

Jezzie melted in disbelief.

"Do your parents also agree with usury and filth?" she asked, attempting to trap him.

"If you're still hoping for an engagement, don't mention this to anyone," he warned with a glare.

Cornered at her own game, she stormed off.

Favor headed to the horse's stables and reached for a handful of grain in a bucket. He held it close to the horse's mouth.

"Rozzie, eat up, boy. You're going to need it," Favor coaxed as the horse licked the food from his palm.

The horse stood perfectly still while being saddled as though knowing they were on a special assignment.

"Let's find this Son's Camp," Favor said as he mounted the noble steed. The horse nodded and snorted as if saying, "Let's go."

Favor's thoughts vacillated between pleasing his parents and the threat of being disowned if he married outside his class.

"I don't know what to do. I'm dizzy with indecision. Every time I'm around Jezzie, she has this strange, wicked pull on my reasoning. Purity is everything I could ever want in a wife, but my parents will never accept her status."

Favor raced through the acreage of Shadow Brook Estate, not quite knowing what direction to take. He called out several times, "Purity! Purity, do you hear me?" In response, there were only echoes of his lone voice in the treetops.

About an hour into the search, Favor and Rozzie entered a thick cluster of trees. The wind blew through the branches, making an eerie rustling sound. Unaware, they were being followed by invisible dark spirits. One jumped on Favor's back, and a sharp pain hit like a knife. He doubled over—a hopeless feeling of discouragement ripping through his soul.

Another spirit bit at the horse's neck and then coiled around it tighter and tighter. Rozzie began to rear and buck, trying to find relief, and flung the evil spirit against a tree with great velocity.

"Let's get out of here," Favor said as the pain in his back let up.

The Ring of Grace landed and surrounded Favor and his horse. Josiah took hold of the reigns while Toby stroked the horse's side with steady hands. Rocco stood in front of Rozzie and gave the horse the ability to see the spirit realm. Kaleb fed him some stardust, and Sergio shot a fiery dart from his wrist, hitting small bat-like spirits swooping down to attack.

"Let's get them going," Sergio said.

"Follow us," Kaleb whispered in the horse's ear.

Led by the unseen angels, Favor and Rozzie edged by Son's Camp. The sons, keeping watch from the trees above, blew their rams' horns.

"What's that sound?" Favor asked the horse as though he understood. Dutifully, the sound bellowed through the trees. Favor kicked the horse's side, and Rozzie picked up the pace.

"I think we're onto something," Favor said, galloping toward the sound. They slowed under a wooden sign for Son's Camp.

"We made it. Good work, Rozzie."

The sons in camp heeded the warning and grabbed weapons.

David spotted Favor first and ran to him, begging.

"Sir, please let us stay. The boys will die without shelter."

"Where is Purity?" Favor said as he pushed past him.

"Over there," David said, pointing to a shelter blowing in the wind.

"Favor, save us from the witch. Don't send us away," the sons called out.

Favor dismounted and approached the shelter.

"Purity, don't hide from me."

Hearing his voice sent bolts of fear and frustration through Purity's body. She stood and vigorously tried to wipe the drying mud from her buckskin dress, face, and hands.

She stepped out of the shelter, and he thought she'd never looked so beautiful.

"Mud baths are good for the complexion, I've heard," Purity joked, trying to make light of the situation.

"The witch tried to kill her," Andrew interrupted.

"Did she hurt you?" Favor asked with genuine concern.

"What does it matter? I'm just trash—a whore who dances with men so I can feed my sons," Purity repeated the insults with a heavy heart.

"I've seen glimpses of the boys, but I had no idea you were housing them here." Favor looked around at the twelve bewildered boys whose faces were weighed down with worry.

"Can you look away from children living in utter poverty? I've struggled to provide for them. I did what I had to do."

"You should have been honest with me. You've put yourself at risk for others," Favor chided.

"This is your land, and I beg forgiveness for keeping this from you. But it's going to take more for them to survive than pretending they don't exist. I work two jobs because I have mouths to feed, and I'm asking for your help."

Some of the younger sons clung to her body for comfort, waiting to hear the verdict.

"Your secrecy puts me in a predicament with my parents. I'm sure they will find out. We both know it's inevitable," Favor said with concern.

"When will you stand up to your parents? You sleep between clean sheets in the warmth of your lovely estate. You eat at tables of bounty on a daily basis. All of it won off the backs of slaves and the poor. Where's your conscience?"

"You stole my business ledgers. Three were missing from the library. You know everything?"

"Enough to expose murderous greed and injustice. And don't tell me it's all a new revelation for you. Remember reading analysis—what's the author saying to the world? How is he moving your soul? Your father's business practices indicate a man who has not thought of anyone but himself. My soul loathes such usury," Purity confessed.

"Your soul weighs the matter correctly," he admitted with some level of shame.

"But I'm here to discuss this camp."

"We mean no harm. We're ridding your land of wild animals and making it safe to venture out," Danny defended.

Favor turned, inspecting the conditions around the camp. He entered a dilapidated tent. Looking up, he noticed the roof was leaking. Most of the bedding on the ground was soaked through.

"Jezzie was right. This camp is full of squalor and filth."

The threat of eviction pierced Purity's heart.

Jonathan removed the roasted chickens from the fire.

"Will you eat with us, sir?"

"No, thank you," Favor answered with sympathy.

Buckets of dirty laundry sat next to an oak tree. He picked up one of the wet, soiled garments.

"I've never seen such deplorable conditions. Something must be done about this immediately."

Purity pulled Favor aside.

"If you have any affection for me, then embrace my fight against injustice. Make right the wrongs of your family and so many others. Start by helping these boys."

"I do care for you. It's not that easy."

"But it is. I may not be up to your family's standards, but I'm a person of worth, and you respected me when others simply looked past me."

"You don't realize the pressure I'm under." He gazed into her eyes.

"I'm tortured by you. I can't get you out of my heart and mind. Wherever I look, there you are." He looked away, "And Jezzie has some sort of spell on me too. I can't explain it," Favor said with frustration.

"Please give me an answer," Purity begged.

"I need time to figure things out," Favor said as a dark spirit wrapped around his head. He bent over, nauseated.

"Doublemindedness will make you sick. I refuse to beg for your love."

Favor stood.

"I never stopped caring for you."

"And yet you'll marry Jezzie and see her throw us out on the streets. She's your perfect match. You're both spoiled, pampered prodigals hearing the word of God every week, and refusing its power to change your souls. Your life together will be a wonderful misery."

"This is what you think of me?" Favor asked.

"I thought I was in love with you, but now I see I've been in love with a man who was the making of my own imagination—not the real Favor. I fear for you because someday your treasures will rot, and you won't have the power to save yourself."

"You go too far, Purity."

"Does that mean we're evicted?" David asked.

"You'll hear of my verdict soon. And return the ledgers tomorrow if you don't want trouble." With that, he jumped up on Rozzie and was gone.

Truth Revealed

Chapter 16

AT DAWN THE next morning, Favor walked the shipyard. It was engulfed by a damp rot that seeped into the men's souls. Foghorns sounded on the bay as deep-water ships were coming and going. The docked ships swayed slightly with the ebb and tide of gentle waves.

The heavy fog and a chill sank deep into Favor's bones. He was dressed as one destitute, with saggy pants, an old sailor's jacket, and a hat pulled over his eyes.

A large workforce surrounded the many ships with massive metal frames. Men loaded cargo to be sold in Europe. They groaned under the strain of pulling huge vats of rum into the ship's hold with pulleys made of rope and metal chains.

Favor read the worker's faces. Their young smooth skin was becoming leathery with lines of care under short beards. All were nursing sun-scorched complexions from long hours of labor.

"What ya standing there for. Get working," the supervisor griped. He yanked Favor into one of the work lines and slapped a pair of leather gloves in his hand. Favor gazed at the man from under the cover of his sailor's cap.

"You object? I got this for ya," the supervisor threatened and pulled a metal pipe from his jacket.

Favor deflected his eyes, resisting a response, and became one with the men around him. He listened as they worked side by side.

"I can't take anymore," an older worker groaned in pain, removing a bloodied hand from his glove.

"There's no gettin' away. They have our passports. At least we can eat," his friend sympathized.

"If they don't kill us first," replied the man with the bloodied hand.

Favor's head remained low, and his arms shook wearily from the weight of the cargo he'd helped move. Another load of rum was added to an empty pallet. The men in unison pulled on the ropes and chains, lifting it inch by inch to the ship.

Evil creatures of darkness descended with swords of fire, undetected by the human eye. They flew around the workers and surrounded the heavy load. In unison, they blew with pursed lips gusts of wind, causing the weight to shift.

Ahaba appeared, giving the order, "Cut it."

A dark being slashed the straps and chains with vicious blows that looked like sudden lightning strikes. The load of rum went tumbling onto the workers below.

"Let's go. We have more lives to ruin," Ahaba growled as his hordes followed in submission. They gathered as one large dark cloud and flew away.

Favor narrowly escaped the avalanche of heavy wooden crates. He was knocked down by other men trying to escape. Broken rum bottles released a stench of alcohol into the air. Shattered glass and cracked, slivered crates covered the workers and blanketed the dock. Several men lay motionless in pools of blood.

Those unaffected began digging out the workers buried under the debris. The injured men moaned, and many surfaced with large cuts oozing blood. Several suffered fractured arms and legs and screamed with intense pain.

Favor jumped to his feet.

"Call for help. These men need medical attention."

"This goes nowhere. Little accidents can't be helped. Who do you think you are?" a supervisor growled, raising a fist to smash a hard blow.

Favor caught his hand in midair with an aggressive move and swiftly pulled off his hat, revealing his identity.

The supervisor retreated in shock.

"Disguised deception. What ya doing dressed like a dirty sailor?"

Favor grabbed the man.

"Get these men help, or I'll kill you and consider it one more little accident."

The other supervisors descended on the exchange and readied to attack the rebellious sailor until they recognized who held the gun. They withered in disbelief at their boss's shoddy appearance.

The police arrived shortly afterward, with clubs drawn, ready to bounce any disobedience.

"Who's in charge?" an officer asked with authority.

"It's my responsibility. I'm the owner of Wisedor Shipping," Favor said, stepping forward. They eyed his shabby attire with suspicion.

"I'm Favor Wisedor. Excuse my attire," he said, showing his identification.

"Please, come with me."

They walked into the main building, to his office, where he answered all the officer's questions.

"I promise you, stricter safety protocols will be established immediately," Favor assured them. The officers took their report and left.

A few journalists from the local newspaper burst through the door, demanding an interview.

"Who is paying all the medical expenses? What do you have to say about your labor practices?" a reporter pressed.

"All the medical expenses will be paid. I won't abandon the men. But my labor practices are none of your business," Favor said, wanting to avoid a public scandal.

"They are now," another reporter proclaimed.

One of them snapped photos, but Favor blocked the view with his hand while pushing them out of the office. He dropped to his office chair and sat, numbly pondering the shameful treatment of his workers.

One of the supervisors rushed into the office door, "There's been an explosion at the rum distillery."

Favor reached for the sailor's cap and jumped to his feet. He drove with speed through the streets of Bristol. Finally, he turned onto Chestnut Road and watched fire rage from the rooftop of the factory. As he stepped out of the car, more blasts rocked the building. He dove to the ground, hoping to avoid the force and debris blasting through the air.

Over three hundred workers stood outside. They were saturated in perspiration, chilled by the cold breeze blowing off the Narragansett Bay. Men with serious burns writhed in agony while being carried from the burning building. He turned from the horrid sights of flesh hanging from the arms and legs of the victims.

"My God, stop the pain, stop the pain," one worker groaned.

Rescue teams from the Bristol Fire Department helped the injured. Ahaba's forces moved throughout the distraught men and whispered violence in their ears. A group of angry workers surrounded Favor's father shouting with rage.

"You slave driver. You'll kill us all," one worker yelled, landing an angry fist into Mr. Wisedor's gut. Others joined in, pulling at his clothes and throwing more punches.

"How dare you?" Mr. Wisedor shouted in protest, throwing punches.

"Let's kill him!" someone shouted.

Favor ran and pulled his father from the vicious mob, wielding his gun and shooting it three times in the air. The men released him long enough to escape. They headed to one of the storage buildings and locked the door behind them.

"I suspect it was sabotage. I'll find the guilty and kill 'em myself," Mr. Wisedor threatened, rubbing his aching chin.

"It's our fault. We deserve what they're suffering. Justice is due, can't you see it? Judgment's descending, avenging the blood of innocent men," Favor said with conviction.

"I heard about the shipyard accident. That's business. Don't take it personally," his father snapped.

"Nothing has changed in the last four generations. You're a slave driver. I'm ashamed you're my father," Favor raged.

He was drawn to the window as the workers outside became more restless. A riot was brewing.

"I'm going out there."

"You're not going anywhere. I've had enough of your nonsense," Mr. Wisedor warned, grabbing his son's clothing. Favor fought back, and the two wrestled like angry dogs in the shadows. His father tired and let go.

"Stay here if you want to live," Favor warned.

"And leave if you want to die," Mr. Wisedor yelled after Favor.

Favor approached the riotous men without fear. He jumped up on a wagon to get the workers' attention. A mob tried grabbing him, but he pulled a pistol from his coat and shot it in the air. The men backed off.

"Hear me. Today you'll be paid threefold in back wages. Your paperwork will be returned, and all debts forgiven. You're free to leave, but to those who stay, I promise change as God holds me accountable. I need your help to close this factory. Work is available at the shipyard."

"It's a death trap," one worker yelled.

"Revisions in safety are in process. Your wages will be more than fair."

"Over your old man's dead body," someone yelled with skepticism.

"I'm in charge. Change starts now," Favor eyed the men hoping it would calm a storm of rage.

* * *

The next morning, Naomi ran from the kitchen door of Shadow Brook mansion. The front page of the newspapers flapped in her hand.

She entered the small cottage in a rush. A photo of Favor dodging the press was plastered on the front page. The headline read, "Wisedor Empire Crumbling."

"Favor's on the front page. What does it say? You know I don't read well." Naomi thrust the paper under her daughter's nose.

Purity was still in her robe, sipping on a cup of tea. She snatched the paper and read in haste.

"Don't tell me justice is finally calling. Let's see. It says men were seriously hurt at the shipyard, and an explosion burned several workers at the distillery."

"Serves them right. It's a shame about the men, but it's about time hardship found the Wisedor's too," Naomi said with bitterness.

Purity read on.

"Protesters are planning a labor march against all the factory owners, demanding higher wages and safer working conditions. They're expecting large crowds at Bristol town square at one o'clock. From there, they'll march. Are you going?" Purity asked, raising the ornate teacup to her lips.

"And who's going to pay our bills if we're fired?" Naomi asked in fear.

* * *

Favor sat in his office at Wisedor Dish Factory. He felt paralyzed, pinned to his chair, holding the morning paper. The weight of all the injured workers and the added pressure of discovering more of his father's unethical business practices made life unbearable. Public scrutiny brought personal shame regarding his association with such corruption.

Flashbacks ran through his mind from the last few days. Jezzie's ranting about the whore and her sons. Purity's confronting insults. The injured victims screaming in horror, flesh hanging, and broken bones jutting through bloodied skin. Fire blazing from the distillery rooftop. His father's snarled face defending fatal business practices. Each event caused his stomach to lurch.

His eyes shifted to the mound of paperwork on the desk. With a violent thrust, he threw large stacks into the air. Each paper floated to its own special place on the floor, and for once, he didn't care about the mess.

Purity's righteous scolding echoed, "I thought I was in love with you, but now I see I've been in love with a man who was the making of my own imagination—not the real Favor. I fear for you because someday your treasures will rot, and you won't have the power to save yourself." A feeling of doom cut through his soul.

The mountain of orders was proof Wisedor china was in high demand. The orders came in from far and wide for the delicate dishes of Bristol's very own fine dish factory. Each item was hand-painted with gold or silver trim and designed with ornate colors. Some designs featured flowers such as roses, orchids, and violets. Others had ornate patterns. It was every local bride's dream to have the best for entertaining.

With business booming, and the need for inexpensive labor was vital for profits. It was an inescapable fact that the children working in the factory were looking younger and younger. They knew little English.

Mr. Wisedor entered the office ready to battle regarding all the rumored business changes. He noticed the paper mess on the floor.

"You've lost your mind," he growled impatiently at his son.

Favor straightened his shoulders.

"Father, I need to speak with you regarding our labor practices."

"The managers are responsible for supplying the workforce. They receive hefty bonuses for keeping expenses down, I might add. Our profits have been exceptional. Who works for us, and where they come from, isn't your concern."

"I've gone over the books. How are the men supporting their families on what we pay them? And the boys aren't even on the payroll."

"Their wages are comparable to other factories in the area," Mr. Wisedor insisted.

"We're paying mere pennies a day."

"These matters are settled," Mr. Wisedor threatened.

Favor stood his ground.

"Nevertheless, I'll conduct my own investigation."

Favor left the comfortable, plush office and started on the first floor of the three-story building. He rarely ventured past the office area in the factory, but since he was the new administrator, it was time to face the conditions.

The first floor of the factory was where the dishes were sculpted and kilned. There were seventy pottery stations with two adults at each, shaping the dishes and vessels made to order. The managers noticed Favor and changed their harsh tone toward the workers. Each employee worked feverishly. He smiled slightly at them and noted their diligent work.

Then he ascended the squeaky wooden staircase to the second floor. Another sixty adult workers were stacked in tight workstations, painting the dishes.

"Do they stop for breaks? How long are their shifts? Ten or twelve hours?" Favor asked.

"Twelve hours a day, six days a week, thirty-minute lunch breaks," Dagon, the floor manager answered.

"And where do you find the workers?" Favor asked.

"Here and there," Dagon answered, reluctant to elaborate.

Just then, Orion, the boy from the streets, descended the third story steps. He had worked night and day since being sold to the factory by the sailor. Exhausted, he struggled under the weight of the stack of plates he carried up the stairs. He missed a step, and the dishes fell from his grasp, shattering into an awful mess.

Dagon's eyes bulged in anger. He tried to control festering rage. The child collapsed in fear, realizing a beating was to follow.

Favor approached and reached out his hand.

"Don't trouble yourself, child. It was an accident. What's your name?"

"Orion," the boy said, fearing eye contact.

"And the children? Where do you find the children?" Favor asked Dagon, expecting answers.

"The streets. They're rescued from begging bread. No one knows where they're from," the man confessed.

The workers didn't dare look at Favor, realizing he had the power to terminate their position at any moment. They had suffered much at the hands of the managers who often fired workers for the slightest infractions.

The air was stale and ventilation poor as the windows were only slightly open. Each worker sat on a small chair at their own table—supplied with paint and a stack of dishes.

Favor went over to the windows and opened them.

"These workers need proper ventilation from the paint fumes. I dare not see these windows closed again," Favor ordered and began to ascend the staircase leading to the third floor.

"You shouldn't go up there," Dagon warned.

"I own this factory. Do you dare restrict me?" Favor scolded. He took Orion's hand and led him up the stairs.

Slowly, they climbed to the third floor. Favor couldn't believe his eyes. The room was filled with at least seventy-five boys who were packaging the fragile dinnerware into boxes.

A few adults labeled the orders and prepared them for shipping. Others carried the completed packages out the back door and down three flights of stairs where the wares were loaded on waiting trucks.

The chatter hushed as Favor stood in their midst. They realized by his dress and stature that he must be someone important. He noted the workers varied in age from about five to sixteen years of age. They were of all skin colors: pale, dark, yellow, and red.

Favor rested his hand on Orion's head, then pulled it away, noting the oozing green pus.

"Get me a rag. It's putrid. And you knew about this awful infection? He could infect the other boys," he glared as Dagon grabbed for a clean cloth and handed it over.

"Don't worry, Orion. Help is on the way," Favor said, wiping the green pus off his hand. Then refocusing, Favor asked a teenager, "Where are you from?"

"Poland," the teen shyly replied.

"And you?" Favor asked a light-skinned boy with blonde hair.

"Denmark," the boy replied.

"And you?" he asked another boy with dark hair and eyes.

"Romania," the teen answered politely.

"What's your pay, Orion?" asked Favor.

"Food and a blanket, that's all."

"And where do you sleep, boy?" Favor pushed. Dagon made a stern face. Orion begged with his eyes to be released from the questioning.

"Tell me, I insist," Favor pried.

"We sleep on the floor," Orion responded loudly for all to hear.

Favor's eyes scanned the large room, noting a pile of rolled pallets stacked against one of the walls, confirming the boy's answer.

The manager's face filled with rage. Dagon clenched his fists as though revealing the dark secrets jeopardized his own interests.

One orphan started, and the others joined in singing, "Call of the Orphan."

> Hear the call of the orphan child, a forgotten, desperate soul
> Come, ease our pain, don't look away from our shame
> You're the only one who can give a hand
> We're the children of the world, lost and all alone
>
> Do you care, hear our cry, help us in our despair
> We come from far and wide, making your wares
> Don't look away when we're cold and tired
> Working from dawn to dusk, without rest or care

Hear the call of the orphan child, ease our misery
We're the children of the world, hoping for a better way
Come, ease our pain, don't look away from our shame
One by one, you're the one, who has the power to make change

Lift a hand and take a stand for a better life
Be a voice for the voiceless in the land

A boy coughed and appeared too weak to stand. Favor extended his hand and felt the boy's forehead, then turned to Dagon.

"He's too weak to work and burning with fever. Why are you exposing the other workers? Get a doctor for him right away. I'll return and check on his condition."

"Yes, sir," the manager said.

"Come with me, boy." Favor took Orion's hand and moved through the orphans.

"I promise, I will come back for you," Favor called to all the boys.

Outside the Factory, a huge gathering of protesters stood. They bombarded the entrance, waving signs demanding change and yelling chants. Purity and Natasha held signs that read, "Higher Wages" and "Stop Abuse."

As Favor left the building, and the protestors addressed him.

"Who owns this sweatshop?" the protest leaders asked in agitation.

Favor noticed Purity among the protesters. They locked eyes. She stared without wavering as though trying to prove her point.

"I do, sir," Favor replied, almost defiantly.

"We're demanding higher wages, safer working conditions, and sick time. We want eight-hour shifts, five days a week. Your workers deserve better," the leader demanded.

"You're growing wealthy on the backs of others. Many of them are defenseless children," a protester yelled.

"That issue has come to my attention. Let me deal with it," Favor said defensively.

"We'll make sure of that," the leader spouted. Favor pushed Orion to safety as the men pulled him into the crowd. Some began ripping his clothing while others slapped and punched him.

Purity ran to the men attacking him.

133

"Stop! You're going to kill him," Purity protested and tried to pull the attackers away. One of the men pushed her violently aside.

"Choose your battles, or you're next," the man yelled.

"Stop. He's a good man," Orion begged.

Favor reached into his jacket pocket for the pistol and fired it into the air.

"I'll have you arrested for assault," Favor warned as his nose and lip bled.

"It's you who needs arresting," one protester argued.

"Blood's on your hands," someone else chimed in.

"People die on your watch," a woman complained.

Others screamed obscenities.

"I'm aware of the conditions. I promise change as God holds me accountable," Favor yelled with conviction.

The mob of protestors couldn't believe their ears and quieted.

"We'll meet next week. Then we'll see how serious you are," the leader said, glaring.

The protesters continued their march down the road to the next factory.

Favor headed back inside the factory to clean himself up, Orion by his side.

Mr. Wisedor had cowered behind the factory door, taking in the whole exchange.

"Sick time and eight-hour shifts. You'll do nothing of the sort. You're out of your mind colluding with those brutes. The unions have no business nosing in on our labor practices," his father screamed, grabbing Favor and slamming him against the wall.

Orion hid behind a large barrel and began to cry.

"You're out of your mind with greed, Father."

"You'll be the end of us. Bankruptcy? Is that your plan? I'll see you disinherited first," Mr. Wisedor threatened.

Favor quickly escaped his father's grip and pushed him to the wall. He pulled back but stopped his fist just short of his father's nose.

"May God strike you and your profits. Give me full authority to make a change, or I'm running from this insanity. I won't be a part of your slave mentality any longer. Do you hear me?"

Favor took Orion by the hand, and they left in his new car. The ride was quiet. The boy didn't dare speak to this stranger nursing a bleeding lip.

Favor finally broke the silence.

"Where's your family, boy?"

"We were separated at the shipyard. I don't know where they are."

"I'll do my best to find them," Favor promised.

Favor parked in front of the house at Shadow Brook Estate. Orion had never seen such wealth. He stared up at the grandeur of such a place, speechless.

"This way." Favor led Orion to the stables. He let the boy pet one of the horses as he saddled Rozzie. Favor mounted his faithful steed, then pulled the boy up in front of him. He grimaced at the foul smell from Orion's sore.

"Let's go, Rozzie. Take us to Son's Camp," Favor ordered the horse. Rozzie took off through the majestic hillside, tall grasses, and thick trees. The silence was broken with the sound of ram's horns on the wind.

"Orion, don't be afraid. You'll be in good hands here. I promise I'll look for your parents," Favor said, helping the boy slide from the tall horse.

"Yes, sir. Thank you, sir."

Favor dismounted Rozzie with ease. Taking Orion's hand, they made their way through dense brush and trees. In a few hundred yards, they reached Son's Camp. The ram's horns stopped as the Son's recognized their esteemed visitor.

"We come in peace," Favor shouted.

David blew on his ram's horn, signaling the sons to put down their weapons of defense.

Favor spotted Alexis and dug into his money pouch.

"I need your help. Please, care for Orion until I can find his parents. His scalp's infected. This should cover his care and medical expenses," Favor said, handing over a substantial amount of money.

Alexis noted Favor's swollen right eye and fat, blood-stained lip.

"Someone's beaten you,"

"Nothing like the school of hard knocks. It's been quite an education," Favor said, wincing as his lip split, trying to smile.

"I'll let Purity know. She's tending to important business."

"Our paths crossed. I know all about it," he said, leaving with the weight of many burdens on his shoulders.

Clawed by the Devil

Chapter 17

MAVE'S OF BRISTOL was cloaked in darkness. Purity worked the kitchen now since dancing with the men gnawed at her conscience. She finished scrubbing a pile of dirty pots and looked out the window, trying to make out who arrived.

Mave snapped the whip on an old horse. It grunted in protest, straining under the weight of a heavy wagon as it navigated into the back driveway of the hotel. Looking about her, Mave stepped down and headed to the back of the wagon that was covered by an old tarp.

Purity's eyes were opened to the spirit realm. She saw a dark figure clinging to Mave's back. Its weight bent her over in agonizing pain. Black crows descended on a nearby tree branch.

Mave peeled back the heavy tarp with an angry yank. Five heads popped up, gasping for fresh air—four young boys and a teenage girl.

"Don't pretend you don't see me. Get out here now," Mave yelled, eyeing Purity through the window. She leaned on the wagon and winced in back pain.

In moments, Purity burst through the kitchen door wearing a soiled apron.

"You're back to scrubbing pots, hey? Here's some kitchen help. The girl goes to my office. Find a nice robe for her and pour some tea." Mave headed inside to the bar area.

Purity passed the boys off to the other kitchen workers.

"Wash and feed them. I'll help the girl," Purity ordered.

Alone in Mave's office, Purity helped the teen get ready.

"What's your name?" Purity asked with urgency.

"Ellie," the teen replied.

"What's your story?"

"I fell in love with a man named Roberto. He promised to marry me, but he's nowhere to be found," Ellie said, in a sea of tears.

Purity's memory was jolted by the name.

"Roberto. What did he look like?"

"He's tall, with dark hair, and very handsome," Ellie said with obvious pain.

"Where are you from?" Purity asked, anxious that her time with the girl was short.

"An Armenian village in Turkey." Her English was broken but understandable.

Purity provided a beautiful silk robe and poured a cup of tea.

"Please, help me," Ellie begged, realizing she was in trouble.

The sound of Mave's voice echoed down the hallway, "I've got a beauty for you."

"I hope so," a man replied.

Purity hid in the closet after giving the teenager a hand signal to remain quiet. The teen understood the gesture and appeared as a living statue paralyzed with fear.

Ellie was sitting on the couch and jumped as Mave and the man entered the office. Chin Lu followed behind Mave and waited by the door.

"Calm your nerves, my dear. Ah, you're quite lovely." Mave examined Ellie's flawless skin with her long fingers and stroked the teen's shiny brunette hair.

The man settled in a chair nearby and inhaled the teen's features with desire. His back was to Purity as she peered from the closet—most of his face hidden by a large hat. But it didn't take long for Purity to flinch at his deformed left hand. It was shaped like a claw, with a thumb, pointer, and middle finger, and glazed over with thick crusty, leathery skin.

Dark spirits from Ahaba's forces filtered in to witness the sale. The man's claw began to throb in discomfort as the dark spirit wrapped tightly around it. The stranger winced in pain.

"A stunning investment, isn't she?" Mave said, not fazed by the man's discomfort and pressing for a quick sale.

The stranger shook his hand forcefully, and the dark spirit went flying across the room.

"How much English does she know?" he said with concern.

"A little. But no worries. It's all about work experience, and she'll get plenty of it. I won't go cheaper than a hundred dollars for this one. She's never been used. You'll make a fortune," she said, reaching for a cigarette. She lit it and took a deep drag.

Ellie tried to run, but Mave caught the teen, saying, "Last time I heard, there was no way out of hell."

The stranger stood and stroked Ellie's hair with his claw, adding to her panic. The teen screeched in fear at the appearance of the deformity. Unfazed, the stranger scanned her developed body through the revealing robe. Ellie burst into tears, terrified.

"I want her branded." He handed the cash to Mave.

"Chin Lu, we need a branding," Mave said as she left the office.

"Yes, Mave," Chin Lu said dutifully.

In a matter of moments, two men entered with a hot branding iron. It was immersed in a bucket of hot coals. Ellie panicked as one of the men held her still in a vicious vice grip. The other pulled the robe from her right shoulder and pressed the red-hot branding iron with the letter "M" into her soft skin. Her blood-curdling scream did nothing to stop the pain.

"Put her in the car," the stranger said, raising his deformed hand.

Then without discussion, the men bound Ellie's hands with rope and chained her feet. Ellie tried to battle, but it was fruitless. They carried her to a car waiting outside.

Purity opened the closet—the office was empty. She quickly climbed out the window and caught sight of "The Claw"—her nickname for the stranger whose name remained a mystery. He helped the men put his new purchase into a fine automobile.

"I can handle her from here," The Claw assured them.

Purity heard the wind rattling the loose tiles on the roof of Mave's of Bristol. The wind picked up and grew stronger by the moment. The sound of stampeding horses thundered from above.

"Captain, I need you," Purity shouted, looking to the sky. New strength and courage enveloped her soul.

Gusts of wind swirled around, kicking up more dust.

She covered her face with a scarf, tying it around her neck to conceal her identity. She hopped on one of the patron's horses and followed behind the car, riding far enough behind so as not to draw attention.

The streets of Bristol were clogged with traffic once again. Horse-drawn wagons and newly invented cars slowed everyone down. She followed the car across town to the rear driveway of the Metacom Hotel.

The Claw opened the car door and dragged Ellie off the fine leather seats. The teen, still bound, did her best to fight off her new master. The man raised his claw and used it to slap the girl into submission.

Purity charged at The Claw with the horse, knocking him down. His identity remained hidden by the large hat as he hit the ground hard.

Transparent, fiery hands appeared from the Ring of Grace. They grabbed Ellie and pulled her up on the horse.

The Claw pulled himself up and grabbed at the horse's reins. Purity fought the man off.

"Who are you, vicious girl? How dare you rob me? Help, I'm being robbed!"

The Claw grabbed Purity's hair, pulled her close, and scratched her face raw with his deformed hand. With a swift kick, Purity hit the man's rounded abdomen. He grunted as she knocked the wind out of him.

Heads began to turn, and men on the street rushed to intervene. Purity kicked the horse's side, yelling, "Captain of the Lord's Army, help us!"

Stampeding armies above sounded like a mighty swarming wind. Swords clanked, and warriors yelled out, "Hold fast for the victory!"

Ahaba's army flooded the sky above. It sounded like thunder cracking as the two forces clashed.

Captain of the Lord's Army appeared on his white horse with a vast number of warriors following behind.

"Mighty army, it's time to fight," the Captain declared.

A battle cry arose, and the horses rode out to face their enemies. His archangels swooped in, wiping out vast numbers of Ahaba's army.

Purity's eyes and ears were miraculously opened to the unseen battle that raged above. The horse rode bolted forward as it was shot with an arrow of fire from the unseen realm.

A man chased on foot, trying to stop them from getting away. Dark spirits covered his head and whispered in his ear, "Kill them. Don't let them get away." In response, the man pulled his gun and fired shots.

The Ring of Grace shot fiery arrows at the bullets, and they were deflected. The angels knocked the gun from the man's hand and then shot arrows at a handful of other men chasing behind Purity and Ellie. Each man was picked off and tumbled to the ground.

Purity and Ellie galloped away, down back alleys, making their way out of town. Captain's forces kept Ahaba and his minions from advancing after them.

* * *

Purity settled Ellie at Son's Camp on Shadow Brook Estate late that evening. The sons helped loose the teen from her chains. They sang and danced around the campfire with homemade instruments, hoping to relieve Ellie's heartbreak.

"You're safe with us. Get some rest," Purity said, walking Ellie to her tent-like shelter specially prepared by the sons.

"Don't go back. It will be your death sentence," Ellie warned, fearing for her new friend's life.

"Don't worry. I've got this for them." Purity picked up a bow and arrow. She shot the arrow into a nearby tree. Alexis approached with Orion, and Purity threw the bow aside. Purity didn't recognize the boy.

"I saw you at the factory, helping Favor," Orion boldly declared.

"Someone clawed you good," Alexis said, noting the scratches on Purity's face.

"The devil himself," Purity replied with loathing.

"Favor saw you at the protest," Alexis said with worry.

"It doesn't matter. Injustice must be dealt with," Purity fired back.

"He brought Orion from the factory and asked us to look after him. That is until his parents are found," Alexis said, pulling out the money Favor had given her.

"And what about the others dying in his clutches?" Purity turned her attention to David.

"David, I need this horse returned to Mave's of Bristol. Can you do it without getting caught?"

"Anything for you, Mother."

Purity picked up the bow again and found a quiver of arrows nearby. She slung both across her back and disappeared into the darkness.

"Mother, wait. It's not safe out there," David said, trying to follow her into the darkness. But she eluded him. He stopped momentarily and, with a trained hunter's ear, strained to pick up her trail, but it was futile.

Purity moved through the sprawling dark acreage of Shadow Brook Estate, the moon lighting her way. She was comforted by being alone in the silence, surrounded by nothing but utter darkness. Crickets chirped, then an old owl cooed above in a tree. As she listened, the woods came alive with coyotes, bears, bobcats, and foxes.

Dark spirits from Ahaba's army landed on boulders and trees, searching for something to possess. A bear and bobcat faced off in the woods within eyeshot. The wispy, translucent bat-like spirits flew at them and began their attack. The bear swung large paws in the air, resisting what felt like invisible bites and gnawing at his flesh. The bear roared, spooked by the unseen enemy. The spirits entered its roaring mouth.

The animal's behavior changed—a wild look now in its eyes. With one swipe of his paw, the bear sent the bobcat flying. The bear seemed in agony as it resisted the inner demons. It twisted on the ground, rolled in somersaults, grunted, roared, and frothed at the mouth. Trying to escape, it took off running with great speed.

Close by, Purity gazed into the star-filled night, hoping to get a glimpse of the New Earth.

"Was it all a dream, the New Earth? Captain, are you listening? Are you near?" Purity called. The only answer was her voice echoing through the trees.

Large black crows landed on the tree branches above, showering dead pine needles onto her thick, long hair. Purity brushed them off and quickly surveyed the area. Sensing impending danger, she readied her bow and pointed it rapidly in several directions.

Heavy breathing stalked closer and grew louder and louder until hot breath panted on her soft neck. Turning, she stared into a pair of eyes glowing red in the darkness.

"They got you, Mr. Bear," Purity whispered, aware of his demon possession. She took one step backward, then another and another. The bear stepped closer, inch by inch, growling and hissing. He charged in a fit of rage.

Purity ran her fastest, but the bear was gaining on her.

"Captain, help," Purity yelled to the heavens.

Ahaba and his army hovered above, gleefully excited to see the end of one of the Captain's vessels.

"Attack! Attack," Ahaba commanded the evil spirits in the bear.

The bear's eyes glowed brighter red, and the furry creature mindlessly pursued in a fit of insanity.

Rainbow beings from the New Earth hovered above, appearing as Bright Star. They pulsated as one with in rainbow light.

Purity fixated on the Bright Star as she ran in an erratic path, hoping to evade the bear.

"Bright and Star, is that you?" There was no response.

The Ring of Grace appeared as translucent child warriors, holding fiery swords. This time, Purity's eyes were opened to see them.

"The kid angels. I've heard about you."

They morphed into what looked like a golden vapor and entered the bear's roaring mouth. As the light and dark forces battled inside the bear, the animal collapsed to the ground, jerking, rolling, and twisting.

Within moments, the bear was motionless. He let out one last roar, expelling the vapor. In the tall grass beside him, the Ring of Grace morphed back into warriors, each holding a wicked bat-like creature in their grasp that writhed and struggled to be released.

"Your end has come," Sergio said.

"Revenge, for all your wicked ways," Kaleb shouted.

"Take your last breath," Josiah urged.

"Allegiance to the Captain," Rocco declared.

The evil creatures were extinguished with one swipe of their fiery swords. Nearby, the bear revived and sauntered off in a daze.

Purity sank to her knees, suffering from extreme exhaustion.

"I can't go on," she complained.

The small angels surrounded Purity, each laying a hand of fire on her head, shoulders, and back. She felt a heat radiating where they touched, moving through her body and reviving every cell. The heavy burden of fatigue, fear, and sorrow began to lift. It was replaced with energy, power, and determination.

"I receive the Captain's power," Purity said with hands lifted high and eyes closed.

When she opened her eyes, the angels rolled into a ball of fire and shot through the night sky.

Purity took a few deep breaths. She relaxed in the wonderful peace and love she now felt. Renewed in strength, she pushed forward through the darkness.

* * *

The cottage door creaked, and the wooden floor squeaked under her feet as Purity entered the small cottage. She lightened her step, not wanting to wake her mother, who slept in Papa's overstuffed chair. Naomi's head rocked back and forth in the slow rhythm of slumber. She took another step.

Naomi shifted and snorted herself awake.

"Good Lord. What time is it?" She raised a small lamp from the side table, trying to make out the time on the old grandfather clock. Naomi gasped when the light shone on Purity's face. It was covered in dried blood.

Naomi rose quickly and grabbed a towel and a water basin.

"You've been clawed. Dancing with the devil, I suppose. This saving the world is catching up with you." She wiped the blood from her daughter's face and sang, "Dancing with the Devil."

> You're dancing with the devil
> You better get smart
> Cause he claws and scratches too
> Take my advice, you better think twice
> Cause you're playing with the grave
> What a pretty corpse you'll make
> Make no mistake, he hates the likes of you

You're dancing with the devil
And it won't be nice
He'll do whatever to stop your plans
Your heart is right, helping the fight
Against those who rob and kill
Take my advice, you better think twice
Cause I can't stand to lose you too

"I need your prayers, not your judgment. I don't understand a lot of this myself," Purity said with tears welling.

"You're playing with fire." Naomi sighed in frustration, then lifted a hand of prayer.

"Lord, your will be done, your Kingdom come. I don't want to lose her, too." The prayer was sealed with a gentle kiss on her daughter's forehead.

Minutes later, Purity collapsed into bed. The evening played on repeat in her mind—a haunting cycle. Her heavy eyes beckoned rest, and misty shadows of deep sleep closed out a world fading away.

She was taken into the netherworld of billowing fog and lurking shadows. Purity was sitting in a small boat, moving down a slow-flowing narrow creek. Snakes slithered, gliding upon the waters, striking out toward her as they passed. Decrepit hands of those lost in another time and place surfaced from the murky waters below.

"Get her. There's no escape," a voice echoed over the waters.

Mave, wearing a dark robe, stood on a bridge over the foggy waterway.

"How dare you enter my domain." She pulled a knife from her robe.

Purity saw the flash of metal in the moonlight as Mave threw the blade right for her heart. She woke just before the knife penetrated her chest. She jolted to a sitting position, filled with terror. Her feet hit the cold wooden floors, and stumbling in the dark, she leaned over a bucket, nauseous with fear.

"Do not return to Mave's of Bristol. Do not return to Mave's of Bristol," a still small voice resounded through her soul.

"Captain, is that you?" her whisper broke the dark silence.

* * *

The next evening, rebellious to the warning, Purity reported for duty at Mave's of Bristol.

"I can handle Mave. Besides, I need the money," she reasoned.

Entering the kitchen, she tied an apron around her thin waist and rolled up her sleeves. A large stack of pots and pans needed scrubbing, and she got to work.

Chin Lu tapped her shoulder.

"Mave wants to see you."

Purity dried her hands on a kitchen towel and obeyed the request. Walking down the hall, her knees started shaking, and her hands got clammy. Purity knocked on the office door.

"Purity, my dear. Come in." Mave reclined on the satin couch.

Purity entered timidly.

Mave eyed the scratches on Purity's face with focused interest.

"It appears you've had a struggle. Sit down and let's talk about it." Mave patted the soft cushions next to her with a welcoming hand.

The lace curtains moved as a handful of Ahaba's forces flew in. They settled on the furnishings, expecting a fierce battle. Unseen by the human eye, their bodies were dark and wrinkled.

As ordered, Purity sat. She looked around, sensing evil in the room. One spirit blew his breath in Purity's direction and licked his chops. A chilling shiver made the hairs on her arms stand up. She tried to dispel an inner alarm.

Mave jumped up as a spirit coiled around her neck. She coughed and poured a cup of tea.

"Tea?" Mave offered.

"No, thank you. I have to get back to work."

"You vanished like smoke last night after I brought you more kitchen help. You're such an ungrateful girl. Of course, that was after you helped our little friend, Ellie, clean up."

"I had unexpected business. It won't happen again." Purity avoided eye contact.

Mave locked the office door in a hurry.

"I'm sure it won't. I'm afraid I have bad news. Our friend Ellie is missing. Imagine, kidnappings in this fine city. You wouldn't know anything about that, would you? Or have you added another orphan to your collection?"

145

"You're accusing me of kidnapping?" Purity shot back.

"I should have sold you when I had the chance. You're nothing but trouble, thanks to Mandy. Maybe I should get rid of both of you," Mave threatened.

In the mirror across the room, Purity saw Mave pick up a knife from the tea table and hide it behind her back.

"What really happened last night?" Mave probed with agitation.

"If you think I'm guilty of anything, let's go to the police. If that's not the case, I'll get to work."

Out of nowhere, Mave lunged at her with the knife.

"How dare you step into my domain? Where's Ellie? Tell me, or you're dead," she screamed.

Purity dodge Mave's jab.

"Witch, stop, or you're looking at your own grave."

Before Mave could attack again, Purity landed a swift kick to Mave's bone-thin body. The wind knocked from her lungs, she dropped the knife and collapsed to the floor.

"Wicked girl," Mave grunted.

Bending on one knee, Purity squeezed her neck in a tight chokehold.

"You sell souls into torture. It's your turn to burn." Purity relished the words. Despite a struggle, her tormentor turned blue from lack of oxygen.

"Captain, send her to hell." Purity said with spite.

"Don't become what you hate," a still small voice sounded.

"Captain, is that you? I'm trying to understand," Purity asked.

Mave's eyes rolled back in an unconscious stupor. Reluctantly, Purity released the death hold. She picked up the knife and threw it at a portrait of Mave hanging on the wall, piercing her eye. Then opening the office window, Purity climbed out.

Chin Lu banged so hard on the office door it vibrated down the hallway.

"Mave. Mave, you alright?" she yelled while pulling a heavy keyring from a pocket. She unlocked the door and burst into the office. Mave was motionless on the floor, a dark spirit resting on her abdomen.

"She's dead. The witch is dead," Chin Lu said as her icy heart began to melt with the hope of freedom. She moved closer and kicked Mave's foot.

"You in there?" Chin Lu asked, hoping the long nightmare was over. She kicked Mave's other foot and hoped for no response. Suddenly, it jerked back, and her owner began to stir.

"Hard to kill the devil," Chin Lu sounded with disappointment.

"What was that?" Mave choked out the words.

Gift of Clarity

Chapter 18

SHADOW BROOK ESTATE sat under a cloak of darkness. Purity's steps grew heavier as she narrowed in on the final path to the small cottage she called home. The darkness of the night mirrored her soul. She wasn't sure when Mave would release her revenge, but one thing was sure, it was on the way.

"Captain, I need you more than ever," Purity said in anguish.

Upon entering the cottage, Naomi's snoring filled the atmosphere with some semblance of comfort and safety. Purity dropped into bed, exhausted.

The rainbow beings, Bright and Star, emitted colorful light into her dark bedroom. They lifted their familiar friend from her warm bedding as though she was light as a feather. Purity never knew when the honor of visiting the New Earth would be granted or how she would get there. But each time she went, it was considered a gift. Once again, they escorted her to the glowing planet, traversing light-years in mere moments.

They laid Purity's body in the sailboat moving down the majestic river that flowed through New Earth. This time, playful dolphins surrounded the boat in great numbers. They danced on the fast-moving current, doing flips, jumping high, twirling, and diving deep into the clear blue waters.

Purity woke with a start, rattled by the playful creature's sputtering and splashing. Rising quickly, she watched as they raced alongside the boat.

One of the larger dolphins swam close.

"Jump in Purity. How about a look around?" the dolphin said in a sputtering way.

"What's your name?" "I'm Phin. Let's go," the dolphin said, flipping high into the air.

"But I can't breathe underwater," Purity yelled back.

"Here on the New Earth, everyone can breathe underwater," Phin said with a nod of his head and a big smile.

Purity jumped off the sailboat and plunged into the cool waters. The dolphins surrounded her. She grabbed hold of Phin's large fin, and he pulled her along. They plunged deep into the crystal-clear waters, surrounded by tropical fish and colorful coral reefs. Purity ran out of air and inhaled the river water, but instead of choking, she breathed in clear rejuvenating vapors of life-giving air.

The dolphins traveled a great distance and led Purity to a crystal-clear cove surrounded by trees. Her feet touched down on the soft sand. She waved goodbye to the dolphins, who jumped and twirled one last time before swimming away.

Above, the sky was painted with colors in shades of pink, orange, and yellow. Purity walked along the shore of the cove.

"Captain, where are you? Will I ever meet you? Lord of the Dance, come to me," she yelled, but her voice only echoed off the surrounding mountains.

She reached out to touch one of the ornate leaves on a tree, and it recoiled.

"I won't harm you," she spoke softly.

Then the laughing began, like the sound of a child filled with delight.

"Where are you?" Purity asked, bewildered, as the laughter increased. "Over here," a child's voice responded. And then more giggling.

The voice echoed in the direction of a large field with giant roses, geraniums, chrysanthemums, carnations, and gladiolas. Purity rushed through the flowers as the laughter continued, searching for its source.

"Come find me, Mother," the girl teased, hoping to be found.

"How am I your mother?" Purity called out.

"Because I'm in the Captain's thoughts for you," the child reasoned.

"Then you must be a happy thought. Let me see you." Purity looked about the huge field of giant flowers.

A girl around the age of seven peeked out of an enormous red rose. Purity froze to see such a precious sight. The girl's hair was honey-colored with highlights of gold. Her sky-blue eyes sparkled, enhancing her angelic features.

"Mother, we meet at last. I'm glad you're here," the child said, sliding from the enormous flower into Purity's arms. She hugged her mother's neck, and a feeling of great peace and tranquility filled both of their souls.

"What's your name, Daughter?"

"I'm the gift of Clarity," the child said with a twinkle in her eye.

"When will you come to me, Clarity?"

"At the appointed time. No sooner, no later—right on time. Come this way," Clarity said. She took her mother's hand and led her to a cluster of the most beautiful flowers ever imagined. The whole field of giant flowers began to sing, "Captain's Glory."

We sing to tell the story
Of the Captain in all his glory
Basking in his light
Our colors shine bright

We sing to tell the story
Of the Captain in all his glory
We rise in the winds of life
We take delight like angels in flight
Warming hearts and making all bright
We sing to tell the story
Of the Captain in all his glory

The flowers swayed in the wind, singing away. Sprays of gold and silver erupted like pollen, dusting the air.

In the field, a large book was suspended in mid-air as though an invisible being held it. A pair of transparent human hands opened the colorful book. The hands started turning the pages, then, as though caught by a turbulent wind, the pages turned faster and faster on their own.

"What's this book?" Purity asked in amazement.

"It's 'His Thoughts Revealed.' For He knows the best plans for you. If you don't know his thoughts, life won't be what it should. Weigh your decisions carefully. You must complete your purpose. Have faith, and I'll come to you. It's all about the Captain's timing." Clarity's voice faded out.

Purity woke in her bedroom. She mumbled, "Clarity. Clarity, come back."

"Wake up. Stop your dreaming. You'll be late. You're serving breakfast in the big house," Naomi called from the small cottage kitchen.

Purity could barely open her eyes. With a moan she rolled over.

"I'm exhausted, Mama," she complained.

Naomi sighed and shook her head. Without another word, she grabbed an apron and headed for the mansion.

* * *

Natasha and Alexis eyed Naomi as she entered the kitchen with a look of embarrassment.

"I'm supposed to be off, but I'm working Purity's shift. I can't pry the girl out of bed," her mother groaned. She picked up a fresh tray of pastries and headed for the dining room.

Victoria, Favor, and Mr. and Mrs. Wisedor were enjoying a full course breakfast. Naomi placed the tray of pastries on the table next to the pancakes, eggs, bacon, fruit, coffee, and juice. She stood along the wall, ready to serve their every whim.

Favor picked up one of the exquisite plates made at the Wisedor Dish Factory. Deep emotion jolted his heart. He thought on the hands involved in making that one dish. In his mind, he saw hands forming it on the potter's wheel, another pair painting it, and glove-covered hands removing it from the hot oven.

"Did you hear me, Son? I'll be at the dish factory today," his father said, pounding a fist on the table.

Favor was jolted from his thoughts.

"I'm not working today. I have urgent business elsewhere."

"What's more important than family business?" his father glared.

"It's personal. But good news travels fast. You're sure to find out, eventually."

His father eyed him with uncertainty but didn't question him further.

"I could use a bit of good news." Mr. Wisedor stood and folded the morning paper under his arm before leaving.

Mrs. Wisedor turned to Favor.

"What could be more urgent than assisting your father?" his mother pried indignantly.

"It's a surprise. With your giving spirit, you'll be pleased," he said, half indignant, and finished the last bite of eggs on his plate. Favor carefully wiped his swollen lip from the beating a few days before.

"Look what those brutes did to you. And yet you want to help them. I don't know you these days, Favor," his mother said, eyeing the swollen cracked lip.

"I'm sorry, Mother. I honestly don't know if I can please everyone." He grabbed a pastry from the tray started to walk out.

"I hope our differences won't be permanent. I do love you."

His mother's voice trailed off as he left the room.

The morning's soft light blanketed Shadow Brook Estate. Favor joined a long line of loaded wagons behind the horse stables.

"Follow me," he yelled.

The caravan of wagons traveled along the beautiful hills and meadows of the acreage. Most of the men weren't told what the mission entailed, but that was fine as long as they were paid.

At Son's Camp, several of the boy's sat warming themselves by the campfire, reading the Bible. David was in the meadow targeting a rabbit for roasting, and Jonathan was close behind.

The approaching noise of the clanking wagons and grunting horses caused quite a stir in the forsaken camp. The sons rallied to attention, and ram's horns blew. David panicked and ran to meet those driving the wagons.

"Are you evicting us? Winter's coming. The younger boys won't survive," David begged.

"Help us unload the wagons," one driver demanded.

"Let's get moving. There's work to be done," Favor called out.

David pulled back one of the tarps covering the supplies and was shocked. He and Jonathan whistled for the sons to come and help unload the wagons. They were packed with blankets, clean sheets, clothes, winter jackets, boots, rice, beans, bacon, fresh fruits, vegetables, and loaves of fresh-baked bread neatly stacked in boxes. Other wagons were loaded with building supplies.

"I can't have the boys living like beggars," Favor said with compassion.

"Purity can't stand you, but you've won me over," Jonathan said, hugging him.

"Thanks, I think."

A crew of experienced carpenters began surveying the land. Some began digging the foundation for the new living quarters. Others unloaded the wagons and began stacking the lumber. The sons joined in, helping the men.

* * *

At the cottage, Purity battled depression and exhaustion. Nothing seemed to be going her way, and she was on the verge of hopelessness. She earnestly desired to return to the New Earth and find Clarity.

"Captain of the Lord's Army, I say 'yes' to Clarity. I say 'yes' to your thoughts revealed. But who's her father?" Purity prayed, seeking answers. In her mind's eye, she saw Lord of the Dance. His eyes burned with compassion.

"Lord of the Dance, can you please tell the Captain I accept his thoughts revealed? I will be Clarity's mother," Purity spoke aloud.

"Wait and trust. The answers will come," the Captain whispered into Purity's heart.

"I know that's you, Captain. Don't ask me how I know. I just know. As long as you're listening, I need some help. Are you with me? Give me a sign. Captain, where are you?"

Pounding on the cottage door jarred her prayers. She jumped from the bed and peeked out the window. It was David.

"Wake up, Purity. Wake up," he shouted, continuing to pound the small cottage door.

She grabbed for a robe and opened the door.

"What's gotten into you?"

"Favor's at Son's Camp," David rattled with alarm, and before saying another word, she finished the sentence.

"And he's evicting us. Oh, Captain, how could you let this happen?" Purity agonized, lifting her eyes to heaven.

"Get dressed. We need your help," David demanded. He turned away with a mischievous smirk.

Purity rushed into her bedroom and slammed the door. She washed up, threw on her buckskin dress, and strapped a bow and satchel of arrows over her back.

"If I have to fight my way out of this, I will," Purity threatened.

In minutes, they were running through the acreage with the speed and agility of fine athletes.

"What did Favor say? Is he alone? Don't tell me Jezzie's with him? Captain, how will they survive?" Purity asked one question after the other.

"Who's this Captain you're talking about?"

"He's the only one who can help."

"If you say so."

They reached Son's Camp in record time. Winded, Purity leaned against a tree, trying to catch her breath. With wild eyes, she searched for Favor among dozens of workers. It was difficult to tell what was happening. Some workers were tearing down the old dwellings and creating large piles of debris.

Purity advanced defiantly.

"Stop, this is a crime. I beg you, don't tear Son's Camp down," she yelled, hoping to stop the work.

She looked about as several men ignored her remarks. They continued demolishing the old cabin.

"The men won't defy my orders," Favor said from behind her.

She spun around.

"You're tearing their only shelter down?" she asked, searching Favor's eyes for answers.

"This blemish will soon be eradicated. I refuse this filth on my property."

Purity's heart withered. She pushed him in frustrated protest. He grabbed her fists, and a smile erupted on his face.

"How could you? Heartless fool," she protested.

Favor laughed.

"You're so tough," Favor teased.

"Evicting orphans is a joke? Go clean your own toilets," she yelled.

"Hold your temper. You don't understand," Favor said, looking concerned.

"How can you stand yourself?" Purity said, still trying to push him around.

"Mother, we're getting a new house. Don't be mad," Jonathan said, hugging her.

"A new house?" she softly repeated and stepped back from Favor.

"A new kitchen, too," Jonathan said, with excitement.

"It was all your idea, all this?" Purity asked Favor.

He sheepishly nodded. Overcome with joy, she ran into his arms. She impulsively kissed his cheek, and it pleased him incredibly. Their lips drew close. Then with one steady pull, Favor took Purity's hand and headed to the woods.

"Private meeting. Please excuse us," Favor said to the others as he wove his way among them.

"What's wrong?" Purity said somewhat in a panic.

Once alone in a thicket of trees, he released Purity's hand.

"I want to ask for your forgiveness. You have a habit of seeing clearly, and I'm always in the fog. I'm tired of seeing you pushed in the mud and mistreated. I can't stand the fact you're dancing with men who care nothing about you. Purity, I want you above anything or anyone else," Favor said with sincerity.

"I've waited my whole life to hear those words," Purity said gently. Her heart argued with her mind whether to let him into her heart again.

"How can I love and loath the same person," she thought.

Favor pulled her in gently and pressed his lips to hers, softly at first and then with more passion. Purity felt charged with an inner fire and melted into his embrace. After a few minutes, she came to her senses and pulled away.

"What about your engagement to Jezzie?" Purity said with urgency.

"That's my mother's engagement, not mine. I've made my choice," Favor said. He embraced her again and kissed her neck.

She pushed him away again.

"Have you told her you won't marry Jezzie?"

"My mother is impossible, but I promise you I will," he pulled her in tighter, desiring more.

Purity's heart was troubled. She wanted to believe Favor—that they could be together—but she knew the Wisedor's would never accept her.

"I have to go, but I want to thank you for helping with my sons."

He let her go.

"You opened my blind eyes. I'm the one who's indebted to you," he said with sincerity.

Purity left him there in the thicket of trees.

* * *

Back at Son's Camp, the work progressed. Pastor Ezra, his wife Rebecca, and their children were among the volunteers. They approached Purity after she emerged from the woods.

"Can we speak with you?" asked Pastor Ezra.

Favor had followed a few moments behind Purity and now remained within range of their conversation. He tried to look busy by unloading a nearby wagon.

"We're leaving next week to China. Would you consider the invitation again?" Pastor Ezra asked.

"It would be a great comfort to me and the children if you'd consider coming along," Rebecca said with confidence.

Favor couldn't stand the thought of losing Purity through possible death on the mission field. He stepped toward them.

"Sometimes, the biggest mission field is in your own backyard. Aren't twelve sons enough to handle?" Favor asked Purity, as though longing for her not to consider any other option.

"Thank you, Pastor, but the timing's off," Purity replied, glancing at Favor with a longing heart.

Favor sighed in relief hearing Purity had no intention of leaving Shadow Brook Estate.

"God be with you," said Pastor Ezra. His family departed after giving her hugs of affection.

Later that day, Favor entered the mansion, removed his muddy boots, and tiptoed across the marble floor. Despite his best efforts to elude notice, his mother's voice echoed through the hallway.

"Favor, come here at once," Mrs. Wisedor yelled.

Cringing, he made his way to the grand parlor, passing Natasha, who dusted statues in the hallway.

He entered the room looking like a soiled carpenter, his clothing saturated with dirt and perspiration. His parents stared in disgust.

"Honestly, tell us, Son. A construction project on our property? Surely, this must be only a passing whim. People are talking," his father said.

"Indeed, building housing for delinquents. Did you honestly expect us not to find out? And Purity referring to them as her sons? It's intolerable," his mother complained.

"Truth be known, I found it quite stimulating," Favor said with a curt tone.

"Ridiculous. We've had this conversation already. We forbid your affections to be entertained any further with this maid of ours," Mrs. Wisedor exploded.

"First, it was meddling in our business practices and now this misplaced generosity. If this continues, we'll be as unfortunate as the worst of them. Then what will become of all your charity? Think soberly about your family obligations," his father demanded angrily.

"My family obligations?" Favor asked.

"You're engaged to a lovely young woman," his mother insisted.

"I didn't broker that deal," Favor protested.

"Jezzie adores you," Mr. Wisedor persisted.

"She adores herself."

"It's time to start planning your wedding," his mother demanded.

"I refuse to marry that entitled flirt. Her very presence is like a dark cloud," Favor exploded.

"Jezzie's a prize. Their estate is thriving. Besides your reputations at stake. We know about your little secret," Mr. Wisedor sounded angry.

"My little secret? Explain."

"The baby. We can plan a quick wedding, and then you're off on a honeymoon. It's early days, and none will be the wiser," Mrs. Wisedor sounded with excitement.

Favor felt like he'd just been kicked by a horse.

"Stop right there. You're telling me Jezzie's pregnant, and I'm the father. Is that what she told you?" Favor asked in a disgusted manner.

"We can't say we're completely surprised. Jezzie said you're both deeply in love," Mr. Wisedor said as though annoyed.

"In love, are we? I haven't so much as kissed the fraud. It's all lies. She's forcing my hand into marriage and cares nothing about ruining our family's name. Your ignorance is pitiful. Let me fill you in on her family's little secret."

"Their little secret?" Mr. Wisedor questioned.

"Their estate is bankrupt. Haven't you heard? It's the talk of the town. They've deceived you so you can prop them up with funds from our estate."

"How deceitful. It couldn't be true?" Mrs. Wisedor proclaimed.

"Do you honestly believe Jezzie has the capacity to love anyone? And now she's expecting us to adopt her bastard child. Have you ever stared into her vacant eyes? It's like the devil himself staring back. Would you dare align us with such treachery?" Favor said, glaring.

"It's a spider's web, and we're not the ones spinning it," Mr. Wisedor concluded.

"How are we going to get out of this mess?" He asked his wife.

"Our family's criminal business practices have put us under the cloud of generational curses. I beg you to repent before it's too late," Favor scolded.

"You're being emotional," Mrs. Wisedor said.

"You're more interested in aligning with comparable estates than caring about the bodies and souls of those who make your prosperity possible. Hell will sweep you both away without a second thought," he pleaded.

His mother waved her hand dismissively.

"Understand this, Jezzie's a white-washed tomb that reeks of death. As God holds me accountable, I will never marry such a curse," Favor vowed as he walked out.

Bailey's Ballroom Theater

Chapter 19

A WEEK LATER, a crowd gathered at the Bristol train station. Many were there bidding their farewells to Pastor Ezra's family.

Purity hugged Pastor Ezra's wife goodbye.

"Take care, Rebecca."

"It's a train ride to New York, then a steamship to China. There's a world to see. If you want an adventure, the invitation is always open, my dear."

"It's my dream to travel the world, but it's not my time," Purity responded tenderly.

"The motives. God is always looking at the motives. Are you staying because God told you to? Or because someone's holding you back? Think about it, child," Rebecca asked with the tenderness of a concerned mother.

Pastor Ezra's family boarded their car. Friends and relatives stayed until the train slowly left the station and faded from view.

Rebecca's last words echoed in Purity's heart.

"The motives. God is always looking at the motives. Are you staying because God told you to? Or because someone's holding you back?"

Favor emerged from the crowd and placed his hand on Purity's shoulder.

"Can I take you back to the estate?" Favor asked.

"I'd appreciate it." Fight as she might, his presence made her weak in the knees.

He offered his elbow, and Purity grabbed onto it for dear life. Walking by his side through life was what she'd always wanted. Their passionate kissing at Son's Camp invaded her thoughts.

She had seen a change in him. He was making good on his promises to his workers, and then there was Son's Camp and his care for the boys. She looked up at him with admiration.

He turned to her with a smile and their lips drew near. But he hesitated and pulled back. To kiss her in public was taboo. She was just a maid. It was against protocol, and they both knew they were breaking all the rules.

* * *

Later that afternoon, despite the danger, Purity headed into the city of Bristol. She stepped on the back porch of Mave's of Bristol.

Chin Lu burst through the kitchen door carrying a load of wet laundry, headed to the clothesline. Shocked to see the fired kitchen maid, Chin Lu dropped the basket.

"Get out. Mave's gonna kill you," Chin Lu warned and gave Purity a push.

"I've got work for you at Son's Camp. You better get out before you end up six feet under," Purity said with concern.

"Mave kill my family if I leave. No escape for me." Chin Lu spit out the fearful words in broken English.

"We'll go to the police together," Purity said, trying to sound encouraging.

"Police, they know. Nobody comes to help. No escape for me," Chin Lu's eyes began to tear up.

"Fight or die, piece by piece. Who's going to want you when there's nothing left to buy?" Purity handed Chin Lu a small piece of paper.

"Give this to Mandy. And nobody needs to know," Purity warned.

"Mave beat me if I help you." Chin Lu quickly snatched the note and tucked it in her bra. She left the clothes basket and disappeared behind the screen door.

In a few minutes, Mandy appeared on the back porch and looked around. Purity waved a hand from behind a nearby tree and caught Mandy's attention. In moments, the two friends were reunited.

"I've missed you," Purity said, smothering Mandy with a big hug.

"You're brave stepping foot in these parts. Let's get out of here while we can," Mandy said, looking back at the hotel.

After walking the streets of Bristol in silence, Mandy chose her words carefully.

"It's not the same without you, but you've been replaced."

"I figured that much."

"How's Ellie doing? I saw your sons in town. They told me about her."

"We shipped her home a few days ago. She's a lot wiser now. I could have killed Mave, but I trust the Captain for justice."

"The Captain. Who is he?" Mandy asked with curiosity.

"You know, the big guy up there," Purity said matter of fact, pointing toward the sky.

"Oh, of course. I need him too," Mandy said respectfully.

They kept walking down the busy streets of Bristol and did some window shopping.

"Purity, I can't explain it. Tell me how an uncoordinated klutz like you, with two left feet, has transformed into an incredible dancer. Every step I taught, you repeated in the exact rhythm and with the technique of a world-class dancer. I can't figure it out. But I think it's time to conquer new territory." Mandy pulled on Purity's clothing.

"Come with me." She whistled for a taxi.

In moments a taxi stopped before them.

"Where to ladies?" the taxi driver asked.

"To Bailey's Ballroom Theater," Mandy said as they hopped in.

Bailey's Ballroom Theater was on the ritzy side of town. The theater sat a few thousand and was constantly filled with spectators. It housed an enormous ballroom dance floor for prestigious balls and dance competitions.

The magnificent building was well utilized by the elite, who dressed in high fashion to attend the entertainments held there. The women wore sparkling gowns, jewels, furs, and fancy hats. The men dressed in classy suits and black high-top hats.

As they entered the building, Purity was in awe. Stately marble pillars added to the palatial ambiance, while under their feet, the granite floor shined. Above, huge crystal chandeliers sparkled with newly installed electricity. Ornate furnishings, including tapestry couches, leather accent chairs, Persian area rugs, and expensive carved wooden furniture added to the ambiance. The place was packed with a crowd.

"This reminds me of the New Earth, where dreams come true. What's going on? This place is packed," Purity asked, looking around.

"The New Earth? Stay with me, Purity. This is no fantasy land. We've got work to do. Wait a minute, and you'll see," Mandy said as though right at home.

Patrons and old friends greeted Mandy with wild shock and the crowd parted to let them pass.

"I can't believe my eyes," a young woman said, gawking at Mandy.

"Welcome back, stranger. Never thought we'd see you again," a well-dressed man said to Mandy.

"Never say never," Mandy replied with an edge and kept moving.

"You're like seeing a ghost," a well-dressed woman proclaimed.

The crowd was buzzing about the unexpected guest. Purity didn't know what to think about high-class folks treating her friend like royalty.

"She's a famous ballroom dancer," a reporter said to another guest. He snapped her photo several times.

"Yeah, yeah, get over it," Mandy said, dismissing the attention.

Mandy pushed through two double doors leading into the grand ballroom arena. Purity was now in the exclusive world of professional ballroom dancing. Couples practiced complicated choreography to the rhythm of a well-strung orchestra.

"Watch. See the way they position their heads. Look at their posture and notice their footwork. Do you see how the man leads and the woman follows?" Mandy instructed.

Purity's feet began to move to the rhythm as her eyes focused on their footwork, style, and precision.

"You're looking at some of the best ballroom dancers in the country. They're here getting ready for the U.S. Ballroom Competition being held right here in Bristol next month. And guess what? I'm entering you into the competition. You have a gift, and it won't be wasted," Mandy said matter of fact.

Purity turned and headed for the exit with such speed it was hard for Mandy to catch up.

"Wait. Where do you think you're going?" Mandy's knee started buckling.

"Hey, no fair. Slow down." Catching up, she pulled at Purity's clothing to make her stop.

"I can't do it. It's one thing to dance with drunks, but with professionals? And you're expecting me to win?"

"Ask yourself a question—is this a risk or the chance of a lifetime? The prize money is cash. Ten thousand dollars, split by the winning couple."

"You mean five thousand dollars cash if I win? I could start a school," Purity said, dreaming.

"That's right. A win is a life changer. I could quit Mave's and ask any price for training dancers," Mandy insisted.

"My mother could retire," Purity said.

"One minor detail. I need to find the right partner for you, and I've got someone in mind," Mandy said, looking around the ballroom.

Then with sharp focus, her eyes landed on a fine specimen of a man. He was handsome, fit, and tall. He spun a dance partner around the floor with the ease and technique of a champion.

Grabbing Purity's hand, Mandy dragged her through several dancers, spectators, and members of the press.

The man's dance ended just in time for him to lock eyes on Mandy. Painful emotions surfaced, too difficult to hide.

"Mandy," the handsome dancer said in disbelief.

"Surprise, surprise. It's me, Stephen," Mandy responded as though trying to hide deep pain herself.

"Are you entering the competition?" his voice resonated with hope.

"Yes, if I can find a brave soul to dance with this young lady. Have you registered yet?" Mandy asked with an upbeat attitude.

Stephen's brow darkened with disappointment.

"No, I haven't registered. There's no one like you, Mandy."

Mandy chose her words carefully.

"I've taught her everything I know. Now it's time for the test."

"Oh really. What makes you think this shining hopeful has a chance?" his voice oozed skepticism.

Mandy knew it was all about the approach, and if she sounded too defiant, he would walk away.

"She doesn't unless she's paired with someone who knows what the hell they're doing. Not just anybody—you," she said, trying to sound convincing. He looked away with simmering aggravation.

Purity could sense they had a history together, and some light was dawning. But she was still doubtful of the whole enterprise and tapped Mandy's shoulder.

"Listen, he's right. This is no joke. I'm a barroom dancer, not a ballroom professional. I have to work. I don't have time for all of this," Purity rattled.

Then Stephen joined in the verbal protest.

"You can't just walk back into my life and make demands like there's been no time between us. And now you want me to take a kid under my wing who knows nothing about ballroom dancing. You're trying to make a fool out of me," Stephen ranted.

Mandy held both hands up in defense.

"All right, all right. I'm not thinking about it. I'm doing it. You both have what it takes, but you'd rather forfeit your future than fight for it. Change happens when you step up to the challenge and do something different, and that starts now. So, let's get to work. We've only got a few weeks to rehearse. Start thinking how you're going to spend that prize money."

Purity and Stephen were speechless for a moment.

"Why don't you dance in the competition with Stephen?" Purity asked Mandy.

"My knee would never hold up. My career is over as far as competition, but through you, I could dance again. I mean, what were the chances of a washed-out, knee jerkin dancer like me finding a talent like you to train?"

"So, the two of you were partners?" Purity guessed.

Mandy nodded.

"We won every competition we entered for three years. All that changed last year when I blew my knee out at the World Ballroom Championships in France. Just one wrong move and my world ended." Mandy locked eyes with Stephen.

"So that's what happened to you," Purity said sadly.

Stephen looked away from Mandy.

"Somehow, God's giving us all another chance to fulfill our purposes. I believe one victory will lead to others," Mandy coaxed.

Stephen shook his head and smiled.

"You're so convincing. What makes you think we have a chance?" He asked cynically.

The music changed, and the orchestra banged out a lively number. Purity's feet moved uncontrollably. Stephen looked perplexed as if watching a crazy girl. His eyes rolled in ridicule.

"Mandy, what is this?"

"Take her to the floor and find out," she shouted over the music.

He eyed her with an exasperated look but his curiosity got the best of him. Stephen pulled Purity onto the dance floor, and her feet showed the technique and expertise of a master dancer. They whizzed past some of the best dancers in the country, who became wild-eyed with envy.

"Who is she? Where's she from?" more than a few spectators questioned.

Stephen couldn't believe it. She made him look rusty. He had given up hope of finding a dancer who matched Mandy's talent, but in a moment, everything turned around.

Abundant Supply

Chapter 20

FAVOR STEPPED INTO his office at the Wisedor Dish Factory and closed the door. He opened some mail. There was a letter from the city that officially closed the permits to the rum distillery due to fire damage.

"Good riddance. Nothing wrong with a little sobriety," Favor thought.

On his desk were the blueprints and plans to improve the working conditions of his employees. Most of the children working at the dish factory were orphans, while others worked to help support their struggling families and had no means to attend school.

"Initially, we'll absorb the cost of building the school and tuition. But then I'll recruit other factory owners in the area who may want to contribute. They can send their young employees to school too," Favor thought.

He quickly set to work on more strategies, formulating detailed plans for generating revenue to cover the school's expenses and to support the orphans. His train of thought was disrupted by yelling in the hallway.

Dagon was berating a tardy employee.

"I'll beat you to a pulp."

Favor burst from his office in time to see Dagon landing a heavy blow to a teen's abdomen. He grabbed Dagon by the collar and manhandled him all the way to the door.

"Get out! You and your corruption," Favor yelled with righteous anger.

One solitary clap sounded from a worker, and then others joined in on the applause. Favor nodded in thanks and retreated into the office.

Someone knocked on the door shortly afterward, disrupting his work.

"Come in," Favor said.

A detective entered.

"I'm here in response to your inquiry about the boy, Orion. We've found his parents, sir."

Favor nodded in appreciation and handed him a few large bills.

"Go to my estate. My sister, Victoria, will assist you from this point on."

The man took the money and departed.

That afternoon, workers parked their wagons full of building supplies in front of Wisedor Dish Factory. The work crews began clearing a large plot of land beside the factory.

Mr. Wisedor rushed into Favor's office.

"You're building a new distillery? Splendid idea. I knew you were ready for the challenge."

"Not quite. We're paving the way for others to excel." Favor joined his father by the window, observing the flurry of men working.

"Paving the way for others to excel? What kind of hogwash is that? What's this construction all about then?"

"Go ask the builders yourself. I'm sure you'll be quite pleased," Favor responded with ridicule.

Mr. Wisedor marched out.

Favor watched from the window as his father approached the foreman. At first, his father's face reflected great appreciation. The muffled questioning from Mr. Wisedor seeped through the window. Favor picked up his coffee cup and raised it in a motion of cheers. Then he sipped it, ingesting the rich flavor. Before he'd swallowed the hot coffee, he saw his father's facial expression sour into a fit of rage. His hands flew in awkward directions as though arguing a point. The foreman's pleasant expression faded into submission. Favor put down the coffee cup and ran outside.

"There's a misunderstanding. We have no intention of building a school or dorms for our employees," Mr. Wisedor yelled, turning redder by the minute.

The foreman signaled the men to stop working. Many of them dropped their tools.

"Father, you're out of touch with the needs around you. Yes, a school, dorms, and more than that—a lighthouse for the community. Everyone, children and adults, will have the opportunity to learn. The other factory owners will share the costs." Favor's voice was strong, confident, and unwavering in conviction.

"Why do we have to save the whole world?" his father wailed.

"It's our obligation to make a difference, lest we put ourselves under judgment," Favor said, trying to sound compassionate.

His father was still having none of it.

"Judgment? What are we doing wrong? You've been listening to Purity, that maid of ours. I don't doubt she's behind this. First, it's building housing for delinquents. Now a school and dorms by the factory. You'll drive us into the poorhouse. I can't allow it," his father whined in protest.

"You've given me the responsibility of running our businesses. If my methods prove damaging to the companies, then you can fire me. Until then, let me run things my way," Favor insisted. He gave a signal for the men to resume their tasks.

"Back to work, men." In response, each man picked up his tools, and the work commenced. Mr. Wisedor was about to bluster again but held his tongue.

* * *

That evening, Purity sat at the kitchen table in her small cottage. By the light of an oil lamp, she reread the letter she had recently received from Pastor Ezra and Rebecca asking her to come to China and help with the orphanage. Confusion entered Purity's exhausted soul. Her days were filled with hours of dance practice, working at the estate, and spending time with her sons. But with Alexis and Natasha keeping watch more often over the sons at Son's Camp, Purity allowed herself to think once more about the future she'd always dreamed of living.

"Captain, honestly, I don't know what to do. Is it more honorable to dance or serve on the mission field? I want to do what's right. If I win, the prize money will change everything. If I lose, what was the point?" Purity asked in prayer.

Looking at the clock, she rose and tucked the letter in her nightstand drawer. She reached for the clean apron from the hook on her bedroom door, and with a stomach full of anguish headed to the kitchen door of the mansion. Now that she had dance practice eating into her days, she worked some evenings at the estate.

"I'm so tired of Shadow Brook Estate. The cold walls are keeping Favor and I apart. It's one thing to confess your love, but totally another to do something about it," she sighed as every approaching step grew heavy.

Entering the kitchen, Purity was confronted with wild activity. The aromas of fine foods baking in three large ovens made her hungry. Roasts trimmed with vegetables filled one oven while dinner rolls and desserts baked in the other two. Several maids raced around the kitchen, preparing salads and trays of goodies.

"What's going on?" Purity asked Alexis, who was busy mixing cake batter.

"More prospects. The socialites are swarming like aggressive bees, all trying to win Favor's heart. Rumors are circulating the Coevet's are bankrupt and Mrs. Wisedor is fishing, casting the net for other suitable estates. So, it's another grand dinner at Shadow Brook Estate," Alexis answered with a hushed tone.

"Is Favor attending?" Purity inquired.

"Of course. He's here looking like a Prince."

"I loathe these games," Purity confessed. She fled the kitchen and entered a back hallway, where she wiped away her tears in the shadows.

"I don't know if we'll ever be together. When will he stand up to his parents?" Purity's thoughts raced.

"He has no intention of committing. He's merely used me and toyed with my love. I wonder how many others he's fooling around with."

Heavy footsteps clattered down the hallway. It was Natasha and Alexis coming from the kitchen. They didn't see her and stopped close by—their conversation hushed.

"So, is the engagement to Jezzie on or off?" Alexis asked.

"She's pregnant with Favor's child. I heard it with my own ears when I was dusting outside the parlor the other day," Natasha shared.

Purity clasped a hand over her mouth in shock.

"I don't believe it. Favor would never conduct himself that way," Alexis said with concern.

"Don't tell a soul till it's confirmed," Natasha said looking around.

"Let's get back to work," the maid said, and they rushed down the hall past Purity.

Purity's knees buckled with weakness.

"Favor has betrayed my affection," she thought as a wave of nausea hit.

"Purity, where are you?" Naomi's voice sounded from the kitchen.

Purity dried her tears with shaking fingers and breathed deeply to gather her emotions before entering the busy kitchen.

"I'm here mother," Purity said entering the kitchen.

"We're drowning in work," Naomi said, handing her a tray of appetizers.

"Take these in."

Purity took the tray and plunged into an elite world of privilege. Favor, the most eligible bachelor in Bristol, stood in the grand parlor surrounded by well-dressed, provocative singles—each hoping for some glimmer of interest on his part.

Purity did her best to serve the room full of spoiled, pampered, self-absorbed socialites with a smile on her face. It was a difficult evening, and the conversations were always the same—stories of adventure, buying and selling, and the backroom deals of uniting families in marriage. A few times, Purity caught Favor staring at her from across the room, but he made no moves in her direction. He seemed too aware of his mother's ever-watchful gaze.

Purity poured a glass of wine for a guest. From the corner of her eye, she saw a young woman clasp Favor's hand and say, "Let's take a walk." The woman then tried to pull him along to the secluded gardens. The wine Purity poured splattered everywhere.

"Clumsy maid. You've ruined my gown. Get me a towel," the elegant woman complained.

Shaking, Purity set the wine bottle down and headed for the kitchen. She threw her apron on the kitchen counter and plunged out into the cool night air.

Black Iron Snake

Chapter 21

PURITY LEFT A small envelope on the kitchen table in the cottage. She picked up her bags and, dodging detection, made her way down the long cobblestone driveway of Shadow Brook Estate.

At the Bristol train station, she slipped a ticket into her pocket and tried not to think of her heated argument at Son's Camp the day before. Alexis and Natasha refused to hide their disappointment regarding Purity's decision to leave.

"Just because everything's running smoothly at Son's Camp doesn't mean you can leave. And what about your mother?" Alexis's voice was full of pain.

"Or the dance competition? If you win, it could change all our lives," Natasha added.

"And what if I lose? Nothing here is going to change. Forgive me," Purity begged and walked away.

The conversation echoed through her mind like voices ringing through a deserted canyon.

Purity stepped aboard the train for New York and didn't look back. A haunting whistle blew from the smokestacks, bellowing of an unknown future.

Dark translucent beings from Ahaba's army descended on the roof of the train. They flapped bat-like wings and hissed threats into the atmosphere.

"Easy prey. She's ours," an evil spirit screamed.

More dark beings descended upon the train as it raced through the surrounding towns. As it picked up speed, the train morphed into what appeared to be a black snake slithering down the tracks. The train whizzed on, mile after mile, and lightning flashed in dark clouds looming overhead.

Ahaba's evil warriors hissed and waved their weapons as the Ring of Grace joined them on top of the rail cars. The angels appeared as five illuminated boys, each wearing body armor, a bow, and quivers of arrows strapped to his back. Along with fiery swords in their hands, instruments of praise were attached with magnetic hold to their body armor, arms, and thighs. Harmonicas, when played, stopped the enemy in their tracks with piercing vibrations. Trumpets vibrated with such sound they blew the enemy back with ultra-sonic force.

High above, the five archangels hid in the clouds, observing Ahaba's Army gather rapidly against Purity and the Ring of Grace.

"The Captain has commanded us to standby," Raphael said as his vision pierced through the heavy cloud cover.

"Those kids may need us," Michael said with apprehension.

"Ahaba's forces are well trained," Ariel said, scanning the evil hordes lining up for battle.

"It doesn't look good," Azrael added.

Gabriel raised a lightning bolt in his hand.

"Good thing they've got back up. Only say the word, Captain, and it's on."

"Let's hope they pass this test," Michael replied.

On the train below, the Ring of Grace was up to the challenge.

"Hey, guys. Guess who sent us?" Kaleb, one of the boy angels, yelled.

The wicked warriors drooled threats and waved their weapons.

"You may want to wipe your drool. It's making a mess," Sergio joked.

"Purity won't get away," a wicked spirit snarled, blowing odorous breath.

"What's that smell? Time for a bath, guys," Rocco teased the ugly spirits.

"We're a Ring of Grace sent by the Captain himself," Toby yelled with pride.

"Oppose him at your own risk," Josiah added.

The angels pointed their swords toward enemy lines. In response, the enemy raised their weapons, and Ahaba's ghoulish face appeared in a swirling tornado above them.

"Advance," Ahaba yelled at his dark army.

The Ring of Grace fearlessly advanced toward the enemy, and a violent clash ensued on top of the train.

"We're holding our own," Rocco said to Josiah, unaware of the archangels who held off the evil forces from above.

"We've got this," Sergio yelled at his comrades.

Inside the train, a black Caribbean porter walked the aisles checking tickets. Wearing a dark suit and starched white shirt, he made his way through the long line of cars. Out a window, he saw a windstorm, reminding him that winter quickly approached.

"Ticket, miss?" the porter asked Purity, clicker in hand.

Purity handed her ticket over. She stared out the window, appearing restless as the gusty winds and rain that pounded the windows.

"Cheer up. Where you headed?" the porter asked as he punched a hole in her ticket.

"Shanghai." Purity tried to sound positive.

"Interesting. And you're going alone? Don't tell me, it's just you and your guardian angel," he joked, handing the ticket back.

"I could use a guardian angel about now," Purity said, cracking a smile.

"Well, they come in different shapes and sizes. You never know when one will show up," the porter said, moving down the aisle.

"Tickets! Checking tickets," the porter called out. He came to a group of men playing poker at a table a few rows down. The porter's stomach turned when he saw Mr. Wells. He was a familiar face, sitting with a group of scoundrels. The porter dreaded the long train ride with such passengers.

"Get on with it," Mr. Wells demanded in his usual tone. Smoke flowed from his mouth and nose after a long drag from an expensive cigar. He appeared like a dragon, with a menacing look in his eyes.

The porter punched the group's tickets and moved to the next row.

A dark, translucent spirit slipped through the wall next to Mr. Wells' head. It jumped on his back and wrapped its vapors around his neck, appearing like snakes coiling around prey. The old man coughed as though choking from the smoke and tried to catch his breath. Then leaning into a passing waiter, Mr. Wells made a sly inquisition.

"Roberto, find out if she's alone." He slipped money into the waiter's hand and nodded toward Purity.

The porter overheard the exchange. It was nothing new. He'd seen it before with this crew of gangsters. Another innocent young woman was in peril, but this time, something tugged at the porter's heart. A fight emerged in his spirit.

Moments later, he watched the paid-off waiter, Roberto, approach Purity with a tray of fresh-baked cookies.

"Here, miss. Cookies on the house?" Roberto asked like a perfect gentleman.

It had been ten years since Purity had set eyes on him—when he'd whisked Rachel away never to be heard from again. She was just a child, new to America, and an innocent bystander. He had aged slightly but was still young and handsome. Neither remembered the other.

"Thank you," Purity said and gobbled down the cookie.

"I'm Roberto. Here's a snack for your traveling companion," he said, holding out another cookie.

"I'm alone. But I'll take the other cookie," Purity replied. He smiled, and she took the cookie.

"Where you headed?"

"Shanghai, China," she blurted between bites.

"China. You're traveling around the world... alone?"

"Well, not exactly. I'm meeting friends there," Purity sheepishly admitted.

"You're very brave, miss," Roberto added. He looked over his shoulder and winked at Mr. Wells, who grinned like a Cheshire cat.

Sudden remorse hit Purity like a punch in the gut.

"I'm not feeling good about this venture. Captain, what am I doing? I have no sense." Purity's thoughts oozed fear and condemnation. She squeezed her eyes shut in frustration.

When she opened them, Roberto was standing over her with a lustful gaze. His friendly demeanor changed as he took in her long hair, clear eyes, and bustline. He smirked and moved on, offering snacks to the surrounding passengers. Purity clutched her bag closer, got up, and headed for the bathroom.

As she passed the gamblers, Purity saw their ominous glances. She quickened her steps, trying not to let panic overtake her.

Roberto returned to the gamblers.

"She's alone and headed for Shanghai," he whispered in Mr. Wells' ear.

Wells looked intently at his hand of cards, and a sinister smile uncovered his tobacco-stained teeth. He slapped the cards on the table.

"A Royal flush. Looks like it's my lucky night in more ways than one."

The gangsters moaned, throwing their cards down on the table.

Wells scooped the winnings into a money bag, except for a few crisp bills he handed to Roberto.

"See that it's done."

Roberto left and Wells pulled a fresh cigar from his pocket. He licked the tip of it with his thick, odorous tongue.

"Another round, gentlemen?"

* * *

The sun was setting on Shadow Brook Estate. Favor walked toward the house with a few friends, returning from a night out. He spotted Naomi standing in the doorway to the cottage, anxiety written across her face.

He felt a kick rip through his gut. Something was wrong. A small, transparent hand, appearing like fire, pressed into his back. It was Ora, the angel who appeared as a girl and was often sent on assignment by the Captain to help warn of impending doom or encourage his followers in the right direction.

Ora whispering in his ear, "It's Purity. She needs help."

Favor dismissed his friends.

"Excuse me. I must go."

"What's wrong? Why the sudden change of plans?" one of his friends asked in irritation.

"Urgent business. I've completely forgotten about it. So sorry. We'll play cards tomorrow night if you don't mind?"

"Tomorrow night's as good as any to take your money," his friend agreed.

When the others were gone, Favor went to Naomi.

"What is it, Naomi? Has something happened?"

Recognizing Favor, a sudden rush of tears poured from her grief-stricken eyes.

"Foolish girl," Naomi muttered as she handed Favor the letter in her hand.

He read it quickly.

Dear Mother,

Pastor Ezra's family needs me in China.
I'll contact you when I arrive.

Love,
Purity

"When did she leave?" Favor asked.

"I went to work this morning and haven't seen her since. I have a bad feeling about this."

"She never mentioned anything to me about leaving," Favor complained.

"To leave without saying a word." Naomi prayed, "Oh, God, assign your angels. She means well enough. Keep her from evil, Lord."

"I'll check the train station," Favor offered and rushed from the cottage.

At the Bristol Railroad Station, Favor went straight to the ticket window. The ticket clerk who knew most people in town.

"Have you seen Purity Thomascovich? She may have purchased a train ticket today."

"Ah, yes. Bought a ticket to New York. The train left early afternoon," the clerk said.

"Was she with anyone?"

"I don't recall, sir," the clerk answered in a rush.

"Next customer," he called to the line of customers behind Favor.

Another train rolled out of the station, blowing a loud whistle which rang like a siren of alarm in Favor's soul. He turned away from the clerk in despair.

"Oh, God, keep her safe," he prayed.

Favor left the station feeling hopeless. With hands firmly wrapped around his car steering wheel, his mind raced.

"I'll never see her again. She'll die on the mission field. I've lost her forever. She was the only person who had the guts to be honest with me. Now she's gone without saying goodbye."

It was late when Favor turned into the driveway leading up to Shadow Brook Estate. He entered the mansion in a gloomy mood. At once, a butler took his coat and hat.

"Favor, is that you? Where have you been?" his mother prodded, meeting him in the hallway. Mrs. Wisedor stood as a barracuda, ready to strike.

"Calm down, Mother. I had a prior engagement," Favor said, trying to avoid her wrath.

"We had dinner guests. The daughter of a rich family from upstate New York came and left. Do you realize the embarrassment you've caused?" his mother said in anger.

"I had an appointment with friends. Your plans slipped my mind. I'm so sorry."

"It's obvious what was more important. Naomi told me you went looking for Purity. Somehow the girl thinks she can save the world. Nothing but nonsense."

"You're entitled to your opinions," Favor shot back.

"It's simply inexcusable. My son, chasing after a maid. Her charms have blinded you," she rattled on.

"Well, Purity is gone. That should make you happy. The only competition for your plans is out of the way."

"Nonsense. She was nothing but a foolish crush to be toyed with. And now, you can put it behind you," his mother argued.

"I won't cast her aside so lightly," Favor said, playing into mother's fears.

Changing tact, Mrs. Wisedor put her hand softly on his cheek and looked him in the eyes.

"You'll simply have to, my dear. She'll probably die a martyr on the mission field. Have your cry now and be done. Of course, we'll care for her mother." She patted his cheek and walked away.

Favor fumed and stormed off to his room.

* * *

Purity couldn't hide in the train bathroom forever and had returned to her seat. The lightning strikes out the window next to her were a blur as the train sped along the tracks. They were now miles away from anything familiar to Purity. She was being watched and tried to hide behind the passenger sitting in front of her—a large woman who was snoring.

Roberto stood in the kitchen, recounting the crisp new bills from Mr. Wells. Satisfied, he shoved them into his pant pocket.

The porter was there, preparing a fresh pot of coffee. He turned just in time to see Roberto pour a small amount of white powder into one of the water glasses for the passengers. The waiter's head jerked in guilt, feeling watchful eyes on an evil deed. The porter whistled an old tune, pretending ignorance while he poured himself a coffee.

Roberto placed the water glasses carefully on a tray, then set out on his foul mission. As he made his way down the aisle, the wind outside howled and a hard rain pelted the windows.

"Water! Water," he called. He passed out glasses to several passengers before he approached his target.

"More water?" he asked Purity.

"Thank you," she responded.

He handed a specific glass to her, not spilling a drop, and she ingested half the water.

The porter crashed into Roberto, causing him to knock the glass from Purity's hand. Roberto barely held on to his tray.

"Sorry. I didn't see you. Forgive me," the porter apologized as he bent down on one knee and began wiping the floor with a small cotton towel.

Roberto glared with loathing and grabbed the porter's black jacket.

"Meet me in the kitchen," he snarled with murderous intent and rushed to the kitchen.

The porter slipped Purity a small note before standing and walking in the opposite direction of the kitchen.

Purity unfolded the note. It read, "Follow me. You're in danger." It only confirmed her fears. She looked up to find Mr. Wells leering at her.

Purity had to find her way to safety. Not knowing for sure if the porter was friend or foe, she tucked the note in her pocket and stood. A wave of light-headedness and nauseous rushed over her as the drug from the water took effect. She managed to move her feet in the direction the porter went. At the end of the car, he stepped out from a sleeping compartment.

"This way," he said.

Picking up the pace, they moved through several more cars until they entered a storage compartment where extra luggage and supplies were stored. Purity staggered in with heavy legs and arms.

"I'm sorry I don't even know your name. Thanks for helping me," Purity said slightly slurring her words.

"I'm George Pullman. Don't thank me till we get out of this alive."

"Somehow trouble always finds me," Purity said and almost fell over.

George steadied her and looked around the dimly lit compartment for some way out of their situation.

The battle above the black iron snake train continued to rage. The Ring of Grace fought off the evil forces with bravery as the archangels continued observing with laser vision.

"Purity's our slave," Ahaba threatened with sinister laughter.

"Not on our watch. You'll be chained forever," Rocco yelled as two other angels tried encasing their foe with chains. Ahaba fought back with overwhelming power.

"Captain of the Lord's Army, we need you," the angels yelled in unison.

In moments, the Captain appeared on his white horse. He was majestic in power with a mounted army trailing behind.

"Make ready," Michael said, pulling a galactic instrument from his armor. He blew with power and the trumpet's song rang through the clouds.

The archangels spread their massive wings, pulled out their bows and laser arrows, and descended closer to the battle.

Purity leaned against the wall of the train compartment. Her head spun and her vision blurred. Beams of rainbow light reached through the walls of the train and wrapped around her, strengthening every cell of her body. A heavenly presence poured into her like nothing she'd ever felt. Her eyes closed in momentary comfort.

"Is that you, Bright Star? I feel your peace," Purity mumbled.

George snapped his fingers, and she opened her eyes. He pointed to a large wicker basket with a key in its lock. Asking no questions, she stumbled into it. He closed the lid, locked it, and tucked the key in his pocket.

Roberto kicked open the door. Mr. Wells followed behind, scanning the storage area like a hunter chasing prey.

"Have a seat," Roberto said, pushing the porter down on a large trunk. He drew a knife and held the tip to George's neck.

"Where is she? Our pretty world traveler has vanished," Mr. Wells protested.

Translucent dark spirits erupted through the walls. Their eyes beamed red with evil intent. One pounced on Roberto's back and slowly curled its hands around his throat.

"Is she worth your life?" Roberto threatened, making choking sounds as the wicked spirit squeezed harder.
Beads of perspiration formed on George's forehead and upper lip.
"I don't want to die," he said in desperation.

"That's what you get for sticking your nose where it doesn't belong," Roberto said with anger.

Transparent hands of light appeared on George's back. It was Kaleb and Toby, the child angels, infusing strength.

The rest of the Ring of Grace materialized in a translucent form. Sergio, Rocco, and Josiah extended their hands over the basket where Purity was hidden. Rays of power infused the basket, drenching Purity's being with sobriety.

The archangel's watched from above, their penetrating vision able to see into the black iron train. They rooted for the child angels.

"Get it done," Raphael cheered.

"Come on, guys, you've got bigger wings coming," Michael said with a smirk.

Captain of the Lord's Army wrestled a huge, bat-like, slithering creature that drooled yellow and green secretions. With one slash of his fiery sword, the Captain pierced it with a fatal blow and threw it on the railroad tracks below.

The train screeched to a sudden stop—its brakes spewing sparks and smoke. In the storage car, the abrupt change in speed tossed the luggage about and snuffed out the oil lamps that hung on the walls. The storage car plunged into darkness as screams from jolted passengers echoed in the distance.

With supernatural strength, George flung his knife-wielding enemy, Roberto, to the other wall.

An eerie silence followed, only broken by the sizzle from a lone match being lit. The smell of sulfur and smoke permeated the air. Mr. Wells rose to his knees, and with the light from the match, he found an oil lamp and lit it.

Mr. Wells and George cast their eyes upon a grizzly sight. Blood poured out around the embedded knife in Roberto's abdomen.

Mr. Wells reached for a cigar from his jacket and placed it between his teeth. Then striking another match, he lit it. He inhaled deeply and exhaled a cloud of smoke. He was unaffected by the flow of blood and pleading last words from the dying young man.

"Help me. I've helped you… get the girls… and plenty of 'em," Roberto begged, his breathing labored.

The middle-aged man slowly inhaled another drag from the cigar. Then in his usual manner, he lifted the cigar to his nose to smell the high-grade tobacco. His face took on the appearance of a grotesque mask, weighed down with heavy lines and a sinister spirit.

"Roberto, Roberto. What's that to me, you street rat? I paid you well. Get over it and die," Mr. Wells sounded with disgust.

"I'm afraid to die." Roberto's voice was just a whisper as blood pooled on the floor around him.

More evil spirits seeped through the walls, anticipating the reception of Roberto's lost soul. They relished in their ability to torment him forever once his spirit departed from his mangled body.

The Ring of Grace stood as warriors, bathed in transcendent light and undetected by the human eye. The angels spoke with instant communication, mind to mind, and raised swords of fire to block attempts by the slithering spirits to inflict fear in the porter's heart.

George's eyes opened wide gazing into the spirit realm for the first time. The child angels wrestled the evil spirits trying to get to Roberto. He was speechless.

"Speak, or Roberto will be tormented forever," Rocco urged George with the tip of his fiery sword. Toby and Josiah laid hands on the porter and released more strength into his weary soul.

The evil spirits surrounded Roberto, dripping saliva and flapping their wings. Roberto groaned in agony.

Josiah prompted the porter again with a firm hand. It sent powerful light directly to his heart.

"Speak before it's too late," Rocco urged George, communicating mind to mind without speaking a word.

"Give me the power to speak," George said aloud.

"You're delusional. Shut up," Mr. Wells shouted, unaware of anything taking place in the spirit realm.

George turned to Roberto.

"The demons are waiting for you, Roberto. You'll be lost forever. Ask Captain of the Lord's Army to forgive you and take you home. He has the New Earth waiting for you."

"I said shut your mouth," Mr. Wells yelled as though the porter's words were burning his ears.

Roberto groaned and whispered, "I see them too—the demons. I've served evil all my life. Why not in the next? I'm a thief, murderer, rapist, that's just for starts. It's too late for me."

"Ridiculous. Just die!" Mr. Wells' shouted as a small demon appearing as a fanged rat chewed his right ear. Disturbed by the pain, Mr. Wells slapped his ear.

George recited what the angels told him to say.

"I beg you, call on the Captain. His warriors are here, ready to take you home. He'll save you."

In torturous fear, Roberto's heart changed.

"Captain, I'm a big mess up. I don't deserve it, but please forgive me and take me into your Kingdom." Roberto puffed out these last words with his last breath.

The wicked spirits hissed and thrashed about as they heard Roberto's final confession. The young man's spirit lifted from his bloodied body. The wicked spirits reached for his translucent soul but were unable to take hold of it. Roberto's spirit man stood tall, glowing with light, protected by the child angels.

"That was close," Toby said, blowing out a sigh of relief.

"I don't deserve it," Roberto sighed.

"Nothing like second chances," Sergio said with a smile.

Kaleb, Josiah, Rocco, Sergio, and Toby placed their hands on Roberto. They morphed into a ball of rainbow fire and shot through the roof of the compartment. In the sky above, they met the archangels.

"We knew you could do it," Ariel said with a grin.

"A victory for the Ring of Grace," Gabriel congratulated.

"Everyone passed the test," Azrael cheered.

The Captain appeared and raised his hand toward the child angels. A laser light shot out of his hand and each angel's wings grew.

Rocco flapped his large wings.

"We could get used to this."

The angels surrounded Roberto's spirit once again, morphed into a ball of light and shot through the atmosphere.

The porter was a witness to the whole heavenly exchange. The vision rocked him.

Mr. Wells missed the unseen encounter and turned his attention to the porter.

"Your life's over too. Now you're wanted for murder. But I can make it all go away. Just tell me where she is."

"Never," George insisted

"Don't worry. She's my new business partner, and she's going to make me a lot of money."

"How's that?" asked George.

"High priced johns. Hopefully, she'll like the heroin too. It dulls the pain of the beatings and infections. Once she's addicted, she'll stop fighting." He pulled a small pistol from his jacket and pointed it at the porter.

"Roberto just missed hell, but the angels should have dropped you off on the way," George said without fear.

"You're delusional. I make hell for people. Now, tell me where the girl is."

George reluctantly reached into his pocket, handed the key over, and pointed to the basket.

"Ah, clever. I wouldn't have guessed." Mr. Wells put away the pistol and grabbed for the key. His breathing was heavy with anticipation.

"I need some light over here, idiot. I can't see," Mr. Wells barked, fumbling with the key.

The porter reached for the small lamp and directed the light closer to the lock. Mr. Wells turned the key with shaking hands. Slowly, he lifted the lid of the basket, anxious to exploit fresh prey.

Purity jumped out, swinging and scratching. Together, she and George pushed the old man's flabby body, and it landed inside the basket with a thud.

Mr. Wells threatened and howled like a captured animal.

"How dare you? I'll kill you, like rabid dogs."

George wrestled the pistol from Mr. Wells' pocket and tucked it in his belt. Then Purity slammed the lid down and locked it.

"Let's get out of here," George said, leading the way.

"Do you know the Captain too? Can you arrange a meeting?" Purity asked as they rushed down a dimly lit corridor.

"I just learned about him myself. I can't take any credit for what happened back there. His angelic warriors told me what to say. They're nothing but kids."

"I've seen them too."

"They were small but powerful. I get the sense that if you keep asking for the Captain to reveal himself, he'll show up just in time," George offered.

"If he's such a great Captain, why does he always wait till the last minute?" Purity asked with frustration.

"I guess so you know he makes the impossible possible. It's not by your efforts."

Above the train, the Captain and his army finished off the last of the evil hordes.

"My dear Purity, I'm always right on time," the Captain said, raising his fiery sword.

"To the New Earth and beyond." His great army followed behind as he disappeared.

Back on the train, George and Purity rushed through the narrow cars.

"Slow down. Stay calm. You don't want to draw attention to yourself," George warned. He looked out the train window and recognized their location.

"We're in New York. I'll be accused of murder. Get your things, I'll meet you outside the station."

Returning to his room, the porter quickly packed his belongings, placing them in a worn suitcase. He looked around the small cabin that had been home for a few years. He knew in his spirit that it was time for a change, and this whole scenario was the push he needed.

From his nightstand, he picked up his prayer book. He raised his eyes to heaven and made the sign of the Cross.

"I need you more than ever," he whispered, and then stuffed the book in the pocket of his suitcase.

George turned to step out of the cabin but hesitated, remembering something. He pushed an old chair to a certain spot on the worn carpet and stepped up on its cushion. After lifting a small section of the ceiling compartment, he blindly searched the area with one hand and pulled out a black leather money bag containing his life's savings. He jammed it into another front pocket on his suitcase and left without looking back.

* * *

Purity gathered her belongings with external calm. But inside, her heart was full of emotion. Wherever she looked, visions of the dead man appeared without invitation. Her stomach lurched at the thought that it could have been her or the porter dead on the floor.

Purity pulled her hat low over her brow, hoping for anonymity as she stepped out into the aisle. Passengers pushed and shoved, trying to forge ahead to an exit.

Stumbling off the train with her two small bags, Purity wove her way through the crowds, headed for the station's exit. Her knees nearly buckled, and her heart raced with panic.

As promised, George was waiting outside in the shadows. He wore a dark overcoat, and a black hat shrouded his eyes.

"Miss. Miss. This way," George said, only loud enough to get her attention.

"How could I ever repay George? He'll be a fugitive, running for the rest of his days," Purity thought as her stomach rumbled with anxiety.

They walked side-by-side through the crowded streets of New York, acting like strangers.

"I'm surprised the Captain didn't warn you about me. Run while you can. Trouble found me again" Purity lamented.

"The Captain runs to trouble, not from it. You have a ship to catch. I'll see you off," he said with steely determination.

George asked for directions, and they made it safely to the harbor. They were surrounded by the sights, sounds, and smells of an international seaport. Men loaded several large ships before departure and in the distance stood the Statue of Liberty.

"We passed under Lady Liberty ten years ago. We had hope written all over us then. But Papa died before his time, and Mama works till she can't see straight."

The light of Lady Liberty illuminated a ship full of new immigrants heading for Ellis Island.

"The Statue of Liberty, she's so grand, but the thought of freedom from poverty—can it happen for me and you?"

"All things are possible for those who believe."

George turned aside and approached a sailor.

"We're looking for Pier 39. There's a ship scheduled to leave for China within the hour." He held out Purity's ticket.

The potbellied sailor strained to see the words on the ticket.

"My eyes aren't good, but I can tell ya the ship bound for China left yesterday with a rowdy crew."

"That can't be true. My ticket says today." Purity pointed to the date of the departure.

"You've been swindled, no doubt. The oldest trick in the book—gullible, half-witted girl. I don't care what ya say. This ticket is a counterfeit. Your money's gone. I'd count your blessings. The ship left yesterday, and it wasn't a passenger ship. You wouldn't have made it to open sea without being violated in the worst way with that bunch."

"My God. I have no sense." Purity nerves teetered on the verge of collapse.

George took the ticket and ripped it to pieces.

The old sailor rubbed his rough whiskers and sagging jowls.

"Ya better get out of here. This place can be dangerous. I suggest you rethink what ya doin', miss." The Sailor shook his head.

"If you were my daughter, I'd lock ya up till ya know better."

Ten blocks down, George and Purity reached a dilapidated cafe. They sat in the back, avoiding other customers. Purity's feet throbbed. She pulled one shoe off and assessed a few blisters.

"I've got blisters. What's next?" Purity complained, sounding pitiful. The porter looked about, keeping his hat pulled low over his eyes.

"You're lucky that's all you've got. God has a way of closing doors, and I'd say this one was slammed shut."

"But I'm expected in China." Purity tried to keep her voice low.

"You're blind to the obvious. Don't you get it? You're not meant to go. This venture is cursed," the porter said, looking around.

"At least Roberto made it to the other side. I wonder if he's made it to the New Earth yet?"

"I've heard of the great Captain before. My grandmother told me stories about him, but I never took any of it seriously. Don't get me wrong, I say my prayers. Even got my prayer book. But what I just saw changed everything. Did you see it?" George asked.

"Not this time, but I've been to the New Earth. That's where the great Captain lives. I haven't met him yet, though. I'm not sure what's taking him so long." She took a sip of lukewarm coffee.

"What did you see?"

"I saw what looked like hell itself—wicked spirits waiting for Roberto's soul. I had trouble thinking straight. That's when the kid angels gave me the strength to speak up. I'll never look at death the same. I hated Roberto. He treated me like dirt, and the last thing I wanted was for him to end up in a better place. I'm so glad his soul isn't on my conscience."

"You saw into the spirit realm," Purity said with awe.

"I didn't ask for it, but I'm better for it. I don't think you understand just how close you came. Roberto went quick, but it would have been a slow death for you, existing as a sex slave. The young and beautiful go missing daily on that train. I call it the 'black iron snake.' With no trace, they just disappear."

"What do you think happens to them?"

"They're sold to factories and brothels, used and abused till they die. Mr. Wells deals in human cargo. Roberto was one of his gophers. And there are others. I've overheard a lot of plots and plans but didn't want to make myself a target. I just got tired of looking the other way," he said with regret.

"And you saved my life."

"Mr. Wells won't forget it. He's got eyes and ears everywhere. I suggest you lay low when you get home. Hopefully, in time, he'll lose interest in revenge," George warned.

Purity nodded in understanding.

"I'm sensing you're running from something?" he asked as Purity sat back in her chair.

"We better go. I'm sure my mother's frantic by now," Purity said, trying to avoid a personal conversation.

"Maybe not a something, but a someone?" He wasn't letting it go that easily.

"I thought I was doing the right thing, but it was for the wrong reason," Purity said, pushing out a sigh of bitter recognition.

"If your motives aren't right, what good is it? You've got your angels working overtime chasing after you."

"There's this friend who's engaged—or about to be engaged."

"Are you in love with this friend?" he pried.

"That's personal," Purity shot back.

"So was saving your life. Answer me straight," he prodded.

She didn't want to say it out loud, but he was so sincere. And what could it hurt to tell a stranger?

"Yes, I love Favor. But he's forbidden to love someone like me. We come from two different worlds and society dictates he must marry someone of wealth and breeding," she said with utter hopelessness.

"And this Favor has no idea how you feel about him?" George pressed.

"He says he loves me too, but I doubt him."

"Had he given you reason to doubt his intentions?"

"Yes. I overheard something before I left."

"Ah, you overheard. So you haven't talked to him about it?"

"What's the use. Even if it's not true, his parents will never consent to our marriage."

"Do you believe the Captain can do the impossible for you?"

"I want to. But I've dreamed for so long, and nothing has changed. At times it all looks so clear, and then reality sets in. It's just a fairy tale, and it hurts too much to keep believing the fantasy," she said, tearing up.

"It sounds like you need a dose of faith to receive your miracle. If Favor is God's choice for you, then nothing can stop it."

The words rang true, but she couldn't begin to accept them just yet.

"You talk about faith and miracles. It all sounds so simple."

"The fact your plans didn't work out shows the Captain is orchestrating something better. You need to figure out what he's trying to tell you." His voice was full of compassion.

Purity looked at him with gratitude, realizing his profound wisdom and presence wasn't an accident.

"You saved my life and risked your own. I can't thank you enough."

"I'm not done till I get you home," George promised.

"I'm ready to go," she said with conviction.

"What will you do?"

"I have a son and a daughter I haven't seen in a few years. Who knows. Maybe we can start a new life together. I want to get far away from here," George said with tears welling.

"I'm sure they'll be happy to see you."

He stood.

"We better get moving. It's going to be a long night. I have friends who can hide us on the train back to Bristol."

They left the café and walked several blocks back to the train station.

* * *

The next morning the train rolled into the Bristol train station. It blasted a haunting whistle through the early morning fog.

George stepped off first and grabbed Purity's hand.

"Watch your footing," he said with concern.

"Here's my address, if you need to find me," Purity said, placing a folded note in his hand.

"Thank you again. I'll never forget you."

"You're welcome. Here's my parents' address in Virginia. They always know where to find me." George reciprocated by handing Purity a note.

"I owe you my life," Purity said and hugged the porter.

"There comes a time when you have to stop looking the other way. I regret waiting so long," George said with tears in his eyes.

Purity grabbed her bags and walked away, looking back just before she turned a corner. The porter was already gone.

Face to Face

Chapter 22

IN THE WEE hours of the morning at Shadow Brook Estate, Favor tossed and turned. He battled anger, feeling abandoned by his childhood friend, Purity.

"How could she leave without saying goodbye? What about her sons? What kind of mother is she? To take off for who knows how long?" Favor mumbled in frustration.

The sheets twisted around his tossing body. Finally, he stood up, pulling free from the sheets. Moonlight flooded in through an open window. He walked over to it and looked out.

The only sound was the soft breeze rustling through the tree branches. He hit the window frame with a tight fist and sighed in frustration.

"Ungrateful, selfish girl," he thought.

After a few moments, he returned to bed and fell into a fitful sleep. Captain of the Lord's Army called his name.

"Favor, come to me, my Son. Come to the one who knows your days ahead."

Then the Captain sang, "Come my Son."

> Come to me, my Son
> I'm Captain of the Lord's Army
> Come to where misty shadows fade away
> Crystal clear vision is here to stay

In the days ahead,
You will fight my battles till won
I'm calling you to be as one with Purity
There's no other I've chosen

You'll fight my battles, hand in hand
Till the enemy falls by your side
Come to me, my Son
For I've chosen your bride
I'm Captain of the Lord's Army

Favor's feet touched down on the New Earth. He walked along the river, gazing at the beauty all around. He admired the tranquility of such a place.

A Great Warrior appeared, standing in front of Favor. He had weapons magnetically clinging to his body armor. Favor jumped at the grandeur of this being who carried a weighty presence.

"Favor, I am Captain of the Lord's Army. I break the spirit of witchcraft off your mind now," the Captain said as his fiery eyes penetrated deep into Favor's soul. A dark spirit like a hissing black snake fell from Favor's head. The Captain extended his hand and shot fiery darts into it, causing the spirit to evaporate into a hazy, sulfuric cloud.

"It's gone. All the confusion and double-mindedness." Favor felt as though a great weight of oppression had lifted.

"Where the Spirit of the Lord is, there is freedom," the Captain said, nodding.

"I'm free from Jezzie's curse," Favor said as he rubbed his head.

"Your bride comes," the Captain said and pointed a finger.

A sailboat with billowing white sails moved down the river. Favor squinted, trying to recognize the sole occupant. A slight smile formed as he recognized the familiar form and flowing hair. She gazed at Favor with piercing green eyes that radiated a fiery glow.

The boat stopped a few feet away.

"Purity," he gasped. He ran to her, but just before their hands clasped, he was awakened.

Knocking rattled Favor's bedroom door.

"Favor, wake up. Purity's back." It was Natasha's voice. Her tone was hushed so as not to wake the house.

Favor jumped from his bed, slipped on a pair of pants, and wrestled with a cotton shirt. Sliding his feet into cold leather shoes, he stumbled over to the door in the dim light.

"Where is she?" he asked Natasha.

"I saw her just now out the window, coming down the drive."

He raced past her, bounded down the grand staircase, and shot out the front door. His feet sank into the damp ground from the early morning dew.

The thick morning fog cast its shadows on the silhouette of a shapely young woman. She carried a small piece of luggage in each hand.

At the sight of her, Favor stopped. She walked a few more steps and set her bags down before him. He could reach out and touch her, but he didn't.

"Did your journey take you far?" Favor asked, his voice simultaneously tinged with anger and relief.

Purity ran into his strong arms.

"Too far to ever be the same," she whimpered, on the verge of tears.

"I've been lost without you," he confessed, raising his eyes to heaven.

He slowly spun her in a tight embrace. Their lips drew close as if pulled together by some invisible force. He kissed her gently on the forehead, then each cheek. Lastly, their lips collided in desire. One kiss led to more—neither able to overcome the magnetism between them.

"It's been a terrible mess," Purity confessed between Favor's smothering affection.

"We'll sort it out together. Promise me you'll never leave me again," he coaxed between kisses.

"Someone might see us," Purity said, suddenly aware that their parents would not appreciate the public display of affection.

"Let them see." He kissed her thoroughly.

She didn't know if it was the kiss or exhaustion from the journey, but her knees buckled.

Favor steadied her.

"You must be tired from the journey. Let us sit." He led her a few yards away to a patch of trees near a quiet stream. There was a bench along the edge of the water.

Purity sat, regretting the last twenty-four hours.

He stared at her reflection in the gentle waters, entranced by her lovely image. Then his mood shifted, and he stood to his feet to make a point.

"Help me understand why you left. After I've done so much for you and your sons?" he said with pain.

"Because I can't stand one more dinner party where you are auctioned off to the highest bidder. And because I heard something—Jezzie's pregnant, and you're the father."

"I never touched her. It's nothing but a ploy to bail out their bankrupt estate. You've got to believe me," he pleaded, taking her hand in his.

"I was under a spell of witchcraft, but it's gone. I'm free of her."

"I believe you, Favor. I'm sorry I didn't ask you before leaving."

He sat beside her, still holding her hand.

"I need to tell you something. I've met the Captain. I don't know if it was just a dream or if I was really there, but New Earth was so peaceful and beautiful."

"I've been trying for so long to meet the great Captain face-to-face. Tell me, what did he look like?"

"He's a mighty warrior with eyes that burn bright like the sun. And there's such peace. You never want to leave. Nothing else matters in his presence," Favor said as though in a daze.

"Did he mention me at all?"

"Why do you ask?" Favor tried to hide his blush.

"I was hoping I was on his mind—in his thoughts. Favor, this whole thing, I honestly can't take it anymore. I'm not willing to share you or pretend we don't exist. I refuse to live in the shadows anymore," she said with deep emotion.

Favor kissed her hand and took her in his arms. He began to sing, "I'm Won."

> I see your heart, and I'm won
> Roaring like a lion, strong and bold
> Trouble can't move you
> Money can't buy your soul
>
> You captured my heart

Like kids in a candy story
You're my irresistible craving
I won't be denied

I see your heart, and I'm won
We're flying high, two kites entwined
No more waiting, it's time to be one
Like the morning sun, kissing the earth
A soft rain in the springtime
Bringing everything alive
It's time to grow
Life's journey begun

I see your heart, and I'm won
What's keeping us apart
Take my hand before I miss
This chance to make you mine

I see your heart, and it's our time
I see your heart, and it's our time

"Tell me I'm worth your admiration, my darling. I love you," Favor whispered in her ear. Purity sang, "Music to My Ears."

It's music to my ears
Those three little words
I… love… you

How I've dreamed of the day
When I would be yours
Hand-in-hand
Like two kites entwined

It's music to my ears
Joining our lives as one
I… love… you

Our love is one of a kind
It doesn't matter the color of my skin
Or the class that I'm in

It's music to my ears
You'll be mine, and I'll be yours
I… love… you

"I see your heart, every part. Like two kites entwined, it's time to become one," Purity said and kissed his lips softly.

"I'll handle my parents. Let's agree we'll never be apart again," Favor said with intention.

"Never again," she agreed. With a heavy sigh, she continued.

"I need to tell you what happened on my latest adventure."

"I'm all ears."

Purity started from the beginning and didn't leave out one detail. When she finished, she handed Favor the porter's address.

"He is a marked man. Someday we may need to defend him."

"Indeed," Favor agreed.

"Let us pray Mr. Wells is brought to justice."

Dance Competition

Chapter 23

LATER THAT MORNING, Mandy knocked on the kitchen door of the mansion. Natasha answered.

"Where's Purity?" Mandy asked, driven and to the point.

"In the cottage," Natasha answered, pointing down the path. Mandy marched to the small cottage a stone's throw away. She pounded on the wooden door with bitter resentment.

"Purity! Purity, answer this door. I know you're in there," Mandy yelled through the door.

Purity was jarred from a deep sleep by the racket. She put on a robe and headed for the door, half asleep.

"You're great at disappearing. Where the hell have you been? Did the dance competition just slip your mind? How do you expect to win without practicing?"

"Never mind where I've been. What are my chances of winning, anyway?" Purity's words sounded heavy with sleep.

"No chance if you don't practice. You have the talent, but without discipline, it's as good as wasted. Give me one good reason why you stiffed us?"

"I took a detour, running from disappointment—trying to do the right thing for the wrong reasons. Temporary insanity. I don't know," Purity said, trying to wake up.

Mandy slapped a handful of cash in her hand.

"Don't tell me you're robbing banks. What's this?" Purity asked, gawking at the money.

"You've been sponsored," Mandy said, grinning.

"Who'd be so generous?" Purity asked, fully awake now.

"The dancers at Mave's of Bristol," Mandy said, pausing for a reaction. Purity was speechless.

"Close the door to your past. A new door is opening, and it's called opportunity. And you're the only one who can walk through it. Start believing you've got a gift."

"What I can't believe is this bankroll."

"When God calls, he provides. It's dance practice this afternoon. In fact, give your notice, we've got work to do. The Wisedors can find someone else to scrub their filth," Mandy said as she left in a rush.

Purity counted the cash, and despite all the previous confusion, the fog was clearing. She decided it was time to change her mindset. Returning to her room, with a gentle touch, she opened her music box and watched the dancers spin round and round.

Purity mumbled a prayer.

"How foolish I've been, Captain. Thank you. Forgive my unbelief."

* * *

Bailey's Ballroom Theater was packed with dancers and spectators. Purity and Stephen perfected their routine in a private room off the main ballroom. Mandy coached and choreographed with a keen eye, correcting every flaw.

"Purity, watch your hands. Not so stiff. Like a ballerina."

Mandy didn't hesitate to correct Stephen's technique, either.

"Don't let her strength overshadow your ability to lead, Stephen," she scolded.

Stephen stopped dancing.

"Really, Mandy? Like I don't know how to lead? How many championship wins did I lead you to?" he said with an offended glare.

"This isn't the time or place," Mandy said, looking away.

"This is nothing but the time and place, or else I'm walking out just like you did," Stephen said, holding his ground.

"Take ten. You two have stuff to deal with." Purity picked up a towel, wiped her perspiration, and walked out.

"You've got some kind of attitude, and I'm not putting up with it. What's the real issue?"

"I don't know what you're talking about," Mandy said, avoiding eye contact.

"The hell you don't. We've been dancing around our past, and I refuse to ignore it another minute," Stephen said with insistence.

"Okay. I confess, watching Purity dance in your arms—I'm having a tough time with it," Mandy paused, breaking down.

Memories from that fateful day passed through her mind in slow motion. They were dancing in France at a prestigious dance competition. The place was packed with fans and the press. Emotions ran high. Stephen and Mandy were dancing for first place, in perfect sync, when they hit complicated choreography. In a moment, Mandy's knee twisted in a career-ending direction.

"Seeing you dance again reminds me of everything we lost together. The championships, the awards, the finances. I let you down."

"The injury wasn't anyone's fault, or was it more than that? The accolades, all the wild public attention, the money? Is that all I meant to you? Like I was your ticket to fame and fortune, and when that was gone, you left me?"

"Is that what you think?" Mandy protested.

"Listen, I loved you, Mandy. But I guess that didn't matter when it was all said and done," Stephen admitted with deep emotion.

"Forgive me, Stephen. I left because you were too talented to sit on the sidelines with me. You needed to go on and fulfill your dance career. I was dead weight to you. I left because I loved you too much to stay."

"And you made that decision alone. Why didn't you let me in on it? My whole life isn't wrapped up on the dance floor. There are deeper things than success, fortune, or public opinion, and that's what you threw away when you walked out those doors."

"You're right. I've been such a fool. Dancing was my everything. It was who I was. I'm nothing without it, don't you get it?" Mandy said, drawing closer to Stephen. He reached slowly for her hand. A charge of emotion shot through her like reignited sparks, vibrating through her every cell.

"You're more than a dance champion. That was just a part of who you are. It was never just the dancing for me, Mandy. The day you left me, my world ended. Not the day you were injured. I never stopped loving you." Stephen stepped away and put on a slow number on the record player. He took Mandy in his arms. They swayed in slow romantic rhythms for more than a few minutes. Large teardrops flowed down Mandy's cheeks, and Stephen wiped each one away.

"I guess we can both agree on one thing," Stephen whispered in her ear, sending chills down her spine.

"What's that?"

"We still love each other," Stephen said softly.

"Oh, yes. We do," Mandy said, looking into his eyes with love.

"We don't have to do this competition. I don't need anything else. You're enough for me. Is that enough for you?" Stephen asked with all sincerity.

"It's more than enough for me."

They kissed softly, and Stephen clutched her hand, dancing close, and sang, "Hand in Hand."

Take my hand, it's time to romance
No more running away
Hold me close, this is where you belong
In my arms, for a lifetime, never growing old
The day you left, my heart fell apart
Now, we're beating as one, you're my very heart

Take my hand, it's time to dance
No more running away
In my arms again, we'll dance, never letting go
With one glance, I knew it was you
I'd know you anywhere

Take my hand, it's time to do life
No more running away
We've got what it takes, no more great escapes
It's just that easy, living hand in hand
Lay the past to rest, we've got a future that's blessed

Take my hand, my arms are open
No more running away
We've got places to go, let's get on the road
Take my hand, it's time to romance
Hold me close, this is where you belong

"Glad to see you patched everything up." Purity entered the room and sat with a thud on a bench nearby.

"Ten more minutes, and we're on," Mandy announced, rushing to her notes and wiping tears. She began reviewing the new choreography.

Everyone jumped when a handful of reporters burst through the door and started popping questions.

"There are rumors you've got the winning team. What do you say, Mandy?" one reporter asked, holding a writing tablet and pencil.

"Maybe. So who's interested?" Mandy asked, playing with the press.

Another reporter pushed forward.

"Where did you find such a talent? Do you think Purity has a chance to win?"

"What's your coaching strategy?" a young reporter asked, vying for attention.

"Stephen's got experience, and Purity has raw talent. Put the two together, and we're hoping for the win. Any more questions, ask them yourselves."

In an instant, the press surrounded Stephen and Purity. They snapped photos and barraged them with one question after the other.

"Purity, what's it like to be the new kid on the block?" one reporter asked, pushing others aside.

"Well, I don't exactly know," Purity started to answer but was interrupted.

"With no prior training, do you think you have a chance?" another reporter asked, bullying his way in front of the others.

"I'm being trained by the best, Stephen and Mandy. They're the professionals. I'm not pretending to be anything special, but I'm not backing down. The night of the competitions, I'll be fighting for a win."

"But where did you train? England? South America?"

"I guess you could say… in another world." Purity's eyes glanced heavenward, and a smile enveloped her face.

"Yeah, right. Don't get crazy on us," a reporter moaned sarcastically.

"That's enough. We have a routine to practice," Stephen barked and pulled Purity from the pack of hungry journalists.

* * *

The next morning at Bailey's Ballroom Theater, Purity fastened her dance shoes for practice. Mandy shoved a newspaper under her nose. A large photo of Purity covered the front page, and the headline read "Amateur Dancer Challenges Ballroom Professionals."

"Oh, Captain. Don't let the Wisedors and Mama see this," Purity whispered under her breath. Then a terrifying thought threatened her concentration.

"What about Mr. Wells and Mave? Captain, I need your protection."

"Let's go, Purity. Get your mind on the dancing and off your picture. We've got work to do," Mandy barked in a teasing manner.

* * *

On the far side of Bristol, dark clouds hovered over an opulent estate. Mr. Wells sat in his study behind his fine mahogany desk, puffing on a high-end cigar. The room was stately, decorated with elegant draperies, fine leather chairs, velvet couches, woven Asian rugs, and stained-glass oil lamps.

He read the morning paper between sips of strong coffee. Suddenly, his face contorted. He frantically pulled a round magnifying glass from his drawer. Holding it with a shaking hand, he positioned it close to an image on the front page.

"I've made an interesting discovery," he announced as Mave entered the room carrying a tray of finger foods and tea.

"What new treasure did you find?" she questioned without much interest.

"Your son's killer," he said.

Mave dropped the tray on the ornate desk with a thud. She snatched the newspaper from under his nose. Staring back at her was a familiar face.

"You're sure it was Purity?" Mave's voice screeched with anger and pain.

"It's been too painful to mention, but I was an eyewitness. It was a brutal murder. I narrowly escaped the same fate. I've never dealt with anyone more vicious," he said, pulling a gun from his desk drawer with a clean white cloth.

"It's not registered. I suggest you take advantage of the noise on the night of the competitions." He dropped the gun into her hands.

Rose Garden Dancing

Chapter 24

PURITY AND VICTORIA sat in the library, listening to the teacher drone on about photosynthesis. Victoria was distracted as usual, but Purity took notes so she could help Victoria with the details later.

The teacher abruptly ended the lesson.

"Your focus is pitiful," the teacher rebuked Victoria.

Purity feverishly finished jotting down the last of the lecture notes and then closed the books.

"We have enough to keep us busy," Purity announced.

"Indeed," the teacher hissed, acknowledging the maid was the real student in the sessions.

"Your parents' money is wasted on lessons for you," the teacher scolded.

"If I were brilliant, your services wouldn't be needed. How would you pay your bills?" Victoria said sharply.

"Your disrespect will be reported," the teacher bellowed.

"And yours as well," Victoria called out as the teacher left in a huff.

Victoria and Purity giggled at her frustration.

"You really shouldn't bait her so," Purity scolded.

"I can't help it. I only have one thing on my mind, the rose garden dancing. Mother has hired the best dance instructors. You could learn the newest dances. Why don't you come along?" Victoria pleaded with Purity.

"I could just see your mother, dithering about, all flustered. She'd scream out, 'There's a maid on the dance floor! Preposterous! Such an embarrassment,'" Purity mimicked Mrs. Wisedor with a blustering voice and mannerisms.

"That sounds just like Mother," Victoria said, laughing.

"First, your mother would object. And second, I'm not interested in rubbing shoulders with pampered vultures. I refuse to be a part of the food chain," Purity said, giving a silly wink.

"Be careful, Victoria, of greedy suitors with one thing in mind— your wealth. It could be the end of your happiness."

"You're right. But promise me you'll come," Victoria pleaded.

"I'll promise nothing of the sort," Purity said with agitation.

"That spoils it for me then. I'm personally inviting you to our gala coming up next week. That means you need to know how to dance the waltz. I'm sure you didn't learn such refinement dancing at Mave's of Bristol, wretched place that it is."

"I didn't know about the gala."

Purity still worked at Shadow Brook Estate a few days a week because her mother had not yet found a replacement. She didn't tell Naomi where she ran off to each day. Instead, she endured the skeptical looks Naomi gave her each time she brought home money to pay for food or bills.

"You haven't worked here much in the last few weeks. It seems like you're purposely avoiding my brother," Victoria sounded with concern.

"I've done nothing of the sort," Purity protested.

"The gala is, of course, mother's latest idea. As you know, she wants to increase our chances of marrying the finest."

"Is there anyone in mind for you, Victoria? Someone you're not telling me about?" Purity probed.

"I have a few prospects. What about you? Do you ever hope to marry?" Victoria pried.

The question hit Purity like a sock to the stomach.

"Me, marry? That would be my dream come true. But who would want a woman with twelve children? Who would dare take that on?" Purity tried to laugh it off.

"Well, my brother's taking care of your sons despite my parents' objections. I want you to start thinking about your future," Victoria said sternly.

"I think about my future all the time, but the marriage I want would be a miracle. Victoria, I love you like a sister but stop pretending. I don't come from a marvelous family fortune." Purity stood and looked out the window overlooking the bay.

"Victoria, there's something I haven't told you."

"Don't keep me in suspense. What is it?" Victoria said, wiggling in anticipation.

Purity turned back to her.

"It's a new dream. I want to travel the world and help rescue children from slavery. I've seen it in your factories and at Mave's of Bristol. It's everywhere. Maybe I could help change the laws and provide safe housing for the victims."

"I overheard my parents arguing with Favor. We've abused and cheated our workers. It's a scandal. But when was anyone going to tell me about it?" Victoria asked in disbelief.

"I suppose they feel it's none of your business. Your job is to look pretty and marry well." She sat next to Victoria.

"Regarding marriage, I'm waiting patiently. The man I love has a few things to work out."

"I can't believe it. You're in love, and you never told me. He's a fool if he waits too long. Who is he?"

"It's a secret for now," Purity said with a tinge of hope.

"Tell me who he is. It's not fair you're keeping this from me. I'll be watching your every move. I'll solve this mystery if it's the last thing I do," Victoria said, jumping up.

"Calm down. I don't know if we'll ever get to the alter," Purity said, trying to defuse any excitement.

"You mustn't ever leave. I don't know if I could live without you. You're like a sister to me. Plus, Favor's trying to restore our dark history. He's building a school and dorms, not only for your sons but the orphaned children working in the factories. He's looking for teachers and caregivers."

"He's building a school and dorms to help the children?" Purity repeated in shock.

"Shush. I'm not supposed to know," Victoria said, lowering her voice.

A clock on the mantle chimed. Purity jolted.

"I've got work to do. Mother asked me to cut fresh roses for the tables in the garden." Purity gathered the books and stacked them on the desk.

"And I've got dance lessons."

They left in a rush, each to their own business.

Purity hurried through the busy kitchen where the maids were fixing lemonade and snacks for the guests. She went out the kitchen door and jogged toward the gardens.

Upon entering the garden shed, Purity grabbed a flower basket, clippers, gloves, sun hat, and an apron. She wrapped the apron around her waist and positioned the large hat to her identity before hurrying to the rose garden patio to gather flowers.

It was a maze navigating through throngs of young hopeful socialites who waited for the dance lessons to begin. Purity went right to work, cutting roses and placing them in the basket. She lifted a rose to her nose. The fresh scent eased her worries.

A ten-stringed orchestra started to play a lively number. The music sailed on the wind, and the guests began to dance as the dance teachers belted out instructions.

"Let's start with the waltz. Hold your partner—heads held high," one of the instructors bellowed from a megaphone.

Large blue and white striped tents were set up on the lawn to shade tables filled with refreshments.

"Dance with me?" Jezzie said, grabbing Favor's arm.

"You're avoiding me. I don't like being ignored."

"And I don't appreciate your lies. Stay away from me. You're toxic and determined to ruin my reputation," Favor warned.

"How dare you?"

Before he could rebuff her further, Victoria's shouting interrupted the brewing argument.

"Purity, dance with us!"

Favor searched for and finally eyed the young maid. Purity waved a hand in protest, trying to avoid notice. Favor shook loose from Jezzie and sauntered over. He took the clippers from Purity's hand and pulled the little gardener onto the patio floor.

"Favor, stop. I'm not an invited guest," Purity protested.

"Consider this your invitation. Call it a lesson."

"You seem very sure of your abilities," she said in a feisty manner.

"Maybe you can teach me something, then," he said, taking her basket, gloves and throwing her hat to the wind.

The music changed to a fast Quick-Step, and Purity couldn't resist the temptation to outdance him.

"Shoulders back and watch your feet. Not so stiff." Purity barked instructions, and Favor obliged.

"Like this?" he questioned, trying to adjust.

"Keep moving," she said, intent on teaching him a thing or two.

Their pace quickened, and soon the other couples gave way to their furious dancing. The dance teachers stopped barking instructions. In jaw-dropping admiration, they weighed Purity's talent. Her feet moved in dramatic patterns and new rhythms. Favor just tried to keep up.

"She's the dancer—the nobody from the newspaper," one of the instructors yelled over the crowd.

"She's in the ballroom competitions. Look at that rhythm," another instructor yelled back.

"Disguised as a maid. What a prank. Leave it to Mrs. Wisedor," a pretty socialite bellowed.

"Probably cost a fortune to get her to come," a handsome young guest rattled back.

The music changed again to an upbeat, fast-paced rhythm. The guests clapped and beat their feet to the sound. Wild applause ripped through the garden as Favor and Purity whizzed by and then ended the dance with a flourish.

Mrs. Wisedor rushed into the garden.

"What's all the cheering about?" she asked, squinting her eyes, trying to focus.

Purity ran into the crowd and disappeared.

"Encore! Encore!" the socialites yelled. Favor took several bows, deciding not to chase after Purity.

Factory Collaboration

Chapter 25

THE NEXT MORNING, Favor sat in his office at the Wisedor shipyard. Visions from the rose garden dancing rolled through his mind. He chuckled in low tones. Purity was never short on surprises.

He opened the top desk drawer and pulled out a newspaper clipping. There she was, smiling back at him with a full write-up informing the public about this newcomer to the U.S Ballroom Dance Competitions. He had hidden the front page from his parents the morning it came out. So far, there had been no mention of it.

A knock at the office door shattered his moment of pleasure. He quickly folded the paper and shoved it back in the drawer.

"Come in," Favor said with a grunt.

One of the workers opened the door and peeked his head in, saying, "They're all here, sir."

Favor entered the shipyard's meeting room and closed the door.

"Thank you for attending gentlemen. I've called this meeting to address my concerns for the workers represented by the factory owners in this room. A few weeks ago, I narrowly escaped the most severe beating by protesters demanding change. The incident and other circumstances have forced me to evaluate my family's business practices." Before he could go on, Favor was rudely interrupted.

"What are you insinuating? Are we slave drivers that need correcting? Our employees are free to find work anywhere they choose. Work is a blessing for the poor," one factory owner said.

"Where is your father in all of this?" another factory owner shouted.

Favor's tone changed from accommodating to one of authority.

"I've visited most of your factories. The number of children employed and not attending school shocks me," Favor said with indignation.

"Many are forced to work sick and infected, and the men aren't able to support their families on the wages we're paying them. Reform starts with us, or the violence will follow you home."

"What do you suggest?" asked another man.

"We need to increase wages, improve safety and working conditions. If we pool our funds, we can open a local school for the children working in our factories. It must be enough to hire teachers and cover overhead expenses. I'm also proposing evening reading classes for the adults." Favor held his breath. The factory owners roared with loud opposition.

"That will cost a fortune," a business owner lamented.

"Doing nothing is even more expensive and incriminates us as greedy fools. Act now, or your factories will be vandalized, your workers will take to the streets, and your very lives may be in jeopardy. Let's do this because it's the right thing to do. Think soberly, men. If these conditions continue, we'll answer to God for our greed. We go to bed between clean sheets and eat from tables of bounty. Injustice is difficult to face when you're the one benefiting."

"Your father has the worst business practices in Bristol. But if he's willing to change, I'll join him," a younger business owner called out.

Another well-dressed man agreed and then another. Eventually, the whole room collaborated. The group was soon unanimous in contributing to the school, raising wages, and improving the working conditions in all the factories.

* * *

Favor woke with a start, hearing heavy footsteps above.

"The eagles. I'm going this time," he thought. He rushed from his room and climbed the narrow staircase to the roof, taking two steps at a time.

He opened the rooftop door just as Bright and Star were fastening Purity to Valor's back with soft fibers of heavenly light. She was still entranced in a dream world. The large eagles flapped their wings and, with a running start, barreled over the mansion's roof, shaking the occupants below. Their wings caught the cool, foggy air, and with great strenuous flaps, they lifted into the atmosphere.

"Stop. Wait for me. Take me to the Captain," Favor shouted, running after them. His feet shifted on a few loose wooden shingles, and he began to roll like a log down the sloping roof. His hands ripped through more loose shingles, trying to stop a chaotic descent. Sharp splinters dug into his hands.

At the roof's edge, his hand caught hold of a shingle. Legs dangling, the wooden shingle cracked under his weight.

"Captain, I could use a lift," Favor grunted as his last bit of strength gave out.

Down through the misty fog, he fell. His arms and legs flailed in protest, but he couldn't eke out a scream.

Then suddenly, he saw the rainbow light of radiating beings. They appeared at first as Bright Star then morphed around his body. The brilliance of their light blinded him.

Bright Star acted like a billowing parachute, filling with air in a slow descent. Favor landed on the soft grass below with nothing more than a gentle thud. Their presence hovered, filling every fiber of his being with peace.

Favor sighed, and his eyes closed in a deep sleep.

The next morning, Mr. Wisedor was walking the grounds. He lifted his expensive shoe and tapped lightly on Favor's bare foot, saying, "What on God's green earth is going on?"

"Father, is that you?" Favor looked up, blinded by the morning sun.

"Last time I checked, you had a bed. Don't try to explain this one away. Let's just say you were sleepwalking and call it a day," Mr. Wisedor said, leaning on a walking cane.

Favor sat up and looked around at the bits of wood shingles that had fallen with him to the ground.

"I should be dead."

"Gibberish. Get up before your mother catches wind of this," his father said, taking Favor by the hand.

"Ouch," Favor looked down at the painful splinters embedded in his hands.

"Those are deep. I don't want to know what you were doing up there on the roof."

"I was rescued by a blanket of light. Or was that just a dream?"

"Get some rest, Son. I don't think you're feeling well." Mr. Wisedor moved on.

"Purity, where are you?" Favor asked out loud.

He headed to the small cottage behind the mansion. His hands ached as he knocked on the cottage door.

"Favor, what's happened to you?" Naomi questioned as she answered the door and saw his unkempt, wrinkled bedclothes.

"Where's your daughter? She's got me chasing the stars," he asked, looking past her into the cottage.

"Sounds like she's rubbing off on you. Take my advice and keep your feet on the ground. When I woke, she was gone. Who knows where. The girl's not sleeping well, but she won't say why."

"Tell her I stopped by, please," Favor said and turned away.

* * *

Purity woke on the New Earth once again. Little hands caressed her cheeks.

"Wake up, Mother. The Captain's heard your prayer. He's called you to come to His City of Light," Clarity said softly.

Purity sat up in the deep green grass of a valley filled with flowers and surrounded by splendid mountains and flowing waterfalls.

Valor and Keenan flew over with enormous wingspans and released loud squawks as though saying, "Get ready to fly."

"Come, the Captain has prepared a great banquet. All the nations are coming to honor him," Clarity said with wide sky-blue eyes.

"Lead the way," Purity said, wide awake.

Valor and Keenan swooped down and landed with the wind still rustling their wings. Purity hopped on Valor, and with a running start, Clarity jumped on Keenan's back. They grabbed onto large feathers and nestled into soft patches of fur for the long journey. In no time, they were in flight over the New Earth.

"It's beautiful," Purity said, looking over the land as they gained altitude.

"Yes, it is," Valor said to Purity's surprise.

"Do all the animals talk here?"

"Yes, so don't be alarmed," Keenan answered.

Wild animals—lions, tigers, elephants, and giraffes—marched over the plains alongside throngs of people. They traveled in a caravan together, rejoicing in the journey to the great city.

Purity's greatest desire was to meet Captain of the Lord's Army. The thought of finally being in his presence was beyond any joy experienced on the earth from which she came.

The eagles touched down in a lush forest and were surrounded by glowing butterflies with red, orange, purple, and blue colors.

"What are they called?" Purity asked Clarity as she reached for one.

"They're called New Beginnings. The more you touch them, the brighter they glow."

Sure enough, one landed on Purity's nose, and fluttered its luminous wings, emitting sparks of light. Another one landed in her hand, and flashes of light sparked when the wings touched.

"I shall stay forever. Such wondrous creations," Purity sighed.

"Your time has not come to stay forever. Follow me."

Clarity led Purity through the forest near thunderous waterfalls. Above were shining stars and planets in orbit.

Purity looked up at the sky.

"They are so close I feel as if I could reach out and grab one."

"It's never night here. We live by the Captain's Light," Clarity explained. She reached for a star, and it manifested in her hand. The small baby star glistened like a diamond.

"How do you know so much?"

"Because I'm one of the Captain's thoughts. He knows everything," Clarity said with a giggle.

"Ah, yes, and his thoughts must become my thoughts. His ways, my ways," Purity pondered out loud.

"You're learning," Clarity said with a grin.

"We've traveled so far. How much longer before we reach the city of the great King, our Captain?"

"We've only begun, Mother," Clarity answered with a tinge of sadness. She was concerned if her mother could make the long journey.

Hours later, exhaustion overtook Purity. With each step, her body grew heavy with fatigue.

"Clarity, I'm fading. I won't make it," Purity said, stumbling behind her daughter.

The Lord of the Dance appeared by their side.

"Take my hand, weary traveler." Purity put her hand in his and was strengthened.

"You have a way of making me whole. I'm feeling so much better," Purity said, instantly revived.

Clarity hugged his legs with great excitement.

"Take us with you to the Great Throne."

"Beautiful Clarity. Oh, the plans the Captain has for you," Lord of the Dance said, bending down to make eye contact.

"I can't wait to be Purity's daughter," the child said with expectation.

"You'll be the best daughter and a blessing to so many," he responded.

"Why did you bring me here?" Purity asked.

"Many times, to get the full picture, you have to go higher to see the view."

Instantly, they were standing on a mountaintop overlooking the City of Light. It sparkled like clear jewels, and rainbow colors shone through each dwelling, large and small.

"The brightest light. See it there?" Lord of the Dance pointed to the brightest, most piercing light in the middle of the city.

"That's where we're headed. Let's dance our way there," he said with a laugh.

"Do you mean it? I'd love to," Purity said with joy.

"In the days to come, the Captain will reveal his plan for you in detail. Remember, you're never alone. The armies of heaven are fighting with you."

"I'm coming too." Clarity jumped about with excitement.

Lord of the Dance and Purity danced on air and landed in the great city. Bright and Star wrapped Clarity in light and carried her along behind them.

"Mother, we made it," Clarity said, touching down on streets of pure gold.

Lord of the Dance led them into a palatial building. The archangels were there, towering over the other angels and the Lord's army. Purity's eyes landed on the Ring of Grace as she was led to a long table elegantly set for an elaborate meal. A heavenly orchestra played rhythmic music.

Lord of the Dance pulled out a chair for Purity.

"Have a seat and enjoy," he said, smiling. He did the same for Clarity.

"Thank you. Let the feast begin," Purity said with excitement.

The Ring of Grace were dressed as waiters and approached with plates full of delicacies.

"My guardian angels. You're all here."

"Don't look so surprised. Wherever you are, we're close by. We cook too." Toby set a golden plate of food on the table.

Lord of the Dance sat between Purity and Clarity. A magnificent orchestra played the most enchanting music Purity had ever heard.

She indulged in the decadent foods and a feeling of belonging sunk deep into her soul.

"Can I stay forever?" Purity asked Lord of the Dance.

"Forever has already started in your heart. But you still have much to accomplish on the old earth."

The archangel's Michael, Raphael, Gabriel, Ariel, and Azrael appeared before Purity in illuminated splendor. Raphael extended his hand to her.

Lord of the Dance smiled and began to dance with the small angel Ora. She'd appeared just in time to join the celebration.

"Have you ever wondered where the Captain's angels live?" Raphael asked.

"Where the angels live? I never thought about it, but I'm in," Purity said, taking his hand.

Instantly, she was elevated from her velvet blue dining chair. The archangel Gabriel grabbed Clarity's hand and lifted her too. The palatial ceiling rolled away like a window opening, exposing a sky with glimmering planets that looked like luminescent balls of blue, purple, gold, and silver. Stars began to twinkle.

Like a flashing vapor, they flew into the atmosphere of New Earth. Raphael hit a button on his metal belt, and straps of soft fabric secured Purity on his back for a safe trip. Gabriel secured Clarity in the same manner.

The archangels flew in unison, covering the vast territory of the New Earth within minutes. Multitudes of angels of all ethnicities and with wings of varying sizes surrounded them.

In front of them, high enchanted gates glowed with brilliant swirling colors.

"Is that it ahead?" Purity asked, mesmerized.

"Yes. Welcome to Gabriel's Quarters—home to all the angelic host," Raphael said with pride.

Then everything went dark. Purity woke to Naomi humming in the kitchen.

Each visit to the New Earth left her stronger and more confident, yet she always longed for more.

"What about the Captain? I was so close," Purity lamented. She rose and looked out the window into the bright sky. Then her eyes caught sight of the music box on her dresser. It opened on its own, and the dancers began spinning, surrounded by glistening rainbow lights.

"I still have much to accomplish," Purity thought.

"Who's there? What's that music?" Naomi asked from the kitchen.

"Hey, Mama," Purity said, entering the kitchen.

"I'm sorry I overslept."

Naomi jumped in surprise.

"Last time I looked; you were gone. Or maybe my eyes are finally going," Naomi said, scratching her head.

"Favor came by earlier looking a mess."

"Did he say what he wanted?" Purity asked with concern.

"No, but he was acting strange," her mother replied.

Surprise Purchase

Chapter 26

FAVOR WHIZZED BY the grand parlor, hoping to evade his mother's notice and be on his way. He had much to do today.

"Favor. Favor, come to the grand parlor," she called out.

There was no escaping now. He stopped and stepped into the luxurious room. Mrs. Wisedor sat having tea with Victoria and a handful of highly groomed mothers and their daughters. No doubt they were hoping to secure his mother's favor and a chance to flirt with him.

Word traveled fast that Favor's engagement to Jezzie was off. After the rose garden dancing, she and her conniving parents had been banned from Shadow Brook Estate. Mr. Wisedor had confirmed the Coevet's dire financial state and wanted nothing more to do with them.

People had started whispering about Jezzie's mental state. They often saw her roaming through town, despondent and disheveled. Rumors circulated she was pregnant and sought to blackmail the Wisedors.

Every time Favor went to town, people whispered and looked at him funny. But despite it all, it was open season for the other prominent families in the surrounding areas. An illegitimate child was nothing new, and parents of eligible young ladies could overlook such an indiscretion for the right price.

The visitors were pleased by Favor's presence, each plastering on their best smiles. Several mothers nudged their daughters to sit up straighter.

"Son, join us for lunch? Your favorite dishes are prepared. And afterward, I need you to take Victoria to town. She has errands to run," his mother insisted with a syrupy sweet voice—the one she reserved for company.

"I'm so sorry, Mother, but my calendar is full. Ladies, have a pleasant day," Favor said and kissed her forehead.

"How amazingly sweet. What a son," one mother said.

"As your mother, I insist you join my guests," Mrs. Wisedor said, pulling rank.

"At least have lunch. Mother has indeed prepared your favorite foods," Victoria added.

The guests waited in the awkward silence. One young woman even batted her eyelashes in a ploy to sway his decision.

"As you wish. I'll stay briefly," Favor said, disgruntled.

The available young beauties surrounded Favor at the luncheon. He devoured his favorite dishes and engaged the mothers in conversation. He ignored their daughters as much as possible.

"Can you please engage the younger guests, my dear," his mother whispered as everyone adjourned from the table.

"I thought you'd be pleased. I'm getting to know my potential mothers-in-law," Favor joked. His mother did not find it amusing.

Favor turned to the group.

"It was a pleasure, ladies. I'm looking forward to seeing all of you at the gala Saturday night. Until then." With that, Favor escorted Victoria from the dining room.

As they approached the waiting car out front, Purity ran from the cottage.

"Sorry, I'm late."

"I forgot to mention I invited Purity to help me," Victoria said with ease.

"A pleasant surprise," Favor said as he opened the rear passenger door. The girls slid across the fine leather seats.

* * *

The ride into Bristol was picturesque, with majestic bay views, blue skies, and rolling hills. Victoria was full of vigor and nonstop chatter about the upcoming gala.

"Mother has arranged for the finest foods at the gala. I'll deprive myself all week so I can gorge like a pig. And you're going to love my gown," Victoria said as she reached for Purity's hand and squeezed it.

Purity was a bit on edge, as this wasn't a usual occurrence to be in a car with Favor. From the backseat, she gazed at his handsome profile and muscular neck. It was difficult to forget his warm embrace and passionate kisses. She felt her face flush and shifted her gaze so Victoria wouldn't notice.

"Where are we going first?" Victoria asked in excitement.

Favor didn't answer. He seemed preoccupied.

"Are you well today, Favor?" Purity asked with concern.

"Quite well, thank you. There's just so much on my mind."

He pulled onto a busy street, clogged with traffic and people.

"First stop is McFaye's Boutique, then. We have to pick up my gown. Favor, without your approval, I simply refuse to purchase it," Victoria stated.

"I'm sure it will do," he said in a bored manner.

"I'll start on the errands and be back in an hour," Purity said with a humble nod.

"Have you ever been to a formal dress shop?" Favor asked politely.

"Only to assist Victoria," she said, blushing.

"I insist you stay then." He smiled at her in the rearview mirror.

* * *

The bell above the door jingled as they entered McFaye's Boutique. The clerks readied to attention, recognizing distinguished customers.

"Ah, the Wisedors. It's a pleasure. Miss Victoria, your gown is ready," said the head clerk.

"I simply can't wait," Victoria uttered as the clerk escorted her to the dressing room.

Favor looked around the shop, and Purity browsed in the other direction. They avoided each other, trying not to draw attention. A few stolen glances were all they could manage under the gaze of the staff and other patrons.

The gowns in the shop were elegant made from the most delicate fabrics. Purity admired the gowns as though works of art. Her fingers glided gently over the soft, silky fabrics and intricate beadwork.

Then she paused to admire a rose-colored silk dress with beadwork and a lace overlay fitted perfectly on a mannequin. It took her breath. She could only imagine the feeling of wearing such a creation.

Purity sang, "Splendid Fashion" as she swayed in front of the mirror and danced around the mannequin.

> Splendid fashion, splendid fashion
> Perfect lace and rose-colored silk
> Fit for a princess dressed for a ball
> How would I look in splendid fashion
> What I'd give to ditch these rags
> Dressed to the hilt in splendid fashion
>
> Like a butterfly with wings of color
> Transformed inside and out
> Who would know the new me
> Dressed in splendid fashion
> We'd dance all night
> Teaching him a move or two
> In splendid fashion, in splendid fashion

Purity sensed Favor's presence.

"I think you should try it on." His voice seemed to penetrate every cell of her body.

"Favor, honestly. What's the point?" she protested, avoiding eye contact.

He waved for a clerk.

"Excuse me. The lady wants to try on this gown."

The clerk eyed Purity's maid uniform, realizing her position.

"Excuse me, sir?" the clerk questioned.

"You heard me. The lady wants to try on this gown. Let's not disappoint her."

"Yes, sir. This way, miss," the doughty clerk said. She pulled the gown from a nearby rack and mumbled, "This should fit."

Before Purity could resist, the clerk whisked her away to a dressing room. The clerk moved fast, unbuttoning Purity's clothing and tugging it off.

Purity protested being undressed like a child.

"Wait a minute."

"Mr. Wisedor has made a request. He could buy this shop if he fancied. We don't want to disappoint him, do we?"

The clerk slipped the dress on Purity, and she morphed into a graceful woman with curves.

"I can't go out there. Not like this," Purity protested in a panic.

"Nonsense. The man's waiting. And for whatever reason, he's itching to see you in it," the clerk insisted, desiring an expensive sale.

"Let's just tell him it doesn't fit."

"Embarrassed or not, get out there." The clerk pushed Purity into the main area of the dress shop.

Favor admired Victoria, who modeled an expensive gown fit for a princess.

"You're going to wear it well, dear Sister."

The clerk cleared her throat, demanding Favor's attention. Favor and Victoria turned and gasped in admiration. Purity looked like an angel.

Favor caught her eyes, and she looked to the ground. Purity was a different breed from the spoiled socialites he had been forced to meet. She was a hidden gem. He studied her soft pink lips that matched the color of the dress.

"Absolutely enchanting," Victoria declared.

"I'll take her. I mean, we'll take the dress," Favor stuttered, embarrassed by the blunder. His cheeks heated with a blush.

Purity tried to argue.

"Thank you, but that's out of the question."

The clerk held out matching shoes.

"These will match perfectly with the gown."

"Sold. Wrap everything up," Favor insisted.

"But I have no place to wear this," Purity said, again trying to discourage his generosity.

"Nonsense. You're the guest of honor at our gala this Saturday night," he bragged.

"We wouldn't have it any other way," Victoria agreed with a smile. She studied the love-struck glances between her brother and Purity.

"Mystery solved," she announced, realizing who Purity loved.

"What mystery?" Favor asked, not taking his eyes off Purity.

"Never mind," Victoria said.

"Victoria, you're not making a bit of sense," Purity objected.

The Gala

Chapter 27

SHADOW BROOK ESTATE was a stir with preparations on the day of the gala. Maids rushed about dusting, mopping, polishing silverware, and setting fine tables. In the kitchen, staff prepared a feast to feed a multitude.

Purity hid out most of the day, catching up on much-needed rest. Dance practice had become more exhausting with each passing day.

Naomi burst into her bedroom.

"Get up. You've got kitchen duty. And don't tell me you're sick." Naomi left in haste before Purity had a chance to respond.

Purity rose slowly from the bed, cleaned up, and put on her uniform. She dreaded the evening as she made the short trip to the kitchen door of the mansion.

In the kitchen, Purity smelled roast beef with mushroom sauce and other delectable treats. Naomi handed her a fresh apron.

"Victoria's expecting you," Natasha whispered to Purity.

"She needs help, I suppose."

"I've already dressed her," Natasha assured her.

Purity climbed the long, elegant staircase, rehearsing a few excuses.

"Victoria, my sincerest thanks, but I'm needed in the kitchen. Don't be silly. Your parents would never agree to it." Purity practiced again in low tones as she stood in front of the bedroom door.

Two maids walked by.

"Just daydreaming again," Purity said, hoping they bought the excuse.

A bundle of nerves, she knocked.

"Come in," Victoria sounded a gentle reply.

Purity entered and noted Victoria's appearance. With her jewelry and hair done, she looked even more like a princess than she had at the shop.

"Where have you been? We don't have much time. I have to do your hair and makeup," Victoria scolded.

"This is a bad idea. I'm needed in the kitchen."

"Absolutely no excuses. You're attending this gala, not as a maid, but as our special guest. Who knows, you may meet the man of your dreams tonight," Victoria said mischievously.

"What are you up to?" Purity asked with a smile.

Victoria sat her down on the vanity bench in front of the mirror. Purity's eyes shot up to the ceiling, to a painted skyline full of cherub-like angels. Then she looked to the porcelain angels on either side of the fireplace.

"There are angels all around."

"And you're one of them. I think your hair will look best partially up," Victoria said, playing with Purity's hair. She brushed it out and arranged it with hairpins. Then she added scented oil for shine.

"My favorite hair clip will fit comfortably in the back," Victoria said, clipping a jeweled barrette to Purity's soft, lustrous hair.

"Now, a little makeup—some powder, lipstick for color and rouge." Victoria dabbed each on Purity's face. When finished, she paused, admiring Purity's clear complexion.

"You're a beauty. And remember, tonight, you serve only yourself. If I see you in the kitchen, there will be consequences."

Victoria stood back to inspect her work.

"Perfection." She then walked to the closet and pulled out the gown Favor had purchased for Purity.

"What about your parents? Your mother will throw a fit, then what?" Purity asked while quickly undressing and stepping into the gown.

"Don't worry about my mother. She has conveniently misplaced every pair of her eyeglasses," Victoria said, opening a drawer full of eyeglasses.

"She won't be seeing anyone clearly tonight, and father won't be looking,"

"You little sneak," Purity said with wide-eyed laughter.

Victoria fastened the back of the dress, then directed her friend to the mirror, saying, "You're a dream."

A rap at the door interrupted their giggles.

Natasha entered in haste.

"Your mother's furious you're late."

"Oh no. A storm's brewing," Victoria said and rushed out on a mission.

Natasha stooped down to pick up the pile of clothing on the area rug. She recognized the maid's uniform, then eyed the adorned beauty before her.

"What's going on? Is that you, my dear friend?" Natasha asked in disbelief.

"You mustn't tell a soul. Help cover me tonight, I beg you?"

"But whose dress is this?" Natasha gasped in wonder.

"I can honestly say it's mine," Purity replied.

"It's stunning. I bet you'll meet the man of your dreams tonight and retire this uniform forever," Natasha said, holding the crumpled, lifeless garment.

"A girl can dream," Purity teased, wanting to believe life could be different.

The ballroom music echoed through the mansion, up the staircase, and into the bedroom.

"It's time to step into your future," Natasha said, opening the door.

"I don't know if I can do this," Purity said as a wave of fear pulsated through her.

"Opportunity has wings. Don't let this one fly away. It takes faith to believe God has more for you than this," she said, shaking the uniform in Purity's face.

"When you make it, come back for me," Natasha pleaded.

"We are friends forever. Never forget that," Purity said with compassion.

Natasha thought of her attempted kidnapping.

"I remember well. You saved my life."

"What if someone recognizes me and shouts, you're just a maid? The last thing I want to be is a spectacle."

Natasha grabbed an ornate hand fan from Victoria's dresser.

"Here. Use this." Natasha spread the fan out over her face then handed it to Purity.

* * *

Favor greeted guests near the entry when his eyes landed on a graceful beauty descending the stairs. He abandoned his task and waited for Purity to alight the last step.

"You look…," the words escaped him.

"May I have the first dance?" Favor asked as he took her hand and kissed it.

The sweet smile that formed on her lips made him feel like he was the only man in the room.

"You may," she answered.

Favor led her into the crowded ballroom, where couples dressed in magnificent attire lined up for the first waltz. The conductor struck up the orchestra.

Favor embraced Purity with a gentle touch, and they glided as one across the dance floor.

Victoria danced close by with a handsome partner. She winked at Favor with overwhelming approval.

"Who's the fabulous beauty Favor is dancing with?" an elderly guest asked Mrs. Wisedor.

"What. A fabulous beauty and I know nothing about it?" Mrs. Wisedor squinted as she scanned the room.

"You're slipping, no doubt," the guest answered.

"Does he look interested?" Mrs. Wisedor asked with curiosity.

"I would say very much so," the guest replied.

"Then I won't interrupt. As long as her estate matches ours."

"Absolutely. A must," the guest nodded in agreement.

Favor spun Purity round again, and her eyes caught something in the window. He followed her gaze. David, Jonathan, and the rest of her sons peered through a large bay window. Favor danced them over to Natasha.

"Feed all the guests," he said, nodding toward the boys.

"Yes, sir," Natasha answered.

"I can't thank you enough," Purity said, holding Favor closer.

"Did you know we're having a dance contest? I recommend you enter Purity. First prize is a trip for two to Europe, donated by one of our guests."

Purity stumbled but quickly regained her footing.

"Europe. Only imagine. Mother would love it."

"I do believe you have the talent to win. Wouldn't you say, Purity?" Favor teased.

"What gives you that idea?" Purity asked, avoiding eye contact.

"Lucky guess."

* * *

A short while later, guests entering the competition pinned papers with numbers on their jackets and dresses. Favor grabbed a number and then escorted Purity to the ballroom.

She opened the small fan and flapped it in front of her face. She hoped none of the local socialites looked too closely.

"Is this why you invited me? So you could win the prize?" she asked with a smile.

"What makes you think you're that good?" he teased as he pinned the number on her dress.

"Here we go." Favor urged her onto the dance floor.

Unbeknownst to the Wisedors, Jezzie had slipped into the party and even now led her partner to the floor. She wore a hat with a short veil to disguise herself, and her eyes had something wild about them.

The music rolled loud to an upbeat jazz number, electrifying the crowd.

"Dance until you're instructed to leave," one of the judges yelled.

Purity's feet moved in perfect rhythm to the music. She held the fan close and lifted it anytime a local young socialite got too close.

Over his shoulder, Favor spotted Jezzie.

"What's she doing here," he said through clenched teeth.

Purity turned to see just as Jezzie and her partner danced over to them.

227

"Hello, Favor," Jezzie said in much too sultry a manor.

"Who is your bewitching dance partner?"

"Get out before I throw you out, Jezzie."

"Now, now, Favor. No need to be nasty. You wouldn't want to cause a scene for your poor Mother, now, would you?" She waved her fingers and danced away.

"The gall," Favor groaned.

"She's right. Better not to cause a commotion," Purity assured him.

"What is she plotting?" Favor wondered aloud.

Favor and Purity danced on for nearly an hour. Many of the dancing couples were eliminated after just a few rounds, and now only three remained.

"Five-minute intermission," one judge called out.

Purity gave Favor some last-minute instructions during the break.

"When the dance ends, give me a dip for a dramatic finish." Purity fell back into his arms, her back bowed and arms spread wide like wings. Their eyes locked, and their lips drew closer.

"Let's go, folks. It's time to choose our winners," the head judge shouted.

Jezzie and her partner were up first. Her performance was almost perfect, but her partner missed some key steps.

After the dance, in the commotion of congratulations by onlookers, Jezzie reached into a pocket and pulled out a handful of fine pebbles. She released them slowly, leaving a trail across the dance floor.

It was Favor and Purity's turn next. They danced the samba and mixed in different jazz steps, moving with great speed across the floor.

Natasha rushed to the kitchen to find Naomi.

"Come quickly. You'll be so proud," she begged Naomi.

"If it ain't work, I don't have time," Naomi said, resenting the interruption.

Natasha pulled a tray from her hands and pushed the head maid out of the kitchen. Then she helped Naomi through the crowd and into the ballroom.

"Is that who I think it is?" Naomi said, rubbing her eyes as Purity flew past her.

"Yes, it's Purity," Natasha replied over the music.

"She's got rhythm. Go Purity," Naomi shouted.

Purity felt her shoes slipping.

"It's sand or something," she warned Favor as their steps progressed with feverish momentum.

He nodded in understanding, and they continued to dance with all their might. The guests shouted, cheered, laughed, and exploded in applause at the couple's spontaneous routine.

At the end of the dance, Favor's feet slid out of control on the pebbles. His body contorted as he tried to maintain his balance.

Purity slowed the pace but caught some of the pebbles too. She awkwardly fell into Favor's arms, and he dipped her as planned. Her hair reached to the floor as her back bowed in Favor's embrace. Even with their mistakes, her profile was one of elegance and strength. Both were breathless and exhilarated. He leaned in and kissed her cheek.

People clapped and cheered in a roar of pleasure.

The final couple took to the floor. They did their best, but they were no match for the other couples. At the end of their dance, the judges asked the audience to vote for the winner by a show of hands. It was a tie between Jezzie and her partner and Favor and Purity.

The judges deliberated and returned with a verdict.

"And the lucky winners for the European vacation are Miss Jezzabella Coevet and Mr. Rodney North," one of the judges proclaimed.

Jezzie and her partner were swarmed by a sea of people congratulating their efforts.

"Jezzie?" Mrs. Wisedor proclaimed.

"Who let her in?" She stormed off to speak to her staff.

"Don't be disappointed," Favor whispered into Purity's ear.

"Victory is marked by perseverance."

"And that victory comes in God's timing," she said, smiling.

* * *

After some refreshments, Favor led Purity through the crowds and into the garden. The music faded away as they walked along the path leading to the bay. Waves crashed onto the rocky shoreline, illuminated by a full moon. They inhaled the fresh air of the Narragansett Bay in unison.

He sighed.

"What a night."

"Despite the loss, this night has been the greatest win in my life. I see now that what seemed impossible could be possible," Purity said, gazing up at him.

"I've watched you grow into an accomplished woman. There's no limit to what you can achieve."

"You've been a great teacher. Thank you for that."

"And you've taught me a lot as well, painfully so. I want to ask for your forgiveness. You were right about everything from providing for your sons to my parent's greed and selfishness."

"Of course, Favor. You have my forgiveness."

He gazed into her eyes and took a deep breath.

"I want you to be the first to know that I'm getting married."

Purity was stunned.

"But I thought your engagement was off?" She asked, trying to disguise a trembling voice.

"I've chosen my bride, and I'm hoping to marry as soon as possible." Favor said, searching her eyes for any reaction.

Purity gulped back bitter disappointment.

"I had no idea. What a fool I've been." She started to walk away, but he tugged on her arm and pulled her back to him.

"Can't you see I'm deeply in love? Why I'd marry tonight if possible," he said with deep emotion.

"Do you relish in taking me to the heavens and then crash every expectation to hell below," she said, trying to pull away as tears welled.

He hugged her closer.

"Oh, my darling. You are my very heart. I don't care what anyone thinks. I could never be happy with anyone but you."

Purity stared up at him in amazement.

"You're my perfect craving that no one else can satisfy. And I don't want to exist another moment without you. Purity, please say you'll marry me. You're my only desire in this whole world."

Purity trembled against him. The words cut through her disappointment and quenched the longing of her hungry heart.

He leaned in ever so slowly and kissed her lips, trying to suppress his pent-up passion. She molded deeper into his arms, finding him irresistible and kissing him back with a new passion.

Favor pulled away.

"Does that kiss mean yes?" Favor asked, searching her eyes for the answer.

"Yes, yes, yes," Purity said and kissed him again.

"All things are possible for those who believe. We'll marry right away."

"To be your wife is everything, but there's something you need to know," Purity acknowledged.

"What's this mystery?" he said, showering her face with light kisses.

"I'm dancing in the U.S. Ballroom Competitions. I want you to be there," Purity said, searching his eyes for approval.

"I was wondering when you were going to tell me."

"You saw the newspaper?"

"I snatched it before anyone caught wind of it. I'd be honored to marry to a Ballroom Champion."

"I hope it goes better than tonight," she joked.

The brilliance of the moon and stars above created an irresistible calm in the atmosphere.

Purity turned to him.

"Can I ask you to do something for me?"

"Anything," Favor replied.

"Announcing our engagement will only cause drama and detract from the competition. Can we keep this our secret for now?"

"I can wait until after the competition if that's what you want."

"Thank you."

"Now, when are we going shopping for our wedding rings?" he asked with a glimmer in his eyes.

"As soon as possible," Purity replied with a giddy smile.

Elusive Triumph

Chapter 28

THE NEXT MORNING, Favor knocked on the cottage door. Purity answered with expectation, ready for their outing.

After a sweet embrace, Favor reached for her hand.

"Shall we go?"

"Yes, please," she replied.

They walked to his luxury car, parked in front of the mansion. A gardener looked up at them. Instead of disdain, the gardener cracked a big smile.

"It's a battle, but you're winning, sir," the gardener said.

"It's going to be worth it," Favor said while opening the passenger car door.

Purity glided smoothly over the new leather seats.

"Your car's a jewel," she said, admiring the shiny paint.

"No, you're the jewel. But this one's yours," Favor responded.

"This car is for me? You mean it?"

He nodded.

"Teach me to drive then," Purity insisted playfully.

Favor reluctantly urged her to slide across the seat and take the wheel. He got in on the passenger's side.

It was a harrowing drive to the Bailey's Ballroom Theater. Purity managed to fry every nerve in his body on the hair-raising journey.

Favor's knees were a bit unsteady as they entered the theater. Arm in arm, they walked to the private studio, whispering sweet words of affection mingled with light kisses. Heads turned when several patrons recognized Favor.

"Mandy and Stephen, I'd like to introduce you to Mr. Favor Wisedor," Purity announced proudly.

Mandy and Stephen glanced at each other in disbelief, realizing society forbad a match between Favor and Purity.

"You're Favor Wisedor of Shadow Brook Estate?" Mandy questioned in awe.

He nodded slightly.

Stephen extended a hand and shook Favor's with due respect.

"It's an honor to meet you, sir," Stephen said.

"Let's get started. Favor wants to watch the practice," Purity boasted.

"Fair enough," Mandy said and started the music on the record player.

Stephen and Purity began to dance, and Favor was amazed at Purity's gift. From then on, Favor would insist on taking her to every practice.

* * *

A few days later, Naomi sat her daughter down.

"What's going on? Where's Favor taking you every day?"

"I wanted it to be a surprise, but since you insist, I'll tell you." She twisted her hands in her lap, nervous about how her mother would respond.

"Mama, I'm dancing in the U.S. Ballroom Dance Competitions this Saturday night. I'd like you to be there."

"I knew you could dance from the gala, but competing as a professional? When did this happen?"

"Technically, I'm an amateur since this is my first competition, but I'm competing against professionals."

"Is this why you've been gone so much of late? I thought you were off at Mave's or something worse."

"Just dance practice. I promise."

"Well, that does ease my mind," Naomi admitted.

"But I still don't understand how all this came about."

"You know as well as I that I have two left feet. I've been gifted with the talent of ballroom dancing. It's a miracle. Somehow my feet just know what to do."

"A miracle indeed."

"And the best part—the prize is ten thousand dollars split between the winning couple."

"That's a lot of money."

"We could stop working for the Wisdor's, and I could open a school."

"But what if you don't win?"

"I don't know, but the Captain does. He has a plan for me, and he put this door in front of me. I have to try—for us, for the boys."

"Purity, I'm sorry. Please forgive me."

"For what, Mama?"

"After Papa died, I died too. I took my pain and loneliness out on you. I've lived as a bitter woman, with no hope of anything better."

Purity put her hand on Naomi's hand.

"I lost my patience with you. Every time I looked at you, I was reminded of everything I couldn't do to make your life better. I felt like a complete failure. I had no dreams, and I resented all your dreams."

"Oh, Mama. I miss Papa too. We are in this together."

"You're right. I'll be there, cheering you on Saturday night. I believe in you," Naomi said, hugging her daughter.

Purity held her mother tight.

"Those words mean everything to me, Mama."

Anticipation

Chapter 29

SATURDAY NIGHT CAME in a flash. People from all over the country poured into Bailey's Ballroom Theater.

"Welcome. Welcome to the U.S. Ballroom Dance Competitions here at Bailey's Ballroom Theater," the announcer bellowed.

"Tonight, we have twenty couples from around the country competing for the title of 'U.S. Ballroom Champion.' And don't forget folks, the grand prize is ten thousand dollars in cash to the winning couple."

The crowd erupted in applause.

Purity's knees shook, and she prayed under her breath.

"Lord of the Dance, come dance with me now," she whispered.

Mandy noticed her panic.

"You've got the talent to win this. They're all here for you, everyone you've ever touched," Mandy said with encouragement.

"That's the last thing I need to hear," Purity said as she scanned the audience. Her gaze landed on her sons and then other familiar faces—her mother, Favor, Alexis, Natasha, and all the dancers from the hotel.

"Oh Captain, now look what you've done," Purity said as a wave of nausea hit. Her knees shook even worse.

"Focus. Get your mind on the dance," Mandy demanded.

As the crowds continued pouring into the large venue, dark beings descended on the roof.

235

In answer, the Ring of Grace appeared as five shafts of light, bolting into the area like lightning strikes. They morphed into five children dressed as warriors, welding swords of fire for battle.

The Captain of the Lord's Army descended, followed by a vast army, while the archangels hovered above, waiting to intervene if needed.

Mave strode into the theater. Shrouded in a long black velvet hooded cape, she walked with a cane. A small sequined purse weighed heavy on her wrist.

Her eyes burned with evil intent as she brushed past the excited crowds and settled in a seat near the dance floor. An eerie creature overshadowed her—a dark spirit that clung to her back.

"One shot. Just one shot will do it. Roberto's death must be avenged," the evil spirit whispered into Mave's ear. She nodded in agreement as though well acquainted with the voice.

Ahaba descended on the roof with his massive army of wicked spirits.

"One shot, and Purity's done," Ahaba hissed.

The Ring of Grace raised their swords, declaring, "Fight for the victory!" They advanced with all their might pressing against the enemy.

Captain of the Lord's army moved forward, challenging the enemy army.

"Off with your heads," the Captain threatened.

The hordes battling the child angels pounded with unrelenting violence. Their little bodies were blown back with a demonic vengeance.

"Retreat, Ring of Grace. Let us handle them," the Captain warned as his army advanced.

Inside the theater, the audience was on the edge of its seats. The competition began with an elegant waltz. One couple at a time sat down as the judges flipped a sign with their number on it, indicating they were out of the running. This went on for each category: Waltz, Fox Trot, Rumba, and Quick-Step.

After a few hours of stiff competition, Purity and Stephen were one of three remaining couples. The other two teams went first in the final dance, both giving exceptional performances.

"Watch out for the Russian judge. He's scored you low all evening. Don't give him anything to protest," Mandy warned.

"And finally, folks, the last of our top three couples, our home-grown dancers, Stephen and Purity, from Bristol, Rhode Island," the commentator announced.

"They need a perfect score to win," Natasha complained to Favor. He gulped at the odds.

The Bristol team made their way onto the dance floor.

"We've got this," Stephen assured Purity.

"Let's wrap this up and get out of here," Purity said with determination. She gave a faint smile as the music vibrated through the grand ballroom and prayed under her breath.

Everyone was up on their feet, calculating every move, every step. All the contestants watched, scrutinizing them with trained eyes, looking for any mishaps. It was the same thought on everyone's mind, "Could the Bristol team dance the perfect routine?" Anxiety and anticipation weighed on each face.

Purity and Stephen landed every step with perfect timing. As they moved across the floor, it was as if they floated on air. When the music stopped, the crowd exploded with excitement and relief.

Mandy locked eyes with Stephen, and every win they'd enjoyed together flooded back in like an avalanche of memories. Stephen reached for Mandy. She melted into his arms, crying tears of joy.

It took several minutes for the judges to deliberate. They had never seen such brilliance, rhythm, and control. One by one, each one came up with a perfect score.

The Russian judge seemed to be stalling. He scowled as he reviewed the score sheet.

The other two teams stood side by side on the platform in torturous suspense. The audience grew louder, shouting for their favorite.

Favor left his seat and made his way through the crowd. Purity rushed into his arms.

"I can't look," Purity said as she buried her head against Favor's chest.

Reluctantly, the Russian judge raised the score paddle, marked with a perfect score of ten. The building erupted in thunderous applause.

The commentator took the mic and announced, "With a perfect ten out of ten across the board, the grand prize goes to the Bristol team."

Favor lifted Purity in his arms, and she raised her arms in victory.

"Thank you, Captain," she shouted and blew a few kisses heavenward.

Stephen turned to Mandy and kissed her soundly.

David was drawn from the crowd by a small, bright, burning light only he had eyes to see. He followed it backstage into the darkness. The crowd roared in the background. His warrior's intuition kicked in, and he pulled out his bow and arrow, ready to fire. Something was terribly wrong.

The light morphed into a glowing child angel and flew in front of him, surrounded by golden light.

"What's your name?" David asked in shock.

"My name is Ora," she said gently.

David instinctively sensed her goodness.

"Lead the way."

He followed her deeper into the darkness, behind heavy curtains and stage props. David hesitated, overhearing a soft conversation. Ora put a finger to her mouth as though telling him to be quiet. He listened. Mave and Mr. Wells discussed a plot to harm Purity.

"Remember, Roberto's death must be avenged. Don't disappoint yourself," Mr. Wells said with intensity.

A few of Ahaba's transparent beings descended on David like a hammer. Ora fought them off with jets of fire coming from her hands. In retaliation, they blew the nearby light furnishings in a wild wind that flung them toward her and crashed them to the floor with a loud noise.

Mr. Wells jumped.

"Someone's been listening." He wasn't waiting around and left in a hurry.

A smoky, translucent spirit whispered in Mave's ear and wrapped around her neck. She looked about, and then with an angry yank, pulled back one of the large backstage curtains. David was exposed, with nowhere to run.

"Well, well. Look who's here. It's Purity's little bodyguard."

Mave grabbed for David's bow, trying to wrestle it from him.

"I'll protect Purity if it's the last thing I do." David fought off Mave's swings and scratches.

The evil spirit wrapped around Mave and enlarged up over her body, appearing like a huge, coiled snake ready to strike.

"Don't let him escape," the evil spirit whispered, biting deep into Mave's neck.

She roiled in pain and fought against David with increasing resolve. He defended himself and punched back. Ora wrestled with the translucent snake and fought off other spirits jumping on her back.

David grabbed for her walking cane. She clicked a button, and a glistening dagger popped out of the end.

Ahaba watched from the rafters, hoping for a bloody mess.

David dodged vicious thrusts as Mave lunged at him again and again. Ora tried to shield David, but she was overpowered by advancing evil spirits. A dark spirit tangled his feet with invisible snares.

David tripped and pulled Mave down with him. They wrestled on the floor until spirits wrapped around his hands like constricting bonds. Mave, with an angry thrust, hit David's shoulder with the cane dagger, paralyzing him with severe pain.

"Die alone," she said with a demonic voice before racing away.

David realized he was in trouble. The wound bled profusely.

"Captain, I've heard Purity talk about you. I could use a little help," he mumbled.

Suddenly, Ora appeared before him as a ball of fire.

"Is it my time to die?" David asked, feeling faint but not fearing the light.

The fiery ball drew close, and Ora transformed into a beautiful child. She wore a crown as a princess would.

"Don't fear. You have more work to do," she said, pulling the dagger out. Ora reached out a fiery hand and touched his wound. Her hand felt like it was burning him to his core. David gasped in pain.

Mave stood among the cheering crowd, a wild look in her eyes. Dark spirits swarmed around her head, appearing like black flies on the attack.

"Revenge, revenge. You must avenge Roberto's death," a dark spirit said, attacking Mave's mind. Her shaking hand emerged from her purse, holding a cold metal pistol.

She turned her gaze to Purity, Favor, Stephen, and Mandy, who stood on the stage as the crowd cheered for them with loud shouts and wild clapping.

Mave's aim wobbled as she lifted the gun. A woman nearby noticed and began screaming hysterically.

A piercing pain shot through Mave's hand as a small arrow impaled her palm. With a loud scream, she dropped the gun.

Blood dripped, one drop at a time, and then it flowed, splashing her cape and pooling in a small puddle on the floor. She staggered to a nearby exit and disappeared into the night.

A police officer working the event rushed over. He picked up the gun with a clean cloth, noting the blood on the floor. He questioned those who had witnessed the incident.

A short distance away, David tucked his bow back into his jacket. Ora had completely restored his wound. Even the blood on his jacket was gone.

Ora re-appeared and wrapped her arms around David's neck and gave him a warm kiss on his cheek.

"I couldn't have done it without you," he said to Ora.

"The Captain sent me to help," Ora said, staring into his eyes.

Josiah, one of the child angels, floated by David's side in translucent form, striking fiery darts at wicked forces headed their way.

The other four angels from the Ring of Grace hovered over the winners. Appearing as flashes of colored light, they blocked an onslaught of attacks from enemy forces.

The unseen war moved to the roof where Captain and his army were crushing Ahaba's forces. The Captain whistled loudly and then blew his trumpet, calling for the archangels. In a flash, they were there, slashing with death blows the thousands of evil spirits until finally Ahaba and his evil spirits retreated.

In the theater below, the press surrounded the winners, taking pictures and asking questions. Reporters pressed in, hoping to get the first interview.

"How does this win feel? Will you be going to the World Championships in France after this?" a reporter asked Purity.

"The win's a miracle. World Championships? I don't know," Purity responded, searching Favor's eyes.

"Yes, she's going to fulfill her purpose in dance," Favor answered for his future bride.

"Stephen, you've been out of competition for over a year. How does it feel to be back and a winner?" asked a reporter.

"Unbelievable. A dream come true. It helps when you have the right coaching," he said, hugging Mandy.

Stephen and Purity were awarded the prize money in a short winner's ceremony where they posed with their trophies.

"Speech, speech," yelled the audience.

Purity cleared her throat and spoke into the microphone.

"First, I'd like to thank the Captain up there for giving me the gift and talent to dance," Purity said, all choked up.

"Mandy and Stephen, thank you for shaping my talent. This would never have been possible without you. Lastly, I'd like to thank my fiancé, Favor Wisedor of Shadow Brook Estate, for all his love and support," Purity said with joy.

Favor embraced her, and the audience roared with exuberant applause and surprise.

Stephen approached the microphone with his trophy and prize money in his hands.

"Purity and Mandy, you gave me the will to dance again. Thank you," he said, fighting emotion.

"And while we're at it, Mandy, will you marry me?"

The crowd erupted again as she accepted him with a hug and kiss.

The other dancers crowded the platform to congratulate the winners and mingled with appreciative fans and judges.

In the bustle, Purity handed Mandy some of her prize money.

"I can't accept it. You've got sons to feed. Besides, my man has plenty of money," Mandy beamed with pride.

* * *

Later that night, Naomi and Purity sat at their kitchen table drinking tea. Naomi gazed at the trophy and five thousand dollars in cash stacked on the table.

"Mercy, mercy. It's time to retire," Naomi said.

"Our dreams are coming true," Purity said with renewed confidence.

"I've never been able to dream for anything. Teach me how to dream."

241

"We'll dream together, Mama."

"Is it possible to start over? Am I too old to do something that matters?"

"This is our chance to start over. Most don't get that opportunity," Purity said tenderly.

"Thank God for new beginnings," Naomi said, wiping away a tear that rolled down her cheek. Naomi sang, "Bitter Times."

> Bitter times, bitter words
> It strikes every life
> Taking hold, like a deadly mold
>
> Bitter times, bitter words
> Work over my head, no way out
> A loved one dies, I'm alone again
>
> Bitter times, bitter words
> I can't see the way ahead
> All is lost for years on end
>
> Forgive my words
> Landing like heavy blows
> You didn't deserve my bitter soul
> In the days ahead, I'll try my best
> To reverse the curse
> Misery was my only defense
>
> Bitter times, bitter words
> I put you away
> Realizing this is a new day

"Bitter times have come to an end," Purity said, hugging Naomi.

Purity went to her bedroom and fell into bed. A deep sleep descended upon her. Bright and Star hovered over her body in rainbow lights. They encapsulated her body with New Earth peace and wrapped her in colorful lights as they took her out the window and up to the mansion's roof.

In her dreams, Purity heard the voice of a child calling.

"Mother. Mother, come to me," Clarity called from the New Earth.

Once again, Keenan and Valor waited on the roof for their dear friend, Purity. Bright Star fastened her body to Keenan's soft feathers with strong fibers of intense rainbow colors. With a running start, the large eagles took off, lifting into the air and shaking the roof below.

When Purity opened her eyes, she saw New Earth. Keenan and Valor flew over the billowing sailboat, and Bright Star gently set her down in the vessel.

A light breeze blew through her hair as she sailed down a winding river. The water glistened with hues of gold, silver, and rainbow colors, like diamonds dancing on the surface.

Clarity steered the boat, but the sails sagged without enough wind. The Ring of Grace appeared, filled their lungs, and blew into the boat's sails, propelling it along.

They sailed down the winding river, passing the majestic landscapes. Purity had come to love. This time, however, they also glided through vast cities with great towers and palaces.

"The Captain's calling for you," Clarity said, eyeing her mother.

"Why is he calling for me?" Purity asked, nervous about finally meeting the Captain.

"Because you'll need his strength for the journey," Clarity said, as though she knew the future.

"Three times a year, those on the New Earth celebrate with the Captain. We rejoice in all the victories. You danced in his power and won. You didn't draw back. He's expecting you," Clarity announced.

Throngs of people walked along the riverbank, waving and shouting words of welcome.

"Are you going to another feast?" Purity shouted to them.

"Yes. We'll see you there," they replied.

"Everyone's invited, for the Captain's expecting us," Clarity said as they sailed on.

"How does a person get here, to stay? Do they fly on eagles like I did?"

"You'll soon find out."

Further down the river, they disembarked and walked through a majestic forest. As they came to a clearing in the trees, a windstorm swept in and swallowed them up in its fury.

"What's going on?" Purity yelled.

"You'll see." Clarity held tight to her mother.

Small eruptions burst forth from the fertile soil beneath them. They looked like mounds of dirt at first but then took on the shape of a human-looking body, fully clothed and made of clay. A swirl of golden wind encircled the body, entered its nostrils, and expanded its lungs.

"Look, Mother, a forever life is forming." Clarity pointed to the creative work forming before their eyes.

"A life, never to die again, forming before our eyes," Purity said in amazement.

The body's chest cavity rose and fell as it breathed in and out.

"The breath of life raises them up," Clarity said.

"It's true. It's all true," a new arrival proclaimed in amazement.

Others materialized in the same manner, popping up like an instant harvest of newcomers.

"I'm young again," a woman said, sitting up with a strong new body.

"I'm not sick anymore," a little child said, erupting from the soil.

Ora appeared to them.

"Come, follow me to the great city. The Captain is expecting you."

Clarity gave a wink to Ora, and the newcomers were off.

"Their forever life begins. All pain and sorrow have passed away," Clarity said with joy.

"All those who believe in the Captain come here. Is that right?" Purity inquired, remembering Papa.

"Yes, this is their reward. They will live with him forever," Clarity said with pride.

"I know my Papa's here somewhere. Why haven't you taken me to him yet?"

"Who and what you see here isn't my choice. Yes, my grandfather, Papa, is here. I know him well. But you're here to see the Captain," Clarity said in earnest.

"Your grandfather? Yes, of course, Papa is your grandfather. Why didn't you tell me you know him?" Purity asked, tearing up.

"Mother, why wouldn't I know him?" Clarity said, smiling.

"I'm still learning the ways of the New Earth. I beg you, Clarity. Take me to Papa. Surely the Captain can wait."

"No, Papa will have to wait. Remember, I'm the Captain's thought for you. He says you must meet him first. He comes first above everything and everyone." Clarity stared deeply into her mother's eyes, and it was as if they burned like a fire.

The longer Purity stared into her daughter's eyes, the more intense the fire blazed, pulling her into the vortex of another realm. It was the strangest sensation, as though being drawn into a sacred heart of love.

Next to Clarity appeared a glorious warrior. He was dressed for battle in golden armor, leather, and heavy, sturdy boots. A double-edged sword was tucked in its sheath by his side. His skin glowed, and his eyes blazed with kindness.

"Lord of the Dance," Purity said, shocked by his presence.

He reached for her with his strong battle-scarred hands. A gentle smile covered his face. Then an unseen orchestra began to play, and Purity couldn't utter a word. She inhaled deeply in profound peace and remembered not to worry about knowing the steps and keeping the rhythm. As long as she remained lost in his eyes, her feet knew exactly what to do.

"Shall we?" He took her in his arms.

Purity's nightgown transformed into a gorgeous, sparkling gown. And off they lifted into the atmosphere of the New Earth. They danced over the forests, vineyards, and cities below.

"How can it be you never miss a step?" Purity asked.

"Keep your eyes on me, and you'll never miss a step," he responded.

Purity felt a love beyond the romantic love she had for Favor. Dancing with Lord of the Dance strengthened her resolve to battle for injustice. In his arms, she felt completely safe and whole.

When the song ended, he set them down by the shore of the river where they first met. The trees nearby bowed in reverence.

A short distance away, Clarity called out to them and waved with excitement.

"Mother, how was the dance?"

"It was wonderful," Purity answered.

The Ring of Grace appeared and swooped Clarity up into the clouds.

"We need to talk," Lord of the Dance explained, watching Clarity wave goodbye.

"Yes, I wanted to tell you. I won the dance contest. Does the Captain know?" Purity said, searching his eyes.

"What makes you think he wasn't there? Remember, the Captain knows and sees all. He's Lord of all your victories and all the challenges ahead. So do not fear. Your heart is growing closer to his, and one day, when he stands before you, you'll know it's him." Lord of the Dance gave her a sweet kiss on the forehead.

Purity woke up in her bed. It was still dark outside her window. Lord of the Dance's voice echoed through her mind, "Do not fear, do not fear, do not fear."

Purity threw her fists down on her pillow.

"Lord of the Dance, I wanted to stay. I wanted to tell you I'm engaged."

"What's that?" Naomi shouted from the kitchen.

"Nothing, Mother," Purity replied.

"We need to talk about your winnings and the World Championships. And we've got a wedding to plan. Right under my nose, you were courting Favor. I'm sure Mrs. Wisedor isn't sleeping a wink tonight."

"It's late, Mama. Tomorrow." Purity rolled over, desperately asking to return to the New Earth.

* * *

The next morning, Shadow Brook Estate was abuzz with change. Natasha and Alexis served breakfast, barely able to suppress their joy.

Mr. Wisedor and Favor sat alone at the dining table.

"Son, can we talk?"

"Of course," Favor answered and put his fork down.

"I was there last night. It was the talk of the town, and I just couldn't miss it."

"What did you think? Isn't my bride-to-be unbeatable?" Favor asked, sensing a breakthrough.

"Yes, she's beautiful. I've been wrong about you and Purity. She's not just a little maid anymore." He continued, "And I realize now that she's a person of substance. I don't doubt she's behind the changes at the factories. I'm proud to accept her as my daughter-in-law."

"Thank you, Father. Indeed, Purity opened my eyes to our greed and injustice. If not for her, I would have gone to the grave believing we were entitled to use others," Favor said with sincerity.

Mrs. Wisedor bustled in, shaking the newspaper in a fit.

"Reprehensible. It's a scandal. Our family name disgraced," she pouted.

Mr. Wisedor knew there was no stopping her tirade. He lifted a hand to Favor to indicate he hold his tongue.

"Our son engaged to a maid. A barroom, I mean, ballroom dancer. Foolish nonsense. She's a nobody," Mrs. Wisedor spat in anger.

It was all Favor could do to keep quiet.

"I was there last night, and it was outstanding. Our son knows exactly what he's doing. It's his choice, not yours." Mr. Wisedor grabbed the newspaper with a yank.

"And she's no longer a nobody," He tapped the paper that had Purity's face plastered on the front page.

"Are you mad or just possessed? Her family is of no account and penniless," Mrs. Wisedor argued.

"Purity earned five thousand dollars in one night. Quite a little businesswoman, I'd say," Mr. Wisedor boasted.

"You better start planning a wedding. Favor has chosen his bride."

Mrs. Wisedor's mouth hung open in shock.

Victoria strode in.

"Yes, I'm available to help plan the grand affair anytime, Mother."

"Plan the wedding yourselves. I'll have no part in it," Mrs. Wisedor protested.

"Mother, listen to reason," Victoria begged.

"Who has bewitched my family? That maid has been scheming from day one to inherit all this." Mrs. Wisedor shook with anger.

Favor could not stay silent.

"You have been so bewitched by money and status that a person's character holds no value."

"You dare correct me?" She gestured around the room.

"All of this came at a high cost, and I'm trying to make sure it wasn't in vain," his mother hissed.

"Yes, and the high cost was the lives of others less fortunate," Mr. Wisedor corrected.

"The matter is settled. Favor made his decision, and there will be no more debate."

Auctioned Innocence

Chapter 30

A FEW DAYS later, Purity entered the Weinstein's deli in downtown Bristol. The smell of fresh bread, homemade salads, and deli meats permeated the air. Natasha's parents had opened the shop upon their arrival in America, and Purity visited on occasion when Naomi sent her to run errands.

Natasha motioned Purity into a side storage room.

"Come in here."

"Your note sounded urgent."

"I have to quit Shadow Brook Estate," Natasha said with anxiety.

They were interrupted by Natasha's mother.

"Congratulations, Purity. Your win is national news. Let me feed the famous winner."

"Corned beef on rye, please."

Mrs. Weinstein left to make the sandwich.

Natasha grabbed Purity's arm.

"Forget the sandwich. A businessman came by today. Father owes a debt, and I'm the payment. I start tomorrow."

"What's the job description?" Purity asked, concerned.

"I'm not sure, but he has a big mansion somewhere here in Bristol. Maybe I'll be his maid. He looked as though he could eat me alive."

"What do you mean?"

"It's the way he leered at me. He's picking me up tomorrow, and father says I must go."

"If you're feeling uncomfortable, why is your father forcing this? There must be another way," Purity argued.

"Maybe I could pay the debt. I have money now."

"You are so kind, but the debt is too great. I think my father borrowed money to start the shop, but the interest on the loan was so high he could never pay it back," Natasha explained.

"I'll talk to your father myself. Maybe there is still hope."

"Father won't listen and feels there's no danger. I think he's been threatened."

Purity was adamant.

"I'm going with you to make sure this man's intentions are honorable. I'll be back tomorrow morning."

"Oh, thank you. Maybe if he realizes someone outside the family knows, then I'll be fine."

* * *

The next morning, Purity headed to town, anxious about Natasha. David and the sons followed in the shadows.

"Can I offer my fiancée a ride?" Favor called from his elegant new car as he pulled up beside her.

"I'm on my way into town."

"I need to get to the deli," she said, her brows pulled together in concern.

"You're anxious about something. I know that look well," he said.

"It's Natasha. She's being forced to pay her father's debt."

"Isn't that a family matter?" he said, trying to work out why Purity was involved.

"I'm afraid for her safety."

"Get in."

She hopped into the passenger seat and smiled at him.

"Thank you, Darling."

Favor drove to town like a madman and came to a screeching halt in front of the deli. Purity rushed in as Favor trailed behind.

"Natasha. Natasha," Purity shouted.

They looked in the kitchen and then the storage room, but no Natasha. Just then, a door creaked at the hinges and swung open down the hall. It was Natasha's father. He emerged with a prayer shawl covering his shoulders and a kippah on his head. He was pale, and his hands shook in fear.

"Where is she?" Purity demanded.

"I dropped Natasha off this morning to work as a maid. I went back later to check on her and was told to mind my own business. They threatened to kill the rest of the family if I went to the police. I don't know what to do."

Favor pushed for answers.

"Where did you take her?"

"The Wells Estate," Natasha's father replied.

"Mr. Wells," Purity repeated the name with horror.

* * *

Black crows descended on the high towers of Mr. Wells' Estate. Cracks of thunder rumbled overhead as Ahaba's face emerged from the dark clouds overhead.

"Advance! No retreat," Ahaba ordered his evil spirits.

Like long misty dark translucent fingers, the spirits descended through the atmosphere. Slowly, methodically, the evil mist seeped under doors and through open windows.

"Destroy innocence," Ahaba yelled with urgency.

A loud knock resonated on the back door of the stately mansion. An old maid hesitantly opened the door.

"What do you want?"

"Fresh dinner rolls ordered this morning," Purity blurted out and pushed her way inside.

"I didn't order dinner rolls," the stout old maid snarled with a hand on one hip.

"Mr. Wells ordered them directly," Purity said with confidence.

The maid scanned Purity's trim figure and full bustline.

"Special order, yes. But it's not the rolls he's after by the looks of you. Go up the stairs. The last door to your right." The old maid wiped her hands on a matted apron and turned away in a huff.

Purity quickly climbed the majestic staircase, hoping to avoid notice. The hallway was empty—no sign of Natasha. She lightened her step and made her way to the last door on the right.

The door was ajar. Purity watched through the slit as a man gripped the arm of a young brunette teen. He dragged her in front of Mr. Wells, who sat behind his desk. The sight of him triggered visions of Roberto's crumpled, bleeding body from the train disaster.

Downstairs in the kitchen, the old maid continued peeling a large brown potato.

"I've enough to do. Too much for interruptions," she mumbled under her breath.

An abrupt knock on the large ornate front door jarred her concentration. Another knock sounded.

"Now what? Does no one else do their job around here," she questioned, slamming the potato down. She untied the soiled apron and headed for the stately front door. Stopping by an ornate mirror, she straightened her hair before answering the door.

To her surprise, a most interesting-looking gentleman burst through the door. He had a funny-looking beard, was tall, thin, and awkward on his feet. He was slightly bent over and wore a large overcoat. On his head sat an over-sized hat cocked to one side. He pushed the maid out of the way.

"How dare you barge into this fine home. Excuse me," she barked like a dog ready to bite.

"I'm looking for Purity." He stumbled and steadied himself on a nearby table.

"I'm calling the police," the maid threatened.

"There's no one here by that name."

"You'll do nothing of the sort," the stranger commanded. With an awkward gait, he began searching the house.

A loud banging on the kitchen door distracted her attention.

"I need a raise. Mr. Wells ain't paying me enough for this mess," the maid muttered, rushing toward the loud banging.

Once she was out of sight, Jonathan pulled off the old overcoat, hat, and beard and jumped from David's shoulders. They readied their bows with the finest arrows and rushed to the French doors that opened out onto the garden. The rest of Purity's sons flowed in through the doors, armed with bows and arrows.

The old maid continued to mumble as she approached the kitchen door.

"Open up before I shoot it open," rang a masculine voice from the other side.

The threat caused her old hands to shake, and she immediately unlocked the door.

Upstairs, Purity strained to hear Mr. Wells' conversation. She peered into the office, trying to remain hidden.

"She's a real beauty. You'll make a fortune on this one," Mr. Wells bargained.

"She's a bit young. What's your price?" the man asked, holding tightly to the teen's arm with a hand that possessed only a thumb, pointer, and middle finger with rough scaling skin.

A hat hid the man's identity, but Purity recognized the stranger's grotesque deformity. It was the same claw she'd seen at Mave's of Bristol.

"The Claw... again," Purity muttered, eyes widening in alarm.

A translucent spirit wrapped around The Claw's deformed hand and squeezed it tight.

"Nothing but pain from this old thing," the stranger complained.

The spirit, appearing as a vapor of misty smoke, moved up the man's back and coiled around his neck. He winced.

"Don't worry about her age. Customers like them young." Mr. Wells sounded irritated to be bargaining over such a prize.

Another wicked spirit hovered over Mr. Wells and glided down his arms.

"What's your price?" The Claw asked while inspecting the captive's porcelain skin.

"This one's from Europe. She's never been used. No less than two hundred," Mr. Wells grumbled, lighting a cigar. He inhaled long and slow, then blew the smoke out in a casual manner.

"She's coming into her prime. Your investment will be returned many times over. Make up your mind," Mr. Wells pressed for a sale.

The man stroked the girl's shiny hair with his claw, and Purity strained to get a glimpse of the teen's face.

"Two hundred dollars, cash, or the deals off," Mr. Wells said, determined to seal the deal.

Violent hands grabbed Purity from behind. She dropped the basket and threw wild fists at a guard dressed in a black suit.

"Get your hands off of me!" she yelled as the guard wrestled her to the floor.

Mr. Wells and The Claw were startled by the commotion. The bidder let go of his captive's arm and climbed out the side window, escaping down the fire escape.

The girl ran from the office, but the guard who held Purity snagged her.

Mr. Wells sat his cigar in an ashtray and grabbed a gun from the desk drawer. He rose quickly and rushed from the office.

"Let us go," Purity yelled, picking up the basket of rolls from the floor.

"Not so loud, or I'll kill you both," Mr. Wells declared with a raspy voice. He pointed the gun at his prey.

"Don't worry, boss. I've got 'em," the guard said proudly and dragged them into the office.

"The dinner rolls you ordered," Purity said, throwing the basket at Mr. Wells' feet.

"You look familiar." He squinted his beady eyes and studied her features. Then he sneered at the awful memory.

"Ah, now I remember. It's too bad you never made it to Shanghai. But I hear congrats are in order. You've been a busy girl, snapping up Bristol's most eligible bachelor and winning a stack of cash."

He took in her supple curves and soft hair.

"Forget about getting married. It's not what it's cracked up to be. Let me take care of you. And we'll both forget how you murdered my dear friend, Roberto."

"You can't pin that on me."

Mr. Wells reached for his smoldering cigar, resting in the ashtray, and slowly inhaled another long drag.

"I'm a very powerful man with very powerful friends. Normally I'm the forgiving type, but I'm making an exception for you." He blew out a puff of smoke, clouding the room.

"What's your name?" Purity whispered to the teen beside her.

The guard slapped the teen before she could answer.

"Her name is not your business," Mr. Wells stated through the fading smoke.

"Selling the innocent like meat at the market. You'll pay for your sins," Purity raged in anger.

"I'm just an employer, putting people to work. There's a demand, and I'm the supplier," Mr. Wells clarified.

"I'd rather die than make you a penny," Purity argued.

"Get the wrong customer, and that's easy, but only after I get my share. You cost me another sale, so I'll take what I want, for all the inconvenience, past and present."

"Where's Natasha, you slave driver?" Purity screamed in desperation.

"Natasha, who?" he said, playing dumb.

"Tell me where Natasha is," Purity demanded.

"You're pretty confident for a defenseless ballroom dancer. Natasha's working off some family debt, that's all. Now, it's time for you two beauties to turn some profits. Time is money." Mr. Wells signaled his guard to take them away.

They fought the guard with all their might, but he was too strong.

Mr. Wells grabbed a syringe from his desk drawer and moved toward Purity.

"This should help you remember who's boss."

He jabbed the needle at her, but Purity ducked. The needle sunk into the teen's deltoid muscle. Wells injected the sedative with a snarl of satisfaction.

"Stupid girl. You'll be wishing you had the drugs when you start work."

The teen staggered as the drug took effect.

"Rot in hell," Purity yelled as the guard dragged both of them down the hall.

The guard held them tight as they descended the staircase. Purity looked up and relief washed over her. Favor stood at the bottom of the stairs with a gun in each hand. The Ring of Grace floated above him, their fiery arrows ready to strike the enemy.

"Let my bride go," Favor demanded.

The guard didn't budge.

"I don't work for you."

Sergio shot a flaming arrow through the guard's head, instantly confusing the guard. He swayed with vertigo.

"Step aside, or your blushing bride-to-be is a goner," Mr. Wells threatened from the landing. He pointed his gun at Purity.

The child angels fired arrows at the evil spirits that clung to the guard and Mr. Wells. The arrows hit with such force the men momentarily doubled over in pain.

Mr. Wells pulled himself up on the stair railing.

"It's too bad we meet under these circumstances, Mr. Wisedor. I'm afraid you'll have to forego the honeymoon. Your fiancée is going to jail for murder."

Rocco and Sergio shot flaming arrows through the hand that held the gun. Mr. Wells writhed in pain and switched the gun to the other hand.

"Your threats mean nothing. We have our own witness and a gun smeared with blood found the night of the competition. Maybe you can help the authorities find the owner of the gun," Favor replied.

"I don't know what you're talking about. Now stop obstructing justice. These young ladies have committed crimes and are on their way to pay restitution," Mr. Wells insisted.

The guard steadied himself, pulled out a knife, and pressed it to the teen's throat.

"Stand aside."

"Don't hurt the girl. I'm backing up." Favor slowly backed down the staircase.

When he reached the bottom, out of nowhere, soaring arrows flew over his head, striking the guard and Mr. Wells. The guard staggered back, reeling in pain, and released the captives.

Favor turned and saw Purity's sons put away their bows. He nodded in gratitude, and they raced out the way they had come.

Police officers stormed through the front door and arrested the wounded men.

Purity consoled the distraught teen who was sick from the drugs. She breathed a sigh of relief, knowing one person was saved from a life of abuse and misery.

"She's been drugged," Purity warned the officer who helped the victim out to a police car.

"We'll take her to the hospital and question her later," the officer said with compassion.

"If she has nowhere to go, we can help," Purity offered.

"There's also a missing young woman, Natasha Weinstein. She was brought here this morning and has vanished. I believe Mr. Wells can help us locate her."

The officer took down Natasha's name.

"We'll get it out of him. We've been investigating Wells for some time. He'll need a good attorney."

Favor rushed to Purity and held her tight.

"I don't know what I would have done if I'd lost you," He whispered in her ear.

"But you didn't. Captain was with us." She leaned back and smiled up at him.

Sold

Chapter 31

ON THE OUTSKIRTS of Bristol, black crows gathered on the roof of an old, dilapidated building. Fancy cars surrounded the premises, looking out of place in the muddy parking lot.

Ahaba's evil spirits descended onto the roof amid the crows, appearing as large menacing creatures with sagging skin and wild eyes. They raised hackles of disturbing laughter through the atmosphere.

Inside, the old warehouse was dark, except for dim sunlight that beamed through cracks in the roof and a few oil lamps that illuminated the center of the room.

The dark spirits on the roof seeped through the rafters and hovered over the group of lustful men lurking in the shadows.

Natasha stood on a block in the center of the room, eyes downcast. Only sparse linen covered her shapely figure. Her wrists and ankles were bound in chains.

"This is Natasha, a specimen of European beauty at its finest," the auctioneer rattled.

"The bidding starts at one hundred dollars. Who'll be the first bidder?" the auctioneer asked, watching for hands waving in the shadows.

Voices rang out from the dimly lit room, faces undetected.

"One hundred," answered a man with a gruff voice.

"Two hundred," someone else bid.

"Make that two hundred seventy-five," another man chimed in.

The room fell silent as the evil investors looked for better deals.

"Do I hear three hundred?" the auctioneer called, but there was only silence.

"Sold to the highest bidder for two hundred and seventy-five dollars."

"I'll fight you, bastards," Natasha wailed, struggling against the iron chains.

She was pulled from the auction block and rushed down a dark hallway. A door creaked open, and Natasha's captors pushed her inside, where a young woman stripped off her sparse clothing and replaced it with a simple robe. The woman's wrists were also chained.

Natasha stared intently at the woman, who looked withered with hopelessness.

"I know you," Natasha said, holding back tears.

"They all think they know me. I can't help you, girl. See these? I'm chained like a dog, just like you. There's no escape for either of us," snarled the woman. She had aged beyond her years, her once lustrous hair now dried and brittle. An aroma of alcohol oozed from her pores and permeated her breath.

"I said, I know you. You're Rachel." Despite her haggard appearance, Natasha recognized her old friend from the long journey to America.

The young woman eyed her with suspicion.

"I haven't been Rachel for many years," she said, trying to place Natasha.

"I'm Natasha. We traveled to America together over ten years ago. You were supposed to marry, but we never heard from you again. Our prayers are answered. You're alive," Natasha exclaimed, reaching for Rachel's hands.

"Is it really you? But you're wrong. I'm not alive. I died the day I was sold. I'm what you call the living dead," Rachel said, melting into tears.

They hugged each other in deep sorrow. Rachel eventually collapsed in a nearby chair, and Natasha sat by her feet.

"I worked for seven years, servicing up to fifteen men a day, depending on what they wanted. Twelve to fourteen hours a day, with little rest and only two meals a day. Three years ago, I was set on fire by a john who wasn't satisfied." Rachel stood and dropped her robe, exposing deep, rippled scarring on her back, arms, and chest.

He pulled out a bottle of flammable fluid and poured it on me. I tried to fight him off, but I was so tired. Then he lit a match.

Her body shook involuntarily as she remembered that day.

"I'm worth nothing like this, but they still use me," she said, fighting back the tears.

"How did you end up here?"

"My father borrowed money from Wells to start the deli, but he could never pay it back. Wells came to collect, and I'm the payment," Natasha lamented.

"Mr. Wells never forgets a deal," Rachel acknowledged.

"My parents would never have agreed to this had they known," Natasha said with deep pain.

"I was branded to prove ownership that first night." Rachel exposed the letter 'M' branded deeply into her right shoulder.

"My owner used me all night long, rapist pig. The next day I was gang-raped. They call it breaking a girl in. The worse thing for me was the doctor."

"The doctor," Natasha repeated.

Rachel recalled the nightmare.

"A doctor came to my room about a week later. He had a black case in his hand and wore a white coat. Said I needed surgery."

"For what?" Natasha asked.

"Virgins make more money. He was paid to sew me up like a virgin again. Two men came in and held me down while he sewed me up. He came again and again." She stopped speaking—her eyes vacant as though lost in a living hell.

After several moments, Rachel grabbed a bottle of hard alcohol and raised it to her lips. She took a long guzzle and then set it down. It was as though she was numbing her heart to all the pain.

"I get the cargo ready before they're sent out to work. My heart breaks, knowing their fate, your fate, our fate. My dear Natasha," Rachel mourned.

"Contact Purity at Shadow Brook Estate. You must remember Purity and her mother, Naomi. They were your friends. She'll rescue us," Natasha insisted.

"How could I ever forget them? Naomi, she loved me like a mother. If only I had listened to her warnings. And Purity, I'm sure she's grown into a beautiful woman, just like you." Rachel fell quiet again, this time reliving sweet memories.

She snapped out of it and turned back to the job at hand.

"Don't get your hopes up, Natasha. Hope only makes it harder. Whatever you do, don't forget, the code to the elevator where you're going is 0, 02, 20. Do you hear me? It may save your life," Rachel warned.

Before she could say another word, a man entered the room. It was Dagon, the former floor manager at the Wisedor Dish Factory.

"That's enough. She won't need pampering where she's going." His tone was laced with hatred.

"Where am I going?" Natasha asked, afraid.

"To the depths of despair when they're done with you. Hell will seem like a holiday," Dagon said with a snarl.

"Please, help me. I shouldn't be here. Contact my father at Weinstein Deli. Tell him where I'm going," Natasha begged.

"He's the one who sold you," Dagon hissed.

"You liar," Natasha protested.

Rachel turned away, powerless to intervene as Dagon tightened the chains on Natasha's hands and blindfolded her with a scarf. She protested with such force he had to carry her out.

* * *

The driver of a wagon gave the horse one last whip as he pulled into the back driveway of Mave's of Bristol.

Still blindfolded in the back of the wagon, Natasha listened for any clues to where they had taken her. Loud music and the frightful sounds of men brawling spilled out of an open door.

A bouncer with large menacing hands pulled Natasha from the wagon. He carried her into the kitchen and opened a narrow door that revealed a set of stairs. His boots thudded methodically on the carpeted steps, sounding almost like a death march as he led her to the second story.

Her head and neck ached as her body dangled over his right shoulder. He opened a hotel door and laid her on the bed. His rough fingers unlocked the chains on Natasha's wrists and pulled the blindfold from her eyes.

"Welcome to hell," the bouncer joked, exposing yellowed tobacco-stained teeth.

"No, please. Don't leave me to die," Natasha begged.

He slammed the door shut. The keys rattled as he locked the door. She balled up on the bed and sobbed.

A few hours passed, and Natasha dozed in fitful sleep.

Again, she heard keys rattling outside the door. The lock turned, and Mave entered, holding a candle on a stand. Her right hand was bandaged with blood-stained gauze. She clutched it to her body as though in severe pain.

Natasha gasped at the sight of her, recognizing Mave from the attempted kidnapping and realizing the nightmare was just beginning.

"Let me see your face," Mave commanded. She looked Natasha over, saying, "I hope to be good friends if you cooperate. You can start work tonight or tomorrow. The choice is yours."

"What's the job description?" Natasha asked with anger.

"Pleasing the customers. Simple enough for such a beauty," Mave jested.

"Rot in hell, witch," Natasha spat out.

"Your parents did this to you, not me. If you don't cooperate, we know where to find them. I'd hate for anything bad to happen to them because of you."

"My father was blackmailed. He would never agree to this," Natasha protested.

"Do you remember me? I came for you ten years ago. You were collateral for your daddy's little loan, but your friend got in the way. Be grateful Mr. Wells was feeling generous back then. You're worth much more now with some curves."

"You won't get away with this."

"I think you should start tomorrow. It'll give you some time to think about your precious mommy and daddy. It's dinner and a hot bath for you, then rest up. You're going to need it," Mave insisted, cracking a sinister smile.

As she turned to leave, Natasha grabbed a porcelain figurine from the nearby table and struck Mave in the back of the head. Mave withered to the floor, unconscious.

Natasha slowly opened the door and peered out. She ducked back in as a guard dragged two small boys down the hallway.

"No, please, no more. It hurts too much. Don't make us do what we hate," the older boy cried.

The guard knocked on a door, and a sinister-looking man pulled the boys into the room. Natasha could hear their screams of terror as the door closed.

The guard returned to the elevator and pressed a code into a panel. The black wrought iron elevator doors opened with a clattering sound. He stepped in and descended to the main lobby.

Natasha's heart broke for the boys. She couldn't just leave them. She ventured into the hallway and crept along to the room where the boys were deposited. She thought for a moment and then stepped back and kicked the flimsy door open.

The man inside was undressing, his bulging, naked belly hanging over his pants. He lunged at her in protest, but she kicked with a vengeance, and he doubled over.

She grabbed the boys, and they headed down the hall for the elevator. With a trembling hand, she entered the combination Rachel had given her. The elevator doors opened, and they rushed inside, panting like caged animals. The wrought iron doors shook as they rattled closed.

The angry customer caught up to them and banged on the doors, feeling robbed from forbidden pleasure.

"How dare you. I paid for them," the predator yelled.

"Stay away, you animal," the younger boy yelled.

As the elevator started down to the main lobby and the man disappeared from view, the older boy turned to Natasha.

"Thank you, but they've already ruined us."

The elevator doors clanked as they opened, causing some heads to turn. Two large guards spotted them.

"Run," Natasha yelled.

She threw chairs at the guards to slow their pace, but two other men lunged at them. The boys and Natasha fought with all their strength.

"Help. We're slaves," Natasha yelled to the patrons who glanced at each other but didn't move to help.

The guards overpowered the boys and beat Natasha into submission.

* * *

That same night, Purity slept in her bed. Bright Star, glowing in radiant colors, picked her up and took her to Keenan and Valor on the mansion rooftop. Purity awoke to find herself nestled upon Valor's soft feathers. With a running start, the eagles lifted into the air.

On Purity's way to the New Earth, she saw that the universe raged in battle. Ahaba's forces moved against Captain of the Lord's Army. Swords clanked as enemy lines collided in violent clashes.

Bright Star flew next to the eagles and circled them in a vortex of rainbow colors.

"Danger's ahead," Bright announced with concern.

"There's no going around it. We must battle through," Valor yelled to Keenan.

Bright Star created a sword of fire with a golden handle. They swooped down, appearing as a being of light, and dropped it into Purity's hand.

"You are called to fight the Captain's battles."

"I'm not afraid," Purity said with confidence.

Ahaba sensed Purity's presence and yelled with loathing, "Get Purity! She stops our killing."

Captain of the Lord's Army heard the plot and signaled for the Ring of Grace. The five angels fought off a multitude of dark spirits that hoped to cause mortal harm to Purity. Even so, enemy fire pelted her, knocking the sword from her hand.

"I need a weapon," Purity cried out.

Josiah flew alongside her and dropped another sword in her hands. While clinging to Valor's back, she slashed at several dark foes. The sheer force of the weapon knocked Purity off of the eagle.

To everyone's horror, she tumbled into the vast atmosphere. Bright Star circled back and expanded, trying to create a safety net for a soft landing. Keenan and Valor released thunderous squawks to alert the child angels who fought furiously against the enemy.

At the last minute, Sergio, Rocco, Kaleb, Josiah, and Toby caught hold of her, preventing her from slamming into a gassy meteorite and its dusty ice cloud several thousand miles long.

"We should have warned you the weapons are powerful," Rocco said, grinning.

Captain of the Lord's Army hit the enemy with powerful lightning bolts, destroying everything in his path. He took out major generals in Ahaba's army who dared to stand against him.

The Captain beamed with pride as he caught sight of Purity riding on Valor's back against the enemy. He had not opened her eyes to see him, but he deposited his thought into her heart.

"Be strong in my power."

"Yes, Captain. I will," Purity said, recognizing his still small voice.

A flash of lightning sparked from Purity's sword as she struck the enemy with empowered blows. Ahaba pointed his bony finger and sent strong opposition her way.

The Captain, knowing all things, whistled for the archangels Michael and Gabriel.

"Protect our guest," the Captain commanded.

The archangels flew to Keenan and Valor, warding off attackers while Bright Star blasted the enemy lines with balls of fire.

Ahaba despised the incompetence of his underlings. Purity demolished vast numbers of his ranks with her furious blows. He decided to take matters into his own hands. With frenetic speed, Ahaba headed Purity's way, spitting arrows of fire.

The Captain blew his trumpet, summoning the archangels. The five of them stood together as a shield of protection and forced Ahaba back in humiliation.

"You're defeated. The Captain rebuke you," Raphael shouted to the evil forces.

Ahaba retreated in haste, and his army followed behind.

"Time to celebrate another victory," the Captain said. Raising his hand toward the child angels, their wings grew bigger.

Captain rode on his white stallion, heading toward the New Earth. His vast army followed behind, with the archangels bringing up the rear.

Purity remained on Valor's back, firmly embedded within his feathers. Bright Star retrieved the sword from her hand. At an incredible speed, the group of travelers passed galaxies, giant planets, and colossal star formations.

Once again, they descended into the misty atmosphere of the New Earth. Purity fell into a fitful sleep and was gently laid in a sailboat by the archangels Raphael and Ariel while the Ring of Grace hovered above. Slowly, the boat moved down the sparkling river.

Clarity nestled her mother's face in her small hands. Purity woke with a start.

"What's wrong, Mother? You look troubled," Clarity said, reading Purity's disturbed expression.

"Clarity, I need your help. My friend Natasha is missing. I don't know where to find her."

"I can take you to your book where His thoughts are revealed. Maybe she's in the writings," Clarity offered.

"Take me quickly," Purity answered with urgency.

Clarity hopped up to maneuver the boat.

After a long journey, they ran aground on the river's edge. Clarity took Purity by the hand, leading her into a vast, majestic wilderness.

"I need to find Papa. He would know what to do."

"Be quiet, Mother, and save your energy," Clarity scolded.

As the hours passed, Purity grew tired, and each step grew heavier.

"I can't go another step."

Clarity urged, "You must trust and believe." At her words, the atmosphere changed, and a misty fog surrounded them.

"I believe. Lead the way," Purity said, trying to catch her breath.

"This way," Clarity said in a hushed voice. She pulled her mother along by the hand.

"You never get tired, Clarity. I'll get no rest raising you. You'll be the end of me," Purity joked.

"His thoughts never get tired," Clarity answered sweetly.

They pushed heavy foliage aside and entered the enchanted garden with the giant flowers.

Purity rushed to the pond in the center of it and scooped pure water into her mouth.

"Restore me, living waters."

After quenching her thirst, she rose and turned around. There was the book entitled, His Thoughts Revealed. It remained suspended in mid-air, about ten yards away. Purity remembered the first time she'd seen the book, but that time she'd not been allowed to read it.

"Dear Captain, can I read it this time?" Purity asked.

"His Thoughts Revealed, the goal of our search. Your shoes, Mother. This is a holy place," Clarity said. Kicking off her shoes, she approached the book.

Purity removed her shoes and approached at a much slower pace than Clarity.

"Do we kneel or bow in prayer?" Purity asked, feeling apprehensive.

"Relax. The Captain's done all the work. He makes it easy to understand," Clarity said confidently.

Majestic music filled the air. Purity brushed her hands against some of the large flowers, and they began rocking to the tranquil music.

"It's so peaceful. It's a place where troubles are forgotten," Purity said, tearing up.

"Life is simple here," Clarity said.

The closer they came to the book, the weightier the atmosphere became with a tangible peace.

"I can feel the atmosphere," Purity said.

"The Captain lives in the air. To breathe is to inhale his life-giving power," Clarity said, taking a deep breath.

The eager child pried the large cover open, and the pages turned as if a mighty wind blew each page with furious force. Purity stopped the fluttering pages with eager hands and began reading the Captain's thoughts revealed.

The first entry was dated June 5, 1907.

"But that was a few years ago."

She searched more recent dates, then read aloud an entry dated May 11, 1908.

"She's developing the gift of teaching. Her sons are growing in my knowledge and wisdom. I have great plans for Purity's life and will give her the strength to achieve them all. She must come to me for everything. I am the one who fulfills desires and gives every talent because I have placed each one in her heart."

"He's given me his desires," Purity said, amazed.

"The Captain makes life worth living," Clarity boasted.

Purity turned to pages marked with the year 1909. She read on, "I warned her to stay away from Mave after I helped her rescue Ellie. She needs to obey my specific directions."

Another entry read, "I sent my servant, the porter, to rescue Purity from a terrible fate. It was my will to spare her life. I will use her as my vessel to rescue many lives."

She turned a few more pages and read, "Purity's in love with Favor. He's the one I've chosen for her. Together they will bring many into my light. One puts a thousand to flight, two ten thousand. They are my will for each other."

"The Captain approves of Favor."

"Favor must be a good man."

"He's your earthly father because I'm going to marry him."

Clarity smiled at her.

"No matter who my earthly father is, the Captain is my heavenly King," Clarity gushed with complete devotion.

Purity turned back to the book and read another entry.

"I prevented Mave from murdering my daughter Purity. David, my son, was empowered to shoot the perfect shot as my Ring of Grace guided the arrow. My will was accomplished on this spectacular day of victory at the U.S. Ballroom Championships. I gifted her feet."

Purity's knees almost gave way.

"What? David and a Ring of Grace saved me the night Stephen and I won the dance competition. Who's this Ring of Grace he's talking about?" Purity questioned in awe.

"The child angels you've seen. The Captain knew you would need more than one. He's given you five guardian angels," Clarity answered.

"Yes, I have seen them, but I never realized they were assigned to me. I must be a project to have five personal angels. Have you met them, Clarity?"

"Of course. His thoughts know everything."

"I'm sorry. I have to remember you are fully formed in the Captain's mind."

Purity read on.

"Purity's gravely concerned for her friend Natasha. I hope she'll ask me where to find her. She needs to look in a place where the dancing's free, but souls are sold for profit."

268

Purity gasped.

"Dear Captain. Of course. Mave's of Bristol has Natasha. Why didn't I think of it?"

Purity felt faint as she stared into Clarity's eyes.

"Mother, don't go. Don't go," Clarity's voice trailed off.

Purity felt herself spinning and spinning until all was a blur. She was translated back to the old earth that was passing away.

Purity woke at the crack of dawn in her little cottage bedroom. She threw the covers off and dressed quickly. A loud rap sounded on the cottage's front door. She peeked out the window and saw an errand boy wearing a blue uniform and matching cap. Perplexed, she opened the door.

"Miss Purity Thomas... co... vich of Bristol?" he struggled to pronounce her last name.

"Yes, boy," Purity said.

He handed over a small envelope. She tore it open and read hastily.

Dear Purity,

Your friend Natasha has been sold as a sex slave.
She's locked away at Mave's of Bristol Hotel.
I hope you remember me. Please help us if you can.
I'm locked away at the Metacom Hotel.

Your friend forever,
Rachel

"Could this be Rachel who disappeared years ago? This was dated yesterday," Purity thought aloud.

"Do you know who sent this note?" Purity asked with urgency.

"No, but it was sent from Metacom Hotel," the boy replied.

"Thank you," Purity said. She dug into her purse and handed him a coin for his trouble.

"Thank you, miss," he replied and left.

Purity slammed the cottage door in a fit of anxiety.

"Captain, it's just as you revealed. Mave has Natasha. Angels don't fail me now. I need you to fight for those in chains," Purity cried out, kneeling on the old wooden floor.

Flashes of lightning surrounded the small cottage. The Ring of Grace responded to Purity's cry. They materialized as translucent children and peered through the smudged, dusty windows of the cottage. Josiah, Sergio, Rocco, Toby, and Kaleb watched Purity continue to call out for help.

They rolled into a ball of light, shot through the cottage walls, then surrounded Purity in the form of child warriors.

"My guardian angels who help me in all my distress," Purity said, glancing at each face.

"It is as you say," Sergio responded.

"I need your help. Give me a plan to fight this evil," she pleaded.

"May the Captain give you his brilliance in all your trials," Rocco said.

The atmosphere in the room became weighty as it had on New Earth. Extending fiery hands, the angels transferred the Captain's wisdom and creativity to Purity's mind. They remained for several minutes, then rolled into a ball of fire and shot through the roof.

Above, Purity heard horses galloping and warriors shouting. They rallied to fight against Ahaba's ghastly strongholds in the spirit realm.

"Captain, give me the victory. I'll go for you, and if I perish, I perish," Purity cried out.

Far above in the atmosphere, Captain of the Lord's Army shouted, "Advance!" Purity could hear the heavenly armies and felt strengthened. Then a vision played through her mind, and she knew what to do.

* * *

Purity approached Mave's of Bristol wearing a wiry gray wig and a scarf that covered her face. She hoped her disguise as an old woman would work.

Two black crows swooped down and pecked at her with sharp beaks.

"Ahaba and his forces," Purity thought and batted them away.

She stepped into the kitchen to find Chin Lu arguing with the cook.

"What this? Tastes like dirt," Chin Lu complained, slamming a bowl of soup in the nearby sink.

"Delicious fresh muffins for sale," Purity called in a gruff old voice. Chin Lu turned to her.

"How much, ole lady?"

The kitchen emptied as the insulted cook left, and the busboy went looking for dirty dishes. Purity dropped the basket and pulled off the wig and scarf. She dragged Chin Lu into the side pantry with a knife to her throat.

"Where's Natasha?" Purity asked, forcing the blade deep into her neck, almost cutting it.

"Purity, my old friend." Chin Lu could barely spit the words out.

"Lead the way," Purity threatened.

Chin Lu held up her hands in surrender, and Purity pulled back the knife. Chin Lu picked up a match from a small shelf, then lit a small oil lamp. She waved a hand and led Purity up a dark, hidden, narrow stairwell. Pulling keys from her pocket, Chin Lu unlocked a small door leading to a long shadow-filled hallway.

Black crows landed on the roof of Mave's of Bristol as dark, misty clouds in the shape of a claw rolled in. Ahaba's forces heckled from within the clouds, chanting of revenge.

"Revenge. Revenge," Ahaba shouted, spraying venom and malice over his army. They howled with hatred and landed on the rooftop one by one. Dark creatures, as though from the abyss of hell itself, drooled and sputtered vulgarities.

Captain and the Lord's Army circled above with his mighty warriors.

"Mave belongs to me. I can't wait to take her to hell," Ahaba yelled.

"She refused me long ago. My strength is with those who are willing," the Captain replied.

"Few are willing after we're done with them," Ahaba mocked, laughing at lost souls.

"To those I call, the victory is given," replied the Captain.

"I want Mave. Let her die today. My army desires to feed on her bones," Ahaba asked—almost begged.

"A very tempting proposition. Who knows, she may change her mind about me," the Captain said with a heavy heart.

"I doubt it," Ahaba sneered.

As they walked the dimly lit hallway of Mave's of Bristol, menacing howls of tortured slaves erupted from behind closed doors. Chin Lu selected a long key from the ring, stopped in front of a particular door, and quickly unlocked it.

Purity rushed inside, welcomed by screams of terror. She had interrupted a young man's attack and cruel beating. Natasha's face was bloodied, and her clothing ripped by the assailant.

Purity stalked toward him with her knife. The man fled, leaving his jacket and wallet full of cash behind.

"Coward," Chin Lu yelled after him.

Natasha gasped with relief.

"I knew you'd find me."

"Let's get out of here," Purity said in haste.

China Lu grabbed the man's wallet and stuffed the cash into her pocket.

The three women ran for the back staircase, but Natasha hesitated mid-way there. She pointed to a door.

"We have to help them."

Purity nodded to Chin Lu, who unlocked the door. Purity and Natasha raced in with shouts of war. The boys screamed in shock. Purity and Natasha began beating the partially undressed man, who withered under their blows.

"You have no right. I paid good money for the boys," the molester sounded in rage.

Natasha grabbed the boys, who were stripped down to their underwear. Purity picked up their clothing for a swift exit. Chin Lu locked a bolt on the outside of the door as they left, assuring the man could not follow.

"Let me out of here," the man yelled, banging on the door.

The group raced down the narrow dark staircase. When they reached the bottom, Mave was there with a gun in her left hand.

"Chin Lu, I'm surprised you're helping criminals?"

Chin Lu backed away in fear.

"Kidnapping again, Purity? I won't be robbed. You owe me your life for my son's life," Mave whined.

"Your son?" Purity asked.

"Roberto. You killed him without mercy on the train. Now, you and your friends will get the same," she threatened.

The boys clung to Natasha, anticipating a gory death.

"Mr. Wells is spreading lies again. Your son was struck down by his own hand," Purity said.

Mave pointed the gun at Purity's head, her fingers itching to pull the trigger.

"Revenge. Sweet revenge," a wispy spirit whispered in Mave's ear.

Favor appeared out of the shadows, tackling the madwoman from behind as she pulled the trigger. The bullet ricocheted from the wall, narrowly missing her target.

Mave screamed in rage as Natasha kicked the gun from her hand. Chin Lu picked it up and pressed it to her slave owner's head.

"Don't do it, Chin Lu. You're too close to freedom," Purity warned.

Mave groaned in agony, expecting a bullet and lights out. A few evil spirits from Ahaba's army sensed death and flew in anxiously awaiting Mave's wicked spirit.

"Hell is waiting," they chanted.

One misty spirit whispered in Chin Lu's ear, "Revenge. To hell with your torturer."

Chin Lu agonized. Then after several seconds of indecision, she pulled the gun away and handed it to Purity.

"It's my turn to stop the misery. You're not worth jail time."

Favor hurried outside to flag down a policeman. Moments later, officers swarmed the building. They took everyone in for questioning.

* * *

At the police station, wild arguments broke out as the officers tried to make sense of everyone's story.

"Arrest Purity. She murdered my son. I have an eyewitness," Mave raged.

"You're the murderer. Their blood screams out—those you abused and killed," Purity objected.

"She die in prison," Chin Lu said to the officers, pointing to Mave.

"You little whore. Remember, I know where your family lives," Mave threatened Chin Lu.

"Your threats… no longer… hold me captive," Chin Lu stuttered.

Purity pulled the note from her pocket and handed it to one of the detectives.

"My friend Rachel was kidnapped ten years ago. She was forced to be a sex slave and has no way of escaping. This note was sent from Metacom Hotel."

"Can we rescue her tonight?" Natasha asked with urgency.

"We need to move fast before word gets out Mave's of Bristol was busted," one of the officers advised.

"Rachel's owners may move her. Then she'll be lost forever."

A sergeant stepped toward Purity.

"If you were there when Roberto was killed, you're going to need, you're going to need a good attorney. And stay out of our way tonight, or someone is going to get hurt." With that warning, he left to round up officers to join him at the Metacom Hotel.

An hour later, after questioning, Purity, Natasha, and Favor left the police station. They were determined to see Rachel freed despite the warnings to stay away.

Favor drove them to Metacom Hotel. He pulled out his gun as he got out of the car.

"Stay here," he told them.

"I'm going with you. I know what Rachel looks like," Purity demanded.

He reached into the back seat, pulled out another pistol, and handed the weapon over to his fiancée.

"Natasha, you need to sit this one out," Purity advised.

"You remember Rachel as a beautiful young woman. You'd never recognize her now. I'm going in," Natasha insisted.

"Let's go. There's no time to argue," Favor asserted.

The three of them climbed the back stairs of the hotel to the second floor. Looking both ways, they started down the empty hallway and started knocking on doors.

Minutes later, the police swarmed the building. Some climbed the backfire escape, while others surrounded the building. Several officers stormed the front doors, entering through the lobby. Sirens rang out from the streets, and gunfire was heard throughout the hotel as large bouncers fought the officers.

Throngs of half-dressed businessmen and mobster types fled. Many were handcuffed and arrested on the streets.

Favor, Purity, and Natasha continued banging on one hotel door after the other.

"Open up. Rachel. Rachel, are you in there," Natasha yelled.

"Rachel, freedom's calling. Open up," Purity added.

As they walked away from one door, the sound of heavy fists pounded from the inside.

"Purity. Purity, it's me, Rachel. Help me—the door's locked from the outside. Get me out of here," Rachel yelled through agonizing tears.

"Stand back," Favor yelled through the door. He held up his pistol and shot the lock off the door handle. Then with a kick, Favor broke through the door. They rushed inside to find Rachel crumpled on the floor. Purity was appalled at her aged, worn features. She saw the scarring on her face, neck, and arms.

"My God. What have they done to you?" Purity gasped, remembering Rachel as a fresh, gorgeous teen.

"I'm a hideous sight."

Purity helped her stand and hugged her.

"You're safe with us. Freedom has arrived."

"I'm free. Dear God, you set me free," Rachel cried.

An officer entered the room.

"We're taking the whore in," the officer demanded, pointing his gun at Rachel.

Purity begged to be heard.

"She's innocent. She's not a prostitute but a sex slave. She's been a chained captive for years."

"Then I'll need her statement. Everyone out. We're going to the station," he said.

Indian Country

Chapter 32

NAOMI RAN TO the cottage, the front page of the morning newspaper flapping in her hands. Once inside, she rushed into Purity's bedroom.

"Purity, wake up. Please read this to me," Naomi fussed as Purity rolled over.

"Mama, I'm sleeping," she moaned.

"Read it, girl," her mother insisted.

Purity rubbed crusty sleep from her eyes and cleared a groggy throat.

"Give me a second." She sat up, grabbed the newspaper, and tried to focus her eyes.

"It says Mave's of Bristol Hotel, a blight of crime for the city of Bristol, was raided on allegations of human slavery. Mr. Wells and Mave Murdock are accused of buying slaves and selling the victims for labor and sex slavery. The famous U.S. Ballroom Champion, Purity Thomascovich, and her equally famous fiancé, Favor Wisedor of Shadow Brook Estate, played a vital role in closing the establishment by providing key evidence and witnesses. Sex and labor slaves were rescued after months and even years of abuse and torture."

"Why didn't you tell me? No, it's best I don't know these things," Naomi said, second-guessing her train of thought.

"Mama, I'm called to set the captives free."

"I know, and I'm so proud of you. It's just—I can't lose you too," Naomi said, shaking her head.

"You won't, Mama. Heaven's watching out for us," Purity whispered, still exhausted from the night before.

"I forgot to tell you. A telegram from the World Ballroom Dance Championships came yesterday." Naomi reached into her apron pocket and pulled it out.

Purity grabbed for the telegram in haste and tore it open. She read aloud.

"To: Miss Purity Thomascovich
Shadow Brook Estate
Bristol, Rhode Island

From: Pierre De Rhynel
President, World Ballroom Dance Championships
Paris, France

Dear Miss Purity Thomascovich,

It is a great honor to invite the Bristol team, winners of the U.S. Ballroom Dance Competitions, to the World Ballroom Dance Championships in Paris, France.

Event Information:

The World Ballroom Dance Championships
Date/Time: November 7, 1909 at 7pm
Location: Held at the prestigious Dansante Theater, Paris, France.

Please contact us by September 30th if you choose to participate in this event.

Sincerely,
Pierre De Rhynel"

Naomi chuckled and sat down in a nearby chair.

"It's more good news and coming our way for a change. You won't hear any more complaining from me. I promise."

"It does feel good, doesn't it?"

"The competition is six months away, so we've got time to figure everything out. I'm putting my notice in right away. Goodbye, Shadow Brook Estate and Mrs. Wisedor. The old Warner farm is for sale, I think."

"The farm would be perfect for the school," Purity acknowledged.

Rachel came into the bedroom with a cup of tea and placed it on the nightstand. Purity gazed at her rescued friend.

"You're welcome to stay, Rachel. You're a part of this family," Purity said with warmth.

"That means the world to me. It's going to take time to realize I'm free—no more chains, locked doors, and beatings. I was going to kill myself. Then God sent Natasha. I believed if I could just get to you, my nightmare would end. When I heard you pounding on the door, it was like heaven knocking," Rachel said with gratefulness.

Naomi rose and hugged Rachel like a daughter.

"How did you get the note out to me?" Purity asked.

"I bribed a john to send it. He was just finishing up his dirty business and leaving a room. I was making rounds, checking on the girls. I bribed him with some money I hid away. I thought for sure he'd take the money and throw the note away. I must have prayed all night," Rachel said with tears.

"Looks like heaven heard your prayers," Purity said, relieved.

"I'm so thankful," Rachel said.

* * *

That afternoon, Purity's thoughts were full of the school and helping the poor children of Bristol. It looked like one of her dreams might finally be coming true.

As she stepped off the cottage porch to go for a walk, Purity stopped in her tracks. Chin Lu stood before her, holding a basket of muffins.

"It's my turn to give. Chin Lu knows how to cook. I help the boys," she insisted.

Purity gave Chin Lu one of the warmest hugs she could remember.

"Go on in. Mama and Rachel would enjoy a fresh-baked muffin. And don't you worry, my sons are going to love you," Purity urged.

Chin Lu went inside, and Purity started out toward the wide-open spaces of the estate.

A crisp wind blew through her hair and clothing. Sailboats and seafaring ships headed for Bristol harbor dotted the sparkling water of Narragansett. Seagulls flew overhead, and a quiet solace moved through her body. Just knowing Rachel, Natasha, Ellie, Chin Lu, and so many others had been saved from a life of doom restored her soul. It was amazing that even Chin Lu would find her way to Son's Camp.

Purity inhaled and exhaled deeply. The blue skies overhead poured warm sunlight like an open cathedral. She prayed under her breath, "You heard my prayers, Captain. Everything is coming to pass. We're invited to France for the World Ballroom Championships. I can hardly take it all in. Of course, none of it's a surprise to you." Purity walked through the acreage in open conversation with heaven, basking in triumphant victory.

"Your presence means so much to me. I can't wait to marry Favor. And Clarity? How does she fit? Will she be my first child with Favor or my second? I can't wait to hold her in my arms and see the look on his face."

Dark clouds rolled in, and the sky above darkened gradually without much notice.

"We'll buy the Warner farm and start a school in the barn. We'll call it 'Hope Farm.' It's the beginning of a whole new life. Thank you for everything. I won't forget the slaves, and I promise to help create laws to protect your children if you show me how, Captain."

Black crows swooped down in a violent attack, pecking at Purity's head.

"Get away, you nasty birds," Purity said, batting them off. They squawked and landed on tree branches a few yards away.

A troop of Ahaba's dark spirits moved in and blew gusts of wind around her body. Dirt blew into her eyes, momentarily blinding her.

Out of the brush galloped a horse in full stride, headed right at Purity. It knocked her to the ground. Her head swirled, and her vision blurred.

"You've bewitched Favor and ruined our plans. This estate belonged to me," Jezzie screamed like a lunatic from atop the horse. Evil spirits hopped on her back and melted into her soul.

The Ring of Grace arrived as lightning strikes from heaven. They began battling wicked spirits that had gathered for another attack.

Purity tried to rise from the dirt, but a searing pain shot down her back and blood oozed from her nose and mouth.

Jezzie dismounted her horse and towered over Purity. She grabbed Purity's clothing and drug her to the edge of a steep ravine. The dark wispy spirits, appearing as black smoky vapors, whispered in Jezzie's ear, "Revenge, a bitter necessity."

"Watch your footing. It's quite a fall. Revenge, a bitter necessity," Jezzie ranted.

Purity neared the edge, but the pain was so great she could not fight her oppressor off.

David hunted nearby—his arrow pointed at a plump turkey. Five rays of bright light swirled around him.

"What's going on? What are you?" he asked, terrified.

The Ring of Grace flew around David again and again and then touched down, manifesting as child angels dressed in warrior garb with galactic weapons and fiery swords in each hand. A thick atmosphere, weighty in power, surrounded them. Rocco approached David.

"Stop. Don't come any closer," David yelled.

"Don't be afraid. We are warriors from the New Earth. You've seen us before at Son's Camp. Our Captain rules the universe. We fight against Ahaba's evil forces."

"Come again," David said, not understanding the message.

"Ahaba's evil forces have rendered Purity powerless. We must fight," Rocco said as the other angels lifted their fiery swords and belted out a war cry.

"No offense, but you're a little small. Aren't there any bigger angels up there?" David said in fear.

Josiah, Toby, Sergio, Kaleb, and Rocco threw fiery daggers at the surrounding trees with such force they uprooted them. The angels held out their hands, and like a boomerang, each dagger returned to its rightful owner.

"Is that powerful enough for you? Come, time is not on our side," Kaleb warned.

"I can't move. I don't know what's gotten into me. I'd do anything for Purity, but I'm afraid," David admitted.

"A spirit of fear is attacking you," Sergio answered. He drew his bow and arrow and shot a wicked spirit off David's back.

"The fear is gone," David said, relieved.

The Ring of Grace surrounded David with hands that appeared like flames of fire. Kaleb put his small, radiant hands over David's ears to enhance his hearing. Josiah touched his eyes so he could see into the spirit realm. Rocco pressed a fiery hand on his back to give supernatural strength and understanding. Lastly, Sergio placed a radiant hand on David's head to give discernment.

Toby blew a shofar, and in unison, all the angels cried out with a mighty battle cry, "Together we fight. The victory is ours." In an instant, they rolled into a ball of fire and blazed through the trees.

David followed the ball of fire through the acreage. His heavenly gifts of heightened sensitivity awakened his soul to undetected sights, sounds, and spirits. As he ran, he saw that a battle was taking place in the sky just ahead. It appeared in living color—swords clashing, smoke billowing, and dark spirits hit with what seemed like volts of electricity. The violent clashes of raw power sounded like thunder.

David's legs never wavered but grew stronger and faster just thinking of Purity in trouble. He watched a mighty warrior rush into the battle on a large white stallion. The warrior's sword pulverized the enemy, and they screeched with mind-shattering volume as they vaporized.

"It must be the Captain," David thought.

Vicious shouts from a distance became audible, echoing through the woods. David discerned the direction.

The Ring of Grace manifested as child warriors again, running ahead to Purity's location. They made their way to a trail used by many who lived and worked on Shadow Brook Estate. A strange smoky mist became thicker the closer they got to the voices.

David saw movement up ahead. Jezzie dragged Purity's motionless body, step by step, to the cliff.

Ahaba's Army was there basking in the victory over Purity. They howled and growled chants of Purity's defeat.

The child angels raced on the scene, blindsiding the wicked spirits with swords of fire. Their bodies vaporized into a black substance that reeked like putrid sulfur.

"Stop. Death awaits you, Jezzie," David yelled, sprinting toward the attacker.

Gripped by sudden fear, Jezzie let go of Purity and ran away.

"Mother," David screamed as Purity's defenseless body plummeted over the edge. He leaned over, straining for a glimpse of her. She was sprawled out on a small ledge several yards below—not moving.

David pulled the ram's horn from his side and blew it, again and again, signaling a call to arms. In response, he heard the sound of ram's horns coming from the direction of Son's Camp. Help was on the way.

Jezzie had mounted her horse and started to gallop away. David drew his bow to strike a lethal blow, but the Ring of Grace flew in front of him.

"Stop. Vengeance belongs to the Captain," Toby said.

"Purity needs you," Rocco impressed upon David's heart. He spoke no words— it was a knowing.

"May God judge you, Jezzie," David said, aching for revenge as he lowered the bow and arrow.

David rushed back to the edge of the cliff. He hoped to save the only person who cared enough to redeem his life from the streets. There was no way to climb down himself. David blew on his ram's horn, again and again.

* * *

Favor sat in his room enjoying his favorite chair when the sound of ram's horns floated in through the open window.

"Something's wrong. I feel it," he thought. He rose and headed to the horse's stables, where he saddled Rozzie. He told him to find the sound, and they were off, galloping over the acreage.

Favor and Rozzie followed the horn's direction, but then the ominous sound died out. Favor spun Rozzie in a circle, looking for anything that might lead him to Purity.

A younger son, Mark, ran upon them.

"I came to get you, sir. Purity's been attacked. She needs help."

"Lead the way," Favor said, lifting Mark to his saddle, they

Favor and Mark joined the others at the precipice of the cliff where they'd just managed to pull Purity up. She lay motionless on the stretcher.

"No. My God, no. Hold on, Purity. Hold on," Favor said as he grabbed her lifeless hand.

"What happened?" Favor asked the boys.

"It was Jezzie. She attacked her," David answered.

"We have to get Purity to the hospital. Get the old wagon," Favor commanded Jonathan, who hopped on Rozzie and galloped off in a flurry of dust.

Favor stayed by Purity's side, stroking her hand until Jonathan and Naomi returned a short time later, with Rozzie pulling the old wagon behind. It was the same one that took Papa to his final resting place. The horse neighed several times, as though expressing his understood grief.

Carefully, Purity's sons gently lifted the stretcher onto the wagon.

"My worst fears have found us," Naomi said, holding Purity in her arms.

"Let's move," Favor shouted and took Jonathan's place in the driver's seat.

"Let's go, Rozzie. Take us to town," Favor commanded.

Some younger sons hopped on the wagon like brave little guards with their bows and arrows. The older sons followed behind on foot.

Lightning struck the trees, and a fire started in the dry grasses. Dark smoke rose to the heavens. Ahaba was there, inhaling the stench of trauma with great satisfaction.

"We're cursed. We're cursed. To think happiness was here to stay," Naomi cried over her daughter.

Purity came to for a moment. Groaning in pain, she mumbled, "Captain, I need you."

"Where was your Captain when you needed him most?" Ahaba mocked. Thunder cracked overhead, and a vicious downpour soaked through every layer of clothing.

* * *

Purity had been taken to Bristol Memorial Hospital, where a team of doctors and nurses tended to her wounds. Those who loved her crowded into a small waiting room. Favor and Naomi sat, paralyzed with grief. The sons lingered about, filling the room with a stench of body odor from all of their labors.

283

After a few hours, a police officer entered, looking for witnesses. The sons started rattling what they knew in a loud commotion of emotion.

"Enough already. I need a witness," the officer said, annoyed.

"Jezzie attacked without mercy. I saw it with my own eyes," David told the police officer who jotted down the details.

The longer Favor listened, the more his blood boiled.

"We'll try to apprehend Jezzie as soon as possible. What else can you tell me?" the officer pressed, but his interview was interrupted by the doctor.

"Are you Purity's family?" Dr. Cooper asked with a grim countenance.

"I'm the girl's mother," Naomi said through tears.

"And I'm Purity's fiancé, Favor Wisedor. These are her adopted children," Favor explained.

"I'm so sorry to meet under these unfortunate circumstances. Mr. Wisedor, I'm familiar with Shadow Brook Estate. Can I speak with you and Naomi privately?"

He led Favor and Naomi to a small private room.

"I'm sorry to say this, but there's nothing more we can do. Her spine is injured, and there seems to be internal bleeding," Dr. Cooper explained.

"Whatever it costs. Money is no object," Favor pleaded.

"It's not about the money. Frankly, she needs a miracle to live. There's been some serious damage, and surgery is too risky. I'm sorry," the doctor sadly admitted and left the waiting room.

"Lord, save her life," Naomi prayed aloud. Her knees gave out, and Favor caught her with a steady hand.

The sons flowed in, surrounding them. Each one dropped to his knees and started praying.

Naomi pulled David aside and secretly whispered in his ear, "Tell Chief Wolf we need his help. Try to find the tribe. We don't have much time."

* * *

Favor and Naomi spent the night in the hospital waiting room. Favor woke to someone tapping him on the shoulder.

"Are you Favor Wisedor?" It was the police officer from the day before.

"Yes, sir," Favor answered.

"I'm afraid I have more bad news. Your fiancée has been accused of murder. Mr. Wells is financing a case for Mave Murdock concerning her son Roberto's death. He's hired the best attorneys. I also found Jezzabella Coevet. She's at the police station pressing charges for assault. She's claiming self-defense against Purity. We can't make an arrest until we conduct a full investigation," the officer explained.

"But it's all lies. Purity's innocent," Favor asserted.

"Should she recover, Purity will need a good attorney. She's made an enemy of some powerful people," the officer added before leaving.

"This is a mockery of the truth," Naomi cried out.

That afternoon, Favor left the hospital to change clothes and look into an attorney for Purity—should it come to that. Naomi could sit around and wait no longer. She sent a message to the sons, who returned to the hospital with the wagon.

Under her direction, the boys skirted the medical staff and loaded Purity onto the make-shift stretcher they'd used to lift her back to safety. Then they placed her in the wagon outside. David put fresh-picked flowers in her folded hands. The rest of the sons followed suit and covered her body with floral bouquets. Purity looked as if she had already left this world.

Rachel, Alexis, Natasha, and Chin Lu arrived for a visit just as Purity was settled in the wagon.

"Where are you taking her? She needs to be in the hospital," Natasha tried to reason.

"I know what I'm doing, and don't any of you argue with me," Naomi said with a scowl.

"What's the meaning of this?" Dr. Cooper yelled, chasing after them with a nurse following behind.

"If you take her, I'm not legally responsible,"

"There's nothing you can do, remember? I'm not going to sit around and wait for her to die. And if she survives, no court in Bristol will believe a maid over the lies of Jezzabella Coevet and Mr. Wells. She's going to

Indian country. Hopefully, with God's help, Purity can find peace and healing there," Naomi explained, choking back tears.

* * *

Favor returned to the hospital with a bouquet of flowers. A strange emptiness filled his soul when he saw the empty waiting room. He entered Purity's room but found the bed empty.

"What's going on?" Favor called out. He dropped the flowers and hurried to the nurse's station.

"Where is she? Where's Purity?" Favor pleaded.

"Purity no longer needed our services," the nurse snarled.

"She passed?" Favor asked, fearing the worst.

"No, her care has been transferred to the Narraganset Indians," the nurse said with disgust.

"The Indians? Explain yourself."

"You heard me the first time," the nurse replied.

"According to her mother, her condition isn't our problem anymore. They loaded her up about an hour ago."

Favor drove frantically through the busy streets of Bristol. His fist pounded the steering wheel more than once.

"Unbelievable. Naomi, how could you?" he growled. He searched every street, hoping to stop her.

Just as he started to give up hope, he turned down Ferry Road, which led out of town. Crowds lined the street in parade fashion. A smaller group followed behind a wagon in a slow procession. Favor parked and pushed his way through the mourners.

People cried and held each other. Many placed flowers in the wagon as it passed. David held the reigns and Jonathan sat by his side. The rest of Purity's sons walked somberly on either side. Behind walked Naomi, Natasha, Rachel, Alexis, Stephen, Mandy, and Chin Lu, and crowds from Bristol.

A band of warriors from the Narragansett tribe waited patiently at the end of the road. Each warrior was amazed by the townspeople gathering to bid blessings and farewell to a young woman.

Chief Wolf realized this precious one needed special care and recovery. His high opinion and enduring relationship with Naomi through the years opened a mysterious door into the hearts of the tribe that few understand.

The town's people were cautious and fearful. They'd never seen so many young Indian warriors at one time. A group of men waited for the wagon to stop. Then in unison, they lifted Purity from her resting place and gently laid her on the Indian's specially prepared stretcher made of woven multicolored wool.

The warriors, well-trained in Indian medicine, realized Purity's injuries were severe. They exchanged looks of deep remorse. One of the warriors made her drink a remedy for pain. The journey into their hidden domain, where foreigners rarely ventured, would be long and arduous.

Tears streamed down Naomi's face. She realized Purity's survival rested in God's hands.

Chief extended his right hand toward her and spoke in his native language.

"We promise our best. You saved my daughter, Fair Dawn, many years ago, and I hope to save yours. Good will overshadow evil. She will rise stronger and lead many to victory," Chief Wolf declared in full confidence.

Few in the crowd understood the Indian language, but Naomi nodded her head in understanding. During her time working with the tribe, learning their medicinal secrets, and sharing them with many who could not afford a doctor's visit, she had picked up much of their language.

Favor pushed his way to the front of the crowd.

"Stop. You're not taking her anywhere," he threatened. Before he reached the stretcher, two muscular warriors, with weapons ready, blocked his path. They wrestled him to the ground.

"She belongs with me. You have no right taking her away," he yelled in deep sorrow.

"Serves you right, engaged to a maid," a well-dressed man yelled in disgust.

"You brought this on the poor girl. Jealousy is an awful thing," a bitter woman cried.

Favor tried to wrestle free.

"She's my fiancée. I love Purity," Favor implored.

"Son, let her go. There's nothing more you or I can do," Naomi said.

Chief Wolf raised his bow and arrow, a sign that ordered their departure. Several from the crowd took over for the warriors that held Favor back.

Then the warriors raised the stretcher as one unit and began their march.

"She'll be lost forever," a woman cried out, fearing the worst.

"Only God can help her now," a man said scornfully.

"Indians can't be trusted," yelled a sarcastic teen.

"She's under a curse," an old man mocked.

Naomi turned to Favor.

"Her only chance is with the Indians. They have healing methods we don't practice."

"I'll kill Jezzie," Favor threatened in frustration.

"Then I'll lose you both. How much can one heart take? Let them go. Captain will watch over Purity and if it's his will, bring her back to us," Naomi begged, glancing at the retreating warriors.

By now, the Indians were entering the forest. The townsmen, thinking it was safe, released their hold on Favor. He took off like a bullet just fired and ran with all his might, hoping to catch the pack of warriors. A few men ran after him.

As he drew closer, a single arrow decorated with feathers of bright yellow, red, and blue soared with penetrating precision through the air. Favor ripped his shirt open, hoping it would pierce his breaking heart.

The men that followed him retreated as the arrow flew in their direction with unrelenting speed. It fell short of Favor, plunging into the ground. Favor stumbled to his knees and grabbed hold of the arrow, despairing for life.

"You have no right to do this," he yelled.

A gentle rain began to fall, drop-by-drop. The warriors, realizing their lone pursuer knelt in submission, faded into the forest. The crowds dissipated as the light rain became a downpour.

Naomi sat in the wagon with the reins held loosely in both hands. The sons hopped on the back, their faces covered with grief.

Favor returned to the wagon, his clothes stained with mud and the lone arrow resting in his hand.

"Naomi, how could you?" his voice quivered in grief.

"Your heart isn't the only one breaking. There's nothing your fancy doctors can do. And if she resurrected tomorrow, what chance does she have against high-class attorneys. Come. Let's get out of here," Naomi said, striking the leather reigns with force. The horse jolted in response, and the old wagon creaked as it rolled over deep mud puddles.

Favor fought off a flood of condemnation as he walked back to his car.

"It's my fault. I opened the door to Jezzie, and hell walked in." The rain soaked every fiber of his clothing as lightning and thunder cracked overhead.

* * *

Favor's heavy steps on the marble floors echoed through the mansion's entryway. He walked past the library—the double doors slightly open. The sounds of a heated conversation spilled out into the hallway. Favor lightened his step and held his breath to avoid discovery.

"You'll be hearing from our attorney unless we come to our own understanding," Mr. Coevet threatened.

"What's your price? I don't need rumors circulating about Shadow Brook Estate," Mr. Wisedor replied.

"We thoroughly screen our 'Help.' We've never experienced an incident of this nature." Mrs. Wisedor insisted, her voice charged with apprehension.

"I believe twenty-thousand dollars will erase the unpleasant incident. After all, our daughter was brutally attacked by Favor's fiancée," Mr. Coevet asserted.

"We're not sure why Purity attacked. Such vicious behavior." Mrs. Coevet sniffled and wiped dry eyes with an expensive handkerchief. Her facial expression appeared rehearsed.

"Think of the emotional wounds. I don't know if Jezzie will ever recover, and that's not the worst of it," Mrs. Coevet complained.

"What are you trying to say?" Mr. Wisedor pressed for full disclosure.

"You know full well Jezzabella is pregnant, and Favor's denying he's the father. Your son has disgraced our family name," Mr. Coevet said with boldness.

"God only knows if Jezzie will miscarry the baby—our first grandchild," Mrs. Coevet added.

"Favor has denied fathering Jezzie's demon child," Mrs. Wisedor yelled in defense.

Favor could take no more. He burst through the double doors—fists clenched in anger. Everyone gasped at his filthy, wet clothing and wild-eyed emotional state.

"Purity's fighting for her life, attacked by that pregnant witch. Enough of your blatant lies. Your polished grooming has created a lunatic capable of murder," Favor said, eyes piercing like a knife.

Jezzie sat next to her parents on a couch. She winced at his words and held her abdomen.

"Your whore was merciless. She attacked me from behind," Jezzie shrieked.

Favor lunged at the blood-saturated bandages wrapped around her arms and head and began ripping them off.

"You're hurting me," she whined in protest.

He continued ripping and tearing at the bloodied dressings.

"What animal did you kill to stage this lie?" To everyone's horror, there were deep lacerations on her wrists. All were speechless at the appearance of self-inflicted wounds and no other signs of a beating.

"You used your own blood to cover a murder plot? Or did you attempt suicide out of guilt?" Favor asked.

"So, tell us what happened again?" Mr. Wisedor demanded with skepticism.

"You attacked with murderous intent. What drove you to such extremes?" Favor pressed, trying to shake the truth from his enemy.

"You're my fiancé. How dare you choose a maid—a bar dancer—over a woman of high breeding?" Jezzie shouted. Her eyes grew wild and fierce.

"High breeding? You're a sewage line, pumping hatred and lies. Did I ever arrange an engagement with you? Besides, I never touched you. If you're pregnant, I'm not the culprit, and you know it," Favor yelled, hating the sight of such a depressed, miserable soul.

"My parents paid ten thousand dollars for an engagement," Jezzie cried.

Mrs. Wisedor withered in the nakedness of the truth.

"That was before I knew anything about your scandalous poverty. What did you do, hock your possessions to get it?"

Favor felt crushed by the revelation that his parents had sold him like some animal.

"You sold my future to the highest bidder. Aren't their intentions obvious?" Favor lifted his hands, gesturing the opulence of the estate.

"The disclosure of their financial demise occurred after the payment. I was deceived," his mother wailed in defense.

"The deal's canceled," Favor growled.

"Wait a minute. We have witnesses proving our daughter was attacked," Mr. Coevet said, drooling over the stacks of cash on Mr. Wisedor's desk.

"I have my own witnesses," Favor threatened.

"Don't tell me you're referring to Purity's rag-tag sons. Who would believe them? Or that Purity is innocent when she's being accused of murder," Mr. Coevet said.

"What the hell are you talking about?" Mr. Wisedor asked, horrified.

"More lies. So, a maid isn't worthy of justice? And Jezzie's above the law by social standing alone?" Favor picked up the bloodied bandages and threw them at the Coevet's.

"Look at what you've caused by brokering our son's marriage," Mr. Wisedor accused his wife.

Favor's eyes shifted to the stacks of cash on his father's desk.

"And this—blackmail money to cover a crime Purity never committed." Favor scooped up ten thousand dollars, stuffed it in a cloth bag, and handed it to Mr. Coevet.

"Paid back in full. Case closed. But I'm not inclined to wait for divine justice," he said, reaching into his jacket pocket and pulling out a gun.

Jezzie and her mother let out hysterical screams.

"We're innocent," Mr. Coevet protested.

"Hell's calling. Let me help you get there," Favor said, pointing the gun at each member of the Coevet family.

"Don't kill us. I beg you," Jezzie wailed.

Mr. and Mrs. Wisedor froze in terror, distrusting their son's ability to control his wild emotions.

"Get out before I change my mind," Favor said, keeping the gun fixated on the Coevets.

They ran, tripping over each other, and slammed the library doors behind them.

"Do you realize what you've done? Engaged to a maid accused of murder? Your association with this woman has ruined your reputation and ours. This whole matter's insufferable." His mother shook with bitterness, wasting no time projecting the blame on Purity.

"Calloused heart. You opened the door to this with your conniving ways. You care nothing about the people who serve your every whim. Nothing, as long as your needs are met and your fortune's secure. And you were going to give in to their blackmail," Favor glared at his parents.

"We have a reputation to preserve. You've lived like a king because of that reputation. How dare you judge us for protecting our good name?" his mother yelled.

His father raised a wine glass to his lips and grunted a sinister chuckle.

"Our greedy ways fully exposed. Shut up, woman. You've made a mess of things," Mr. Wisedor commanded.

His wife turned away, momentarily humiliated.

"How dare you address me in such a manner? It's Favor's fault we're in this mess," Mrs. Wisedor said, withering in self-pity.

"Blaming each other won't help. Jezzie and that wicked family cast their spell over us all, and Purity is the one paying for it," Favor yelled and walked out.

He marched to his bedroom and dropped like a dead man onto his favorite reading chair. The unanswered questions haunted his thoughts.

"Will Purity survive? Will I ever see her again?" He grabbed a small, elegant statue from the table to his right and threw it at the fireplace. It exploded into a hundred pieces, but that didn't ease his pain.

A knock at the door jolted his attention.

"Go away," he yelled.

"It's me," Victoria spoke softly.

"Come in," Favor whined.

Victoria entered and kneeled on the floor near his feet, crying uncontrollably.

"Why Purity? It's so awful I can barely breathe," Victoria groaned with eyes searching his for answers.

"God only knows if she'll live or die. The question is, will we ever see her again?" Favor said with an air of defeat. He paced the room, thinking of all the possible outcomes.

Victoria was devoid of words and joined him at the large bedroom window. Fresh air blew the satin curtains, but the evening shadows covered the land with an eerie hopelessness.

"May God be with her," Victoria whispered. She took his hand and squeezed it.

* * * * * *

The Narragansett Indians marched on, moving deeper into the forest. Their sandals sunk into the mud-drenched trails. Chief Wolf forged ahead, riding his tall, sleek black stallion. He saw the warriors stumbling in the mud and gave a hand signal to stop. Everyone welcomed the rest.

"Water," Purity whispered as blood seeped from her nose and mouth.

Chief Wolf's son, Sharp Arrow, approached. A tall warrior with noble features, his muscles flexed with the slightest movement. He was born a prince and shouldered the responsibilities of the tribe with his father. Wiser than his years, Sharp Arrow was stoic and serious but could be lighthearted when the occasion arose. He was prepared for the enemy with buck knives in leather sheaths, carefully strapped to each thigh. A bow and quiver of arrows were fastened to his horse. And most importantly, a rifle was secured to his back. The fate of the tribe weighed heavily on his mind.

Sharp Arrow raised Purity's head with one hand and tipped the water jug to her lips. Water trickled down her chin, mingled with blood. Sip by sip, the cool liquid quenched her thirst. She nodded slightly in appreciation. Despite her best efforts to keep it down, blood-drenched regurgitation seeped from her mouth.

Sharp Arrow felt helpless as he wiped it with a soft cloth.

"Don't fear. I'll kill your enemy," he whispered. The sight of her swollen, battered face angered him.

Purity slowly shook her head in disagreement.

"Mariah, come," Sharp Arrow said sternly.

A rustle was heard among the warriors who remained on their horses. They pulled on their reins and the horses moved to provide space for the maiden to emerge.

She appeared as light dawning from a dark night—radiant in glorious beauty—atop a white horse named Wind. All but sixteen-years-old, she had a slender, toned build, tanned skin, and flowing black hair sprinkled with golden highlights from the sun. Her gray-blue eyes shone brightly, revealing an inner spirit of kindness. A brown leather dress, decorated with beaded handiwork and scattered feathers, flowed over feminine curves. She slid down from the horse with the expertise of a skilled equestrian. Her strong hands quickly untied a bundle of supplies from one of the packs.

"Go," Mariah said, shooing the warriors with a wave of the hand as she approached the stretcher. They responded and moved away to give her privacy.

She bowed at Purity's side, and for the first time, she was face-to-face with a stranger from another world. She tried to envision Purity's beauty as it had been. Mariah rarely saw 'whites' up close, as her life existed in the confines of the remote band of Indians. The small tribe hid away, avoiding the reservations that so many were dying in.

The Indian maiden felt privileged to accompany the greatest and fiercest of the tribe. It was an important mission, as she was the only female granted permission to travel with the warriors. It was dangerous for an Indian woman to travel alone, and many disappeared without a trace. More importantly, it was her chance to prove her qualities to Sharp Arrow.

Mariah dreamed of him from afar and found herself staring at him when he wasn't aware. Even on the trip, she kept a longing watchful eye on him. He was of age to marry but appeared disinterested in any of the Indian maidens. The older Indian men decided that Great Creator will choose his wife.

Mariah touched Purity's soft, pale cheeks with the back of her hand.

"Drink," the Indian maiden encouraged in her native tongue, lifting a small woven vessel to Purity's lips. Then she washed the blood from Purity's face and applied healing ointments to help relieve the swelling.

"Be well, my sister," Mariah said. Purity squeezed her hand in thanks.

Satisfied with the results, Mariah signaled the warriors to return and commence the journey. Sharp Arrow gave a faint smile, nodded his head, and turned his horse around in the ensuing direction. Mariah was thrilled he acknowledged her efforts.

The warriors moved further into the wilderness. Mariah's thoughts drifted to the rare sights and sounds of the city of Bristol. Buildings with storefront signs lined the street. People, horse-drawn buggies, and newly invented cars clogged the roads. The women walked about wearing long dresses made from the best fabrics. They wore fashionable hats and carried baskets filled with items recently purchased from the general store. The men were fully clothed and wore stiff high black hats and long coats. She was bombarded with a new world of possibilities and felt somehow her new friend was a vital key to it all.

Several hours later, they stopped once more. Sharp Arrow called for Mariah again. She wiped Purity's swollen face and cleaned her wounds. Leaning close, she listened for Purity's breathing.

"My teacher," she whispered in her native tongue. She stroked Purity's cheek with a gentle hand. Purity reached for her soft hand, connecting with its warmth.

After caring for Purity's needs, Mariah searched through her new friend's belongings. Her hands sank deep into one pack and hit what felt like a wooden box. She yanked on it and pulled out a hard-covered book. It was the Holy Bible.

"What's this?" she questioned, shaking it with a steady rhythm. Mariah tried to imagine its practical use. She had never held a book. Learning to read and write was foreign in her world. She opened its cover and turned clumps of pages at one time. Her fingers manipulated the thin pages, ripping more than a few. Looking around, she expected wrath from Sharp Arrow, but he was busy with the warriors. Giving it another try, she gently turned one thin page at a time. Her fingers glided over the smooth sheets in wonderment.

"What are these little marks?" she thought, scanning the unknown words on each page. Her mind raced with so many questions.

"What good is something like this?" She shook the book and turned it in every direction, trying to understand its purpose.

"Hurry and leave her things alone," Sharp Arrow called, sounding a bit agitated.

The weather changed, and an icy chill cut through her like a knife. Startled, Mariah dropped the Bible, and to her amazement, the wind rapidly turned the pages.

"A great Spirit lives in it," she thought, wide eyes beaming with curiosity. Closing the book in haste, she shoved it back into the pack.

The warriors once again came to lift the stretcher. Mariah mounted her horse and moved away.

Along their journey, the tribe moved through a steep mountain gorge. Chief Wolf scanned the surroundings, a feeling of tension in his spirit. The warriors talked and joked, oblivious to any concern until Chief Wolf raised his bow and arrow to signal the need for silence. The warriors surveyed the rocky hills, trees, and shrubs for enemies. As trained hunters, they listened for any clues such as snapping twigs, the hum of voices, or the rattle of ammunition being loaded into rifles.

Unbeknownst to them, a band of Indians, whose cruelty was unmatched, followed them. Without a word, Chief Wolf gave hand signals to the warriors. Each responded by engaging his weapons.

Jet-black arrows flew from two opposing directions and pelted more than a few warriors. They scattered, taking cover behind large boulders and thick brush nearby. The stretcher strained from the quick movement as the warriors carrying Purity moved to find protection. Another onslaught of arrows soared through the air. From their place of safety, Chief Wolf and Sharp Arrow scanned the mountainous crags in the hopes of locating their attackers.

The sky darkened as Ahaba's face emerged in the clouds. His army trailed behind, thirsty for another bloody battle. Wicked translucent spirits descended in rapid succession, diving into each enemy warrior. As the evil spirits filled the warriors, their eyes glow red with rage and awful intentions. Some spirits wrapped around their necks. Others hopped on backs and viciously squeezed their victims. The sinister warriors emerged wearing black feather headdresses decorated with ornate beadwork. War paint masked their faces with colors of black, red, and orange.

Another legion of translucent evil spirits dropped like dark rain, trying to inhabit Chief Wolf's warriors. They bombarded the warriors with spirits of fear and a loathsome weakness. Some dropped their weapons, paralyzed with doom. Others repelled them, calling on the Great Creator for divine intervention.

The chief of the enemy Indians climbed a large bolder and stood in defiance. Along with his extravagant headdress and face paint, his body had piercings and strange tattoos of snakes coiled, ready to strike. He gave a hand signal, and more warriors stood up with arrows ready to fire on Chief Wolf's warriors.

Purity strained one swollen eye open. Her vision was blurred, but she could see some of the enemy warriors who appeared as demons erupting from the pit of hell. She prayed silently, "Captain, help us."

Sharp Arrow bravely stood before the sea of arrows pointed their way. He was familiar with the enemy warrior's language but not fluent and struggled to find the right words.

"We bring peace, not harm," Sharp Arrow yelled, raising his hands as in surrender.

"Give us fair one you are carrying," the evil chief shouted.

"Death calls for her. Any abuse from you will curse your tribe," Sharp Arrow reasoned.

The evil Chief stood still in thought as though a battle raged through his mind. A fiery dart shot from Ahaba's hand and coiled around the evil chief's head, squeezing it like a python snuffing out prey. The chief grabbed his head in pain and staggered back.

"Help us, Captain," Purity prayed, having no understanding of the language, but sensing danger. The wind began to blow furiously, and she heard the sound of horse's hooves stampeding above.

Ahaba's invisible dark army hovered in defiance above the enemy warriors.

"Finish Purity off!" Ahaba yelled at his forces. Heavy rain poured from the dark clouds, and thunder echoed in the gorge.

Captain of the Lord's Army appeared, riding on a white horse, with his army following behind. He raised a hand with a fiery sword. His warriors of light descended and placed hands of fire on each brave Narragansett warrior, filling them with power. Then Captain's army shot penetrating arrows through the dark forces. Many spirits fell and withered away with screams of agony. Others retreated in fear of the great Captain.

The Captain himself released a fiery arrow at Ahaba's snake-like hand. Immediately, the enemy chief's mind was released.

The evil chief brooded and then raised his hand.

"We give you passage," he yelled.

Purity's hands gripped the wet blanket covering her broken body. The stress of the whole situation caused Purity's bones to ache even worse than before.

"Captain, I praise you," she whispered.

The enemy warriors slowly retreated, disappearing into the surrounding cliffs.

After marching a few more hours, the weather improved. The sun burst through the dark clouds, and Chief Wolf gave the sign to stop by a rushing stream. The warriors set the stretcher down and refilled their water baskets. Mariah rushed to Purity's side and offered some water.

Purity strained to open her swollen eyes and caught a glimpse of the maiden with soft, caring hands. All she could manage in return was a faint smile.

Mariah hummed a soft melody as she mixed a healing herbal concoction, and she fed it to Purity. She removed the soiled bandages and reapplied the healing balm. With a gentle hand, she stroked Purity's soft cheeks again while singing an Indian song of friendship, "Rise Again."

> Rise again, sister friend, rise again
> Like a shining star, bold and bright
> Rise again, rise again
> My sister friend, teach me
> What my mother never learned
> Evil tried to kill your light
> We will help you back to life
> Rise again, shining star, my sister-friend
> Rise again, rise again, rise again

* * *

After a few days journey into the wilderness, the warriors reached their small village. Most Indians forced onto the reservations were dying slow deaths. This remnant of the Narragansett tribe sought freedom at any cost. They lived off the land and avoided civilization.

Indians of all ages, shapes, and sizes tended livestock. Others worked in the nearby fields of corn and vegetables. Indian children played games and laughed by the river that wound through their crops. Some older girls gathered wood and wove baskets while a group of women cooked deer meat over open fires.

Purity winced as the warriors gave a cry of victory. The village ceased from their labors to welcome the approaching warriors. The Indians greeted them with hugs, kisses, and gifts of flowers, nuts, and tasty fruitcakes.

"We've arrived," Purity thought. With all her heart, she wanted to get up and embrace them all.

A specially prepared teepee waited for their guest. Special gift baskets surrounded the parameter of the teepee filled with clothing, blankets, and woven towels. Inside, it was lined with soft pallets covered with bear fur and ornately woven blankets. Light and fresh air flowed in from a round hole at the top. The warriors gently transferred Purity to a soft pallet.

Mariah refused to leave as an older Indian woman tried to pull her from the teepee.

"She's cursed and will die. Her people have thrown her away," the woman said with scorn.

"I will stay. She will rise and teach me what my mother never learned," Mariah rebuked the woman.

Chief Wolf's daughter, Fair Dawn, entered the teepee with humility. She was a teen, about fifteen now, lovely in form and gentle in spirit. Purity recognized the beautiful Indian maiden.

"Live, my friend. We'll help you live," Fair Dawn said, speaking broken English as she wept by her side.

Day after day, Fair Dawn and Mariah cared for Purity's needs. They supplied fresh hay for bedding, tidied the teepee, and changed her dressings. A special tea was prepared several times a day to expedite the healing process.

One day, they surprised Purity. Carefully, they propped her to a sitting position with her head and back supported. Purity winced in pain as any movement was difficult.

Mariah brushed her hair and added hair ornaments worn by the Indian princesses. After preparing her hair, Fair Dawn lifted a mirror and allowed Purity to see herself. She was relieved to see all the swelling and bruising had subsided.

"You Indian now," Fair Dawn said, smiling.

"Indian and proud," Purity responded with a warm smile.

Moving Forward

Chapter 33

FAVOR WALKED THE Wisedor Dish Factory grounds, inspecting the work on the schoolhouse and dorms. In the new school building, workers plastered the interior walls. The construction supervisor braced himself, waiting for Favor's approval.

"Exceptional work. The construction is coming along nicely," Favor said.

"It should be done on time, by Christmas," the Supervisor boasted.

Favor handed him an envelope.

"You're a trustworthy man. Here's the final payment for the construction. I'm leaving Bristol for a period. Enclosed is my contact information should you need anything."

"Don't worry, sir. We will complete the job on time and within budget. You have my word. What a great Christmas present to so many," the Supervisor said, taking the envelope.

Favor walked back toward his office. Natasha, Alexis, Rachel, and Chin Lu stood by a horse-drawn wagon in front of the factory.

"Come to my office," Favor said with a slight wave of the hand.

They followed him into the factory and settled in the plush office.

"Please have a seat. Tea for anyone?" Favor offered politely. One of the office attendants entered and poured tea for the women.

Favor sat at his desk and started with a confident tone.

"This meeting will be brief. I'm aware of your work with Purity's sons. I appreciate your efforts in her absence." Favor's heart filled with emotion, and he paused to collect himself.

He began again.

"As you know, the school and dorms will be completed very soon. I had hoped Purity's sons would live in the dorms. They can attend the school on a full-time basis."

The women stared in disbelief.

"Furthermore, I'm looking for teachers and overseers. I was wondering if any of you were interested. Of course, you would be paid a teacher's wage, plus tuition expenses for courses at the university when you're ready. I can only hire educated teachers, but if you're in a program, I'm sure the work experience would count for something."

His generosity went above and beyond. He offered them a fresh start.

"Yes, yes, we accept," the women agreed in joyful unison.

Favor left the factory, satisfied with their meeting, and roamed the waterfront in Bristol. He ended up at the shipbuilding yard. The workers waved with respect and admiration, and he drew close to the men.

"Any complaints?" he asked the group.

The men stopped working long enough to express their appreciation. One man spoke for all the workers.

"None here. Thank you for making a change. Our pay is more than adequate. The new supervisors are fair, and there hasn't been one accident since you initiated stricter safety guidelines. Men seeking employment come daily, hoping to find work with your company."

"Mission accomplished," Favor said, shaking several of their hands. He passed out business cards with contact information and said, "I'm leaving Bristol. Please contact me if the conditions change."

Favor entered the office and was surprised to see his father sitting at the desk, staring out the bay window.

"I saw you talking to the men. They respect you—something I never earned," Mr. Wisedor moaned regretfully.

"It's never too late. I'm trusting you'll oversee the positive changes in my absence," Favor said, pouring a cup of coffee.

"Your absence? Elaborate. Have you forgotten I'm retired?"

"I'm leaving Bristol, and there's no return date. Can I trust you to treat the men with dignity? I have new supervisors and managers in place. I forbid you from firing them without cause. Your fortune will continue to grow, but after we've been fair to our employees," Favor told his father.

"Son, you've taught me by example. Your mother and I have been wretched. Please forgive us. I understand why you loved Purity so much. It's not the same around here without her fierce spirit," Mr. Wisedor tried to hide tears welling from a contrite heart.

Mrs. Wisedor entered the office, surprising them both.

"Mother, what are you doing here?" Favor asked.

She stood silent as though searching for words.

"I've hardly slept since Purity left us. Call it remorse or regret, but guilt has gripped my soul. Please forgive me, son. I've been a manipulating, self-centered, scheming fool, and that's putting it politely. Is there any hope for such a mess?" his mother said, sounding deeply remorseful.

"There's always hope, Mother. I forgive you, but it's God we answer too. We've used and abused many," Favor said with deep regret.

Mrs. Wisedor began to convulse under the power of an evil spirit that appeared like a translucent snake. It squeezed her head, causing vertigo, and then moved down her neck. It looked like a panic attack with labored breathing, chest pain, and a wild-eyed expression.

"Let me go. I don't want your lies anymore." She could barely spit out the words.

"What's wrong, Mother?" Favor asked in alarm.

"She's having another attack. We never know when they strike or for how long. We've done our best to hide them," Mr. Wisedor said with grave concern.

"God help us," Favor called out, fearing the worst.

Suddenly, Ora appeared, invisible to all but Mrs. Wisedor.

"I see a ball of fire, spinning around and around," Mrs. Wisedor said, sounding completely incoherent.

"Mother, you're not well," Favor said, concerned.

"She's hallucinating," Mr. Wisedor offered, disturbed to the core.

Ora appeared as a ball of fire circling in mid-air. She spun around the Wisedor family like bands of light. Around and around, she blazed several times, then manifested as a stunning child in golden light.

Mrs. Wisedor stared in disbelief.

"Good heavens. The fire turned into an adorable little angel. What's your name?"

"I'm Ora. The Captain has sent me to help you rest." Ora placed a blazing hand on Mrs. Wisedor's head. A light pulsed through her body and burned the evil spirit out of her soul. It fell to the floor, hissing, and then dissolved into thin air.

"Ora, my little angel, set me free from a wicked spirit." Mrs. Wisedor blew out the words with relief.

"You just about scared me to death," Mr. Wisedor said.

"Good riddance, whatever that thing was. Your mother's been hell to live with all these years," Mr. Wisedor admitted.

"Forgive me, dear," Mrs. Wisedor begged.

"I have not been myself."

Mr. Wisedor looked around the room, trying to address whatever invisible presence had helped his wife.

"Thank you for giving me my wife back."

He hugged her, and they knelt for some time in repentant prayer. That same afternoon, Favor packed his bags and left Shadow Brook Estate. He drove down the cobblestone drive lined with professionally trimmed landscapes. In his mind's eye, Purity was all he could see. There she was, standing on the lawn with her sons gathered around. As he passed them, her eyes locked on him, and she waved goodbye.

He forced himself to keep driving. As he passed under the 'Shadow Brook Estate' wrought iron sign, he thought back to the night of the Gala, holding her shapely figure in his arms as they danced. The music sounded in his ears. Their lips drew close, and he kissed her gently. The vision evaporated as a gentle rain began to fall.

* * *

Purity's condition had improved, but she still suffered from severe back pain. The Indians continued to give her a special regimen of medicinal herbs several times a day.

One afternoon, Sharp Arrow approached Purity.

"In town, when you came to us, I heard people talking," Sharp Arrow said with remorse.

"Yes, Sharp Arrow?"

"They said you're a murderer. Did you take this Roberto's life?" He searched her eyes for the truth.

"Mave or Wells must have talked to the police. The truth is, Roberto wanted to use me as a sex slave. He died by his own hand, not mine," Purity assured him.

"I believe you. You will be safe here," he insisted.

"Thank you for everything, but someday soon, I must return to my family. I'm to be married," Purity said with eyes tearing.

"If you return, you'll never be free. They will lock you up," Sharp Arrow pleaded.

"For now, I will remain with the tribe. And when I am better, we can talk about this again. Maybe my name will be cleared."

The days passed slowly, and the tribe continued to care for their special guest. The warriors even made a special wagon for her and padded it with a soft brush, woven blankets, and bear fur. They escorted Purity everywhere in it.

The Indian children pulled their guest around the village too. They took great pleasure in introducing her to all the members of the tribe. She began to learn the language as they showed her different objects and named them.

One Indian boy lifted a sandal and said the Indian name. Purity repeated the Indian name, then said it in English.

"Sandal."

"Sandal," the children repeated, excited to learn English.

"Very good," Purity coached.

Another lifted a bow and arrow and slowly called out the Indian names. Purity repeated the words slowly in the Indian dialect, then said them in English.

The Ring of Grace circled around and around the Indian children. They laughed and tried to catch the swirls of light that spun and hopped about like rainbow-colored diamonds.

"Lights," an Indian child said, chasing after one.

Purity saw the lights, and her eyes shifted to the sky.

"Captain, please don't forget me. Do you even know where I am?" she mumbled without hope.

In the heavenly realm, Captain of the Lord's Army watched from above. Thousands upon thousands of angelic beings attended him. They also watched over the tribe with great concern.

"Place a shield of protection around the tribe," the Captain commanded. Immediately, warrior angels circled the village, appearing as a wall of invisible fire.

Purity had been with the tribe for several weeks when Sharp Arrow entered the teepee. He spoke to Purity in broken English.

"Time for a walk."

"No. It hurts too much," Purity said, resenting his command.

"I'm not ready," Purity protested in pain.

Sharp Arrow bent down and wrapped one of her arms around his strong neck. Another warrior entered and wrapped her other arm around his neck. Together, they brought Purity to her feet.

Mariah was visibly uncomfortable being in such close quarters with Sharp Arrow. She could barely speak around the handsome prince. Both she and Fair Dawn held any protest on behalf of their friend. Instead, they backed out of the way, watching her whither in torturous pain.

"Walk," Sharp Arrow demanded.

Shooting pain burned down her spine as she put a foot forward. The warriors supported most of her weight, only allowing a portion of it to rest on her feet. Sweat dripped, and her muscles quaked from inactivity.

Slowly, with great effort and strain, she stepped out into the sunlight. The first steps were agonizing, but the warriors were unrelenting, knowing she needed to move.

"Sharp Arrow, it hurts," Purity moaned with resentment.

"Move legs, shut mouth," he responded.

Warriors danced around them and played hand-held instruments, strumming and blowing harmonic rhythms.

"Stop, please. I need to focus," Purity begged as the music grated on her nerves.

The warriors ignored her pleas and continued to dance and play.

She absorbed the sun's warmth on her pale skin. Then a glazed feeling swept across her eyes, and she felt like she would faint.

"I'm feeling sick," she pleaded as a flood of vomit erupted.

The dancing warriors moved away.

"Vomit good. You expel the sickness," Sharp Arrow encouraged. "Now you walk."

Purity groaned with each step, resenting his insistence to move. The warriors slowly turned her around after walking a stretch and headed back to the teepee. By then, she was utterly exhausted and collapsed in Sharp Arrow's arms.

"Rest," Sharp Arrow said, nodding. His muscles flexed as he held her tight. His lips grew close, sending a thrill of temptation to kiss her forehead. All eyes were on him, and any desire was squelched with such an audience. The unexpected attraction embarrassed him.

Mariah couldn't help but notice the embrace and looked away in disappointment.

Sharp Arrow gently laid Purity back down on the soft fur pallet. Fair Dawn began wiping Purity's face with a cool towel while Mariah arranged the pillows behind her back. More medicinal tea was offered, helping with the back pain.

From then on, the warriors came daily for the same routine. Purity's heart grew bitter in her suffering. Her progress was slow, and each day she remained was another day away from her love.

"Does Favor know where I am?" she wondered.

"Does he know I'm alive?"

A week passed, and Sharp Arrow barked orders for the warriors to load the wagon.

"Prepare for the river," he commanded those around him.

The warriors loaded it with a soft pallet of hay, bear fur, pillows, and warm blankets. Several Indians surrounded the ornate teepee playing harmonics and dancing.

"Go away," Purity yelled from inside the teepee, dreading the pain.

Fair Dawn offered the pain-relieving tea.

"Drink. You need it," Mariah insisted, overseeing each sip.

Sharp Arrow entered with another warrior.

"No walking today. I don't feel well. Go away," Purity yelled. She did her best to bat him away, but her fists only bounced off his toned muscles.

Sharp Arrow held her close, lifting her to a standing position. Something about her presence touched his spirit.

"You must stop fighting like a bear," he gently responded.

Purity resigned herself to the pain. Cold air hit her like a slap in the face as she left the teepee. She spotted the wagon many yards away. Each step toward it meant she was that much closer to a rest.

Several times she stopped to vomit and give Sharp Arrow an earful.

"My mother asked Chief Wolf to look after me, not kill me. I haven't seen him in days. Where is your father? You have no authority over me, Sharp Arrow. You don't listen to a word I say."

Sharp Arrow nodded his head as though pretending not to understand a word, but he did.

Purity dripped with sweat when she made it to the wagon. Mariah wiped her brow as though a doting mother. Fair Dawn raised a cup of medicinal tea to Purity's cracked lips, hoping to numb her pain.

One of the warriors tucked her Bible in the wagon.

"Please don't bring my Bible. My great Captain has let me down," Purity said with scorn.

"Bring it. Your bitterness has poisoned your soul," Sharp Arrow said, overruling the order.

"Must you always fight against my wishes," Purity rebuked the prince again as the warriors watched.

"Move ahead," Sharp Arrow gave the word.

Two warriors pulled the wagon, two followed, and one walked at each side. Fair Dawn and Mariah followed behind, waiting to fulfill any need. Laughter filled the air as boys and girls ran alongside.

Sharp Arrow led the group outside the village and into the forest. The Ring of Grace appeared and flew above the entourage, keeping watch for any evil spirits.

Purity felt an invisible hand on her head. Her eyes closed, basking in the warmth of it.

"Captain, is that you?"

Rocco smiled, lifting his hand from her. Josiah, Sergio, Toby, and Kaleb flew over the warriors and children, placing fiery hands on each head.

"Receive the Captain's love," Sergio declared.

The warriors and children began dancing and singing, "Creator of the Earth."

> Creator of the earth
> Creator of all things
> You gave us everything
> We dance, we sing
>
> Creator of the earth
> Who gave us birth
> Direct our ways
> We dance, we sing
>
> To our Creator King
> Creator of the earth
> Creator of all things

They rejoiced as they tracked through the forest and rugged terrain. Eventually, the path opened to a bustling river with a waterfall. The cool misty spray blew over the weary travelers.

Sharp Arrow gave a hand sign for the warriors to be at ease. Some waded in the cold mountain waters. The Indian children played games with sticks and small woven balls of string. An Indian song carried on the wind.

The warriors parked the wagon close to the river's edge in full view of the waterfall. Refusing to relax, Mariah remained with Purity until Sharp Arrow dismissed her.

For the first time, Purity was alone with Sharp Arrow. His features were strong and noble. Indeed, he would be the next Chief, and rightly so. He was not foolish and never took advantage of his status in the tribe. Purity discerned an unseen burden that prevented him from partaking in momentary pleasures as the others did.

"I'm sorry I was upset earlier, but movement means pain. I don't know if I'll ever be free of it," Purity said, still feeling the numbing sensation of the tea.

"You'll be free again, but not my people. We are hated without cause. The Indian reservations are death traps. We are hunted and caged like beasts, forced to die before our time. We have escaped captivity, but we can't hide forever," he said with a sigh of pain. He picked up a few rocks and threw them into the river as though relieving his burden.

"I will do what I can to help," Purity assured him.

He reached into the wagon and pulled out her Bible.

"I had a dream before you came. I was riding on the plains, and I saw a great army coming to kill my tribe. My people cried, 'Sharp Arrow, save us.' Then I saw you carrying books. I heard a voice say, 'Receive my light and freedom.' Purity, how much longer before the slaughter comes? Help my people live."

"Only the good Captain from above knows what you must do," Purity said, raising her eyes to heaven.

"Who is this Captain? If he knows, you must ask him. It's a matter of life and death," Sharp Arrow insisted.

"I've heard he hears every whisper, but I'm not so sure anymore. Look what's happened to me," Purity complained.

"This good Captain has brought you here for such a time. I feel it in my bones. You must help us."

"I'm here because the Captain was too busy to defend me. When I needed him most, where was he? My family came from across the sea. We hoped for a better life, but we've only found heartbreak," Purity said, feeling weak from chronic pain and disappointment.

Sharp Arrow opened the Bible, thumbed through the pages, and noticed the fine print.

"What are these marks?"

"I used to believe they were the Words of life," Purity said with remorse.

"You must teach us the story. Stop mourning what you've lost and accept what you will gain. If you're here, find purpose in it. My dream will come to pass. We need you," Sharp Arrow declared.

"But you don't understand. I have no strength to help you," Purity said with a broken heart.

* * *

That evening, Purity tried to sleep but wrestled pain in her heart and body. Mariah and Fair Dawn were fast asleep next to her. Footsteps sounded outside, shifting her focus away from her earthly woes. In the bright moonlight, the shadows of five child warriors showed through the walls of the teepee. Their forms were illuminated like shining stars. Instantly, they appeared in the teepee. Purity was speechless, but no one else stirred.

The Ring of Grace spoke to her mind-to-mind.

"We have come to set you free from your pain," Josiah said as the others surrounded Purity.

Raising their hands, they directed what looked like laser beams toward Purity's battered body. Immediate pain relief and healing flowed through every cell of her body. It felt like wave after wave of soothing heat.

"Never forget, the Captain knows all and sees all," Toby whispered.

"He knows where you are," Rocco added.

"He hasn't forgotten about you," Sergio said with a smile.

"I'm sorry I doubted him," Purity said out loud.

In unison, the angels nodded, and as quick as they came, they disappeared, leaving the atmosphere charged with an electricity she could feel.

Purity rose the next morning, completely restored. The tribe stared in awe, wondering at her quick recovery. She walked through the camp without pain, carrying her Bible.

"It was the great Captain who healed me. He sent forth his power, and I'm whole again," Purity tried to explain.

That day, Purity began to teach Chief Wolf, Sharp Arrow, and the warriors to read the Bible.

Soon afterward, the Indian girls and women came to her in secret.

"We want to learn the message in your book, but the warriors forbid it," Mariah said tearfully.

Purity sent a message to Chief Wolf, asking for a visit to discuss the matter. A few days later, Chief Wolf, Sharp Arrow, and several warriors summoned her to the center of camp.

"Purity, we have heard the women and children want to learn to read, but it is not our way. We seek your wisdom. Is this wrong?" Chief Wolf asked with concern.

"The women and girls must be taught to read, or there will be division in the families. All must learn the teaching within the pages," Purity replied.

He thought for several moments without saying anything, then spoke with the warriors.

"The old order is dying away. We must embrace the new. All must learn to read, including the women, the boys and girls," Chief Wolf declared with confidence.

"All must read the book," Sharp Arrow confirmed to Purity and all those gathered.

Purity pulled the Bible from her backpack and read from the New Testament.

"In Christ, there is neither male nor female, but all are created equal in the sight of God."

A smile of satisfaction erupted on Chief Wolf's face, and a deep peace filtered through his soul.

"Good. You teach the warriors, and they will teach the women and the children," Sharp Arrow declared.

"Captain, forgive me for being angry with you," Purity whispered in quiet prayer.

"I believe that through the worst, you bring the best."

Every evening the tribe gathered together. As Purity read through the Scriptures, Chief Wolf and Sharp Arrow translated the Bible stories to the tribe. They absorbed the messages with interest, and most received the Good News of the Savior. The bickering between many of them stopped. They began to work together without complaining or gossiping. Others reported dreams and visions from heaven. They asked for wisdom, direction, and knowledge on how to conduct their lives. Prayers were answered.

* * *

Even though Purity was well, Sharp Arrow came each day to walk with her. He asked her many questions, and she taught him everything she could remember.

Mariah's devotion to Purity was unquestioned, but the attention Sharp Arrow lavished on their guest stung. Her hope of one day capturing Sharp Arrow's attention dissipated the longer Purity stayed.

She'd stood by and watched as Sharp Arrow had presented an exquisite white fox fur cloak with slits for the arms. He'd placed it on Purity's shoulders and secured it with leather straps.

It was an honor to be singled out by the prince in this way. And others in the tribe noticed his regard for Purity. Mariah had overheard the women as they'd sat around the fire weaving ornate baskets.

"Sharp Arrow no want Indian bride?" a white-haired grandmother had asked.

"He wants Purity," a beautiful maiden had confirmed, a touch of disappointment in her voice.

"Prince Sharp Arrow too good for Indian girls," a stout woman with great standing in the tribe had chided.

Mariah had been unable to stay silent any longer and jumped in to defend the prince.

"He will marry Indian bride when he's ready."

The women had laughed at her.

"He's too busy in white girl's tee-pee. Stop hoping. He no wants you," a snotty Indian teen had scolded.

* * *

Purity's beauty and strength had returned in the few weeks since her healing. She now dressed as an Indian maiden in an ornate leather dress with soft moccasins. Her deepening relationship with the tribe only confused her more.

"Captain, do I belong with the tribe? Do you want me to stay forever? If not, I'm ready to go home," she'd spoken aloud to the heavens on more than one occasion. She longed to return to the New Earth for answers but hadn't been allowed to journey there since her arrival at the camp.

Memories of Shadow Brook Estate filled her thoughts most days. She thought on her sons and her mother, wondering if they were safe and happy. But most of all, she thought on Favor.

She'd lost track of time there with the Indians. She had no idea how long she'd been gone until she'd asked Mariah. Five months.

"How has the time slipped by so quickly?" she asked herself.

"I wonder if Favor has moved on. Did his mother marry him off? Is he lost to me forever?"

Times and Seasons

Chapter 34

Purity was sweeping her teepee when Fair Dawn and Mariah waved for her to come. She threw down the dry broom and rushed to her friends, ready for whatever adventure they had in mind.

They led her out into the surrounding forest. This wasn't the first time they'd dodged the warrior's surveillance and escaped from the Indian camp. If they were caught, they'd receive a swift rebuke. Leaving camp unchaperoned was strictly forbidden for safety reasons.

After a long hike, they rested by a majestic river with a cascading waterfall that emptied into a deep pond. They jumped in, cooling themselves off after the journey.

Several hours passed as they swam and feasted on dried fruit, deer jerky, and roasted nuts.

Purity noticed a flock of black crows that landed in a nearby tree. They shook the branches and thrashed about, squawking. There was something about the sound that rocked her soul. Her countenance changed from relaxed to one of fear and dread.

Mariah noticed Purity's expression and looked to Fair Dawn.

"Let's go," Fair Dawn said, sensing the danger. She scanned their surroundings and spotted three white men amid the heavy brush. They were mounted on horses and watched the women as they gathered their things in a rush.

Ahaba's dark spirits hovered above them, looking for someone to devour. The dark spirits pounced on the lustful men, taking full possession.

Purity felt the demonic spirits waging war against her soul. She saw the men too and warned Mariah and Fair Dawn in their native language.

"Get ready to run."

They nodded in understanding. Purity bolted to the trail, taking the lead. Mariah and Fair Dawn followed close behind.

The thunderous pounding of horse's hooves sent terror into every cell of their bodies. The ground shook as their pursuers gained speed.

"Do we have weapons?" Purity asked.

"No," the Indian maidens answered.

"Run and don't look back," Purity yelled.

As Mariah and Fair Dawn rushed ahead, Purity slipped back, trying to distract the riders. She picked up a few jagged rocks and launched them one at a time with targeted precision.

The horses bucked and neighed in protest. One man was thrown from his horse and rolled around on the ground in pain.

Another other pursuer pulled a lasso rope from the back of his saddle and twirled it above his head, hoping to catch fresh prey. The rope spiraled close. Purity grabbed it with both hands, gave it a wild yank, and pulled the man to the ground. He was knocked unconscious by the force of his fall.

The last tormentor dismounted his horse and stalked after her in hopes of fulfilling his lustful desires. Purity threw one last rock, hitting his head. Blood poured from the fresh laceration.

"Get back here, dirty Indian," his voice quivered with malice. He continued his pursuit as demons clung to his back and bit his neck.

"Dam spiders," he said, reacting to the pain.

He came close enough to grab her braided ponytail, but Purity gave him a swift elbow to the abdomen. He bent over momentarily but carried on, determined to finish the assault. He lagged behind her, out of breath.

One of Ahaba's evil spirits manifested in the form of a black snake on the ground. It slithered along, then morphed into a large tree root. Purity's feet tripped over it, and her body sailed through the air, plummeting to the ground.

* * *

Sharp Arrow and his warriors had noticed the women were missing and now searched for them. They pounded on handheld drums, hoping for any response from the missing maidens.

"Mariah, Fair Dawn, Purity," the warriors called out.

Ahaba hovered above, appearing as ghostly clouds. He blew ominous winds in their direction. The warriors shielded their eyes from heavy dust and fought against flying tree branches. The warriors interpreted it as a bad omen.

"Evil fights against us. Captain, help us," Sharp Arrow shouted.

Fair Dawn and Mariah made their way through the forest with the speed of well-trained athletes. They heard the familiar drum beat.

"Sharp Arrow, warriors, help us," Fair Dawn cried out.

The warriors heard their cries and pushed through the raging wind until they found them.

"Where's Purity," Sharp Arrow asked.

"She's fighting like a warrior. Three men were chasing us," Mariah said.

"Great Captain, show us the way," Sharp Arrow cried in anguish.

The warriors responded, bellowing out deafening war shouts. In response, the Ring of Grace appeared as five child angels glistening in heavenly light. The Indian warriors took a step back in fear. Kaleb whistled while Josiah, Sergio, Rocco, and Toby waved fiery hands for them to follow. The warriors followed the child angels along the trail.

* * *

The last predator stood over Purity. He pulled a gun from its holster. Blood trickled down from his brow and splattered his clothing.

Purity panted breathlessly as his dark shadow covered her withered body. The man pressed the gun into her back, hoping to intimidate her into submission.

"You move, I'll kill you," he threatened in the tribe's dialect. Then he returned the gun to its holder.

"Fresh Indian. What a find." He raised a sleeve to his wound and wiped away the blood that obscured his vision. His stubby fingers unbuttoned the sweaty shirt that clung to his body. He pulled his shirt open, exposing a bloated, hairy belly.

He leaned down, preparing to take what he wanted by force when Purity rolled over and gave him a solid kick to the abdomen.

"Not if I kill you first. I'm Purity Thomascovich from Shadow Brook Estate, Bristol, Rhode Island."

"Yeah, and I'm the President," the man mocked.

"You're not even a man. I'll have you arrested for rape," she said, panting with a quivering voice. She silently prayed the threat would deter his crime.

He furrowed his brow in disbelief.

"The Wisedor's are high-class folks. They'd have nothing to do with you, looking like a dirty Indian," he argued.

"I'm engaged to Favor Wisedor," she insisted.

The man snarled and pulled her from the ground.

"Where's your ring then. Let's see it." He looked at her empty hand. "I didn't think so."

Purity kicked and pounded her fists, but it wasn't enough to break his grip. His hands ripped through her clothing.

"You wanna be Indian? I'll treat you like one." He raised a hand to slap her, but an arrow pierced his back, penetrating his heart. Blood drooled from his mouth as he dropped to his knees. His eyes remained locked on Purity until he keeled over, dead.

The Ring of Grace rolled into a ball of fire and shot through the atmosphere so fast it thundered.

Sharp Arrow emerged with his bow in hand, followed by the warriors. Purity ran into his arms, crying tears of relief. He held tight and kissed her forehead. His love for Purity was clear for all to see. Mariah looked away in humble acceptance.

Purity felt the awkwardness and pulled back from him. She did not want her gratitude to send Sharp Arrow the wrong message.

The sun was setting when they made it back to camp. The fearsome news spread rapidly through the tribe. They identified the attackers as those who frequently traded supplies with Indians on nearby reservations. Chief Wolf was deeply disturbed by the incident and remained very quiet for several days.

* * *

A few days later, the camp was full of activity. That morning, the men collected firewood for the bonfire that night. In the afternoon, they painted their faces, chest, and arms. Then each man put on tribal dance attire, decorated with ornate beading, shells, and feathers.

The women cooked deer meat on open fire pits along with corn, vegetable dishes, and rolled flatbread. Purity had never seen such a feast since joining the tribe a few years prior.

"What's going on?" Purity asked Mariah.

"Chief Wolf is seeing into the heavens," she answered with concern.

"What's he seeing?" Purity said, wondering if the great Captain was involved. Purity had felt a strange foreboding in her spirit ever since the trader was killed.

"Trouble is on the horizon. Chief Wolf's bones ache with worry," Mariah said.

"We prepare a feast tonight to ask for the Great Creator's wisdom."

The Indian maiden lifted a soft buckskin bundle from an ornate storage chest and handed it to Purity.

"Gifts for my teacher," Mariah said humbly.

"What's this?" Purity asked, untying the leather bindings. Inside was a bleached white deerskin Indian dress.

"It's beautiful," Purity said, holding the dress up to her frame.

"This, too," Mariah said, unwrapping another bundle. She pulled out an exquisite deerskin cape with white mink fur lining the hood and borders. Both garments were decorated with elaborate beading, seashells, and rare bird feathers.

"Thank you. But these are priceless," Purity said, feeling uncomfortable with the gifts.

"Dance in these. We must please Great Creator," Mariah pleaded.

Reluctantly, Purity put them on. She'd never looked more like an Indian maiden. Standing, completely restored, she looked up at the heavens through the opening at the top of the teepee.

"Lord of the Dance, teach me to dance again," Purity pleaded, wondering if her body had the strength.

"I want to dance too, Lord of the Dance," Mariah added, eavesdropping on the prayer.

Purity hugged her dear friend.

"Yes, of course. He'll teach you too."

That evening, the sunset left bright swirls of pink, orange, and yellow in the fading sky. Singing erupted from the middle of the camp as the young warriors and maidens began playing the drums and tribal instruments. As the camp darkened, the light from the bonfire illuminated the faces of the tribe.

The tribe watched with great anticipation as the young warriors danced to the Great Creator. During her time with the tribe, Purity had watched with keen interest as the warriors practiced their tribal dances. The dances were passed down from generation to generation, each preserving the precise rhythm and choreography.

Purity watched from the shadows. Her eyes focused on the movement of one warrior at a time, digesting the timing, rhythm, and choreography. As the warriors danced around the bonfire, they suddenly appeared as flames of fire. Each one jumped and twirled with furious speed and precise timing. A holy presence descended, appearing as a misty white fog, blanketing the small tribe Indians.

Purity emerged from the shadows and mingled with the tribe as they sang, clapped, and joyfully watched the dancers by moonlight.

The beat of the drums changed to a fast-paced rhythm. Sharp Arrow danced with incredible ability. His muscles flexed as he hit every step with precision. He circled around by Purity, clearly admiring her new attire. On his next trip around the bonfire, he reached for her hand. For the first time, the tribe witnessed Purity's gift of dance as she joined in.

"We praise our Creator in heaven, the great Captain," the tribe shouted in unison.

Purity's feet moved in perfect step with Sharp Arrow and the other warriors. The Indians were filled with amazement because only the warriors were trained in these dances.

Chief Wolf joined the dance, trying to keep up with the younger, more agile warriors. He beamed, watching Purity with Sharp Arrow dancing together.

The tribe worshiped with joy for the Great Creator.

"We praise the Great Creator," the tribe shouted in exaltation for all his blessings. Many were overtaken with a heavenly bliss and bowed low in humility.

"Great Creator, give us your wisdom. Lead us where we can serve you. Don't let evil destroy us. Please show us what is coming," Sharp Arrow cried out, kneeling with humility.

The tribe wailed in sorrow, each asking for forgiveness, guidance, and protection.

"You see beyond the mountains. Captain, guide these people to a better place," Purity asked with eyes raised to the heavens.

After much prayer, the tribe rose and danced again with all their might. As they worshiped, a shining heavenly Warrior appeared among them, illuminated like many suns. He began to dance with all his might. The Indian warriors danced with him in perfect rhythm.

"Honor to the Great Shining One," Chief Wolf shouted.

"Lord of the Dance," Purity called to him.

The rest of the tribe dropped to their knees in humility and watched. The musicians played on, but their song was joined with the sound of a heavenly orchestra.

Lord of the Dance was handsome, with eyes like blazing fire, glowing skin, and toned muscles. He wore the garment of a great Indian warrior. In his right hand, he held a sword of fire. The blade glistened and projected sprays of fire as he danced, burning up the dried grass below.

A vast army of warriors, mounted on horses and in full battle armor, were visible above him. They surrounded the camp.

Then Lord of the Dance evaporated into a billion particles of gold dust, blanketing the camp.

"Lord of the Dance, don't leave us," Purity yelled, mesmerized. Visions of meeting him on the New Earth rolled through Purity's mind, and she was transported back to where she first encountered Lord of the Dance. He was by the river's shore, splashing about and pouring cool water over his head with a golden chalice. He looked at Purity with his eyes like flames of fire. Her knees collapsed and sank into the soft sand. Gently, he scooped cool water into the cup and raised it to her mouth.

"Drink deep. Drink it all," he said.

Purity's thoughts shifted back to the tribe. The blazing bonfire shone brightly against the growing darkness beyond its reach. The light reflected off of faces covered in heavenly gold dust. The whole tribe rejoiced in the awesomeness of seeing who they believed was the Great Creator. Rising to their feet, they continued with praise and dancing into the wee morning hours.

Purity, Mariah, and Fair Dawn returned to their teepee, exhausted from all the dancing and singing. They fell onto their soft fur pallets, and Fair Dawn and Mariah quickly settled into a heavenly sleep. Sleep eluded Purity, who tossed like a wave as uncertainty tormented her soul.

Eventually, Purity dozed, and one by one, the Ring of Grace entered the teepee. They circled in rapid rotation, appearing as small wheels of fire and lightning strikes. Bright and Star came in rainbow light and waved their hands, encircling Purity in pure light. Gently, the light lifted her body. The Ring of Grace laid fiery hands on her head, releasing deeper sleep and peace for the journey.

In moments they were soaring through the atmosphere and into deep space, passing galaxies and large planets with orbiting moons. Bright and Star supplied the needed light to navigate the way, and the universe echoed with choirs of angels singing.

Sergio, Toby, and Kaleb batted asteroids and ice debris from their path. Josiah and Rocco flew before them, breaking through dark energy and gravitational forces from the surrounding planets. Purity slept through all the turbulence along the way.

Ahaba's evil forces detected their presence in the universe.

"Invaders. Capture them," he yelled, summoning evil forces. He blew on a black horn, making an ominous sound. Its sound alerted wicked principalities to prepare for war. Within moments, legions appeared as ghoulish figures with haunting eyes and translucent bodies.

A foreboding of evil saturated the Ring of Grace. Rocco placed his fiery hand on Purity's shoulder, waking her from a deep sleep. Sergio shot volts of electricity into her hands, and fiery swords manifested. The Ring of Grace raised their hands to heaven, and instantly their fiery swords appeared for battle.

"Captain of the Lord's Army. Your Kingdom come, your will be done," the Ring of Grace bellowed in unison.

Josiah shot another blast of electricity, and it penetrated Purity's back. Giant wings of electric light appeared, flapping with great speed. Rocco and Toby fused them to Purity's back with hot hands of fire.

"Meet Soar, your wings for the battle," Toby said with a wink.

"But I don't know how to fly," Purity said.

"Don't worry. Soar was born to fly. Just turn in the direction you want to go, and he will follow," Sergio yelled, raising his sword.

"Get ready to battle," Rocco screamed, raising both his swords.

Purity's wings flapped with ease. She moved her shoulders to the left, and the wings flew to the left. Then she moved her shoulders to the right, and the wings flew to the right.

"I've got this," Purity said, feeling confident.

The enemy attacked at incredible speeds. Their hissing screams, murderous blows, and foul cursing taxed the small company of angels to a breaking point. Still, they fought on against the enemy army, flying through vast expanses at the speed of light.

"My arms are breaking," Purity complained to the Ring of Grace.

"Call out his name. He's our champion. Captain of the Lord's Army. Do it," Sergio commanded.

"Captain. Captain, I need your strength," Purity breathlessly called out as she fought off several saliva-dripping demons.

The Captain appeared with his army of warriors.

"Captain, is that you?" Purity called out, seeing a spectacular warrior on a flying white stallion a long-distance away.

His voice resounded in her heart.

"I'm here, my love. Do not fear. I will strengthen you." Every fiber of her body was strengthened instantly.

"Archangels, report for battle," the Captain's voice commanded. He pulled a small trumpet from his body armor and blasted a call to battle.

"At your service," the might archangels yelled in unity. Then they pulled out their galactic weapons and lasered thousands of enemy spirits in a short time.

The sound of trumpets echoed as Purity, and the Ring of Grace approached a glistening planet. Purity saw legions of angels appearing as electric beams of glistening light who blew trumpets to alert New Earth's inhabitants that a new arrival approached. Purity and her escorts soared with even greater speed into the enormous planet's gravitational pull. They entered through the majestic, radiant blue arches with electromagnetic gates of silver and gold fibers that automatically opened for them to pass.

The New Earth glowed in vibrant colors wrapped in glistening gold and silver. Purity's heart sang with thankfulness at the unexpected invitation after so long.

"Safe at last," Purity said, relieved as she descended into New Earth's atmosphere. Peace and extreme love permeated every cell of her body as she floated down through misty rainbow colors and tranquil clouds.

"Someone's calling your name," Bright called out.

"Mother. Mother," Clarity's call vibrated through the atmosphere.

"She really missed you," Star said with a smile.

"Clarity, I've missed you so," Purity yelled as the glistening river appeared.

"Mother," Clarity called from the sailboat that moved slowly through the water.

Purity's wings glided through the atmosphere with precision and deposited her into the sailboat. Soar disengaged from Purity's back and hovered for a moment, then flew away.

"Thank you, Soar. Good work," Purity said, waving goodbye.

Clarity's small hands encompassed her mother's face with caressing love.

"Mother, the Captain's timing is perfect."

The sailboat maneuvered to the river's edge and landed with a thud. Nearby trees extended gold-laced branches that morphed into loving hands, helping Clarity and Purity disembark.

"The trees love to help. This way, Mother." Clarity ran ahead into a nearby vineyard and disappeared into heavy foliage.

"Clarity, wait. Don't leave me alone," Purity shouted as she lost sight of her daughter.

A farmer, wearing a large sun hat, was tending vines a few rows down. He sang, "Captain of the Lord's Army" with all his might, accompanied by the echo of an unseen choir and orchestra.

> He's Captain of the Lord's Army
> He gives the victory
> Captain of the Lord's Army
> He gives the victory

We stand, we fight
We give it all our might
Until the battle's won
Until the battle's won

He is our victory
He is our victory

Purity approached, listening to the familiar tune. She remembered hearing it the first time she came to the New Earth. The ground had shaken under her feet as the army had sung together as one.

"Sorry to bother you, but did you see a little girl pass by?" Purity asked, tapping on the farmer's shoulder.

The man jumped, startled, and turned to look her straight in the eyes. His eyes were deep blue and sparkled like diamonds.

"You mean my granddaughter?" he questioned.

Purity gasped.

"Papa, is it really you?"

On the New Earth, Papa looked years younger and more vibrant than ever. Purity melted into her father's arms and burst into tears.

Papa held his daughter tight.

"You're going to be alright, sweetheart."

"You don't know what I've been through," Purity said with great sorrow.

"I know all about it. Don't worry. No matter what happens, the Captain's in control," he said, stroking her hair.

Clarity returned, carrying a basket full of grapes in one hand and snacking on a cluster with the other.

Purity had so much to tell Papa.

"Mama's well, but it's been a rough road for me. I was engaged to the love of my life and won a dance competition, but then..." Her voice trailed off.

"Take heart, my child. Quiet your soul. The Captain fights your battles, and he holds the key to every victory. You have to trust him."

"I have so many questions for the Captain. I thought I was doing everything right. Why did he allow me to suffer? Was there something I missed? I worked so hard, and I still lost everything."

"My heart breaks knowing yours was broken but cheer up. You must believe the Captain is working through the good and bad. You must learn to battle through the tough times and count your blessings when everything's running smoothly," Papa said. He picked a few grapes and offered them to his daughter.

Eating a few pieces of the sweet fruit, her mood shifted.

"You're right, Papa. Look what the Captain's done for you. What's it like here?" Purity asked, looking around.

"His presence is our light. He provides all we need. We live in perfect unity—one people, one language, one spirit. I completed my purpose, and this is my reward," Papa sighed with contentment.

"But we better hurry. Your time here is running out. I need to speak with you about the tribe."

"You know about the tribe? We need the Captain's guidance," Purity said with keen interest.

"He knows the tribe's kingdom purposes. On earth, as it is in heaven. Captain chose me to give you his answer to the tribe."

"Yes, Papa, what is it?" Purity asked with urgency.

"Come, there is more to know," Papa said, taking Purity and Clarity by the hands.

Keenan and Valor appeared overhead, squawking to alert those below. They landed gracefully with extended wings. Papa raised a hand, signaling for Purity and Clarity to mount the large eagles.

They climbed onto Valor, who stooped slightly to make an easy mount. His feathers were soft and smelled of Frankincense. Purity breathed in, and all her stress melted away.

"You smell good, Valor," Clarity said to the giant eagle.

"Thank you, child," Valor said, giving a wink.

"Enough chatter. Let's get going," Papa said, hopping on Keenan's back.

Each one grabbed some feathers, holding tight for take-off. The eagles ran and lifted off, flapping enormous wings on the wind.

They flew countless miles over New Earth. Towering snow-capped mountains, lush forests, and majestic vineyards created endless captivating views. The eagles flew low near a roaring waterfall, the cool mist refreshing each rider.

With great speed, the eagles flew up an enormous mountain where an outdoor stadium had been carved out of the rock at its peak. Roars from the capacity crowd reached their ears and thunderous applause echoed through the high mountain range.

Visions of the old earth were projected on a large transparent screen for all the Cloud of Witnesses to see. They were those who lived on the New Earth—each one having been resurrected to new life. The praise of those in the stadium united with those worshiping and praising on the old earth that's passing away.

Angelic hosts numbering in the thousands hovered above, radiating rainbow colors. They danced to the upbeat songs rising from below.

Valor and Kenan deposited their riders at the base of a long flight of jagged stone steps that led to the stadium entrance. Papa and Clarity climbed with ease, but Purity huffed and puffed under the exertion. The mountain was so high that the air had thinned. Wild praise and adoring songs kept her going until finally they reached the stadium and found three empty seats.

Scenes of events happening on the old earth flashed before the multitudes. The visions loomed larger than life in vibrant color. Purity saw those who praised the Captain of the Lord's Army—from every tribe and nation.

Many were being tortured and mistreated because they refused to disown the Captain's name.

"Reject the Captain of the Lord's Army, and you'll keep your head," a young extremist threatened a believer.

"No, the Captain deserves my life and my death," the believer said, refusing to recant.

"You've made your decision," the militant said and killed the martyr.

Instantly, the believer was translated to the center of the stadium for all to see. Many hugged the newcomer and welcomed him there.

"He's entered into his eternal reward. Guess what's next?" Papa asked.

Suddenly, a vision of the Narraganset tribe appeared. There was Purity and Sharp Arrow, along with the mighty warriors, dancing with all their might. Lord of the Dance appeared in their midst.

"To the Captain, who lives forever," the Cloud of Witnesses roared in exaltation, sounding like a thunderclap.

"That's my mother," Clarity bragged to those standing nearby.

"The Captain received our praise," Purity said, humbled by the sight.

"Come. I have his answer for you," Papa said, leading them out of the stadium.

They hiked down the magnificent mountain, dodging falling rocks and slipping on the pebble-strewn path from time to time. Then the landscape leveled off, and the thick forests teamed with exotic animals. They journeyed for what seemed like hours to Purity, taking refreshments several times along the way at quaint villages.

"Cool water for weary travelers," a child offered, sinking a bucket into a deep well and pulling up living water. He ladled it into tall mugs. It had a life of its own that sparkled in colors of blue, purple, and gold.

The River of Life flowed nearby, saturating the underground streams and lands with life-giving sustenance. The inhabitants worked the land, bringing in crops, tending vineyards, and building homes. And, of course, they danced in praise and feasted at tables of bounty.

Purity saw that multitudes of children roamed the land.

"There are so many children in the land. Why?" Purity asked Papa.

"On the old earth that's passing away, so many don't live long because of disease, abuse, and poverty. Here, they get a choice to remain as children or grow up," Papa said, pointing to a pack of forest-dwelling children.

"Like a good father, the Captain comes and plays games with them and teaches them many things. Oh, how they love the Captain," Papa said.

Moving on, their little group came to a high mountain cliff. Purity spotted a great plain with steaming hot quicksand pools. Vapors rose, then dissipated in the gentle breeze.

"What a wretched place. It couldn't be a part of the New Earth?" Purity insisted.

"Wait and see. That's where we're headed," Papa said as he walked on.

"You can't be serious, Papa," Purity said, holding Clarity close.

"You can't avoid some things in life." Papa gently took Purity's hand.

Soon, they entered the vast wasteland. Their feet started to sink as they stepped into the sandy pits, and the strong smell of sulfur rose from the steamy mist. Then a fierce wind began raging around them.

"Hold Clarity tight," Papa warned.

Purity grabbed for the child as her feet sunk deeper with every step.

"Help, Mother," Clarity complained, fearing the suction pulling her body into the sand.

"What is this place?"

"It's called Premature Landings—where they enter too soon," Papa answered.

"What do you mean? Who enters too soon?" Purity asked with a confused stare. With each passing moment, Purity sunk deeper.

Clarity helped pull her from a sinking pit with supernatural strength.

"You're just a child, and your strength is that of a warrior," Purity said in amazement.

"The Captain is my strength."

"That was close. Thank you, Clarity." She took a few steps forward, still struggling for solid footing.

"Papa, help me understand this place?"

"Premature Landings are for those who believe in the Captain but, for whatever reason, failed to complete their purpose. This is where they enter the New Earth, disappointed because they chose not to believe all was possible in the great Captain. Fulfilling our purpose comes with many trials and at a great cost. But ultimately, he fights for us against the darkness. He gives his life for all who will receive. He was the first to rise again and live forever. So, we follow in his footsteps."

A short distance away, eerie ghost-like figures emerged from the heavy fog. Clarity grabbed hold of her grandfather's leg and squeezed tight.

"Papa, I'm scared," the child said, trembling in fear.

"Let's get out of here," Purity insisted.

"Premature Landings aren't pretty. Some come alone—others in groups. They come too soon because they didn't discern the Captain's will or disobeyed," Papa shouted as the wind kicked up and sand pounded against their skin.

Purity shielded Clarity's eyes and squinted, trying to avoid the painful sand particles. She tried to focus on the ghost-like creatures advancing in their direction. Papa pulled her and Clarity toward the approaching figures.

"Papa, no. I'm afraid. They look like the walking dead." Purity fought Papa's hold, but Clarity, like an obedient child, moved along. A horror filled Purity's soul—like nothing she'd experienced on the old earth that was passing away.

A dark cloud with cracking lightning enveloped those entering New Earth.

Papa yanked them to a halting stop.

"This is as close as it gets," he murmured.

The wind blew Purity's hair in wild fits, but between the strands, she recognized Chief Wolf, Sharp Arrow, Fair Dawn, Mariah, and the whole Narragansett tribe.

"They've come too soon," Purity cried out.

"The tribe will be killed—their purposes cut short—if they don't listen. The Captain was honored by their worship. He has released his wisdom. Tell the tribe to migrate northwest. He will lead them to a new place—a place of fulfilled destiny where they will live in peace and purpose. The Destroyer is coming soon. Tell them to head northwest in three days, three days, three days," Papa's voice echoed as it trailed off.

Purity woke in a panic, back inside the dimly lit teepee. She wiped what felt like dust and sand particles from her eyes. It was dawn, and the rising sun promised another day of sweltering heat. Most of the tribe still basked in sweet sleep.

She prepared to meet the Chief by washing and fixing her hair. Mariah and Fair Dawn heard the stirring but only rolled over in their deep sleep.

Purity emerged from the teepee with puffy eyes, squinting at the bright morning light.

"Where is Chief Wolf," she asked a few of the warriors guarding the sleeping tribe.

"On the sacred ground," one warrior said and pointed to familiar caves at the edge of the village.

Purity walked to the sacred caves guarded by many warriors.

"The Captain has a message for Chief Wolf," Purity spoke in their tribal language.

"Come. His spirit is in heavenly places," replied a warrior.

Another warrior grabbed a torch, lit it, and motioned for her to follow.

They entered the dark cave and journeyed through jagged, steep caverns. The torch illuminated ancient drawings of Indian villages and buffalo hunting. The cave's narrow walls squeezed tighter the further they went. She thought more than once of turning around as the darkness and isolation made her nervous.

"Captain, hold it steady," she thought as her foot slipped and her hands clutched the cold stone walls.

The warrior helped steady her with one hand while holding the torch with the other. It was as though he sensed her vulnerability and gently reassured her everything would be alright.

"Thank you, my brother."

Up ahead, the narrow path opened into a spacious cave. The cavern was dimly lit with torches, and burning incense clouded the air.

Warriors sat cross-legged and looked to be in deep meditation. They hummed in unison with the beating drums and the whistle of Indian harmonics. Entranced by the Holy Spirit, they started singing, "Dancing Warriors."

> Dancing warriors of the King
> Seeking His will, to save our lives
> Dancing warriors of the King
> Giving visions, he leads us on
>
> The King came down and danced in fire
> By his Spirit, heaven came down
> In him alone, our lives are found
> Light the way to go, we call
>
> Dancing warriors, till Kingdom come
> Dancing warriors, dancing warriors

There in their midst was Chief Wolf, sitting on a mound of furs with his eyes closed. She wondered if he was away on the New Earth with Captain of the Lord's Army.

Purity drew near, fell at his feet, and began to sob softly. Without opening his eyes, Chief Wolf extended a hand, permitting her to draw closer.

"Give us the answer," Chief Wolf demanded.

"The Captain received our praise," Purity said, raising respectful eyes to his face.

"The Captain has spoken his will for the tribe. What is, what could be, and what is to come. You are his messenger," Chief Wolf said slowly.

Purity knelt in a praying position and spoke loud enough for all to hear.

"The tribe must complete their purpose. Then you will enter the New Earth with your destiny fulfilled. The Destroyer is coming with deadly blows. Your tribe will die unless you move northwest in three days. The Captain will show you where to settle. Don't look back. If you stay, your people will die before their time. This is the word from Captain of the Lord's Army."

The drums pounded with intensity in response.

"No," yelled a warrior who jumped to his feet.

"We will not die."

"She speaks lies and knows nothing," an older rebellious warrior complained, drawing a knife from its sheath.

"We must fight for our land," another warrior urged, lifting his spear.

Other warriors grabbed Purity and raised their machetes to kill.

"The Captain is giving you a new land. If you stay, your blood will flow like a river," Purity protested.

Chief Wolf raised his spear and called out, "Let her go. She brings good news. The enemy devours those with blind eyes and deaf ears. The season has changed. We're surrounded on every side. They come to take the land and rip our lives like a bear claws prey. The choice is yours. If you stay, death will find you. Move forward, and you will live."

"You agree with this foreigner?" another warrior asked, jumping up in defiance.

"Captain of the Lord's Army's appeared to me last night. The message was the same. Purity confirms his will. We must move on the third day and fulfill our purpose." Chief Wolf turned to Purity.

"If you wish to go home now, we will escort you as we leave this place," Chief Wolf said with kindness.

The news soon circulated among the tribe, and many arguments broke out among those who refused wisdom.

Sharp Arrow tried to convince them.

"Violence comes like a storm. Why choose death over life. You are mighty warriors. We leave not because we are afraid to fight, but because we're obedient to the Captain who knows all things."

"We don't know this, Captain," a rebel shouted.

"You heard his will, yet it is as if you are deaf and dumb. Your blood and the blood of your children is on your own heads," Sharp Arrow shouted, then turned away with much sadness.

On the third day, most of the tribe left before dawn. They waved tearful goodbyes to those who chose to stay. As one group, the tribe moved north, avoiding towns and cities. On the second day, they were within hours of Bristol.

"We'll camp here tonight," Chief said, and they settled by a slow-moving river.

Purity put her white cape around her shoulders to keep warm in the cool night air. She headed to the river alone, wanting to think and pray. At the river's edge, she gazed at her image in the water, thinking back to the time she had sat with Favor by the water at Shadow Brook Estate.

A small pebble skipped over the water, and she turned to see Sharp Arrow. He motioned for her to walk with him along the river.

She reflected on her time with Sharp Arrow as they walked side-by-side in silence. She'd taught him everything Favor and Victoria had taught her regarding reading, culture, history, and science.

The Indian children played a short distance away, rattling sticks, batting woven balls, and singing songs. Mariah looked after them but also kept a keen eye on Purity and the Indian prince.

Purity looked in Mariah's direction.

"Should I call for her?"

"We must speak alone," Sharp Arrow said, reaching for her hand. He led her to a more secluded area, out of reach from prying ears.

Sharp Arrow stopped and held both of Purity's hands. His eyes seemed to search for some type of confirmation.

"It's time for Sharp Arrow to marry."

"There's an Indian maiden who loves you with her whole heart. Mariah's the wife for you," Purity said.

"Mariah? But she gave her wedding dress and cape to you." He touched the white cape on her shoulders.

Purity's eyes widened at the revelation.

"Her wedding dress and cape?"

"Yes. She saw what you refused to see," Sharp Arrow said with boldness. He paused for several moments and then, as though mustering great courage, looked intently into Purity's eyes once again.

"Be my wife. I'm in love with you." He leaned in to kiss her lips, but Purity stepped back.

"I didn't realize what it meant," Purity whispered.

He drew her close again.

"Tell me your heart," Sharp Arrow said, hoping.

"I've grown to love you, but not as your wife," Purity admitted. She took off the cape and handed it to Sharp Arrow.

"I do not understand," Sharp Arrow replied.

"The Captain has another plan for me. After your father departs to the New Earth, you will lead this tribe. My time with your great people is over. I owe you my life, but my heart belongs to someone else. I'm forever grateful, and I'll never forget you, great man of God. Promise me the tribe will continue with their studies," Purity said, choked up.

Sharp Arrow held the cape tightly and embraced it as though it were the only thing he had left.

"You will be missed. I promise we will study," his voice sounded with calm resolve.

"I will take you home when the sun rises."

Purity placed her hand gently on his arm.

"Sharp Arrow, Mariah loves you. Please consider her as your wife."

"But she does not have my heart," he confessed.

Distractions in Maine

Chapter 35

FAVOR'S SPIRIT GROANED as the afternoon party dragged on. He'd left for Maine soon after Purity's attack six months prior. John Matthew's family estate was one of the finest in Ogunquit, Maine. It was settled on the coast with rolling lawns, large gardens, and opulent fountains. John was his closest friend. They'd met back in their school days.

"How about a game of poker in the grand parlor?" John asked as he approached Favor.

"Thank you, friend, but I'm only interested in some fresh air about now," Favor replied.

"See you at dinner then." John walked away with a few friends.

Favor wandered through crowds of distinguished guests, trying to get away undetected. He'd kept his reasons for leaving Bristol to himself. Even John didn't know the full truth. No doubt the gossips probably spread all manner of tales about him—he'd seen the whispers and nods. Unfortunately, none of their stories seemed to keep the young ladies at bay.

John's younger sister, Debra, was a sweet girl. She always seemed to find Favor in a room full of people. He tried not to give her any reason to hope, but it was hard to avoid her in the same house. She'd always been more like a sister and having her around made him miss Victoria.

Favor found his way outside and wandered through a small garden that led to a grassy meadow filled with yellow daisies. The bright sunshine warmed him as he stepped into a patch of flowers.

"Captain, please let me know if Purity lives," he silently prayed.

He took a few more steps, and when he looked up at the horizon, it was as if he saw into another realm. Purity stood before him, dressed in a beautiful white buckskin dress with a cape trimmed with white fur draped over her shoulders. He recognized the traditional Indian attire.

He fell to his knees.

"You're alive," was all he could get out.

Then he saw a handsome Indian warrior who took Purity by the hand. They walked by the river's edge together.

"No. You belong with me," Favor gasped.

Gentle footsteps fell behind him, distracting him from the scene. The vision disappeared, and he snapped his head toward the person intruding on the moment.

There was Debra, standing a few feet away, looking like a pampered princess.

"Are you alright, Favor?" Debra asked.

"You left the party in a rush."

"I'm sorry. I needed to be alone," Favor said, avoiding eye contact.

"I'll go then," Debra sounded apologetic.

Favor sighed.

"I don't mean to be rude. You don't have to leave."

"I was wondering if you'd like to take a walk. But if you'd rather be alone?"

"I'm sorry. Something is weighing on my mind. Please excuse me," he said and disappeared back into the garden.

Debra watched after him. She brushed away a rogue tear that found its way down her cheek.

* * *

Favor retreated to his well-furnished bedroom and opened the window. Puffs of misty ocean air blew the curtains. He sank into a nearby chair, exhausted from living in the desperate disparity of having everything at his fingertips, yet never fully grasping what he desired.

"Purity, I miss you," he whispered.

His heart ached with painful memories. With eyes closed, his mind drifted back to Shadow Brook Estate. The Rose Garden patio teamed with the rich and spoiled, waiting for dance lessons. Purity was in her maid's uniform, cutting roses.

"Dance with me," Favor demanded.

"I don't need lessons," Purity said in a feisty manner.

"Maybe you can teach me something," he said.

They flew across the dance floor, Purity giving instructions along the way.

"Watch your feet. Not so stiff."

The memory faded, and Favor squeezed his eyes shut tighter, trying to conjure up the rest of the memory.

The air from the open window flowed in and out like deep breathing, caressing his face. For a moment, it felt like Purity's soft hand gliding over his cheek. He reached for it, but nothing was there.

* * *

The next day, Favor walked through the busy seaside town of Ogunquit. The echo of a ship's horn blasted in the distance. People scurried about, busy with life, business, and family matters. He'd never felt more alone and desperate for answers.

Passing a chapel, he stepped inside. Soft light streamed through stained glass windows—the rainbow reflections bouncing from place to place. He found a pew in front of the altar and knelt for several minutes.

"Captain, show me how to move forward. I need your direction. I thank you I shall have it," Favor prayed, focusing on the large cross beyond the altar. He lingered a bit longer, then rose and left in haste.

Loneliness sank in again as he returned to the busy streets of the town. Despite the noise and crowds of people, nothing could relieve his aching soul. He dodged people scurrying about, and for some unknown reason, he was drawn to a jewelry shop.

The bell jingled above the door as Favor entered. An excited young couple was there, trying on wedding bands.

"It's perfect," the soon-to-be bride boasted, giving a gentle kiss to her beloved.

"It's perfect because you're perfect for me," the groom said with loving admiration.

337

Favor browsed the jewelry cases, not knowing why he was there. His mind drifted back to his proposal the night of the gala. He and Purity had never had the chance to buy their rings.

The shop owner, a round, middle-aged, balding man, approached, eager to make a sale.

"I've got that special ring, don't doubt it. She won't be disappointed," he said, winking.

Favor's felt nothing but intense sorrow looking at the rings.

Misinterpreting Favor's look as one of confusion, the owner continued, "Let me help. I've got the best quality diamonds in the country."

"I honestly don't know what I'm doing here," Favor stuttered.

"That's what they all say. What's her name?" the shop owner chuckled.

Favor broke into a cold sweat.

The owner's face reflected concern.

"Sit down. I've seen nerves, but you have the look of one struggling with commitment," the middle-aged man said, directing Favor to a nearby chair.

"Honestly, I don't see anything worth buying," Favor sounded arrogant, wiping the perspiration from his forehead with a white handkerchief.

The shop owner brushed off the offense, and his eyes scanned Favor's high-priced suit and shoes.

"Wait a minute. Just wait one long minute. You won't be disappointed," the shop owner said in hasty tones and hurried into the back room.

In a moment, he returned with a small red velvet ring box and opened the contents under Favor's nose.

"This ring is called 'Radiance.' You won't find it anywhere else. I cut this diamond myself and personally designed the setting," the man boasted.

Favor was mesmerized by the stunning quality of the enchanting ring. He grabbed the gemology magnifying glass, and holding it to his eye, examined the quality of the diamonds. It was a princess-cut, two-carat diamond set in platinum and surrounded by another two carats of begets.

"These diamonds are priceless," Favor said, still examining the ring.

"Total weight is four carats for your special bride. What do you say?" asked the shop owner.

Without even knowing what he was saying, he blurted out, "I'll take it."

Favor returned the next day to settle the transaction. He stepped into the shop where a few customers browsed. To his surprise, one of Debra's acquaintances was in the shop with her fiancé, picking out engagement rings. He recognized her at once and tried to walk past them without notice.

"Favor, you're the last person I'd expect to see here. Don't tell me you're looking for an engagement ring?" the woman said with a loud, obnoxious voice that startled every ear in the place.

"If I was buying a ring, what concern is that of yours?" Favor said, trying to shut her down.

The shop owner eyed Favor and headed for the back room. In moments, he returned with the red velvet box. He approached Favor with a giddy payday smile.

"Just what you ordered, young man. What I'd give to see the look on her face when you pop the question," the owner spouted.

"It's not what you think," Favor said, addressing the nosy young woman who watched him.

With his stubby fingers, the shop owner opened the box, exposing the one-of-a-kind ring.

The young woman saw the ring and squealed with excitement as she moved in for a closer look.

"Fit for a queen. Lucky girl."

Favor snapped the box shut.

Debra's friend grabbed her fiancé's arm.

"I want one just like it," she begged.

Her fiancé looked intimidated.

"Let's think about this," the young woman's fiancé groaned. He took her hand and headed to the door.

"What do you mean, think about it? I've been waiting long enough," she complained.

Favor pulled a stack of cash from his pocket and slapped it on the counter.

"Thanks for causing a ruckus," Favor said, dreading the rumors to come.

"I'm sure I haven't heard the end of it."

The shop owner pounced on the large sum of cash and counted it with a hungry expression.

"You won't be sorry. She'll be ecstatic, whoever she is. Not another one like it in the whole country," the owner bragged.

Favor pocketed the ring and left.

* * *

Later that afternoon, the woman's fiancé reported the purchase to John during a friendly game of cards. The man lamented the high standard to which he was now to be held by his fiancée.

"Surely, I would know if Favor were ready to propose to a woman, and I've heard no such thing," John insisted.

It wasn't long before word of the ring spread to others in the household. At tea with his mother and Debra, it was the main topic of conversation.

"John, tell us truthfully, do you know who this lucky young lady is?" John's mother asked.

"I know nothing of the matter. I admit Favor has been very quiet the past few days, but he has given no hint of anything of the sort."

"Hopefully, it's our Debra who's the lucky girl. You can't mention the Wisedor name without people drooling with envy. Thankfully, we're just as rich, so it's a match if you ask me."

Debra blushed a deep rose color.

"Mother, do not speak of such things."

"What?" She turned to John.

"You're Favor's best friend, and he might as well marry your sister."

Debra's countenance lifted at the thought, and John noticed.

"Let's not get ahead of ourselves, Mother," John insisted.

Debra left the room realizing the ring wasn't bought for her. Finding a quiet study, she talked out loud.

"Favor's chosen someone else." She sang, 'Fantasy.'

> Fantasy, fantasy, you're everything I need
> I dreamed you were the one for me
> A hot romance and a wedding day
> Finding it hard, to live without
> My 'gotta have it' fantasy
> Fantasy, fantasy, in my dreams
> You were the one for me
> We're holding hands, in sweet romance
> Living out life in my head
> Oh fantasy, fantasy you steered me wrong
> Cause he's not asking and I'm alone
> Oh fantasy, fantasy
> I wasted my time, living a lie
> Believing in a future, nowhere to be found
> Fantasy, fantasy, I'm worse off than a clown
> Oh fantasy, fantasy, where are you now

* * *

The evening before Purity was to leave the tribe, Sharp Arrow sat around the campfire, staring into the flames. He was brokenhearted that she had refused his offer of marriage.

Chief Wolf sat close by his son, trying to lift his spirits.

"It's a new season for the tribe. Trust the Great One to heal your heart. Until then, our place in the world is waiting," Chief Wolf said with authority.

A peace entered Sharp Arrow's soul as he surrendered his future into the Great Creator's hands. He lifted his eyes to the stars and whispered, "You know the plans you have for me. Plans not to hurt me, but to give me hope and a future. Creator of the great lights, I trust you for the days ahead."

In the middle of the night, long after the tribe had retired, a lone rider galloped into the makeshift camp. The warriors keeping guard raised their weapons in defense. Then they recognized an Indian from their tribe—one who had remained behind—and they lowered their weapons.

The Indian dismounted the horse and fell to the ground from exhaustion. Several warriors dragged him into one of the shelters and gave him water to drink while the others summoned Chief Wolf and Sharp Arrow.

The bloodied, worn warrior could barely speak.

"Everyone's dead. Killed. The Destroyer came and slaughtered without mercy. I narrowly escaped," he said with heartbreaking regret.

A spirit of fear spread throughout the camp. Great cries of distress ascended to heaven.

"You have no reason to fear. We have obeyed. The great Captain has promised a new life. Those who rebelled died as expected. We will move forward without delay," Chief Wolf insisted.

A reverent peace came over the tribe with a new resolution to reach their new land. The tribe began to break camp.

Purity approached the man who had become like a father figure. Chief Wolf raised his hand, granting her permission to draw closer. He sat on layers of bear and elk furs with a look of confidence. She took his hand, kissed it, and sat down beside him.

"If it were my choice, you would stay forever," he said, looking straight ahead.

"You're like a father to me and your tribe, my family. We'll see each other again. If not here, on the New Earth."

"We know the Captain's power because of you. We promise to keep learning," he said, hugging her as a beloved daughter.

"Thank you for saving my life," Purity said, giving one last hug.

She returned to her shelter, unable to fight an entrancing slumber.

"I'll rest a bit," she mumbled as Fair Dawn and Mariah gathered their belongings.

Purity spiraled into a deep sleep and woke on the New Earth, lying in tall, green grass.

"Papa, Clarity, where are you?" she called, sitting up and looking around.

The bushes rustled nearby, and Clarity emerged and ran into her mother's arms.

"Soon, I'll be yours, dear mother. I'm coming soon," the child proclaimed.

"But I'm not even married," Purity said, looking into Clarity's deep blue eyes.

Another rustling from the bushes caught their attention. It was Bright Star, who appeared as a ball of rainbow light, then morphed into two separate beings of pulsating light.

"I have a message from Lord of the Dance," Bright said softly with full confidence.

"Follow the pilgrims to the great city. Don't give up," Star said, pointing to a distant city that shone like the sun.

Then before their eyes, Bright and Star morphed into a ball of fire and evaporated into millions of gold particles.

"Let's go. I hear the people singing," Clarity coaxed with enthusiasm.

Purity trailed behind her daughter as they marched with those going up to worship the Captain of the Lord's Army. Hours passed, but with each step, Purity felt invigorated. The atmosphere closer to the city was charged with a revitalizing power.

A great warrior appeared, and Purity recognized him. Trumpets blew, announcing Lord of the Dance.

"Take my hand. You'll need strength to complete the journey," he said with deep compassion.

"I've been beaten, left for dead, accused of murder, stripped of any success, and cast away from loved ones. I've lost everything. Please help me. My heart needs healing," Purity asked earnestly.

"It's during the trials, when the battles rage, that your faith must stand."

"Help me with my unbelief."

Their eyes locked, and she inhaled a deep supernatural love radiating from him. She looked away and then back, but he was gone.

"We're almost there, Mother," Clarity insisted.

In no time, they entered a great city that sparkled like a precious gem. The walls were broad and high, with twelve gates, made from a single pearl, guarded by twelve angels. There were three gates on each side of the eastern, western, northern, and southern walls. The city had twelve foundations made from jasper, sapphire, agate, emerald, onyx, carnelian, chrysalides, beryl, topaz, chrysoprase, jacinth, and amethyst.

The city had no need of the sun or moon, for the Captain of the Lord's Army's glory illuminated it. A pure river, known as the River of Life, coursed through the center of the city. On each side of the river grew trees of life, bearing twelve crops of fruit, with a fresh crop each month. The Captain used the leaves for medicine to heal the nations.

They followed the crowds heading to the Great Throne. Vast numbers of people worshipped the Captain on clear streets of gold.

Purity beheld the most magnificent golden throne engulfed in a rainbow of fire. Her knees buckled at the sight.

"Will I meet him now? After all I've been through," she thought.

Shouts of "hallelujah" and "praise the Captain" echoed through the city.

Lord of the Dance stood at the foot of the stairs leading to the throne. All Purity's anger melted away, and she loved him with all her heart. Her love for him eclipsed any human love ever experienced on the old earth that is passing away.

He reached for her hand.

"Do you love me, Purity?" Lord of the Dance asked with a gentle voice.

"Yes, since the moment I first saw you by the river. I wanted to stay with you forever," she confessed.

"You must know, Captain of the Lord's Army is King of Kings and Lord of Lords," Lord of the Dance confessed.

"Take me to him so he can heal all my pain," Purity begged.

"You're speaking to him now. I am the great Captain of the Lord's Army, and my name is Yeshua," he said, smiling at her.

Purity was speechless as Lord of the Dance transfigured into the mighty, Captain of the Lord's Army. The worshipers cheered with such exaltation that the pillars of the temple shook.

He was clothed as a mighty warrior king, dressed in a purple robe covered with jewels. On his robe were written the titles, 'Faithful and True,' 'Word of God,' 'First and Last,' and 'Almighty Captain.' His eyes shone bright, like flames of fire, and on his head were many crowns.

Purity fell to her knees, proclaiming, "My Captain, let me stay forever. Why was I blind to your identity?" Purity asked.

"Sometimes it takes time getting to know me before you realize who I really am," the Captain said with compassion.

"What matters is, I know you now," Purity said with awe.

"The time for you to remain has not come. Your purpose is not complete. You must return to fight injustice and share my love," he said and gently kissed her forehead.

"Only by your strength," she said, melting in his presence.

"I will restore sevenfold everything you've lost. Now, let's go in my power," the Captain proclaimed. He led her by the hand out of the temple.

His majestic white horse with a huge wing span was waiting. His saddle was ornamented with many jewels. He climbed on the horse, and a warrior handed him a golden shield. With his other hand, he reached for Purity.

"Ride with me," the Captain said, lifting Purity to the saddle. She sat in front of him, and turning her head, peered into his blazing eyes.

"To the nations," he shouted as they galloped away.

"Captain," she shouted as she woke up, shaking. She was back with the tribe on the old earth.

Mariah and Fair Dawn stared in amazement.

"You finally met Captain of the Lord's Army?" they said in unison.

Purity was unable to speak and trembled in his holiness for more than an hour.

Sudden Change

Chapter 36

NAOMI WINCED AS the skin on her knees rubbed raw on the old farmhouse porch. In a systematic motion, she scrubbed back and forth with the thick scrub brush.

"There's always a mess to clean," she grumbled.

The soap foamed and turned brown as it mixed with the built-up dried mud on the splintered wood. Again and again, she submerged the brush in the soapy wash bucket, brought it up dripping, and scrubbed some more.

"God, I can't take it. I need my daughter back," Naomi said with bitterness of soul, raising disappointed eyes to the sky.

"Forgive me. I sent her away to protect her, but without Purity, my life doesn't make sense."

The wind kicked up and howled an eerie sound that echoed around the old farmhouse. Naomi rose awkwardly, looking old and worn from years of labor. The heartbreak seeped deep into her bones, lapping up any joy.

Suddenly, the old porch vibrated as Rachel ran up the stairs, her feet kicking up dust.

"Now you've done it. More dirt," Naomi complained.

"Indians. Indians are coming," Rachel said, hopeful it was a good sign.

"Indians," Naomi repeated and squinted, causing her wrinkles to fold like lines on a map.

Sure enough, coming up the road were two Indians—a warrior and a maiden. With instant recognition, Naomi ran toward them. Rachel followed behind.

Purity slid from the horse. Naomi rubbed her tired eyes, blinking several times in disbelief.

"It's you. I'd know you from a mile away," Naomi said.

Purity looked completely restored, and they embraced each other for several minutes, crying tears of relief and joy.

"That was the fastest answer to prayer," Naomi said, giving Purity another hug. The reality of seeing her daughter resurrected to a healthy state replenished her soul like water on dry ground. Naomi turned her attention to the Indian warrior.

"She lives because of you. Tell Chief Wolf I'm forever thankful," Naomi said with deep emotion.

Sharp Arrow nodded, accepting her gratitude.

Loud galloping broke the focus of the sweet reunion. A cloud of dust erupted behind a speeding horse, rapidly approaching. To everyone's surprise, it was Mariah, the beautiful Indian maiden.

She dismounted from her horse, Wind, and fell at Purity's feet.

"My sister-friend, don't leave me behind," Mariah begged.

Sharp Arrow looked annoyed.

Purity took her aside.

"It's your chance—what you've always wanted. Stay with the tribe and marry Sharp Arrow. You're Chief Wolf's choice for him now," Purity urged, trying to sound convincing.

"I have more to learn, my teacher, my sister-friend. Let me stay with you," Mariah begged again.

"You belong with the tribe," Sharp Arrow barked, overhearing the conversation.

For the first time, Mariah defied his order.

"I won't marry a man who doesn't love me, even if he's Chief's son. One season ends, a new one begins. I'm never going back," Mariah said with resolve.

Sharp Arrow held his anger, and after a few moments, nodded in agreement.

"Stay, Mariah. You have my blessing," Sharp Arrow said with a change of heart. He then turned to Purity and said, "Thank you. I will never forget you." He turned his horse around and galloped off.

That evening, Naomi fixed a fine dinner, and they talked till the wee morning hours.

"Mother, please tell me what's going on with Favor? Did they clear my name in the court cases? Jezzie's case that I was the one who attacked her and Roberto's death? Will they arrest me?" Purity asked, trying to ward off a fear that hurt into her heart.

"The last I heard, Favor left town. Where? I don't know. And the court cases are still pending, I think. I can't lose you again."

"Captain will defend me. I'm not afraid," Purity said, her confidence rising.

Naomi grabbed her hand.

"How did you find me?"

"We talked about buying this old farm. It was my first guess."

* * *

The next day, Purity walked the property. She followed the sparse fence that marked the boundaries of their land. It was made of old pieces of wood, hammered to posts dug into the ground. Flowers and trees spotted the green pastures that surrounded the area.

The old farmhouse had a sturdy foundation, but the rest of it needed work. It was a three-bedroom single-story structure with wood floors. The kitchen had large windows that allowed a flood of light to stream in each morning. A family room with a stone fireplace was off the kitchen and was furnished with a blue velvet couch with fabric accent chairs. Naomi had made decorative silk pillows to dress each chair.

The dining area was Purity's favorite place, adorned with multicolored woven rugs that covered the rough, worn areas on the wooden floors. Naomi had purchased a used dining table and chairs, but with some light sanding and paint stain, it showed with elegance. A crystal vase with fresh flowers, picked from the meadow a stone's throw from the house, brightened the room. It also complimented the floral painting hanging above an ornate marble-topped sideboard recently purchased from a moving sale.

While Purity was gone, Naomi had spent most of her time repairing the inside, trying to make it presentable. It was a far cry from Shadow Brook Estate, but with a little elbow grease and fresh paint, it was home.

That same afternoon, Purity stopped in front of the old barn and stared at the double doors. A fresh wind blew over her long, wavy hair. She scanned every nook and cranny of the dried knotted wood on the front of the large structure.

"It seems sturdy enough for a school," she said, trying to open one of the large doors with a few hard tugs. The door dragged on the ground, making a grinding sound as though protesting her entrance.

A rush of odorous air that smelled like hay and animal excrement poured out from the barn. Some chickens flew past her head, squawking, and pigs raced over her feet, grunting.

"Captain, I think I've found my school," Purity said, peering into the dark barn.

"Anybody home?" she called out. Her voice ricocheted off the walls.

She opened the other door to air out the stale odors. Then she picked up a rake and started piling up the scattered mess of hay and animal excrement.

* * *

Word of Purity's return traveled quickly through Bristol. Many of her sons found the farm and helped with the renovations. Each one had remained healthy and strong while she was away. They cried at the sight of their dear mother, resurrected and restored to complete health.

Alexis, Natasha, Chin Lu, and many other friends also rejoiced in seeing their friend again.

Purity gave testimony regarding that wonderful night heaven invaded earth, and the Captain's power healed her.

She was grateful her friends had prospered in her absence—teaching at Favor's school and working on their degrees.

Not long after her return, Purity's dream of opening a school and teaching Bristol's poor children came to fruition. Within just a few days of opening, Purity recruited more students than anyone could handle.

Mariah, Rachel, and David worked as co-teachers, sharing responsibility as they taught reading and math basics.

The sons took a break from the school Favor had established and moved from the dorms to Hope Farm with Purity. They decided to continue their studies there and help teach. They made comfortable beds up in the hayloft above the classroom, and each night they sang praise songs and played their instruments. During the day, they saw to it that everything on the farm was well-groomed, and they even helped the students plant a vegetable garden.

* * *

Mariah continued studying, and David became her personal tutor. One day, as they played a game of tag with the children, David chased her into a grove of trees. He'd never set eyes on anyone more beautiful than the Indian maiden.

She ran like the wind, and he laughed at the challenge.

"Get back here, Mariah," he teased.

She ran behind bushes, and David lost sight of her.

"Come out, Mariah. You win," he said, admitting defeat.

She jumped out from behind a tree and startled him.

He gazed at this lovely one and took hold of her hand.

"Are you really staying for good, Mariah?" David asked with a serious tone.

"Yes. I'll go to college and become a real teacher," Mariah said with pride.

"What about Sharp Arrow and the tribe?"

"I'm not Sharp Arrow's choice, and he's not mine."

"Then you're not going back for sure?" David asked, relieved.

"My life is here with my new family, the children, and... you," she said, gazing into David's eyes.

"We can go to college next year, together. If we believe, God will make a way," David said in faith.

"I'll study hard. I promise," she said, blushing.

David gently leaned in and kissed her soft lips.

"Has anyone ever kissed you before?" he whispered.

"No," Mariah said with complete innocence.

"I'm so glad," David said and held her tight.

* * *

Purity sat correcting homework papers at her desk after school. Many students had stayed late for after-school tutoring.

A businessman in a suit entered.

Purity was surprised to see him and set her papers aside.

"Can I help you?" she gulped, wondering who he was and why such a visit was necessary.

"Are you Purity Thomascovich?" he asked in a severe tone.

"Yes, sir," she answered hesitantly.

"I'm from the bank that's financing this property. Did you know you're three months behind on the mortgage?"

Purity was shocked and embarrassed by the news.

"I had no idea, sir."

"If you don't pay up by next month, I'll begin the foreclosure process. Here's your notice," he said frankly, handing her an envelope and leaving in a hurry.

Naomi stepped into the classroom.

"I didn't know how to tell you. Your prize money covered the down payment, renovations, and some expenses. But there's nothing left. God knows we're not making a dime running this school," her mother complained.

All eyes were on Purity.

"The best we can do is pray," Purity encouraged the students, Rachel, Mariah, and David, who looked on with concern.

"Captain, we need a breakthrough," Purity whispered in prayer.

The next afternoon, a horse-drawn buggy made its way up the drive to Hope Farm. Purity wondered who it could be as few visitors came to the farm. She worried it might be someone from the bank again.

Her eyes squinted, trying to make out faces as the buggy bumped along the dirt drive. Then her feet couldn't take her fast enough. It was her dear friends.

"Pastor Ezra. Rebecca, it's been too long. When did you get back from China?" Purity called out.

The buggy stopped, and Pastor Ezra helped his wife Rebecca down.

"Not long ago. My how the time passes. We've missed you," Rebecca said, rushing to embrace Purity.

"Good to see you. Show us around," Pastor Ezra said, receiving a warm hug from Purity.

Purity gave them the grand tour around the farm. Then they stepped into the makeshift school in the barn. The student's stopped studying and eyed the visitors with curiosity.

"Presenting my students," Purity said, introducing the Pastors.

In unison, the students bid their hellos. Rachel, Mariah, and David continued with the lessons as the visitors stepped into a makeshift office.

"Purity, this place is remarkable. We're so proud of your work," Pastor Ezra offered with enthusiasm.

"I have a wish list, but the budget is a little tight right now. Most of our students can't afford to pay tuition," Purity explained.

"What's a visit without a blessing? A few days ago, the congregation took up an offering for your school," Rebecca said with pride. She handed over a large envelope filled with cash.

Purity lost her footing and landed with a jolt on a nearby bench.

"I don't know what to say," Purity responded, clutching the envelope for dear life.

"The old barn needs a roof," Pastor Ezra said, looking up at the light coming through.

"I'll talk to some of the men in the church about replacing it. Oh, and one more thing," He reached into his coat pocket and pulled out another roll of cash.

"This is from an anonymous donor."

"Who cares so much, Pastor?" Purity asked, receiving the money.

"Don't question it. God uses those who say 'yes.' Don't worry, this donor is filthy rich," he said with a chuckle.

"Take it and use it for yourselves. I'm sure you have bills to pay," Rebecca said with encouragement.

"The Captain's answering all our prayers," Purity confessed in amazement.

"Keep doing his work, and he'll supply," Pastor Ezra said with a chuckle that shook his belly.

"Purity, I had a dream about you last night," Rebecca said matter-of-factly.

"I saw you in the most exquisite gown, standing in a grand mansion, holding a wedding bouquet."

"You're sure it was me. It's simply impossible," Purity said, sounding doubtful.

"Unbelief will get you nowhere. Receive it as a sign from heaven," Rebecca scolded.

"When God gives my wife dreams, they come to pass. He's trying to tell you something, girl," Pastor Ezra said with authority.

The noise level from the children started to raise the roof.

"Purity, they're getting wild," Rachel said, rushing in, looking flustered.

"Excuse me," Purity left the office and returned to the makeshift classroom.

"Get your spelling words out and start studying. We have guests, and I expect you to behave," Purity said, giving a stern look to the mischievous children. They immediately obeyed.

"Rachel, David, and Mariah, you're in charge. Feel free to give out detentions to anyone who disobeys," Purity ordered.

She returned to the guests and announced, "Teatime."

Naomi just about fell over when the special guests entered the farmhouse.

"Look what the wind blew in?" Naomi said, wiping her hands on her apron.

"I was just baking. You're just in time."

After affectionate hugs, Purity took Pastor Ezra and Rebecca on a tour of the house.

Naomi scampered to an antique chest and pulled out an elegant tablecloth. She quickly covered the dining table with it and retrieved a crystal vase from the kitchen cabinet. She rushed outside to cut fresh flowers, and in moments the vase filled with flowers was placed as a centerpiece.

The guests returned from their quick tour and sat at the dining table.

"Nothing like fresh flowers," Rebecca said, inhaling the fragrance.

"Freshly picked for our guests," Purity said and ran to the kitchen to heat some water for tea.

"Get out of the kitchen. I'll handle the serving," Naomi commanded.

Moments later, Naomi served the hot tea as though serving the fine folk at the mansion. She set out Wisedor plates, teacups, saucers, and an ornate teapot. Then she brought out freshly baked banana bread on an ornate Wisedor serving tray.

Emotion flooded in as Purity recognized the ornate pattern and bright colors.

"This is Wisedor China. How did we ever afford it?" Purity asked.

"It was a gift from our dear Victoria when I resigned," Naomi said, feeling a tad strange mentioning Shadow Brook Estate.

"Wonderful tea and banana bread, I must say," Rebecca interjected, trying to divert heated memories.

Pastor Ezra and Rebecca feasted on big bites of the moist baked goods and gulped down the spiced tea.

"There was nothing like this in China. It's so good to be home," Rebecca said with contentment.

"Mama learned a lot working for Shadow Brook Estate. Baking was one thing," Purity said.

"It's so moist. No wonder you lasted so long at Shadow Brook Estate. I've heard dreadful things about Mrs. Wisedor—hard to please and all," Rebecca said, shaking her head.

"You don't know the half of it. I'm so glad to be out of there. The stress that woman put me through was nothing short of hell," Naomi recited like remembering a bad dream.

"It's true, Mama, she's not an easy person, but Favor was not like her."

"And look at the trouble Favor caused. You almost died because he made a pet out of Jezzie. It's a miracle you survived," Naomi said as tears welled.

"Favor never loved Jezzie. It wasn't his fault. And Captain used it all for good. The Indians will never be the same."

"We heard all about your attack and legal troubles. The letters came daily, reporting all the news from different folks. Good news travels fast, but bad news travels even faster," Rebecca said.

"Forgive me for not going to China. If only I could have predicted the future. I can't tell you the pain I've endured," Purity's voice quivered, trying to control her emotions.

"Don't second guess yourself. There's a time for everything. You weren't meant to go," Pastor Ezra encouraged.

"God used you in other ways, I'm sure. You were saving the slaves and helping orphans, and the devil got mad. Retaliation was sure to come. I declare God will restore seven-fold everything you lost, my dear." He slammed his fist on the table to prove a point.

"Thank you. I sorely need that. Forgive me for asking, but I must know. Have you any word of Favor and Victoria?" Purity asked.

"I've only been home a short while. Mother said Favor disappeared."

"We're just finding out ourselves. We haven't been home from China long. However, we've heard Favor's returning very soon," Pastor Ezra confirmed.

"Part of the reason for our visit today is to relay the good news. We just heard from reliable sources that he settled all of your legal issues. It took the last six months and the best attorneys."

"Can it really be true?" Purity asked.

"Rest assured. You won't be going to jail. The murder charge against you was dropped," Rebecca rejoiced.

"Favor found a witness—someone working the train that night stepped forward. Do you have any idea who it could have been?" Pastor Ezra asked Purity.

"Was his name ever reported?" Purity stalled, not wanting to mention the porter.

"I don't know, but everything will hit the newspapers shortly, I'm told," Rebecca said with relief.

"Another positive, Mave and Mr. Wells, were convicted of slave trading. To think of the hell they caused so many," Pastor Ezra said, wagging his head.

"Then justice is served," Naomi said.

"And was Jezzie ever charged for trying to kill me?" Purity asked with anticipation.

"No, my dear. The judge let her go. Lack of evidence, he said. It's rumored someone bribed him. But God will avenge all the injustice," Pastor Ezra assured her.

"Then, I'm free. The nightmare's over," Purity repeated in a whisper as tears welled. Rebecca handed her a soft handkerchief.

"Yes, you're completely free to start again, to love again. But be careful. There are rumors," Pastor Ezra warned.

"Now what?" Naomi asked in fear.

"It's Jezzie. She's gone mad and gets worse by the day. There have been sightings—strange sightings. In the midnight hours, she rides through Shadow Brook Estate, cloaked in black, screaming at the devil. Be on your guard," Pastor Ezra warned like a caring father.

"That gives me the shivers," Naomi said in a fit of anxiety.

The thought of Jezzie put Purity on edge.

"I don't know if it's in me ever to forgive Jezzie."

"We might as well get everything out," Rebecca said to her husband, sensing Purity needed to know.

"There's more?" Purity asked as she blotted her tears.

"Favor spent the last five months in Maine. He was living with his friend, John. The maids at Shadow Brook Estate have reported rumors that—" Rebecca stopped as though contemplating whether to carry on.

"Don't stop now, Rebecca. Finish what you've started if you have any compassion at all," Purity said, bracing herself for bad news.

"John has a sister named Debra," Rebecca started with hesitation.

"We've heard Favor will ask for her hand in marriage.

Purity looked away, trying to control a flood of emotion.

Rebecca squeezed Purity's hand.

"Does he know you are well, my dear?"

"I do not know," Purity admitted.

"I hope he is happy," she said, trying to stay strong.

"Favor's due to arrive soon for Victoria's wedding," Pastor Ezra reported with haste.

"Victoria is getting married?" Purity said, surprised by the news.

"I haven't heard from her since my return."

"Victoria hasn't been in town. She's been in Cape Cod with her fiancé's family, but she's due to return any day," Rebecca explained.

"Who's the lucky gentleman?" Purity asked with keen curiosity.

"He's a fine man from New York, from a highfalutin family. He adores the girl, and she'll be set for life," Pastor Ezra exclaimed.

"Victoria's wedding will be the event of the year. And our very own Pastor Ezra is conducting the ceremony," Rebecca said, giving a loving glance at her husband.

"I'm glad to be retired. I can't imagine the back-breaking work. Just the thought of it makes my feet hurt," Naomi sighed.

"We're happy for you Naomi. Well, we must get going," Pastor Ezra said taking his wife's hand.

Rebecca turned to Purity as they left and said, "Remember, my dear, God will restore all that has been lost."

They left, and Purity tried to digest all the big news. She was so relieved her legal worries were over—they had enough to worry about with the bank about to take the farm.

Naomi started clearing the dining table, grumbling under her breath.

"If that pampered Mrs. Wisedor gets one more blessing, I'd say that Captain of yours is completely cold and unfeeling. Isn't that what you call him? Captain of the… Captain of the… what's he in charge of again," Naomi hesitated, trying to recall his full name.

"Captain of the Lord's Army. And stop judging who's got more blessings, the rich folk or the poor folk. For a long time, I felt abandoned too. But, Mama, I'm alive. We've got the farm, the school, and we're helping the poor. And we've got each other. Anything else is the icing on the cake. And most of all, we've got Captain of the Lord's Army," Purity said with thankfulness.

"Purity, did you honestly see him? This Captain?"

"Yes, I've seen him. Mama, I saw Papa on the New Earth too," Purity said, trying her best to encourage Naomi.

"You saw Papa? Why didn't you say so? What's he doing up there?" Naomi asked, welling with emotion.

"He's doing great. He's still gardening."

"I would hope he's looking down on us with a whole lot of prayer. It's not so easy down here," Naomi admitted. She lovingly stroked Purity's hair.

"Are you okay, Purity? With the news of Favor?"

"My heart is breaking," Purity said, reaching a new low.

"I still hoped…"

Trying to divert her heavy heart, she walked to the dining room window and saw the school children pour out of the old barn, each headed home.

David stood with Mariah, watching the children go. He looked at her, and the gleam of love in his eye was unmistakable. It was the exchange Purity needed to see—one of new love. Purity's hope for Favor had died, but not her love. A faint smile turned up her lips as she realized David was a young man with plans of his own.

* * *

Later that afternoon, Purity hiked the hills beyond the farm and picked flowers. She inhaled their sweet smell, and it comforted her aching soul.

Overwhelmed, she dropped to her knees in prayer.

"Captain, your will be done. You've healed and set me free. I'll be content with you. Just tell me—have Victoria and Favor forgotten me? Do they think I died?"

The snapping of twigs and the shuffling sound of a horse kicking up dust sounded from a thicket of trees. Purity's eyes strained to see a dark shadow cloaked in black, galloping away in thunderous speed.

Purity dropped the fresh-picked flowers and ran back to the farm.

Naomi and Rachel jumped as Purity frantically entered the house. Her hands shook as she struggled to lock the bolt on the door.

"Who's after you, girl?" Rachel asked in an alarmed manner.

"I don't know. Someone in black. Maybe it's Jezzie coming back to finish the job," Purity sounded with dread.

"I hoped the trouble was over. We've been followed before by a black rider," Naomi nodded with certainty.

"When?" Purity asked anxiously.

"On our midnight rides helping the poor, when we worked for Shadow Brook Estate. Whoever it was trailed behind, watching our every move," Naomi said, shaking her head.

"My eyes were blind to it," Purity replied, bewildered.

"If he or she wanted to harm us, that would have been easy."

"Mama, that's no help," Purity scolded her mother.

"Get some rest, girl. Tomorrow's at our heels," Naomi advised, heading to the kitchen.

* * *

It was the crack of dawn a few days later. Purity sat comfortably near the fireplace, staring into the flames. The farm was quiet as the school children hadn't arrived. She took another sip of freshly brewed coffee. The dark liquid reminded her of the black rider who had been spotted again. She tried to shake off a cloud of doom.

She thought back to Rebecca's dream of her in a fancy gown with a wedding bouquet. How bitter it seemed, knowing she could never have that beautiful picture—not with Favor at least.

"Thank you, Captain, for another day. Bless the children," she heard Naomi pray from the kitchen.

"Help the teachers with those rascals. If it were up to me, I'd string them up by their toes, but don't take my advice."

Purity chuckled and went to give her mother the good news.

"I went to the bank yesterday and paid all the bills," Purity said with confidence.

"Well, that's a glimmer of hope. Captain sure did come through and fast," Naomi said, shaking her head.

Unbeknownst to Naomi and Purity, Captain of the Lord's Army peeked into the kitchen window, eavesdropping on their conversation. Beside Him, the Ring of Grace piled on each other, trying to get a glimpse through the glass. Rocco stood on Toby's shoulders, and Josiah stood on Sergio's shoulders. Kaleb was next to the Captain with his wings buzzing, peering in as well.

"Watch it. You're pinching my shoulder," Sergio said to Josiah, whose boots were digging in the wrong direction.

"Hurry up. It's our turn. Time to switch," Toby said, tired of holding Rocco.

Behind them, the Captain's vast Army waited patiently on their horses.

"That's the Captain for you. He loves to listen when people talk about him," one of his warriors said to the others.

Naomi and Purity rattled on in the kitchen, oblivious to the heavenly visitors.

"Pastor Ezra sent a message. A crew of men is coming next week to replace the roof on the barn. The Captain is faithful, and we should expect a sevenfold return," Purity said, smiling.

"The Captain's not only faithful, but he's also able to do above and beyond all we could ever imagine," Naomi agreed.

The Captain nodded his head.

"Naomi's coming along. Life has been so hard that she had trouble believing I could turn it all around. Shall we go?" the Captain asked the Ring of Grace.

"The battles are waiting, but there's no contest. We have the victory," Kaleb declared.

Then as fast as they came, the great company dissolved into a billion particles of gold falling on the premises.

The children started arriving, some by foot and others by horseback. They played in front of the old barn that had been transformed into their new school.

"I don't feel like teaching today," Purity said, looking out the window. She longed to speak with Favor. It felt like she'd lived a lifetime apart from him, yet surely time had not erased everything between them.

"You can't go by your feelings—duty calls. Get going, now," Naomi said, taking the coffee mug from Purity's hand as she pushed her out the door.

The morning dragged on as Purity's heart weighed heavily with sorrow. It was a relief to dismiss the children for recess. As they poured out of the barn, Purity looked up at the blue sky, spattered with white puffy clouds.

Out of the corner of her eye, she saw a fancy car coming up the long road to the farm.

"Look at that fancy car," she said out loud.

Rachel, David, and Mariah gathered, gawking too.

Naomi was doing laundry on the farmhouse porch and noticed the car bouncing over the uneven road. She dropped the dirty garment and dried her wet hands on an apron.

The car pulled to a stop, and the chauffeur hopped out. He opened the rear passenger door. A delicate hand emerged, followed by a petite figure wearing a fine dress.

To Purity's surprise, standing on the grounds was none other than her childhood friend and confidant from Shadow Brook Estate—Victoria. Purity's lungs tightened with anxiety and disbelief.

"Victoria, is that you?"

"Purity, who else would I be?" Victoria asked with open arms.

Purity ran to her, and they embraced one another.

"God, I've missed you," Victoria exclaimed.

"The maids told me you survived. I mean—that you returned. I've heard all about your work with the children, and I had to see for myself."

Purity and Naomi gave a grand tour and introduced Victoria to the children.

"I'll be mentioning your work to the woman's guild for fundraising. I've missed you both dearly. Life isn't the same at Shadow Brook without you," Victoria said with deep compassion.

Naomi blushed at the compliment and nodded her head in appreciation.

They entered the farmhouse, and Victoria looked around in amazement.

"It's grand," Victoria complimented.

In minutes, Naomi placed a fresh pot of tea and a small plate of cookies on the table, and they sat.

"I've been out of town until recently. The maids told me where to find you. I wanted to be the first to tell you the good news," Victoria said, giggling.

"And what could that be, dear Victoria?" Purity asked, knowing the answer.

Victoria extended her ring finger.

"I'm getting married."

Purity and Naomi inhaled the glory of the four-carat diamond engagement ring.

"It's incredible. I've heard he's lovely. I mean, he surely must think you're lovely," Purity stuttered, concealing her knowledge on the subject.

"I never dreamed of finding this kind of happiness in life," Victoria gushed.

"As soon as I found out you were alive, I mean recovered, I was determined to see you and make an urgent request. Forgive me for being so forward. So much time has passed between us, but I've come to ask you a very precious thing."

"Yes, I'm listening," Purity said, all ears.

"My wedding wouldn't be complete without you. Will you be my Maid of Honor?" Victoria asked with utter sincerity.

Naomi's teacup crashed to the wooden floor and shattered into pieces.

It was like a dream come true and a nightmare colliding all at once. A flurry of thoughts begged for her attention.

"What will Mr. and Mrs. Wisedor think? Will Jezzie hear of it? I'll have to face Favor and his fiancée. People will recognize me."

"Did you hear me?" Victoria said, snapping her fingers in front of Purity's eyes.

"We heard you just fine," Naomi said, trying not to sound too annoyed.

"Out of all your choices, why me? So much has happened," Purity said, trying to discourage Victoria's decision.

"The time between us hasn't changed our friendship. You taught me everything I know, and what I don't know is all my fault." Victoria reached for Purity's hand.

"I don't know what to say," Purity said in total wonderful, horrifying shock.

"Dear Purity, I won't take 'no' for an answer. Please, my friend. Stand by my side on the most beautiful day of my life? I prayed every day for your return, so you owe me," Victoria said with a playful wink.

"Victoria, you're making it impossible to say no," Naomi mumbled.

"That's the intention. I have everything arranged. 'Yes,' is all I need to hear."

"But I have nothing to wear," Purity was trying to think of any excuse.

"I still have the dress Favor bought for you—the rose-colored ball gown. That will do nicely," Victoria suggested.

"I suppose. But to be honest—"

"No more excuses," Victoria interrupted and stood.

"The invitations are in the mail. You'll be hearing from me in the meantime. My drivers will pick everyone up on the day of the wedding. I'll send three cars as your sons are invited as well. Here's money for Naomi's dress and suits for your sons," Victoria insisted, placing the cash in Naomi's hand.

And off she went, leaving a cloud of emotion behind.

* * *

362

David boldly entered the Wisedor shipyard office building. He'd heard Favor had returned and hoped to find him there.

One of the supervisors spotted David and stopped his search.

"We're not hiring right now," the supervisor growled.

"I'm here to see Mr. Favor Wisedor," David said boldly.

"What makes you think he's got time for you?" the supervisor said condescendingly.

He grabbed David's shirt and pulled him toward the door. The men almost went to blows as David wasn't going to be pushed around.

"Tell him David, Purity's son, is here," David shouted. His eyes remained steadfast on the bully.

"He's an important man. Too busy for you," the supervisor growled and left the room.

"Captain, I could use some help," David quietly prayed and lifted his eyes to the high ceiling.

After a few minutes, Favor rushed into the room, looking expectantly among the workers. Spotting David, he hurried over and hugged the boy as though seeing a long-lost brother.

"David, it's been too long."

"Yes, sir," David answered respectfully.

"Come to my office," Favor offered.

David followed him through the building to the plush office, where he sat in a comfortable chair. A secretary handed him a refreshing cup of coffee and left a tray of fresh pastries.

"You've heard of my return. What brings you here?" Favor asked with curiosity.

"Old times, I guess. Did you know Purity's come home?" David said, getting to the point.

"I just heard from Victoria. I've not been back long."

"She's more beautiful than ever," David replied, hoping to see a spark of interest.

"Then, she's well and in good spirits?" Favor asked, pushing for information.

"Yes, and she's started a school. I've been teaching there with some of the other sons."

"She taught you well and always spoke of starting a school," Favor acknowledged.

363

"She bought the old Warner Farm on Bay Road. You can't miss it. There's a sign posted for 'Hope Farm.' I'm sure she'd want to show you around, sir," David nudged.

"It's been a long time."

"A man knows his heart. Follow yours, and you'll never regret it," David said as he shook and shook Favor's hand.

Holy Desire

Chapter 37

THE DAY OF Victoria's wedding arrived. Three luxury cars bumped over the long dusty road leading to Hope Farm. It was a glorious day with the sun shining over blue skies.

Naomi, Rachel, and Mariah wore new dresses with matching hats. David escorted the ladies to one of the cars while the rest of the sons, wearing fine new suits, piled into another vehicle.

Purity walked out onto the farmhouse porch full of nerves. Victoria had delivered the dress Favor had purchased for her, and thankfully, it still fit. She drew in a deep breath and descended the steps.

"How did I get myself into this?" she thought.

Naomi stood beside her with a smile from ear to ear.

"Get in, girl. You're going to make us late."

The chauffeur opened the car door for Purity, and she slid onto the back seat. The cars moved in a slow procession toward Shadow Brook Estate. It had been over six months since Purity set foot on the property.

Her heart was divided. One half desired to see Favor—to inhale his handsome features and lose herself in his eyes. It was a foolish wish, knowing he now loved another. The other half of her heart shook with dread, fearing everything that could go wrong. She braced herself for the rejection and ridicule that would likely come.

David sat by her side. Sensing her unease, he grabbed her hand.

"Mother, try to have an enjoyable time."

She squeezed his hand.

"Thank you, David. Good advice from my first son."

Shadow Brook Estate was as magnificent as Purity remembered. Cars and horse-drawn buggies lined the long driveway, waiting to deposit their guests at the main entry.

The attendees descended on the palatial property from far and wide. Everyone was in high spirits, anticipating the event of the summer.

"Captain, I need your strength," Purity whispered as her car stopped to let them out.

The chauffeurs opened the doors, and everyone piled out. Mariah stepped out of the car, overwhelmed by the estate.

"It's time to live it up. I could get used to this—coming in the main entrance," Naomi snickered.

Purity's group entered the mansion—this time as invited guests. Victoria had instructed the maids to disperse these special guests. She hoped her mother wouldn't recognize the sons in their fine dress.

Naomi fluttered into the kitchen to reminisce with the maids, while Rachel and Mariah mixed in well with a multitude of stylish young females.

A maid escorted Purity up to Victoria's room without delay. The bride-to-be was still in her robe, but her hair and makeup had been done to perfection.

"Victoria, you're going to make a beautiful bride," Purity declared, admiring the wedding gown hanging from an ornate Armoire cabinet.

"It's fit for a princess," Purity said, looking over the lace, fine silk, and fitted bodice embroidered with pearls.

"Your presence makes my wedding day complete," Victoria affirmed.

Purity tried to hide a mountain of apprehension.

"I'm honored and privileged to stand by your side."

"Remember this lovely hairpin? You wore it the night of the Gala. It's yours," Victoria said, sitting Purity down and placing it in her hair.

"I have another surprise for the Maid of Honor," Victoria said as she pulled out an exquisite gown from one of the closets.

"I told you not to buy me anything," Purity scolded in a joking fashion.

"Only the best for my wedding," Victoria said with a sheepish smile. She placed her hands on Purity's shoulders and felt the tension in Purity's shoulders.

"You can do this. Think how nervous I am. And tonight's my honeymoon. I don't know quite what to expect," Victoria said, hoping Purity could help.

"I'm sorry. I'm just as lost," Purity said, and they both laughed.

"Let me help you with your gown. It should fit," Victoria said, shaking out of her silly mood. She helped Purity slip into the delicate gown.

"It's magical. I love it," Purity exclaimed.

Victoria fastened the back and tied a lace sash around her waist. They peered into the full-length mirror together.

"A resurrected princess, that's what you are," Victoria said with the admiration of a beloved sister.

"I feel like one. From death to life," Purity said, admiring her figure in the mirror.

Victoria jumped as though she'd just remembered something urgent.

"I forgot my bouquet. How silly of me. It's in the grand parlor on the piano. Get it for me? I'll be right down."

A maid entered the bedroom.

"It's time to get dressed, miss," the maid said, reaching for the ornate wedding dress.

Purity nodded and left the bedroom. She made her way down the grand staircase, which was decorated with fresh flowers. Then she went directly to the grand parlor, keeping a watchful eye for Favor along the way, hoping to avoid him for as long as possible.

Purity's hand shook as she turned the knob on one of the ornate carved wooden doors to the grand parlor. Slowly, she stepped into the room, looking about for any guests. It was empty.

The grand piano still stood in front of the large bay windows overlooking an elaborate garden. There, on the shiny black piano, lay Victoria's wedding bouquet.

Purity picked up the bouquet and inhaled its sweet aroma. A wave of apprehension crashed over her.

"Why did I agree to this? I'm not ready to face Favor, nor anyone else for that matter. Captain, this is a nightmare," she thought.

She lowered the bouquet and held it like a bride, imagining what might have been for her had things been different. She watched the guests mingling in the garden through the bay window. They were groomed, sophisticated, accomplished citizens. Muffled conversations, laughter, and happy greetings filtered through the window.

"Big day today?" she heard a guest called out in the hallway.

"Yes, it is." Favor's voice resonated as he stepped into the parlor.

The voice vibrated with such authority and simultaneous compassion she instantly knew whose it was. And every cell in her being responded with longing. If she ever wanted to run, it was now. Purity stood like a statue, unable to breathe.

"Excuse me. You must be the Maid of Honor. Victoria asked me to retrieve her bouquet," he said as he closed the door.

She lifted the bouquet to her nose, hoping it would mask her identity as she turned to face him.

Favor drew closer, and her hands went all clammy. She looked away—anywhere but at him. Neither said a word for several moments.

Then it happened. He reached for her hand, their fingers touching gently. Slowly, he lifted her hand to his lips and kissed the top of it.

"My Purity," he choked her name.

"I'd know you anywhere."

She lowered the bouquet but didn't meet his eyes.

"Purity," he said again. This time, it came out clearer.

"Look at me?" he asked.

Purity raised her brilliant eyes, brimming with tears. His eyes danced with the joy of seeing his long-lost love.

"Are you real or an angel who's about to fly away?"

Before she could respond, he lifted her in his arms and swung her body in circles of adoration.

"My Dove, you're beautiful and completely restored."

He put her down but didn't release her. She felt his hands draw her in closer.

"I never thought I'd see you again. My world crumbled without you," he said as their lips drew close.

"Hope has brought us together again," Purity whispered.

"Does that mean…?"

Their lips drew close with such magnetism, a swirl of gold dust circled their heads. It was Ora, the sweet child angel, blowing the love dust of heaven over them.

Purity didn't have time to answer him as a loud pounding vibrated on the parlor door. Victoria burst through the doors, the other bride's maids following behind her.

Purity pulled away from Favor's embrace.

"It's time to line up. I need my bouquet." Victoria took the flowers and winked at them.

"Can we talk after the ceremony?" Favor whispered to Purity.

"Of course," Purity said, trying to calm her nerves.

"Isn't it grand? We're all back together again," Victoria giggled with childish mischief.

Favor extended one elbow to the bride and the other to the Maid of Honor.

"Shall we ladies?" he said with a handsome grin.

* * *

The garden overflowed with tasteful decorations, and a fabulous gazebo drenched with flowers waited for the bride and groom. Distinguished guests sat with heads held high, dressed in the latest fashions.

An orchestra played a whimsical melody as the wedding ceremony began. Favor and Purity were the first to march down the aisle together. Naomi nearly fell over at the sight of them together while Mrs. Wisedor struggled to make out Purity's face without her glasses.

Slowly, the pair moved toward Pastor Ezra and Benjamin, the groom, who stood under the gazebo. Favor helped Purity to her rightful spot as the Maid of Honor, then stood next to the groom. His heart was full knowing Purity stood only a few feet away. He kept expecting her image to vanish, as she had so many times before during the past six months. He closed his eyes and opened them again. She was still there, radiant and more beautiful than he ever remembered.

The other bridesmaids and groomsmen followed—each couple separating as they reached the decorated gazebo. They waited patiently for the beautiful bride to appear.

Benjamin beamed with anticipation as Victoria, accompanied by her father, slowly glided down the red carpet. When they reached the gazebo, Mr. Wisedor gave her an affectionate, fatherly kiss. Benjamin took Victoria's hand, and they turned to Pastor Ezra.

Favor's eyes landed on Purity's soft features.

Pastor Ezra's wife, Rebecca, watched Favor and Purity stealing glances at each other. Purity looked every bit like the princess from her dream.

"God, don't fail them now," Rebecca whispered under her breath.

"Restore seven-fold, Lord," she prayed silently.

Pastor Ezra's voice rang out, and the music softened.

"We are together to join lives, hearts, and families. Victoria Wisedor and Benjamin Ward, we are honored guests at your wedding. Father God of heaven, we ask you to bless this union between Victoria and Benjamin. They are your children and walk in the light of your love. Help them to reflect your Holy Spirit in their home throughout the years. As they walk together, may they express your words in action. Lord, give them strength when challenged with disappointment and refreshment all their days. With your help, dear Lord, may their love remain deep and committed," Pastor Ezra prayed.

Then he gave a short message and proceeded to the vows.

"Do you Benjamin take Victoria to be your wedded wife?"

"I do," Benjamin nodded, looking into Victoria's deep blue eyes.

"Victoria, do you take Benjamin to be your wedded husband?" asked Pastor Ezra.

"I do with all my heart," Victoria answered lovingly.

The music and ceremony faded into silence as Favor gazed longingly at Purity.

"This might have been us," he thought.

"Benjamin, place the ring which symbolizes God's eternal love and your love for Victoria on her finger," Pastor Ezra instructed.

Favor shook himself back to the present and handed the ring to Benjamin, who gently slipped it on Victoria's slender finger.

"Do you have the symbol which shows your love for Benjamin?" Pastor Ezra asked Victoria.

She turned to Purity, trusting the ring was safely in her possession.

Victoria took the ring from a little black box.

"With this ring, I thee wed," Victoria said as she placed the gold band on the groom's left ring finger.

Victoria and Benjamin's eyes locked, realizing this was the grandest moment of their lives.

"You may kiss the bride," Pastor Ezra instructed with joy.

Benjamin leaned into his new bride and gently kissed her with the adoration of a doting husband.

The crowd burst into jubilant applause as Pastor Ezra said, "I'm pleased to introduce to you, Mr. and Mrs. Benjamin Ward."

The new couple walked down the aisle in unison, followed by Favor, Purity, and the rest of the wedding party.

A buzz of curiosity echoed among the guests as many young women, including Debra, questioned who the lucky Made of Honor was on Favor's arm. It didn't escape their notice that Favor couldn't take his eyes off of her, and it wasn't long before the news spread that she was the famous dancer, Purity Thomascovich.

The guests filed into the well-prepared reception area in the mansion. To accommodate such a crowd, the staff had placed elegant tables in many of the main rooms and the gardens.

Purity slipped away to the punch table and sipped on the cool liquid.

Two women gossiped nearby for all to hear.

"I bet Debra is hoping for that big ring tonight. John is Favor's best friend, so to marry his sister would be a perfect match."

Purity felt sick to her stomach. She put down the elegant punch glass and scanned the multitude of guests roaming the mansion. Her gaze landed on Naomi at the nearby dessert table. She was sampling all the fine pastries and desserts and wrapped some in a cloth napkin. Purity knew the treats would be for coffee the next morning.

Purity rushed over and grabbed her mother's arm in a panic.

"The wedding's over. It's time to go."

"Stop such crazy nonsense. This is the event of the year. And guess what? We're not the maids doing all the work. It's high time we enjoyed the fruits of our labors. You couldn't drag me out of here if you tried," Naomi barked, lifting a champagne glass from a maid's tray.

"We don't belong here," Purity insisted.

"Stop running, and maybe something good will happen to us. We're staying for dinner and the wedding cake too. I'm not leaving a moment sooner," Naomi chastised. She shook her arm loose from Purity's grasp and moved on to another table piled high with food.

Someone cleared their throat behind Purity. She turned to find a handsome man looking down at her.

"Regretfully, we haven't met. My name is John Matthews. I'm a close friend of Favor's," he said, extending a firm hand.

"Purity Thomascovich. I'm glad to meet you," she said, shaking his hand.

"You're the famous Purity?" John said with curiosity.

"So, you've heard about me? I grew up with Favor and Victoria on the estate."

"Ah, here is my sister, Debra," John said, waving Debra over.

Purity's heart dropped. This was the woman who had won Favor's heart. She was beautiful, to be sure.

"Debra, I present to you Purity Thomascovich," John said with respect.

"It's a pleasure to meet you," Debra said, extending a gentle hand.

"After all Favor and I have been through, this is the woman he's going to marry," Purity thought as she took Debra's hand.

"You look as lovely as the bride," Debra offered.

"You're so kind. It's an honor meeting you both," Purity said, giving a slight curtsy.

The orchestra switched over to a waltz, and Purity watched as Favor approached with intention. She thought he must be coming for Debra. But then he took Purity's hand in his, and she felt warm all over.

"Excuse us. Purity, I believe the first dance is mine," Favor insisted.

He pulled her onto the dance floor before she could even respond.

"I don't remember you asking for a waltz," she teased.

"Dancing seems to be the only way I can get a moment alone with you." He pulled her close and placed his hand on her back. Tingles shot down her spine.

They glided over the ballroom floor in perfect rhythm. It felt like home to be in his arms again.

"You haven't lost your touch. You never miss a beat, do you?" Favor said, spinning her.

"My short-lived dance career is over, I'm afraid. These days all I have time for is the school. Mother bought a farm with my prize money, and the sons and I have recruited far too many students. That's my new exhausting mission."

"Despite all the trials, you still think of others," he said with admiration.

She started to imagine the look he gave her was more than just admiration.

"She's beautiful," Purity blurted out, bringing herself back to reality.

"Who?"

"Debra," Purity confirmed.

"Ah, yes. I've known her for a long time. She and John were there for me when I needed them most."

Her plan worked. The spark she'd felt fizzled out like she'd been doused with cold water.

The dance came to an end, but Favor still held her hands in his.

"I need to tell you something, but not here. Will you meet me at the overlook to the bay in a few minutes?"

Purity tried to think of some excuse. She couldn't bear to hear from his own lips that he would wed another—especially at the very spot where he'd pledged himself to her.

"Surely they'll be serving dinner soon."

"There's still time. Please. It's important," he insisted.

As much as she wanted to, she couldn't refuse him.

"Very well."

He kissed her hand and dashed off into the crowd.

* * *

Debra watched Favor kiss Purity's hand and turned away, trying to hide her tears.

John noticed and turned to her like a caring brother.

"Why didn't you tell me about your feelings for Favor?"

"What? My embarrassing, one-sided love affair? I've been Favor's friend, like a sister, because you're my brother. But I thought now that I was older, he'd feel differently. I guess life doesn't always turn out like the dream."

"Favor only spoke to me of Purity once. I think it was too painful for him. They parted under the worst of circumstances, and he thought she was lost forever. Who could have imagined he'd be reunited with his first love at Victoria's wedding? I must admit I can see why Favor felt so lost without her. She's a breath of fresh air."

"Indeed, she's lovely. And I wish them all the happiness."

"Cheer up, Sister. God has someone for you. You'll meet him when you least suspect it. Come, shall we dance?" John asked, offering his elbow.

"We shall," Debra said, smiling as she took her brother's arm.

* * *

Favor rushed up the grand staircase and down the long hallway to his bedroom. He walked deliberately to his nightstand and pulled the top drawer open. Underneath a stack of papers sat a small red velvet box. Slowly, he opened it and gazed at the sparkling ring he'd bought in Maine.

"God, give me the words to say," he prayed.

Then he turned and made his way back to the party. In his distraction, he bumped into his poor mother on the stairs.

"Mother, I'm terribly sorry," he said as he steadied her.

"But where are your glasses? You can't see where you're going."

"Don't blame your mishap on me," she chastised.

"You're right. I'm so excited I wasn't paying attention."

"Of course I'm right. And you have every reason to be excited for your sister's big day."

"I'm excited for Victoria, but it isn't that."

"Don't be so cryptic, dear boy. I don't have the patience."

"You'll find out soon, Mother." He gave her a big kiss on the cheek and dashed off to find Purity.

* * *

A gentle breeze blew over the Narragansett Bay, and the moon was rising in full splendor. Purity's hair blew gently in the breeze as she looked out over the water. She dreaded the conversation to come. Favor would tell her he now loved another and that the spark she'd felt between them was just his joy at seeing her walking among the living again.

Captain's book, His Thoughts Revealed, had said Favor was his choice for her—she was sure of it—but maybe the Captain had changed his mind. She had turned the matter over again and again in her mind since she'd heard of Debra. The exercise only left her more confused.

She heard the crunch of footsteps behind her but didn't turn. She inhaled the fresh air, trying to muster the courage to face him.

"Victoria pulled it off. I had no idea it was you—the mystery Maid of Honor. You made Victoria so happy today," Favor started as he stepped up beside her.

"She made the most beautiful bride," Purity said in an almost whisper.

"She's grown into an accomplished young woman and now a wife. In a few years, a doting mother," Favor stated with certainty. Before she could stop him, he took her hands in his.

"These hands are truly God's hands."

"I am just trying to follow the Captain's lead." She moved to pull away, but he held her hands a little tighter.

"Purity, I told you I had something important to say."

Here it was—the moment that would confirm the heartache she'd felt these past few days.

"But first, I have to ask. Much has happened since we parted. Is there someone in your life? Perhaps you met an Indian man during your time with the tribe."

His question startled her. Was he wanting to see if she, too, loved another before breaking the news?

"No, well, there was a man who wanted to be more, but I belong here," she said decidedly.

"The strapping warrior by the lake?"

"That's very specific," she replied, growing suspicious.

"I had this vision, or was it a dream? I don't know. I thought maybe you felt for this man."

"We parted as friends. He must lead his tribe, and I must do as the Captain has written for me."

"Do you still want to travel the world?" he asked.

"What was the thing you wanted to tell me?" she said, trying to get him back on track and get it over with.

Favor took in a deep, steadying breath.

"I'm proposing to the woman of my dreams tonight."

"I wish you and Debra my congratulations." She pulled away from him and turned to go before he could see the tears welling in her eyes.

He rushed after her and grabbed her arm.

"Wait. Debra?"

"Yes, it's all anyone can talk about. Your mother will be happy, no doubt, with an estate like theirs."

"No, you have it all wrong," he insisted, turning her to face him.

She ducked her head to hide her tears, but he put his hand under her chin and lifted her eyes to meet his.

"It's okay, Favor. Let me go and be happy."

"That is what you want?"

"I...," she couldn't make herself say what she really felt. She wanted him to stay, wanted him to hold her for the rest of their days.

The waves gently rolled back and forth over the rocky crags, creating a relaxed rhythm in the silence. The feeling between them was electric.

Favor caught her hand and drew her close. Then he pulled out the small red velvet box from his suit pocket. He opened it and pulled the ring from its clasp.

"With all my heart, there's no other woman. Spending the rest of my days with you would be a true privilege. I never stopped loving you, Purity."

She marveled at the blazing diamond. It was more beautiful than any ring she'd ever seen.

"But what about the rumors—Debra?" She had to be sure he hadn't just changed his mind in the heat of the moment. Seeing each other again did things to her head, and maybe he was confused too.

"Someone saw me buying this ring and assumed. It was only ever meant for you, dear Purity."

He slipped the ring called 'Radiance' on her delicate ring finger.

"Will you marry me?" He looked into her eyes, waiting for her answer.

She was overcome, and it took her a moment to collect herself. When she did, she flung herself into his arms.

"Yes, Favor. I have loved you my entire life. Nothing would please me more." She grinned from ear to ear.

He leaned in and kissed her soft lips again and again. She never wanted him to stop.

"We'll marry right away. I can't live through any more delays," he declared.

"Hell itself has tried to keep us apart. But Captain has won the battle," Purity said with confidence.

* * *

When Favor and Purity returned to the bustling mansion, the dance floor was full, and guests were engaged in lively conversations. Victoria and Benjamin made the rounds, greeting their friends.

Favor led Purity to the orchestra and shouted for everyone's attention.

"Attention, attention!"

The music stopped.

"I have an announcement. I have a very important announcement," Favor said as the large ballroom fell silent.

"I'm officially announcing my engagement, again, to this fine woman, Miss Purity Thomascovich. I'm honored to marry such an esteemed woman of integrity," he said, lifting her left hand to show off the sparkling ring.

The mansion thundered in applause as no one could deny Purity's lovely spirit and beauty. Victoria clung to Benjamin and smiled in elation, not minding such an announcement on their special day. Naomi was so overcome with joy that she pulled David into a big hug.

"Get me a chair. I shall surely faint," Mrs. Wisedor barked to her husband as her knees buckled.

He did as she bid and whispered in her ear as she sat.

"No one tops Purity, my dear. She is a woman of quality."

"It's not Purity. I just thought for sure he was after Debra. What a match that would have been," Mrs. Wisedor lamented.

"Young people marry for love these days. Arranged marriages like ours are becoming a thing of the past," Mr. Wisedor assured her.

"Our marriage may have been nothing more than a business deal between estates, but I couldn't wait to be your wife. I've always loved you."

Mr. Wisedor almost choked.

"I know I haven't always shown it. I do wish to change—to bridge the distance between us these past years," she said sincerely.

377

He took her hand in his and gave it a gentle squeeze. She smiled up at him, hopeful.

The music resumed, and Favor led Purity to the dance floor.

"Darling, shall we dance?"

She nodded, and he held her tight as they swayed to the music.

"I never thought I'd see you again. My forever love," he said, kissing her lips gently.

"Forever and ever, my love," Purity said, ecstatic with hope.

Debra watched the happy couple when a handsome young man approached.

"How can it be a beauty like you isn't taken?" he lifted her hand to his lips and placed a gentle kiss on her knuckles.

"May I have this dance?"

"You may," she said, a grin forming as she took his arm.

* * *

After an elaborate dinner, the guests celebrated as the happy couple cut the cake and departed for their honeymoon.

Favor and Purity stood arm in arm in front of the house and watched Victoria and Benjamin drive away.

"Favor, my teacher, my friend, my soon-to-be husband. Happiness has found us again," Purity said as she leaned into him.

Favor kissed her on the forehead.

"And nothing will ever break our love."

They stood there in each other's arms for a moment longer.

"I'll help drive everyone back to Hope Farm," Favor insisted.

While they waited for the cars to pull around, Naomi, Mariah, and Rachel admired Purity's ring. She even got a few hugs and kisses from her sons before they loaded into the cars.

It was late when they arrived back at Hope Farm. Naomi invited Favor in for tea, and everyone continued to celebrate. Some of the younger sons fell asleep and had to be carried to their beds in the barn.

Purity walked with Favor, who carried one of the little ones. It was dark and quiet. A twig snapped, and Purity jumped.

"What is it?" Favor asked in a whisper.

"I've seen a rider, dressed in all black, watching us. I'm afraid it might be Jezzie waiting to finish the job," Purity confided.

"Purity, you have nothing to fear."

"How can you be so certain?"

"Because I am the rider in black," he admitted.

Purity gasped.

"It started years ago. I used to follow you and your mother at night. At first, it was curiosity, but then I wanted to protect you—make sure nothing happened to you as you helped others."

"But why now?"

"I had just returned and didn't know how to approach you. I had to see you, but I wasn't sure you would want to see me. I thought maybe you had some strapping Indian husband." He laughed at the thought.

She swatted his arm.

"I'm relieved it was you. But you should be more careful. I might have pulled a pistol on you."

Clarity Prevails

Chapter 38

A FEW DAYS had passed since Victoria's wedding, and Favor hadn't set foot on Shadow Brook Estate. Nor could he bring himself to return to work. He had someone bring some clothes from his house and had spent his nights bunked up with the boys in the barn.

The days with Purity on the farm, helping teach the students, hiking through the acreage, and planning the rest of their lives together, were the sweetest he could recall.

They sat together on the farmhouse steps, relaxing after the long school day. It was the first moment they'd had alone the whole day.

"We need to get married soon. I'm tired of sleeping in the barn with the boys," Favor said, kissing Purity's neck.

"What are we waiting for?" Purity said, gazing at her engagement ring.

The postman came running through the barnyard, scattering the chickens.

"I've got a telegram for Miss Purity Thomascovich," he blustered.

"For me? I hope it's not bad news," Purity said with concern.

Favor took it from the man.

"Let me know if you win," the postman said as he left.

"What's he talking about?" Purity asked.

"It's from the World Ballroom Dance Championships," Favor said, reading the address.

"How did they find me? It's been over six months since I won."

"Your future's an open road. I'm with you every step of the way. Read it," he coaxed.

Purity took the telegram and read.

Dear Miss Purity Thomascovich,

As the winner of the U.S. Ballroom Dance Competitions of 1909, Team Bristol is eligible to compete at the World Ballroom Dance Championships in Paris, France. The event is on November 7. We did not receive a reply to the first invitation. Please telegram the committee with your response and participation plans by September 10, 1909.

Sincerely,
Sir Pierre De Rhynel
World Ballroom President

"Favor, did you have something to do with this? Don't deny it," she asked, petrified at the thought of a dance competition.

"So what if I did? You love to dance, and you're not quitting now."

"There's no time for dancing. We're getting married, and what about our sons and both of our schools?" she protested.

"Dancing's a part of you. Your talent won't be wasted. I'll be there cheering you on."

"They need an answer in a few days. I've lost track of Mandy and Stephen. I can't dance alone," Purity objected.

"They shouldn't be too hard to find. Let's take a walk and figure this thing out," Favor suggested.

She took his hand, and they walked a familiar path through the trees. It was a time of quiet reflection for both. The decision to re-enter the dance world weighed heavily on Purity's heart.

Before she knew it, they crossed over a two-way wooden bridge entering Bristol's city area. They stopped, watching the river flow below. An occasional tree branch floated past, snagging on the rocks.

"The river reminds me of life. Sometimes we just don't know where it's going to take you," Purity said in deep thought.

"True, my dear. But the question is, do we swim with the current or against it? Let wisdom decide," Favor said as he gently kissed the top of her hand.

Bristol was as busy as ever. Cars, horse-drawn wagons, and pedestrians raced past them.

"Let's walk down to the river," Favor suggested.

A narrow, steep dirt trail led to the river's shoreline. Purity followed his lead to the water's edge.

Looking into her eyes, Favor chose his words carefully.

"Listen, my dove. A door of opportunity has opened. Don't let it close in regret. We can go to Europe for a honeymoon and stop in Paris."

"Then we'll marry immediately," she stated, settling on the idea.

Favor slid his hands around her waist and kissed her lips.

"Let's get married today if we can. We've waited long enough," he said with a passionate groan.

"I agree," Purity said, returning his kisses.

Favor released his Bride.

"Mandy and Stephen may still be in town."

"Rachel said no one had seen them since my return."

Clouds developed overhead and darkened the sun. Black crows flew overhead, screeching with irritation. Five lightning strikes cut through the sky, followed by the loud rumblings of thunder.

A large ball of fire landed in the river near Favor and Purity. They jumped at the sight.

"What was that?" asked Favor with a hint of fear.

"The Captain's near. It may be the Ring of Grace," Purity said, watching steam bubble from the cool water.

As they focused on the rising bubbles, the sound of a loud collision and cracking wood permeated the atmosphere. A car busted through the bridge fencing and soared in their direction. Favor pushed Purity to safety, and it missed them by mere inches.

The car plunged into the cold river, sinking fast in the rapid current. They could see a male driver slumped over the steering wheel, bloodied and unconscious. The young woman on the passenger side struggled to open the door. Muffled screams and flailing fists hit the window in her final attempt to flee before the car fully submerged.

Purity and Favor dove into the river in a rescue attempt. The cold rushing water chilled them to the bone. They tried to pry the passenger door open in hopes of releasing the sinking prisoners.

Favor manhandled the door open with his last breath. Water filled the car's compartment.

Purity went up for air and gasped at the surface. Favor broke the surface with a young unconscious woman in his arms. They both recognized the victim. It was none other than Jezzabella Coevet.

"It's Jezzie," Purity gasped, still treading water.

Favor stopped his aggressive rescue effort as confusion filled his heart. Immediately, he released her lifeless body, allowing the current to take her face down. Her body flowed away like a rag doll and sank rapidly.

"Don't let this be on our conscience. Our marriage cannot start with revenge on our enemy. It's nothing but a curse," Purity insisted.

"She's cursed us both. How can you defend the witch? After what she did to you. She deserves to die," Favor said in anger. An inner war raged in his heart.

"Let the Captain decide that," Purity warned.

Changing his mind, he swam frantically in the direction he last saw Jezzie's body. He took a deep breath and submerged under the murky waters. Despite blurred vision, Favor spotted a human form swaying lifelessly in the current. He came up for air, inhaled deeply, and dove down again. Purity dove down after him.

Jezzie's features were ghost-like. She had milky white skin, her lips had turned blue, and blood flowed from a head gash. She remained lifeless, with her dark hair flowing with the current.

Favor grabbed hold of her clothing and yanked. She was snagged on something. He and Purity surfaced. Favor pulled a pocketknife from his belt, opened it, and inhaling deeply, disappeared. Purity followed in rapid succession. It was a frantic race for life. The seconds ticked away.

The knife cut through Jezzie's wet clothing, and together Favor and Purity tugged her clothing free from a submerged tree branch. They pulled her lifeless body to the surface with their last bit of strength and gasped for air.

Breathless and exhausted, they swam Jezzie's dead weight to shore. It was only when they rolled her onto her back that they saw her swollen abdomen. She looked as though she might give birth at any moment.

"She's really pregnant," Favor said, stunned.

The deep cut over Jezzie's left eyebrow poured blood. Purity ripped her dress and applied pressure to the gaping wound.

"Captain, don't let her die on our watch," Purity prayed.

They took turns blowing breath into Jezzie's lungs. After several breaths, she began coughing and gasping for air and woke with a start.

"Where am I?" Jezzie muttered.

"Don't worry. You're safe now," Purity said, trying to calm her nerves.

"Purity, is it you? I tried to kill you, and you've saved our lives." She reached for Purity's hand.

"Help. Help," Favor yelled frantically as a crowd gathered.

"Help's on the way. We've called a doctor," a man responded.

A few men who had gathered dove in to try to find the driver. It was a longshot with the current, but they had to try.

"We're taking you to the hospital," Purity said, reassuring Jezzie.

"No, take me home," Jezzie whispered weakly.

Favor flagged a truck down.

"Can you take us to the Coevet Estate?" Favor asked with urgency.

"Mr. Favor Wisedor, is that you?" the man asked.

"Yes, I need your assistance," Favor answered.

"Whatever you need, sir," the driver obliged.

Favor, Purity, and a few bystanders helped carry Jezzie to the truck. Favor instructed one of the rescuers to send the doctor to the Coevet Estate.

* * *

As they approached Jezzie's home, black crows swooped low over the truck and landed on the black iron sign that read 'Coevet Estate.' Dark spirits spiraled in the clouds above and hovered over the mansion, appearing as a misty dark fog.

Jezzie was carried inside on a makeshift stretcher.

"Miss Jezzie. Miss Jezzie. What's happened to you?" the wicked chambermaid who'd introduced her to witchcraft yelled. The cries of distress echoed through the cold mansion.

"What's the commotion about?" Mr. Coevet asked as he rushed from the library. They set his daughter down at his feet. She looked like a corpse, barely moving.

"There was a car accident," Favor started to explain.

Mrs. Coevet rushed from the grand parlor and screamed when she saw her daughter's bloodied face.

"We're cursed. I knew something horrible was going to happen. It's all your fault." She gave her husband an angry shove.

The sight of Favor and Purity only made her angrier.

Mr. Coevet sank into a chair, seemingly overcome with anguish.

"It was a curse, sending our daughter away right before she delivered. You wanted to hide her pregnancy—stop the rumors and the embarrassment—to save her chances of marrying well. Now, she and the baby might die," Mrs. Coevet howled in anguish.

Mr. Coevet rose and raised a hand as if to strike his wife.

"Another word and I'll kill you myself," Mr. Coevet threatened.

"Enough. This isn't helping matters," Favor said, grabbing the aggressor's arm to halt the blow.

Mr. Coevet yanked himself free of Favor with resentment.

"What does it matter that the child is not yours. You had a chance to marry her and make her respectable."

"You would blame this on me?" Favor replied.

"Get out before I throw you out," Mr. Coevet raged.

Sharp contractions hit Jezzie's abdomen like a swift kick. Her legs drew up, and she rocked from side to side in pain.

"She's going into labor," the maid said with alarm.

"Stop fighting and get her upstairs," Mrs. Coevet yelled at her husband.

"Very well," Mr. Coevet conceded through clenched teeth.

The truck driver, Favor, and Purity lifted the young pregnant woman with care. The maid led the way as they slowly carried her up the grand staircase and into her bedroom, where they placed her on the fine silk bedding. Wishing the young lady a quick recovery, the truck driver tipped his hat and left.

The maid filled a small water basin and began wiping the blood from Jezzie's face. Jezzie's water broke, saturating the plush bedding.

"There's a doctor on the way," Purity assured everyone in the room.

"That's not necessary. We'll take it from here. Get out. Get out," Mr. Coevet snapped.

"You ungrateful fool," Favor said.

"Should I have let Jezzie and your grandchild die? She left Purity for dead. Nothing like returning the favor."

Mr. Coevet approached like a mad man, swinging his fists in the air. Favor twisted the older man into a headlock. The men wrestled back and forth, crashing into furniture and knocking expensive vases and lamps to the floor. Favor's pent-up anger over Purity's mortal wounds flared into a rage he refused to control.

"Stop, Favor, he's not worth jail time. Don't let them hurt us again," Purity said, trying to wrestle Favor off the old man.

The doctor entered the bedroom and, dropping his black leather bag, helped break up the brawl.

"We don't need any more casualties," the doctor screamed.

Mr. Coevet wiped the blood from his busted lip. Favor glared at him as a warning, willing to go another round if he was triggered.

"Let's get out of here, Purity," Favor said, resisting the urge to finish the old man off.

"Not so fast. I may need help delivering the baby," the doctor warned.

Purity eyed Favor with a torn heart, realizing the baby was the innocent victim in all of this.

"I said we're leaving," Favor threatened and reached for Purity's hand. They made their way for the bedroom door.

Mrs. Coevet became nauseous at the thought of helping with the delivery.

"We're sorry. Please stay and help," Mrs. Coevet begged.

Jezzie screamed out in pain. The Coevets started to leave.

"You can't leave us. This is your daughter and grandchild," Purity reprimanded.

"This isn't in my job description," the maid protested.

"Stay, or you're fired," Mr. Coevet demanded.

"We will wait outside," he declared as he took his wife's hand and pulled her from the bedroom.

It was hard, agonizing labor. The expectant mother lapsed in and out of consciousness after a few hours. Dark, invisible spirits from Ahaba's army hovered over her.

"This isn't going well. She's too exhausted to deliver the baby," the doctor said.

"Give up and die," the evil spirits hissed in Jezzie's ear. They pierced her body with unseen hot pokers, and she flinched in pain.

"Shut them up. Help me. I can't take it. I can't do this," Jezzie howled, using all her energy to fight the unseen tormentors.

"Demons torment you," Purity said.

"When did you let the devils in?"

Jezzie foamed at the mouth, her wild eyes glaring back at all of them. Purity grabbed her chin and looked her in the eyes.

"It was with my chambermaid," Jezzie confessed.

"I gave evil full possession of my soul," she sputtered, gasping in pain.

The chambermaid cowered at the revelation.

"You witch, casting spells," Favor yelled at the maid.

"Do you realize the hell you've unleashed on all of us? You're using witchcraft on her now?" Purity asked as she backed the maid into the corner.

"Captain, deliver this witch. Get the hell out of her by your power," Favor yelled.

The maid wrenched as the Ring of Grace manifested in translucent form. They raised their hands and sent bombarding fire toward the maid. She withered back and fell to the ground, slithering like a snake. After several moments, she lay as though dead. Favor took her by the hand, and the doctor helped drag her from the room.

"That explains your dark heart," Purity said to Jezzie.

"Wickedness wants you and the baby dead. You must deliver this baby. In the name of Yeshua, great Captain of the Lord's Army, every demon must go. Get out."

"Help me, I'm so sick," Jezzie whispered as dark spirits flowed out of her mouth, appearing like black translucent smoke.

The Ring of Grace pierced the wicked spirits with their fiery swords. Then the five angels drew close to the expectant mother, and each placed an illuminated hand on her head or shoulder, strengthening her body. Jezzie's dark eyes changed, and peace came over her body.

"Purity, forgive me," Jezzie muttered, searching for mercy.

"You're forgiven. I hold nothing against you," Purity answered with compassion.

"All my insanity and jealous hatred. I deserve to die." Jezzie forced the words out, gasping as another contraction riveted her body.

"The Captain forgives you. Push. Push again," Purity coached.

Jezzie couldn't muster the strength.

"Look at me. You have a baby to deliver," Purity insisted.

"And if it's the last thing you do, this baby is coming out. Ask for the strength."

"You don't deserve to be forgiven," a lingering wicked spirit taunted in her ear.

"He won't hear my prayers. I don't deserve it," Jezzie groaned.

"I'm beyond forgiveness."

"Say it. Captain, help me," Purity demanded.

"Captain, help a wretch like me," Jezzie moaned as another contraction hit.

"Help me sit her up," Purity asked as Favor and the doctor came back in the room.

"What the hell are you doing?" the doctor scolded.

"I'm going to deliver this baby, with or without you. Help us sit her up," Purity demanded.

A ball of light appeared.

Jezzie saw it first, asking, "What is it?"

Purity glanced at Favor and the doctor, who strained to move the expectant mother into a seated position. No one else seemed to see it.

"Captain, let's get this done," Purity prayed.

Jezzie looked deathly pale.

"I have no strength left," she whispered.

"Stay with me. This baby is not going to die! Do you hear me?" Purity scolded.

"Let us die together," Jezzie gasped in defeat as a wicked spirit perched on her shoulder.

Kaleb slashed his fiery sword, splitting the wicked spirit in two. It dissolved into powdered black dust.

"You may have given up, but don't give up on your baby," Purity coaxed.

A petite angel appeared as a little girl bathed in shining golden light.

"I'm Ora. It's time for the baby to come forth," she spoke to Purity.

Ora placed her small, light-emitting hands on the expectant mother's rounded abdomen for a few minutes. Then the little angel swirled into a ball of fire and shot through the ceiling.

After several more agonizing pushes, Jezzie delivered a beautiful baby girl.

"You have a daughter," Purity declared.

Purity and Favor cleansed the newborn in a basin of warm water while the doctor tended to Jezzie. They were amazed at the perfect baby.

"Favor, she's stunning," Purity said, drying the baby off and wrapping her in a small blanket.

"Indeed. None of this is her fault," he said with admiration.

"I'm dying. Favor is not her father." Jezzie's voice was faint as a massive hemorrhage saturated the bedsheets.

The doctor knew there was nothing more he could do. He pulled Favor aside as Purity approached the bedside with the newborn in her arms.

"Don't leave us. You have a daughter to raise," Purity begged.

The new mother grew ashen.

"I'm not going to make it. She is your daughter now," Jezzie whispered.

"Who's the father, so that we can notify him?" Purity asked in a panic.

"He was married. I loved him," she admitted.

With her last bit of strength, Jezzie raised a weak hand. Purity lowered the baby so Jezzie could caress her newborn's cheek.

"What's your baby's name?" Purity asked, urgently realizing that privilege was due to a dying mother.

"Clarity. Her name is Clarity because it's all so clear to me now," Jezzie groaned in pain.

"Clarity? Are you sure?" Purity asked with tears welling as she looked over the baby's sweet features.

The dying woman tugged at Purity's skirt, and looking intently into her eyes, requested one last favor.

389

"Look in my drawer. Everything's explained in the letter." Jezzie released her last words with her last breath.

Holding the baby in one arm, Purity pulled the nightstand drawer open. There was the letter, with a key attached. She quickly hid the letter and key in her skirt pocket.

Favor and the doctor moved to the side of Jezzie's bed. The doctor closed her eyes with a gentle hand.

Jezzie's parents were brought in and stood by the bedside in shame. Mrs. Coevet wailed loudly with uncontrollable cries of pain. Mr. Coevet's countenance reflected a hard man trying to suppress a broken heart.

The baby squirmed in Purity's arms.

"Clarity, Clarity," she repeated, staring at the beautiful bundle with chubby little hands and feet.

"You've finally arrived."

Favor wrapped his arm around Purity. They approached the grandparents with the newborn and tried to hand her over.

"Our daughter's dead. We can't raise a bastard child. God only knows who the father is. Jezzie's plan was adoption. She shamed our family," Mr. Coevet rebuked.

Favor and Purity eyed each other with compassion for the newborn.

"You, liar. The baby was sold to a brothel. We were paid for her life. The buyer was the driver of the car. God struck him dead—cursed for his evil," Mrs. Coevet admitted, breaking under the weight of her grief.

Purity gasped.

"Clarity was sold as a newborn to be used as a slave?"

Mr. Coevet raised his hand from his jacket pocket.

"The woman's deranged. Don't believe her lies."

Purity gasped at the sight of his deformed hand. It was the claw, with a thumb, pointer, and middle finger.

"I've seen that claw at Mave's of Bristol, and you were at Mr. Wells' estate too." Purity's voice trailed off in alarm.

Mr. Coevet turned on her.

"I owned Mave's of Bristol before you helped close it down, and Mr. Wells was one of my best friends."

"You're a slave trader, and your daughter paid the price," Purity accused without fear.

"I'll see to it you're locked up for a lifetime," Favor said as he grabbed for Mr. Coevet.

They wrestled again, throwing fists, and the doctor joined in. Mr. Coevet pulled a gun, and the other men backed off.

"Don't try to follow us, or you're dead," Mr. Coevet warned and pulled his wife from the bedroom.

The doctor pulled himself together and wiped the blood from his lip.

"Let's give them time to get out of here. Then we'll get to the police," Favor said.

The doctor covered Jezzie's lifeless body with the sheets.

"No child deserves to die in a brothel," the doctor insisted.

"This baby needs a home. I'll put a good word in for you to adopt her—if that's what you want?"

"Yes," Favor said, gazing into Purity's eyes.

"She'll be our daughter, and we'll take her wherever we go."

"Clarity. Our daughter," Purity said, excepting the responsibility. She rocked the baby and sang, "Clarity."

> Clarity, Clarity
> It's so clear to me now
> You said I'd be your mother
> I never guessed how
>
> Clarity, Clarity
> It's so clear to me now
> Just as you said
> Our paths crossed again
>
> What a surprise
> Adoring your clear blue eyes
> The Captain's thought became reality
> And what a joy you'll be
>
> Clarity, Clarity
> It's all so clear to me now

Purity gave Clarity over to Favor.

"Take the baby. I've forgotten something. I'll be right back, Favor," she said.

"Be careful," he warned.

"There's no telling which way the staff's loyalties lie.

Purity nodded and made her way downstairs. She found the library empty and proceeded to read the letter she'd hidden in her pocket.

To whoever finds this letter,

My name is Jezzabella Coevet. I have been sold to a brothel, and my baby will suffer too. My very own parents have cast us on a bed of suffering, and the money is in their pockets to prove such a crime. Please help us. I don't know where we are headed, but report this to the police. Our lives depend on it. Enclosed is a key to my father's office. All the records of past transactions are there, proving my accusations.

Jezzabella Coevet

A maid passed by carrying cleaning supplies and fresh linens. She was clearly oblivious to what transpired upstairs.

"Where's the office?" Purity inquired.

The maid looked at her curiously but decided not to argue.

"Down the hall, the last door on the left but it's locked."

Purity rushed down the hall, slipped the key in the lock, and opened the door. She entered and closed the door quietly behind her. Then she began searching the drawers for evidence. In the bottom drawer of the desk was a ledger labeled "Mave's of Bristol Accounts." The pages were full of transactions in human commodity.

Robby Wright, age: 13 years, sold $100 to Shapel Factory.
Clara Striselberg, age: 14 years, sold $75 to General Store.
Ellie Strosberg, age: 13 years, sold $100 to Mave's of Bristol.
Natasha Weinstein, age: 17 years, sold $275 to Mave's of Bristol.

In a rush for time, Purity's fingers floated over several more pages, looking for more recent dates. Her heart skipped a beat as her hand stopped over fresh ink.

> Jezzabella Coevet, age: 20 years, sold $300 to Metacom Hotel. The unborn baby of Jezzie Coevet, birth expected anytime, sold $100 to Metacom Hotel.

Shivers blew down Purity's spine.

"Clarity, my God. Born as a sex slave," she thought.

The office door was kicked open and bounced off the wall. Mr. Coevet rushed in, waving his claw in wild fits, a gun in the other hand.

Purity jumped with terror and braced for a fight.

"Hand over the evidence, or you'll make a pretty corpse," he yelled in disgust.

"It's all here—your dirty business. You're destined for hell," Purity screamed.

"There was no other choice. I lost thousands when Mave's of Bristol closed, thanks to your handy work. I have bills to pay."

"Your deeds have found you out. It's over," Purity replied.

"The Coevet family secrets will rot with your corpse," he protested.

Purity clutched the ledger to her chest as he started to pull the trigger.

In a split second, Favor jumped him from behind, upsetting his aim. The bullet shattered a porcelain vase across the room.

"You're going away for a very long time," Favor said as he subdued Mr. Coevet and took the gun.

New Season

Chapter 39

IT WAS EARLY evening when a police officer dropped Favor and Purity off on the road leading to Hope Farm.

Naomi ran out of the house to greet them.

"Thank God. I've been worried." She looked down at the baby in Purity's arms.

"Who's this little bundle?"

"This is Clarity. She's ours—or she will be once the adoption goes through," Purity beamed.

"Who's the mother?" Rachel asked.

Favor and Purity poured over every detail of the tragic day. Naomi and Rachel took turns holding Clarity by the warm fire.

"You're both exhausted. We'll take the night shift," Rachel offered.

"Get some sleep. You're going to need it. She's your new boss," Naomi chuckled and carried the newborn to her room.

Purity walked with Favor onto the porch.

"I've never loved you more," he said, kissing her.

"I can't accept the invitation to the World Ballroom Championships, not with the responsibility of Clarity," Purity insisted, breaking the mood.

"You're making excuses again. We'll be honeymooning in France anyway, so you might as well dance. Naomi can come with us to watch over the baby," he said, trying to reason.

"I don't know. She's quite young to travel," Purity argued.

"You're willing to pass up the opportunity of a lifetime? It's been a long day. Get some rest, and things will look better in the morning." He kissed her on the forehead and walked to the barn.

In her bedroom, Purity washed and readied for bed.

"He has no idea what it takes to care for a newborn," she complained out loud.

She slipped into bed and spiraled into a deep sleep.

Bright and Star from the New Earth came and lifted her body above the bed. Keenan and Valor waited by the barn roof, ready to transport their friend. They carried her through the expanding universe, and this time Ahaba and his forces were nowhere to be found. After what seemed like hours, they descended into the atmosphere of the New Earth.

A sailboat, with billowing sails, waited on the gentle river. Purity woke as the Ring of Grace appeared and lowered her into the sailboat.

"Clarity. Clarity," Purity's voice echoed over the waters.

"She's not here," Sergio said.

"You've embraced the Captain's thoughts for your life," Rocco added.

"Yes, she's with us now," Purity said, realizing the dream of raising Clarity was just beginning.

The boat sailed down the river through the vast cities of the New Earth. Its occupants waved and celebrated her return.

"You've returned just in time," many proclaimed as they once again made their way to the great city to feast with the Captain.

Valor and Keenan flew overhead, and Purity yelled after them.

"I want to see my Papa. Can you tell me how to find him?"

"Yes, of course, but another time. We have other things planned this trip," Keenan yelled from above.

"You need to understand the Captain's plans for you," Valor clarified.

Instantly, the sailboat stopped along the shore. The Ring of Grace appeared again, escorting her to an open field. She walked cautiously toward the large book entitled His Thoughts Revealed.

"This is your book. What do you want to know?" asked Toby.

"Should I dance in the World Ballroom Championships?" she asked, stepping toward the book.

The book opened on its own. The pages turned as though a furious wind blew them to the desired place.

"And should we take Clarity with us?" she asked again as the pages continued to turn.

The pages stopped turning and rested on a specific page. The date of the competition was neatly written at the top of an empty page in bold ink.

"November 7th, 1909. Here's the date of the competition, but nothing's written. Is this a joke? I don't know what to do," Purity complained, disappointed.

"Does this mean my life is over by some tragedy?" she thought.

A gentle hand landed on her shoulder. It was Captain of the Lord's Army, King of the New Earth. Music from a heavenly orchestra floated on the air.

"Shall we dance?" he said with smiling eyes.

"Yes," Purity said, taking his fiery hand.

He whisked her away, sweeping her over soft currents of air. They danced for a long while, and she asked no questions in his presence. All her concerns and problems melted away.

After an unknown period, they landed by the sailboat.

"It's time for you to go. Clarity needs to be fed," the Captain said with eyes full of compassion.

"Nothing was written for the date of the championships. I need your guidance," she begged, searching his eyes for the answers.

"Hand both schools over to David and Mariah. They will gladly take over. Don't disappoint Favor—Paris is a great place to honeymoon. And Clarity will travel well. Remember, I'll be with you. You're blessed to be a blessing.," the Captain said with loving eyes.

Purity woke with a start to the cry of Clarity, who was throwing a fit for Naomi.

* * *

In less than two weeks, Favor and Purity had planned a grand wedding. The day had finally arrived for them to join their lives as one.

A fine carriage pulled up in front of the Bristol Church. It was decorated with fresh flowers. Inside, Purity held Clarity in her arms. Purity was the picture of loveliness—even with a fussy baby.

Purity's bridesmaids, Victoria, Alexis, Natasha, Chin Lu, Rachel, and Mariah, had all squeezed into the carriage together, along with Naomi.

"Shh, Clarity. Mama's getting married," Purity said, trying to quiet the newborn.

"Of all days to be gassy," Naomi admonished.

"You're late. Let me take the baby."

Purity handed Clarity over, and the coachman opened the door and helped her step down. She waited outside with Naomi as the bridesmaids walked into the old Bristol Church and took their places for the ceremony.

Inside, Favor and his best friend, John, stood at the altar, waiting for the wedding party. The music started, and the wedding party filed in slowly toward the front. Each bridesmaid had a petite bouquet of fresh flowers and held the arm of one of Purity's sons.

The attendees stood and turned, awaiting the bride's entrance.

Purity took a deep breath, looking at the doors to the church.

"We've got company," Naomi said.

Purity turned to see Chief Wolf, Sharp Arrow, Fair Dawn, and members of the tribe wearing full festive Indian attire. Several warriors stood basking at the sight of the beautiful bride.

Purity ran into Chief Wolf's arms without hesitation.

"I never thought I'd see you again."

"Not one perished on the journey. Great Creator led us to a safe place, and we're still reading the books," Chief Wolf said, hugging her as a daughter.

"We heard you were getting married today."

Purity turned to find Stephen and Mandy.

"Favor and I have been looking for you two," Purity said as she hugged them.

"Where have you been?"

"We beat you to it. We got married," Mandy said, showing off her wedding ring.

"We've been on our honeymoon," Stephen confirmed.

"Congratulations," Purity pronounced.

"Welcome home, Purity," Mandy said, hugging her again.

"Looks like we're all headed to France for the World Ballroom Championships. Are you ready for another adventure?" Stephen asked.

"With you two and my family by my side, I'm ready for anything," Purity said with a grin. She looked over the group of well-wishers.

"Thank you for coming. I wouldn't be here today without all of you," Purity said.

Naomi directed the guests to special reserved seating close to the altar, and then she sat in the front row with Clarity.

Mrs. Wisedor caught sight of the last-minute guests and welcomed all with a big bright smile. Mr. Wisedor wrapped his arm around his wife, and she leaned into his affection.

Purity walked slowly down the aisle toward Favor. She dazzled with her stunning gown of French lace and a jeweled bodice. And there was something else—a heavenly light that shone in her eyes.

Purity recognized the train porter, George Pullman, off to her right. He winked at her, and she nodded. And there was Debra, seated next to the young man who'd asked her to dance at Victoria's wedding. Purity's heart was full, gazing on the loving faces of the people who'd been a part of her journey.

A smile erupted on Favor's face as he watched his love walk toward him. He extended his hand as she reached the altar.

"I would have waited a lifetime for you," he whispered to her.

Not a sound was heard in the church as Pastor Ezra officiated. Many songs of love and worship were offered to Captain of the Lord's Army. At the end of the ceremony, Clarity fussed as Pastor Ezra pronounced them man and wife. The couple turned and faced the crowd, which erupted in applause.

Stepping down from the altar, Favor reached for Clarity and carried her with them down the aisle. Purity was by his side, in total admiration of the man God had given her.

* * *

Their small group traveled to New York to catch the Le France—a modern steamship headed to France. They were escorted to the ship by crowds of well-wishers, family, and fans. People waved hats and scarves as tears of joy flowed.

"Win for us at the world championships," many yelled.

Favor and Purity felt the excitement of starting their new life together as they boarded the ship. Naomi trailed behind them, Clarity in her arms. Stephen and Mandy stepped up beside them at the deck railing.

Favor's family was there, standing proudly amid the joyous throng below. The sons, Natasha, Alexis, Chin Lu, and Rachel waved with excitement. David held Mariah in his arms, completely taken by his Indian Princess.

"Happy honeymoon," others in the crowd shouted to Favor and Purity.

"Good-bye. We love you," Purity and Favor shouted to their family and fans.

"Lead the way, Captain, and we will follow," Purity released the words on the wind.

"Let the adventure begin," Favor agreed, smiling. He turned to Purity.

"Anywhere with you is an adventure."

Favor took her in his arms and kissed her sweetly.

Printed in the USA
CPSIA information can be obtained
at www.ICGtesting.com
LVHW041634290923
759463LV00036B/327

9 781956 001877